STONE AND WATER

BY DANIEL FOX

Dragon in Chains

"Fox captures the foggy mysteries of feudal China in exquisite style with this rich fantasy series opener. . . . Fox's concisely elegant style mirrors the light brush strokes and deep colors of ancient Chinese paintings, finely balancing detail, emotion and action. Where many Western authors try and fail to capture the nuances of Chinese culture and mythology, this melodious tale quietly succeeds."
—*Publishers Weekly* (starred review)

"Daniel Fox tackles his material (loosely based on the myths and history of Old China) with a combination of insight, innovation, and sheer command of language that transforms it. . . . Now I'm waiting for the next book, with all the impatience of a dedicated fan!"
—*Locus*

"*Dragon in Chains* is a compelling blend of high-stakes action, well-drawn characters who I really cared about, and a gorgeously painted landscape. This is the kind of fantasy I love to read."
—KATE ELLIOTT

"Intense passions and wild imagination . . . a mythic China intimately imagined."
—A. A. ATTANASIO

"A rising star . . . With talent like Fox's, the future of fantasy is in good hands." —TANITH LEE

"Fox masterfully weaves multiple story strands into a smooth braid. . . . A rousing fantasy adventure." —BookLoons

"Daniel Fox's poetic prose . . . makes even the mundane seem marvelous. . . . Definitely a novel—and a series—that should be on every fantasy reader's radar." —Fantasy Book Critic

"Fox is a lyrical writer whose greatest strength is evoking the mood and feel of a place—Taishu feels as solid and real as the chains that restrain the titular dragon." —RT Book Reviews

Jade Man's Skin

"Brutal, brilliant, complex, and startlingly clear all at once, this series does a magnificent job of taking the reader into a culture, a time, a place that most of us have never considered."
—JAY LAKE, author of *Pinion*

"[Builds] on the brilliantly subtle groundwork laid in 2009's *Dragon in Chains* . . . Readers who enjoyed Fox's delicate descriptions and leisurely prose will be thrilled to find more of the same, along with greater depth of story as the numerous characters are pulled together by schemes and destiny."
—*Publishers Weekly*

"Fox's love of all things Chinese shines through this sequel to *Dragon in Chains,* which should appeal to fans of Asian-themed fantasy such as Lian Hearn's *Across the Nightingale Floor* and Barry Hughart's *Bridge of Birds.*"
—*Library Journal*

"This is both a stand-alone story and an excellent continuation of Fox's previous novel. Set in a richly detailed, feudal, Asian-style empire, the plot revolves around rebellion, betrayal and bonds. . . . All told, it is a tale that's hard to put down until the last line."
—*RT Book Reviews*

BY DANIEL FOX

Dragon in Chains
Jade Man's Skin
Hidden Cities

Hidden Cities

Moshui

THE BOOKS OF STONE AND WATER

Hidden Cities

BOOK THREE

DANIEL FOX

BALLANTINE BOOKS
New York

A Del Rey Trade Paperback Original

Copyright © 2011 by Daniel Fox

Published in the United States by Del Rey,
an imprint of The Random House Publishing Group,
a division of Random House, Inc., New York.

DEL REY is a registered trademark and the Del Rey colophon
is a trademark of Random House, Inc.

Library of Congress Cataloging-in-Publication Data
Fox, Daniel.
Hidden cities / Daniel Fox.
p. cm. — (Moshui: the books of stone and water ; bk. 3)
ISBN 978-0-345-50303-9 (pbk.) — ISBN 978-0-345-52433-1 (ebk.)
1. Dragons—Fiction. 2. Magic—Fiction. I. Title.
PR6106.O96H53 2011
823'.92—dc22
2010042070

Printed in the United States of America

www.delreybooks.com

2 4 6 8 9 7 5 3 1

Book design by Mary A. Wirth

*A book without a dedication
is like a kiss without salt.
Or something.*

'Nuff said.

To Ride the Dragon

one

*D*id he think she was angry, before?

Well, yes. He did think it, and he was not wrong. He had felt the slow stew of her anger, fed over centuries in chains below the sea; he had seen the sudden flare of it when she was suddenly free, when she destroyed a whole fleet of men and ships for their impertinence, abroad upon her waters; he had endured the storm of it when she found herself not so free after all, when she raged through the typhoon.

He had faced her in her fury more than once, eye to eye and far too close.

He still thought he had never seen her quite this angry, and entirely at him.

LITTLE THING, *you promised.*

There were proverbs Han knew, teaching people how very foolish it was to make promises to a dragon.

I know I did. She loured above him, where he stood too close. *I did promise, and I am sorry. I had not meant for this to happen.*

She knew that, she was in his head.

Because she was in his head, she must know this too: that there were just two things he would not willingly relinquish, out of all the world. Despite all terror, and all betrayal. Tien was one of them, and actually this was the other: this constant grinding oppression of scale, this teetering always on the edge of a catastrophic fall. This revealed savagery, this terrible landscape, eternal wrath, this dragon.

He had tried to free her once, and failed. Her chains—or were they his chains?—were more than simple iron, and not so easily cut. He had promised it again, and meant it truly. And had betrayed her anyway, and now he could not free her anywhere this side of death. She was written on his skin, in some spell-crafted liquor more potent than mere ink. And that was Tien's doing altogether, and what he knew the dragon knew, and . . .

I will eat her. If I cannot eat you, little thing. Which they had absolutely established by now: not eat, not drown, not crush or starve or dement him into suicide, no. *I will eat your vicious girl instead.*

No, he said. *You will not.*

You cannot always keep her close. You cannot always watch her.

Right now he did not want her close. But, *I don't need to,* he said. The dragon was in his head, overwhelming; he was in hers, mortal and tiny and insignificant. She was written on his skin, and she could not close him out. *If you go near Tien, I will know. I will not let you harm her.*

Betrayal made no difference, apparently. He was no more free than the dragon; he could still not relinquish Tien.

He couldn't even match the dragon's anger. Tien understood about sacrifice, where he kicked like a rabbit in a snare. She would have sacrificed herself without a thought. Seizing an opportunity, she had sacrificed Han instead.

He knew. He had been there, helpless under her hands.

He was always helpless, it seemed, except when it came to dragons.

She said, *You have to sleep, little thing. Little mortal thing. While you walk in nightmare, I will kill your girl and everything you care for.*

No, he said. *I don't believe you can. A part of me rides with you, that doesn't need to sleep.*

His body was the least of him, it seemed to him these days. Like the paper of a book: fit for writing on, but not itself the words. Not the idea, not the book itself. Not Han.

If that was true of him, of course it must be true of her too. If her body was a vastness, a sodden hulk that reared above him like the stormclouds of her temper, her spirit was immeasurably greater.

He felt the grip of it, and slithered free like a pip between two fingers.

He felt the mighty weight of her mind bear down on his body, cramping and cruel; he rolled writhing in the mud, all pain, all overwhelmed.

But still there was that little part of him that huddled in her head, watchful, untouched. And no mud could smear those words that Tien's needle had driven into his skin, words for sleep and stillness, that he could spill like ink into the turbulent waters of her will.

THE PAIN was unbearable but Han bore it anyway, with something close to patience, till it ebbed. Then he dragged himself shudderingly into the stink of her where she lay slumped and barely aware, sullen and seething, a storm in a bottle.

He sat on one great sprawled foot and stared into the slit of her eye, and even that deep shimmering jade seemed clouded; and he shook his head and said, *You can't. However you come at me, however you hurt me, the words will overrule you now. This isn't something we can break. Either of us.*

Not till I die, he said, *and my skin rots and the words rot with it. Not till then. You'll just have to wait.*

You can do that, can't you? he said. *Just wait. Another sixty, seventy years. You've waited centuries.*

We can find a way to live, he said, *for one puny mortal lifetime. The two of us together.*

You might enjoy it, even, he said. *Once your temper cools. It'll be like nothing else.*

When you swim, he said, *you'll still have to swim alone; but we can learn to fly together.*

And he walked up that unresisting leg, high onto the spine of her; and settled himself like a man astride a roof ridge and loosed her mind from the weight of his words, clinging on grimly with nothing more than his hands now as she rose.

two

Sometimes Mei Feng got confused, a little, and thought she was the empire, the Hidden City of his heart.

Never more so than now. Now it was almost true.

Her poor feet were sore, from too much running on hard stony roads after too much pampering. She lay in a luxury of cushions, and her boy—no, her man, father of her child-to-be—Chien Hua sat with her poor sore feet in his lap and his imperial fingers smeared with a camphor-scented balm, stroking them down Mei Feng's tender soles until her toes twitched. He smiled, and pressed his powerful imperial thumbs into the balls of her little feet until she gasped, until she closed her eyes and fell back among her cushions and groaned softly in an agony of pleasure.

There was the touch itself, the simple physicality of it, shivers of delight. Riding that like a mage on a serpent came the greater pleasure, whose hands they were. That he was willing to do this—no, better, devoted to it—unbuttoned her from the inside out. This was how they ought to be: kind and careful with each other, intimate and demanding, robust and certain sure.

It was the seedling child in her belly that had brought him back to her. The assassin had helped too, at least a little, but it was the child mainly. Being proved right was negligible against being proved fertile, carrying his baby.

She might tease him with that later, scold him for it, but she didn't truly care. He was who he was, what his mother had made

of him. He had dynasties in his blood, written on his bones. Mei
Feng loved him regardless.

And now—well. He was lord of all the world and lord of her
too. Lord of her body. And she was pregnant with his child. His
hopes all lay in her. Which meant, yes, she was the Hidden City for
this little time at least, under his hand. All its walls and palaces
and people her skin, her belly and her blood. Her feet in the emperor's lap.

She wiggled her toes for his attention, and smiled with a greedy
contentment as his astonishing eyes came sliding sideways to find
hers.

"Press harder," she murmured, "lord of my feet. You don't need
to be so careful, I won't break."

Which was nonsense, of course. He had jade in his bones as
well as dynasties. He was the Man of Jade, impervious apparently
to steel blades. He could tear her simple fleshly body between his
hands like a well-cooked chicken. He knew that, and had always
been too cautious. Now he was tentative almost beyond bearing,
unless she goaded him.

"Mei Feng, you're pregnant . . ."

"I am." The doctor they had found might be a fraud, but his girl
seemed competent and was sure. Which was enough for Mei Feng,
who had been sure enough already. Between the two of them, they
had convinced the emperor. His mother would want more surety,
but she was the other side of a storm-tossed sea. "Still, I am pregnant in my belly, not my feet. Work harder, idle majesty," and she
slipped one foot free of his loose grasp to poke him in the ribs with
it, to make him squirm and splutter.

Tonight she would make him less careful of her belly too, less
careful of her altogether. She was not suddenly made of paper,
and she meant to persuade him of it, physically and at length. It
had been too long.

For now, his close attention to her feet was enough. It seemed to
stand for everything she lacked. Perhaps he understood that; he

gripped the errant foot more firmly and worked it between his thumbs until she was the one who was squirming.

"Mmm—yes, lord, like that, exactly . . ."

Her feet were sore, or had been; they were mending beneath his touch. Her heart had been sore too, and was mending too. His touch, his smile, his constant tender services were the best medicine for now. Later they could lay words down like dressings, make promises like stitches to bind open wounds. Better, they could trust the deeper talking to their bodies, oaths sworn in heat and hunger, sealed in satisfaction.

Later.

Now, though: now the last whisper of the dragon's typhoon still lashed the walls, rain and wind together. Coming and going, men let the weather in. Even so, Mei Feng had refused to move from here. Even in this strong windowless stone warehouse, even with his most lethal guards around him, one assassin had come close enough to test a blade on the emperor's bare unprotected back. The blade it was that broke, she'd seen the shards. That needed thinking about—and testing, perhaps, with needles: his body, her exploratory fingers and fine needles jabbing, jabbing—but in the meantime she'd keep his precious green-tinged skin as safe as she could manage. Which still meant here, until someone gave her better reason to move on. Built to keep his jade secure, for now it held only the one piece, original and best, the Man of Jade, her own . . .

Holding her cup below her chin and breathing steam because it smelled sweeter than the rank dank air, she watched the doctor and his girl make their way among the injured. No proper cots: men lay on the wet floor, except where their friends had raided godowns for timbers, pallets, bolts of silk, anything to soften the hard time of their waiting.

Left to himself, she thought the doctor would not be going anywhere near those common soldiers. Afflicted as he was, though—well. She watched his girl lead him from one makeshift bed to the next. Even from distance, it was clear which one of them had

the knowledge and the confidence to use it. The girl lifted off rude
dressings and examined wounds, asked questions, diagnosed, pre-
scribed. The doctor, who should have been her master: he carried
the bag of medicines. And nodded, stroked his beard, for all the
world as though he tested and trusted his young apprentice.

If they went on following that line of patients along the wall,
soon enough they would come to the corner where Yu Shan
crouched above his clan-cousin Siew Ren.

Mei Feng set down her cup, kicked herself abruptly free of the
emperor's beguiling grip and swung bare feet to the rough stone
floor.

Startled, he was still quick; his hands arrested her, shoulder
and hip.

"Mei Feng, what are you doing?"

"Going to help."

"There are any number of men here—"

"Yes, and none of them is doing anything useful."

It wasn't true, quite, but almost it was. Some of the hurt had the
attentions of their friends, but not enough. Mostly the healthy sat
in huddles, quiet and dripping and overwhelmed.

He said, "If you give orders, they will be obeyed."

That was, undoubtedly, true. And would be useful to the needy,
and not at all to her.

"I want . . ."

Lacking the words to say what she wanted, she gestured with
empty hands. That was it, exactly. She wanted to busy those hands
and numb her mind and stop watching Yu Shan. Time and again,
her helpless eyes came back to him. Even the emperor wasn't quite
distraction enough, even at her feet. This whole building smelled
of defeat; defeat breeds sorrow, and what she saw in that corner
was the root and the fruit together, black welling misery.

"We need light," she said, "and air. And tea."

"You have tea," he said. "Is it finished? I've had enough, but . . ."

"Me too," she said. "And who else? Who else has had enough?

If I can't make people better, at least I can bring them tea and tell them that the rain will soon be over."

"So can other people do that."

"Yes, but they're not."

"Mei Feng," his long arms around her, and that was better than sharing his cup, better than his attentions to her feet, except that he was stopping her from doing what she wanted, "I will send men to find cups and kettles, to make tea for all. They will get wet, and the fire-smoke will make us cough, but I will do it anyway. Only I will not sit here and watch you bustle about like a servant—"

"Come with me, then," she said. "We can do it together. The emperor should be servant of his people. And things will happen twice as fast if you are there," clumsy, unpracticed, adorable: oh, she knew. It ought probably to be what she wanted.

"Things will happen," he said, "as fast as they may, if we only give the orders. You and I, together. Sitting here, supervising. *Together.* You are pregnant, and you are not going to risk our baby by—"

She was laughing, almost, into his sleeve as he held her. His name was a sweet cake in her mouth as she mumbled it against the fabric. "Oh, Chien Hua. I'm not one of your delicate palace ladies, scared to lift a finger. Peasant women work until their waters break. If there is risk in movement, then I have risked our baby so very much already: on my feet all day and running so far, crossing that angry river on a mad raft in the end because I had to reach you somehow . . ."

"Yes," he said, as if she had made his point for him. "You have risked so very much already," his hand on her belly now, as though he could guard the little life inside it just by touch, "I can't let you loose again. It is a joy to see you, but you really should not have come."

"Oh, and what was I supposed to do, sit quiet at home in your horrible empty palace with all those people all around me, trapped between Ping Wen and your mother, while you were off fighting a traitor's war for him and letting assassins close enough to test their blades against your *back* . . . ?"

"There was only the one assassin," he said mildly. "And his blade broke, in the event. And you didn't know about him until you had crossed the water."

"No, and how many others are there, that neither of us knows about? So many soldiers, so many strangers," and she glowered around the jade store, trusting none of them, "you don't know who might be next, sneaking up to you with a blade in their sleeve. And maybe the next one won't break. You're not immortal, you only think you are. You're not very bright, either, letting Ping Wen trick you into this even before Tunghai Wang put his eunuch at your side. You're not safe this side of the water, not any kind of safe."

"It was you, as I remember it, who brought the eunuch to me. But wait," he went on frowningly, "I thought we were talking about you, and how you should not be this side of the water?"

"I wouldn't need to be, if you had listened to me back on Taishu. What have you gained here, truly?"

"My city of Santung," he said, meaning *my victory, my first,* seeming not to notice that they were once again not talking about her.

She snorted. "Oh, and what are you going to do with that? You haven't defeated Tunghai Wang, only seen him washed away in rain. He would have defeated you, you would have lost your city and your army and your life too in his ambush, if it hadn't been for the dragon. Everyone says so, when they don't think you're listening. One thing for sure, you can't go chasing after him into the country, he'll just ambush you again and again and again. So tell me, where do we go from here, mighty warlord . . . ?"

"We go straight back to Taishu," he said. "I *take* you back to Taishu, because I can't trust you to go by yourself."

Which was of course exactly what she had come for, to shepherd him back by means of playing sheep. She hid her triumph in his sleeve, while he stroked her belly and explained to her with utmost firmness that he would never allow her to move, never to lift a finger again, "No, not even to make tea for my army. Peasant girl," his lips at her ear, more touching than talking, "I will teach you to be idle and delicate and ladylike, fit vessel to carry my son."

"Ohé, a boy, is it? I say a girl. I thought I'd give you a bevy of girls. I'd like to see you mobbed by a pack of daughters . . ."

It was banter and distraction and delight, a return to delight, and still not enough to keep her eyes from straying to that shadowed corner, the brutal stillness of the figures there. Which was why she wanted so very much to be doing something more. But there was no moving him—literally, no shifting against his grip—and besides, here came someone else now, free to do what Mei Feng could not.

Here came Jiao, striding in through the rain-blown doorway with men struggling under the weight of steaming cauldrons. Jiao who had the gift of it, lucky Jiao, not to glance once into that corner as she called out, "Tea, then, here's tea for all if you only come and get it, lads. Tea and soup, your choice, take one in each hand if you're hungry, if you're lonely, if you've got no friends needing help to bring them something in a bowl . . ."

Just her voice brightened the room, rough and carrying, as good as a shelf of lights. Scents too, wafting on the steam: tea like grass and something richer, darkly savory. Mei Feng couldn't guess what the woman might have found, to make soup in a starveling city. She was what the occasion demanded, exactly: a pirate used to raiding, used to handling men.

Mei Feng leaned her head on the emperor's shoulder in utter surrender, saw his smile and knew he thought himself victorious once more. And couldn't tell him otherwise, wouldn't unpick the day any further to show him how very much was lost here, how much more was uncertain. Let his mother do that on Taishu, when he was safe.

Meantime, thinking how to make him safe, thinking *Ping Wen,*

Ping Wen is on Taishu, she said, "The dragon is in the sky again, and we only have two children blessed by the goddess, to guard us in the crossing."

He said, "Two is plenty. They can herd all our fleet back to Taishu between them."

"Yes, lord, but then?" He frowned, not understanding. She kissed his nose and said, "Emperor of two cities, if you want to keep Santung you will need to appoint a governor, and speak with him after. Back and forth constantly, men and news and instructions. And only two boats safe, and the dragon always watchful. It won't be easy."

"Nothing is easy," he said, shrugging. "You don't need to worry about that, our baby is your concern."

At that she made a noise, quite startlingly rude. "Our baby," she said, "will look after itself, mostly. My worrying will not sour it," though no doubt his mother could find someone to tell her that it would. "And there's a game my grandfather and I used to play . . . No, listen. This is important." If he wouldn't let her bustle about like a servant, he couldn't stop her plotting like a general. "The game has one boat and a farmer, who needs to cross the river with his sack of rice, and his ducks who will eat the rice if they're allowed to, and his bad dog who will eat the ducks if he turns his back, and his leaky sampan will carry the rice or the ducks or the bad dog but no more, not any two at once; and . . ."

three

Like a tortoise drawn into the safety of its shell, Chung hunkered high in the arch of the bridge—his back arched against the underside of the boards above, right at the apex, he could be no higher—and was very glad to be there.

This bridge was becoming curiously important in his life, although he'd never crossed it.

He'd nearly died first, herebelow, among its beams and buttresses. Then he'd killed a man. Then he'd nearly fallen and so nearly died again, except that the emperor had saved him.

Now, though—now there was death everywhere else, death all over and only the bridge was safe.

Perhaps.

This last little rise, the underside of its peak, squeezed between one death and another. This bubble, this shell, that he had to share with a handful of prisoners and a barrel-load of fire barely contained, barely understood . . .

CHUNG AND his prisoners had been stranded on the rocky island, fierce river on either side, fire between them and the bridge as the rebels' engines burned. As the fire died, so the emperor's abandoned guards showed on the bank, calling for their lord. Chung called back through the smoke to say that he'd been here with Yu Shan and swum ashore again, they should chase him upriver; then he settled back to wait till the fire was dead entirely.

Settled back on his pot-barrel, last survivor of the projectiles the rebels had been hurling across the water. Where they struck, they broke; where they broke, they burst into flame. Chung was curious, and this one he was keeping.

By the time the rain came, the riverbank was a mill of soldiers. Chung saw no chance of shepherding his prisoners safely through, never mind his precious lethal pot. He stayed put, and the rain kept coming.

The rain kept coming and the wind blew, air turned to iron, splinter-vicious. The river rose, and flung its waters across the rock.

There was no hope that it would stop rising, while the typhoon squatted like a toad above the valley. Chung yelled above the wind, telling his prisoners to go if they wanted to, cross the bridge and lose themselves among the army as it scattered. Let them find what shelter they could. No man would care, beneath this dreadful weight of water. Afterward, they could do as they liked.

Only, if just a few would stay to help him with his pot, he would see them safe and settled. Here or on Taishu, with the emperor's own word to shield them . . .

Half a dozen stayed. They carried the pot among them to the footings of the bridge, but already that high arch was a dangerous path; they watched the last of the leaving men blown off his feet and almost over the rail, saved only by the grip of his companion.

Thought of trying to carry the barrel over, rising step by step into a harder blast of wind with no hands free to hold on to each other or the rail; and shook their heads, set the pot down, stepped back.

Looked at Chung, who was almost defeated but not quite.

"Under the bridge, then," he screamed. "Look, where the footings will shelter us. Bring rope . . ."

There was plenty of rope, kept spare for the machines that hurled the pots. The stone footings were a strong wall at their backs, the boards of the bridge above made a roof that barely leaked, and a roof and a wall together made better shelter than they would find across the river now. They huddled beneath the sheer blast of rain, and didn't move.

And the river kept on rising; and with water hissing at their heels he said, "Tie the rope around the pot—carefully!—and we'll hoist it up into the beams. We can tie it off up there, hold it as safe as anything can be. We can rope ourselves together too, and cling to the beams, and be safe as long as the bridge lasts . . ."

THE BRIDGE creaked and flexed, but it had stood through any number of typhoons, and this was just one more.

The river kept on rising, but the bridge arched high. They climbed up and up, hauling the pot with them until they were squeezed into the last space that offered, barely sheltered from the hurl of the wind above and the stinging spume of the river beneath. If the waters rose higher yet, Chung thought the men would kill one another—or kill him, rather, kill him first—just for that little extra breathing-room before they all drowned anyway.

He thought Shen might be angry, if he drowned.

But the rain finally stopped battering on the planks overhead, and the wind slacked at least a little. There was still a valley's worth of water to funnel off, and the river would have to keep rising; but now a bold man—or, lacking that, himself—could worm his way out between the beams, haul himself over the parapet of the bridge and try to stand.

Cling hard to the rail, he did need to cling, but his hands weren't ripped from their grip and his body wasn't flung out like a banner behind him. He could look up, even, and see clear sky behind the shredded clouds.

And so call the men out to join him, leaving the pot securely tied among the beams beneath. If the river reached it, the rope should hold it in its nest of wood, and it could hardly be wetter than it was.

· · ·

SOON ENOUGH, Chung said, "Who among you is the bravest?"

None of them spoke, nor moved except to glance sideways among themselves.

He smiled. "All right, then. Who among you is the most afraid?"

That was easy, apparently. They all glanced the same way, and the one they glanced at—the youngest of them, barely more than a boy—did take half a shuffling pace forward.

"Good, then. Take this," Chung's yellow sash, rain-washed and startlingly bright. "This marks you out as an imperial messenger, which is barely even a lie: I am an imperial messenger, and now you are mine. No one will touch you, with this. As soon as the water drops back, as soon as you can reach the bank in safety, I want you to go into Santung and find the emperor. He will be at the docks or close at hand, waiting to send a boat across the strait. Your sash will take you past his guards. Say that Chung has sent you; I am Chung. Say that I am keeping one firepot on the island here, with some men to guard it. Say that I hope to learn its secrets. And say this too, that I am sending you to Taishu to fetch Shen."

The boy nodded uncertainly, gripping the sash. "And then?"

"And then, I want you to go to Taishu and fetch Shen. Like the emperor, you will find him somewhere around the harbor," watching that first boat come in: impatient for news of victory, news of survivors, losses. Scanning the faces on the boat, wondering who lay wounded belowdecks, who had been left behind too hurt to move. "You will know him by his temper, which is foul. And by his shoulder, which is hurt, but mostly by his temper. When you find him, bring him here. If you have to, say that it is an imperial order; the sash confirms it. But see first if he will come for me."

four

$\mathcal{B}$iao had been a thief in his time, and a thief-taker too.

When he was young and hungry—*young and pretty,* he liked to say, without worrying whether it had ever been true—he sold his body, often and often. More than once he sold himself more literally, into formal bondage; and stole himself back again each time, running in the dark with the bond-fee tucked safe into his cheek.

For a while he had been an itinerant magician, until the people he impressed grew too urgent and too demanding, wanting proper magic, curses that worked and fortunes that might actually come true. That time he walked away in daylight, more dignified but no more honest, leaving promises that held as much value as his horoscopes.

That time the fees they paid swung in a purse inside his robes, from where his own nimble fingers could not have stolen it. He felt like a stallion with his worth hung between his legs, ponderous and heavy.

He became a doctor by happenstance and crime, the way he had lived all his life. He might have used the money in his purse to buy himself the knowledge that he needed; indeed, he swore that he would. He found a mentor and paid upfront, half of what the old man asked. Traveled with him for a season, learned what he would need—the tricks and patterns of a doctor's speech, the names of herbs and cures, the proper size of fees—and then denounced the old man to a magistrate as a fraud and felon.

Provided evidence enough to see his mentor's head struck off.

Paid the magistrate his due share of the old man's goods and moneys, kept the rest and called himself a doctor in the next town that he came to, and the next.

He hadn't meant to stay long with the army—he never meant to stay long anywhere, never long enough to see his patients die—but soldiers can prove reluctant to see a doctor go. Sometimes he was lucky, some men recovered. Some men always will, despite their doctors.

That kind of luck wouldn't last, he knew. Luck has a way of turning sour, like soup let sit too long. The wrong man would die, or too many men too close together.

Santung was a mistake he should have walked away from. But the real doctor's empty tent had been too tempting and the road too long, too hard. He was suddenly tired of always moving on. He could discover a taste for staying still, the same roof every morning, the same path outside the door, not walking it.

This was not the place, the tent no enduring roof. It was a mistake. He knew it. And yet, and yet: he stayed. Some wiser part of him was only waiting to find catastrophe, but he was a fat man and that worried whisper was small and buried deep.

When Tien came, he thought at first that she was the catastrophe.

Then he thought she was a blessing. She had the knowledge that could destroy him, and decided not to use it. She could doctor, but she was too young and the wrong sex; he had authority to match his ignorance. Together they were stronger than either one apart. His luck had brought her to him, good sense should make her stay, and she was sensible. She must see that. And yet, he did not trust her. She had a secret purpose, something more than putting rice in the bowl each day and accumulating comforts in the tent.

Also there was her woman, the silent servant that she called Mu Gao. Biao disliked her entirely. How could he beguile someone who would not speak to him? She washed the clothes and cooked the meals, did all the work of the tent and he detested her.

Every night in the darkness, Biao's private self told him to go. His days were easy, though, and hard to walk away from. He was cozened by comforts, a full belly and a dry bed. Tomorrow, perhaps, he would just pack and leave . . .

ALWAYS TOMORROW; and now perhaps tomorrow was too late. Today the emperor had come back to Santung, war had come and the dragon with it.

Or the dragon had come, and war with her.

Biao had seen the dragon flying, with some poor captive thing in her claw.

He knew all the inner shades of fear from intimate experience, but he had never been more terrified. When the clouds broke because she broke them, when she hung like a line of wet brushwork against the paper sky.

Biao could not read, but he knew the character for death, and she was it.

He would have run then—why not, when everyone was running?—but that it all seemed suddenly too late. He was fat and tired, and could not outrun a dragon.

Neither could he outstubborn Tien. She said she was going down into the city, to treat the wounded of whichever side. And taking Mu Gao to help her; and him too, taking him.

Her scorn was a whip that his fear hardly needed. In the end, indeed, he came down ahead of her, while she dallied over some stray unexpected boy. He and Mu Gao, doing whatever they could between them. War was simple butchery, by and large, and called for simple medicine. Complications saved themselves for later days, for putrefying wounds and sweating fevers. He would happily leave now, and leave those to Tien.

Tien came to find them, sooner than he might have wished.

And then the storm came, the dragon's typhoon; and then the emperor's guard, desperate for a doctor, him.

Her.

Him.

AND SO this, a warehouse of stone, a shelter for the wounded and the half-drowned. And the emperor too, half naked and extraordinary, fussing over his pet girl. His *pregnant* pet.

That was an opportunity, but Tien would waste it. She would let the emperor take the girl back to Taishu, to his own imperial doctors, when she might instead attach herself with just a few worried words, a gesture of kindness, a hint of hidden knowledge.

Biao could not read but he could see this written, a secure horoscope, a new life under the emperor's broad roof. He could see Tien spurn it or simply not understand it, let the opportunity go by. He wouldn't care, but he could go with her, where he could not go alone. Master Biao was nothing here, but the mentor of Mei Feng's private midwife, oh yes . . .

Tien apparently preferred to doctor the common soldiery, going from one bleeding groaning nobody to the next. Biao really had no choice but to go with her, carrying the bag of herbs and staying close, where he could at least seem to be an equal voice. From a distance, to anyone who couldn't overhear.

Here again, blade-wounds and broken bones were the most of what they saw. At least he could treat cuts himself, and set a bone as well as anyone. He could let Tien get a bed ahead of him, even. He could have this man's friends hold him still, jerk the leg clean and sharp into its proper alignment, tie off a splint and dispense a simple mixture of herbs to ease pain, reduce swelling, help the bone to knit.

He could turn to catch up with Tien and find her oddly still, oddly quiet, far from her usual brisk competence. Kneeling above a half-naked figure with a man who sat beside, both just as silent and unmoving.

And the man was barely more than a boy, and something about him reminded Biao very much of the emperor; and the one he crouched over was a girl, and hideously burned. Hideous in her burning, Biao thought, and she would heal worse, her flesh twisting and contracting as it scarred.

If she healed at all. He thought it would have been kinder to slit her throat and leave her in the street. She might die yet, but it would be a slow death now and cruel of the boy to drag her through it.

From her silence, he thought that Tien was thinking much the same.

And couldn't say it, of course, not possibly. When at last she stirred, when she did speak, she said, "I can make you up a brew to bathe her skin. I will give you a tea in the meantime, to ease the pain and help her sleep. No dressings, it will be best to let her wounds dry in the air, when they are done with seeping."

The boy said, "She cannot bear to have them touched, that's why I . . ."

Why he had left her lying naked, uncovered, his gesture said. Among all these men, one perfect breast exposed, one ruined.

"Yes," Tien said. "We will find her a room, where the two of you can be private."

But the boy was shaking his head, saying, "I am taking her home. To Taishu, as soon as the first boat sails."

"Impossible," Tien said sharply. "She is too hurt to move, she could not bear it."

"I carried her here, and she bore that. We belong in the mountains, she and I. I have the emperor's promise, I can take her home."

Tien shook her head again and almost seemed to look around for the emperor, to have that promise withdrawn. Biao took advantage of the moment to ask a simple question.

"What does she have in her mouth?" A leather thong hung from her lips, and looped around the back of her neck: something she wore as a pendant, that she was sucking now.

"Jade," the boy said, impossibly. And reached a hand to his own throat and touched the stone that hung there, glimmering green; and no, it couldn't possibly be jade, and yet . . .

That was what this boy had in common with the emperor, Biao realized: a faint green cast to his skin, as though it were dusted with jade. He said *the mountains,* he said *Taishu,* they must come from one of the mining clans; and it still made no sense, it was utterly unlawful for mere mortals to be wearing jade, but Biao was beginning to believe it.

He said, "How can she . . . ?"

"The emperor allows us. His private guard and me," without quite saying who or what he was himself. "It helps her now, I think, it keeps her strong. Strong enough to make the journey," defiantly, almost flung across the silent bitter body at Tien.

Who shook her head, defiant too; said, "She will need treatment daily, if she is to heal well."

"There are other doctors. Imperial doctors, on Taishu already . . ."

" . . . Who do not know my remedies, don't have access to my books. And will not be willing to travel up into the mountains, live there months among your people. It will take months, to bring her back to health."

"Teach me," the boy said. "Give me the herbs and show me how to use them."

Again, Tien shook her head. "It needs a doctor. These drugs are dangerous; I would not trust them to anyone not used to giving doses and observing the results."

"You come, then."

"No. My work is here," with a gesture around at so many others hurt.

"Some of these too will be coming to Taishu."

"And some will not. And I don't belong to, to the army," *to the emperor* Biao thought she had nearly said, nearly, "the city needs me here; and the books are here too, that I need," and she had her secret too, something to do with the dragon and a boy, and no, she would not leave.

"The emperor will make it an order, if I ask him to."

"And still I will not go; and what then?"

Then, inevitably, they would come down to threat and counter-threat, *the emperor will have you carried away in bonds* and *I will not treat your friend then, not treat anyone, not be a doctor if I am a prisoner*—and Biao forestalled them both.

"I will go," he said.

They stared at him.

"I am a doctor," he said, with at least some evidence about him. "I will . . . confer with Tien, what remedies she thinks best, what treatments," when they could be alone, when she could show him exactly, "and I will come with you."

A roof, safe shores, the end of the weary road. A reputation he could bring with him, a task within his powers if the girl should live, and small blame on his shoulders if not.

And jade: a fortune that could be worn on a boy's neck, sucked in a girl's mouth. Jade in the valleys, freshly mined, and himself right there, oh yes.

five

andan was surprising herself, surpassing herself.

She felt like a knife: chilled and forged and sharpened, lethal, *meant*.

It astonished her.

Till now, till this she had thought herself so placid, so content.

She had had a life and she liked it, in the jademaster's palace. Then the emperor came and all his entourage, his eunuchs; and the jademaster made a gift of her along with all his things, his other things, to serve the emperor. Which meant, she thought, to serve his eunuchs; but they picked her out and paraded her before his mother the dowager empress.

Who picked her out and gave her to his girl, his favorite, Mei Feng. It was understood—at least by the empress—that Dandan was to be her spy. Along with all the other women that she picked, and the eunuchs too.

But Mei Feng picked out Dandan in her turn to be a confidante, and Dandan thought that perhaps the empress had spies enough, while perhaps Mei Feng was short of friends. When Mei Feng wanted to sneak over the water to Santung, of course Dandan went with her, though she had never left Taishu before and did not want to now.

And when they had crossed the strait in the dragon's shadow and survived; when they had gone ashore to give thanks to the goddess and Mei Feng had nudged Dandan aside and stolen her away, even then Dandan had been willing. Someone had to stay

with the little fisher-girl, however wild she ran. She was the emperor's favorite, his only love; and, what, should she go ramping
off in wartime on her own? It was unthinkable. Unpardonable.
There would be heads hewn from necks if it was discovered.

Besides, Mei Feng was her friend, which made it unthinkable in
a whole other way.

And besides again, Dandan knew a secret. Mei Feng was pregnant. Or might be. Or hoped that she would prove to be, perhaps.
It was a slithery kind of secret, different every day, depending on
her mood: whether she had quarreled with the emperor again, or
with his mother, or with the court. Pregnancy was a weapon that
she didn't know how to use.

For her own sake, Dandan would have gone. For Mei Feng's
sake, she would have gone. For a baby, an imperial child, just for
the possibility—well. There was no question.

Which Mei Feng knew, even before she asked it.

DANDAN WAS neither built nor dressed nor fit for a hard slog on
mud roads. No more was Mei Feng dressed for it, but then they
met Jiao and her soldier-troop along the way. Mei Feng slit her
skirts and kept up with the pirate, trading one companion for a
better, leaving Dandan to flail along at the troop's tail.

And then there was a boy come from somewhere, bare-legged
and bruised, and they could flail together. Dandan had decided by
then to be angry with Mei Feng, that this was not at all the behav-
ior of a friend.

She took the boy in charge because that was her nature, and,
yes, because she had been told to. That was her nature too. The
troop moved more slowly, coming into the city; there was time to
find him trousers, time and breath enough to bully him a little. He
was called Gieh, and he was a peasant through and through. Like
any peasant he had been hungry even before the soldiers came.
Then he had been hungry and afraid. Then he had been hungry
and afraid and charmed, a little, by rough kindnesses. Now he was

all of those things and hopeful too. What peasant boy couldn't be lured away by a passing army, gifts of food and the promise of another life, sweeter and more interesting, less hard . . . ?

She might have struck him, just for his simplicity. She might have struck Jiao for laying those casual inducements, except that the woman was taller and stronger and certain to strike back even while she laughed. And was besides at the head of her troop, while Dandan and the boy were raggle-taggle at the tail.

It was easier to stay resentful, and cloudedly angry at Mei Feng. Even when she dropped back to walk with you after all, pale and shaken from some rooftop adventure that she didn't want to talk about. Even then. You might stop seething because she was after all your friend, and needed perhaps to hold your hand for a while, till the trembling in her fingers stopped. Your anger might fall like sediment to leave your spirit clear because she needed you as she knew you, calm and accepting and unchanged. Even so, it was still there like sediment and could be stirred up again.

You might learn so when she dragged you back a little, you and the boy both, to allow the troop to pull ahead; when she tugged you suddenly into a shadowed alley and away, the same trick again, without a word again, with only the boy at your heels; when once again she ran ahead and left you, with only the vaguest instructions what to do and how to follow her.

DANDAN AND the boy together found their way up to the governor's palace, arriving at the great gate just in time to find Mei Feng tumbling out. This time she couldn't be forestalled, couldn't be delayed. Babbling incoherently, some threat against the emperor, conspiracy and traitors—but Mei Feng was always unreliable about traitors, seeing them everywhere at court, even among the emperor's generals—she barely paused long enough to give fresh orders. Find two men in the palace, guard them and give them over to Jiao, who should bring them before the emperor as soon as might be. Where was she going? Why, to the emperor, of course, to save his life from traitors. Why couldn't she take the men herself? Because they would be too slow, she had to go *now,* see her go, pell-mell away in hopes of a boat across the river . . .

Dandan stood and watched her go, felt herself abandoned one more time, felt the anger stir and start to rise.

It was an old friend, almost. Dependable. She was beginning to understand how some people lived so constantly angry at the world.

Thought she was.

Didn't know how thin, how weak and selfish it was, that discontent that she called her anger.

Not until she turned and trudged in at the gate with the boy Gieh at her heels, wondering just how the two of them were supposed to search a whole palace and all its grounds for two particular people—whom Mei Feng had not of course described, in all her heedlessness and hurry—when there would no doubt be dozens, maybe hundreds of people here taking shelter from the war, hiding in whatever darkest cubby-hole they could.

Perhaps the boy and she should wait right here in the courtyard for Jiao. Especially as this errand was really Jiao's in any case, Dandan only the messenger. *Take these people to the emperor,* yes; no harm, surely, in letting it be Jiao who sought them out as well? *Find these people, and take them to the emperor.* Yes . . .

Except that here they came, two men finding themselves, finding Dandan and the boy. Looking for them, perhaps. There must be some urgency that would bring them out squinting into the sun, as if they had lived long in the dark. Something that would pull them toward the gate when one was twisted and broken and needed a crutch to shuffle himself along, while the other stood straight enough but even so could barely keep up with the first.

Dandan watched their slow and painful progress and broke all too soon, long before she thought she should.

She hurried across the courtyard to prevent them. "No, no, please. Look, here is a bench, sit, sit. Both of you, just sit down. Do you want water? Here . . ."

The boy Gieh had her bottle. The two men—both of them gray-haired and grizzle-bearded—seemed glad enough to sit, to drink, to pass the bottle between them and then have the boy run to fill it again. He would have gone to the fishpond in the court-yard there if she hadn't snapped at him to go find a well or a kitchen cistern. Food too if he could do that, if he could sniff it out.

Meantime she had a handkerchief, a square of silk that she could dip into the fishpond to wipe the scouring sweat from the old men's faces. The breeze was cool up here and clouds were blowing in but even so they sweated, as though they shared a fever.

She thought she knew already what they did share, nothing so easy to treat. Nor so easy to catch. One man certainly could pass it to another, but only over time and only with care and concen-tration, deliberately, an act of will.

She thought they hurt, deeply and consistently. She thought they had *been* hurt, deeply and consistently. This wasn't the kind of hurt that comes from birth or accident; nor the kind that comes in war. As a precursor of war, perhaps, or in its aftermath, but not from stabbing or slashing or crushing, not from blades used in anger or terror in the heat and confusion of battle.

No. She thought both these men had been hurt methodically and slowly and with intent. She thought they had been tortured.

Really it wasn't—or at least it shouldn't be—a surprise. Of course Tunghai Wang tortured prisoners. He was a traitor and a rebel; no doubt torture would be commonplace to him. No doubt these were loyal supporters of the emperor. She still didn't see why Mei Feng wanted him to meet them quite so urgently, but that wasn't important quite yet.

She introduced herself in the simplest way she knew: "Please, my name is Dandan. How may I serve you?" She had her instruc-tions, *get them to the emperor,* but there are ways and ways to hide one purpose in the shadow of another. Ways to hide a disobedience also. The emperor was on the wrong side of the river, in the middle of a war. Whatever these old men had to tell him, it could wait. She was not dragging two cripples half across the city in chase of him, not even for Mei Feng.

Besides, whatever the old men knew, Mei Feng clearly knew it too. She could tell the emperor herself.

For now, they could all sit here in the sun. Old bones appreciate heat; she didn't want to move them until she must.

One man, the taller—or perhaps he was only the straighter, they were much of a height sitting down—smiled at her from somewhere, from a well of grace. "Sit," he said, in a voice worn thin she thought by screaming. "Sit with us. We have seen . . . entirely too much of each other, in recent days. A fresh face is a blessing."

"Sit and talk," said the other. "We have talked so much together, I no longer know which is his voice and which my own. In either case, I think I prefer yours."

She sat, then, on dry and dusty stone at their feet, and looked up and shivered at something that shrouded them: not quite a smell—they and their clothes were scrupulously clean, as though they had most carefully washed and dressed each other—but the memory of a smell, perhaps, if memories could cling. Their nostrils flared together at the sea-breeze building.

She said, "I think you two have been prisoners together."

"We have shared the same cell, certainly." That was the crippled one, crutch laid carefully to hand beside the bench. The other had held his elbow, to ease him down when he sat. There was a courtliness between them that she liked extremely.

"And you have not been treated kindly." They might prefer not to speak of that, but it was in her nature to be direct.

The tall one smiled again. The other had a solemnity that suggested he would rarely smile. Perhaps that was only because she looked up from below, saw all the lines of pain and their shadows; but she was seeing them both from the same angle. And most of the people she had to deal with in palace life, sooner or later she saw them from her knees. One way or another. She was accustomed to making judgments from below.

The tall one said, "We have . . . shared the same suffering, also." That odd little break in his voice was almost laughter, she thought, though it was also almost pain, as though the two instincts were somehow the same physical spasm, and needed the same little catch of breath to carry him over.

"Yes," she said. "I am sorry for it. But the emperor has come now, and he will see you safe."

"The emperor may not be so pleased to see us at all."

"Not? But Mei Feng was quite determined . . ."

"Yes. I think she is probably quite often quite determined. And for sure he will want to know what we have told her. But whether he will want to see us afterward, if he survives it—well. Perhaps. Or perhaps only our heads, he might appreciate that more."

"Your heads? I don't understand."

"Of course not. You don't know who we are. Or who we were, perhaps. Now we are only two ruins sitting in the sun, watching a storm blow in. With the dragon, I think, riding above it. My eyes are not so good just now, but I think that was the dragon."

She would not turn her head to look, not be distracted. "Who you were? Who are you, then?"

"Two ruins; I have said. But once I was Li Ton the pirate, and the enemy of your emperor. Before that I was General Chu Lin, a loyal servant disgraced and banished by his father."

"And this?"

"Oh, this is Ai Guo. Tunghai Wang's most excellent torturer. I have been . . . the object of his attentions for some time now. I said, we have shared the suffering: he at the eye of the needle, I at the point."

BLESSEDLY, HERE came Gieh running back with the bottle filled and a string of dried figs glistening with water. He had found them, he said, dropped in the stable yard in someone's hurry to be gone. He had washed the muck from them, and they were perfectly good. He thought they should be good, he amended hastily, not realizing that a streak of fig-seeds on his wet chin was giving him away; and did they think there would be a typhoon? Only the sky seemed so dark suddenly, and the wind was turning vicious . . .

She hadn't realized, but he was right. With or without the dragon, a storm was on its way. Li Ton pulled himself to his feet by way of Gieh's obedient shoulder, and leaned on the boy quite heavily as he started his slow shuffle toward shelter. Dandan held Ai Guo's crutch for him while he drew himself up, then paced him at his crablike scuttle in the other man's wake.

Behind her, at the courtyard gate, she heard voices.

She turned around and there was Jiao, with a string of men at her back.

"You, girl—is Mei Feng with you?"

Dandan shook her head, against the mercenary's exasperation.

"Where's she gone this time?"

"Down toward the harbor, I think, looking for a way across the river. Looking to find the emperor."

"She'll be lucky if she finds a boat. But—well, we will leave her to her luck. Someone will look after Mei Feng; someone always does. What are you doing with these two?"

"Right now, helping them indoors before the rain comes. Staying with them, until the emperor decides what to do." *If the emperor wins his battle,* but that was taken for granted. "They're my prisoners, I suppose. Can you leave me two men, just for comfort?"

"I doubt you'll need them, but—you and you," picked out with a flicking finger, "follow Mei Feng down to the harbor. When you don't find her there—and you won't, but we'd best be sure she hasn't run into trouble on the way—double back up here and guard these for me. Understand?"

The men's grins said they understood entirely. They would be spared the battle, and they had a whole palace to pillage. Dandan wished they wouldn't leer quite so openly.

THEN THEY were gone, all of them, at a run; and here came the rain, a sudden squall that was really only a precursor, a scudding cloud before the storm.

From the great public courtyard of the governor's palace, the closest doorway led of course into the great public hall where he held his audiences.

Not a comfortable place. Not a place for hurting old men to stand, however strange, however bad they were; not a place for anyone to stand whose clothes ran with water onto the polished floor.

"Where are your quarters?" Dandan demanded.

"Mine are . . . in the lower levels. And insalubrious." That was Li Ton, of course, still almost amused despite his pain.

Ai Guo only shrugged.

"Wait, then." She didn't know this palace, but palaces, yes, those she knew; and the minds of the men who built them. Somewhere here, behind one of these concealing doors—this one, yes— would be a robing-room. No lord of men would willingly wear his public robes longer than need dictated. Here they were, the governor's magnificent silks . . .

She whistled shrilly down the hall, beckoned hugely.

Waited by the door there, watching the men's slow progress. Growing angry.

It wasn't either of the men she watched that she was angry with. Not Li Ton the traitor, nor Ai Guo his torturer. It might have been Tunghai Wang, for employing anyone so broken, so cruel, so calm; it might have been the emperor, for being so easy to betray. She didn't understand it, quite, though it was a cold clear thing, a rushing mountain stream risen up from deep.

She herded them all into the robing-room, and had them strip:

"Come on, quick, before wet and hurt marry into something worse, lung-fever or joint-fever, both. You too, idiot, Gieh. You may be young, but you're not immune to anything except good sense . . ."

When she had them naked she rubbed them dry herself, with half a closetful of silky shifts. She felt all their individual shivers and worse, she learned the first and most obvious truths about their bodies: that Gieh had been starved and beaten but no more than was common for boys and easy to mend; that Li Ton had been cut and tattooed, tortured then and tortured now again, fresh scabs too prominent even to be hidden by the crude black characters that covered half his skin; that Ai Guo his torturer had been tortured himself but less well and long ago, so that his bones were twisted and his legs were bent, he had no way to stand un-aided and every hop-step, every touch must hurt him savagely.

And by the time she was done with that intimate exploration, by the time she had left all three of her charges to dress one an-other in whatever they could find of comfort while she stalked through the corridors in search of somewhere fit to house them— by then she was angry in a way she could not measure. Angry like an arrow, seeking a target. Anger with clarity, that helped her focus: anger that helped her think that she had found something right to do, to be. Which was not, or not only, angry.

six

*R*ain in her hair, rain in her eyes.

It had almost stopped now, the rain. There were still teeth in the wind, though, blowing against wet skin, wet hair, sodden clothing. The wind was warm, like a dog's breath; it still had teeth, like a dog's mouth biting.

Jiao didn't care.

The wind was warm, but Jiao not. Inside she was cold the way a blade is cold, the chill of a steel edge waiting to bite.

She had done . . . what she always did, what lay in her nature to do.

After a hard day's fighting, through victory and defeat and recovery, she had brought the desperate Mei Feng across the swelling river in the tail-end of the typhoon. Which was a victory in itself, and deserved more acknowledgment than it had received so far.

Jiao had seen the girl safely to the emperor—which had brought Jiao necessarily face to face with her own great loss, something worse than defeat. She had found Siew Ren her rival gravely burned, and Yu Shan palely with her. Utterly with her, seeing only her ruined face and the pain behind it, thinking only of his bare intent to take her back to the mountains that they came from.

Jiao did what she could, all that she could. After a battle, won or lost—or abandoned, as this one had been—the wounded are the first priority. She wouldn't offer false comfort to anyone, friend or foe, rival or lover or herself; she would offer her time, her help, her company wherever it was welcome. Here, not. Not to Siew Ren, and Yu Shan didn't know how to look at her. She said what little she had to, and came away.

Talked to the other wounded, up and down the line. Let them tell her everything they'd done, everything they'd seen, how it had been for them. She gave them what little she had: a drink, a chew, a word of praise, a hand to hold. Her attention, her time. Not enough.

After a battle, the soldiers are their own priority. Crude comforts: heat in their bellies, dry clothes, somewhere to sit or sprawl, somewhere to talk until they were ready to sleep. She did what she could. Tea, food, what plunder they could scavenge from the docks. That kept her busy for a while.

Not enough. Everyone had closer friends, every duty someone else to cover it.

The emperor and Mei Feng were absorbed entirely in each other, no time even to look about them to see what they might have missed.

Eventually, Jiao simply couldn't be in there any longer.

She came out into the rain and the wind, ready to lie if anyone should ask her why. She might plausibly be going to check that men were keeping proper watch at the city's edge. A fire isn't out until the last cinder loses its glow; if she had been Tunghai Wang she would have brought her army back into the city on the very heels of the typhoon, if she still had an army she could bring.

No one did ask, but she made a point of checking anyway. Where she found troops, she talked to them; when she knew where to look, on rooftops and under sheltering archways, she sought them out. It was all hollowness, all show. She didn't care.

Doubt was bad, self-doubt was worse. Worst was what underlay it all, her folly, her absurd attachment to Yu Shan.

She was too old to be besotted. He was too young to be of any abiding interest. She believed both those things profoundly.

In theory.

In practice—well. If there were one thing almost as foolish as doting on a mountain boy, it would be denying the clear fact of it. Jiao had always dealt with the world as it was. As it came to her. Which might well be at swordspoint, but might just as well be in the tumbled covers of a bed. Either way, she reckoned her successes and her failures and moved on with whatever she'd achieved, coins or scars, experience either way. Tales to tell.

She didn't dwell on faces left behind, she didn't moon over lost beauties. Jealousy had no grip on her; she walked away. It was easy. She expected to keep nothing, except what she could carry or wear.

Except . . .

Physically, of course, he was delightful. His body was more than commonly lovely, more than commonly strong. Couple that with the charm of innocence, and she had treasured his presence in her bed, for so long as she could keep him there.

He was not so innocent now. She couldn't lament that, when she'd been mostly the cause of it. She had loved, indeed, having him to train, to educate, to corrupt: to take the boy and make a worthwhile man of him.

Apparently she had been working for Siew Ren's benefit and not her own, but she ought not to care so much about that. She ought not to care at all.

It was the jade, of course, in his blood and bone that made him such a pleasure, that gave him a literal charm. She did understand that. There was magic about a man of jade, that drew the eye and the heart together. How else could one man command an empire— and why else would he want to keep the stone to himself? Yu Shan should have died and died again, for his abuse of jade. More than once, it had been Jiao who saved him.

That didn't matter. It wasn't the kind of debt a boy had to repay. No.

She walked in the rain, and everything that did matter was a weight on her back and an ache in her breast. She had been angry for a long time now. Tonight she was mourning, but that anger was only banked up, not extinguished. No fire is out till the last cinder has ceased to glow.

Still, it was a relief to be so full of sorrow that her temper had no room to rise. It seemed more proper, somehow. Anger was a cloak she wrapped around her, but sadness welled up from within.

Sad, then—and wet, very wet—she walked the empty streets of a city fallen twice. And here was a well-wall, and no, she had no thought of jumping in; but still she could get no wetter, in the well or out of it, so there was no reason not to sit on the wall and dwell on all the losses of her day, the losses of her heart. The loss of herself, that could bring her here and to this, glooming in the rain in the hours after battle when she ought to be exultant, a survivor, drunk and gleeful with her men . . .

She tipped her head back: rain in her face, warm rain, it was almost like taking a bath with her clothes on. Her fighting-clothes, but the fighting was over now, for a while at least. If she went back to Taishu with the emperor, it might be over forever. Unless she fought Yu Shan. Or she could fight Siew Ren, of course, but that was the same thing now, Yu Shan would come between them and she'd have to fight him instead. Fight and lose. She wasn't used to losing fights, but she thought this one was lost already.

There was a noise, a yowling protest that sounded even above the constant fall of rain. Jiao was already smiling before she saw the cat.

Young cat, almost still a kitten, walking out of an alley. Soaked through and through, fur spiked with water, so wet there was no reason not to walk in the rain. Though he was certainly going to complain about it.

Jiao chirruped at him. "Hullo, little cat."

It was always a surprise when cats came to her, she was an unlikely friend. Twice a surprise today, in this city, in the rain.

"Lucky little cat," she murmured, stroking his head with a finger, watching water squeeze out ahead of it. "Nobody's eaten you yet. Perhaps they were waiting for you to grow?"

The cat spoke again, brief and assertive; and leaped from her lap to her shoulder, stretched himself across her neck, spoke directly into her ear.

"Oh, you think so, do you? Well, your choice. I may eat you yet. If you stay, if I get hungry. You might do better jumping down the well. Maybe you live down the well anyway, you're that wet. Maybe you think it's safer, smart little cat, and you've come to grumble at me for sitting on your doorstep. Are you chasing me off, or inviting me in? I wonder how deep it is, your home . . ."

There was a loose stone in the capping of the wall. She had been rocking it back and forth, picking away flakes of mortar, wanting vaguely to pick it up and drop it childishly down the well just to hear the splash.

Now she had an excuse. It was almost a reason.

It was a big stone, but if the well was deep she'd need a big splash just to hear it. The rain had filled her ears and soaked into her head.

Loose it might be, but she still needed both hands to wrench the stone out of its bed, where it had tried to wedge itself between its fellows.

Hoisted it high, held it poised for a moment above the mouth of the well—like a priestess at an altar, before a congregation of a cat—and let it fall.

Listened for the splash, and heard a drier, duller impact first. And then, together, a wetly disappointing sound as of water swallowing a stone that hasn't fallen very far at all, has had its true fall broken by something else just above the waterline; and a grunt, almost a cry, however hastily it was swallowed down.

And the world was different, the rain was just a factor, the cat was a fool if he stayed where he was on her shoulder. She was on her feet already, her tao was in her hand and she was calling down into the dark. "Come out. I know you're there and you'll have to climb up sooner or later, so it might as well be now. I expect it's getting rather full down there, isn't it? And there's sure to be more water on its way. You really might as well climb up . . ."

WHOEVER HE was, he heard her; more to the point, he listened. She could hear him splashing and scrabbling, muttering to himself, his voice echoing oddly in the rocky round of the well.

She heard the scrape of steel over stone, and stood ready. He'd be a rebel, sure. Caught out by the emperor's sudden arrival, cut off from his friends, hiding up and hoping to sneak out of the city after dark. He wouldn't be the only one: just an unlucky one, caught by a random stone dropped by a foolish woman feeling sorry for herself.

Now she was all fighter, poised and eager. Here came his head, ducking up: a broad weathered face, a veteran soldier, running with blood where his scalp had been torn open by her stone. He was lucky perhaps not to have been knocked unconscious, not to have slipped down into the rising well and drowned.

It was an odd kind of luck, that would save his life one minute and snatch it back the next. She should take it right now, hew his head from his shoulders while she had the chance, while he clung precariously to the well-wall. Why not? She meant to kill him anyway.

But then his body would fall back into the well and rot there, tainting the water for weeks. Months.

She waited, then, while he heaved himself mutely over the wall. A lash of rain across her eyes; she cleared them impatiently, and now he had his own tao drawn.

Well. Here was a fight, what she most wanted: something she could do, to remind herself of who she was. Pirate, lethal, merciless . . .

"So," she said, because Yu Shan was right, perhaps, she would still be talking when they buried her, "you follow Tunghai Wang, I suppose?"

"All the way," the man said. "From the Hidden City, and before."

"All the way to this rat-hole, to hide down in a well," and die here in the rain. "Was it worth it?"

The man shrugged. "You follow the emperor, and hide on an island and eat fish. Is that worth it?"

Well, she did eat fish, that much at least was true. The rest she wasn't sure of. She wasn't on Taishu now, and didn't much want to go back. Did she follow the emperor? It was Yu Shan she had followed into the emperor's service. She might have stepped up to be chief of the imperial guard, the position was there for her to seize—and she had deliberately stepped away, choosing to cross the strait in the second fleet this morning, putting together her own rough troop and leading them almost in her own separate battle, fighting because it was there to do, not for the emperor's glory or his enemies' defeat.

It was Mei Feng who had brought her across the river and back to the emperor; and what she'd found in his shadow, well . . .

Oddly, she found herself stepping back now, lowering her blade. Not wanting to set the seal of steel on his charge, suddenly refusing to commit herself.

"Oh, get out of here," she said. "If you can. There's a watch on the river and the valley roads, but go up high and you could be lucky. Everyone's ducking the rain, anyway."

He hesitated; she said, "Go on, go! Give my respects to Tunghai Wang, if you can find him. Tell him he might as well come back, no one could defend this city; but tell him there's no point, he couldn't defend it either. Why waste lives?"

It was only not to waste another life, that's what she told herself, watching the man turn and start to run. What did they have to fight about? He was a soldier, she was a pirate. He was committed, she was not. She had given no thought to the emperor before this summer, when she all but tripped over him. Except to think about stealing his jade, of course. Every pirate in the land likely thought of that a time or two, but she at least had tried it. That was something.

Maybe she should have another try. That would be something else, a reminder, where her own roots lay.

The cat was still on her shoulders, seeming quite settled there. She eyed him askance and said, "No point getting comfortable with me, little cat. I'm not offering anyone a home, I'm not staying. Here or there, either side of that dragon-infested sea. I may have to go back to Taishu one more time, but then I'm off. In a hurry, maybe. You wouldn't like that so much. The road is like the rain, only it doesn't ever stop. Maybe I'll give you to Mei Feng, something to cuddle and fuss over till the baby comes. She'd like that. So would you, I'm guessing. Maybe I'll do that . . ."

seven

Tunghai Wang was a soldier first and foremost. Before he was a general, long before he was a generalissimo with generals under him, with ambitions to rise one last little step higher: before any of that he had been a soldier. How many campaigns had he marched on, how many battles fought, how many winters waited out before spring came with its inevitable orders to march again? He couldn't count them all. Someone might actually do that, he supposed, when he did finally achieve the throne. Some eunuch clerk would have the task of recording all the details of Tunghai's life, numbering every battle, praising every stroke of sword and strategy . . .

Let him do that. Tunghai was concerned with the thing itself, writing it in history, not on the page. Blade and blood and the march over land, not brush and ink and paper.

Right now blades were like to rust, there was no blood and the march was something close to a retreat, the next worst thing. The land was all mud, broken terraces and ruined paddy.

He had pulled his men back, back and back, out of Santung-valley altogether. There was no organizing anything in the typhoon; in its aftermath, in the spewing rain there was no land to stand on between the rising river and the hills of liquid mud.

How many times had the weather ruined a perfectly good battle-plan, a sudden strike, an unassailable position? There was no counting that either, though someone no doubt would try. Time and again he had done this, trudging wearily against the wind, away from what he wanted. This was soldiering, the heart

of it, the real thing; and it had never been more bitter, he had never
been more sullenly resentful.

Typhoons came and went, but not like this. Half a day's march,
the setting sun glimpsed through broken cloud brought them to a
settlement that had barely felt a fling of wind all day. Here he
could regroup, send parties out to gather all his scattered men behind him, draw his generals and commanders together in a straw-
strewn barn.

He could say the impossible thing, the thing no soldier should
be obliged to face: "The dragon is against us."

"Sir . . ."

"No, hear me. The dragon destroyed my fleet when we went to
invade Taishu; twice now she has let the emperor's boats across
the strait to attack me. And this today was a dragon-storm, nothing natural. I saw her fetch it in. Just when we were poised to crush
the emperor, when he had walked entirely into the trap we laid; we
had him between our fists there, and the weather defeated us. The
dragon defeated us. Not him."

They stood in silence, in acquiescence.

"So," he said. "The emperor is in Santung. Likely he will go
back to Taishu, his people will insist; they all know now, Santung
cannot be defended. We have proved it, and so has he. There will
be boats, going to and fro. Perhaps they have an arrangement with
the dragon; perhaps she can be reasoned with, or bribed. We need
to know whether she can tell which boats are loyal to the emperor
and which are not. Send men to steal a boat and try the strait. If
they can cross in the emperor's wake, let them go to Ping Wen and
learn his news. If not—well, we learn by that. Send more than one
boat. Send a dozen, if you can find them. We need to know if we
can get through.

"But more than that," he said, "we need to know how we can
fight a dragon. She has been chained before; she can be chained
again."

eight

*O*hé, old man!"

The cry came unexpectedly, across the creak and toss of many boats. He looked up from another captain's deck, saw a cluster of lanterns on the wharf and was surprised how bright they seemed. He'd been splicing a snapped cable, old gnarled experienced fingers working by touch in his own shadow, and he hadn't noticed the set of the sun.

"What do you want?" His back ached, now that he was noticing. He was hungry and tired and wet, and would quite like to stop soon. He should find Pao and take him away in search of supper. They would sleep on his own boat, which had taken no harm in the typhoon; the bedding might be damp, but old bones were used to that and young bones were learning. Pao might not know it yet but he was the boat's next master, if he wanted it. He might never learn the ways of the goddess, he wasn't born to her service and hadn't grown up in her regard, but that was true of half the fleet these days. At any rate, there was no one else.

"You," the call came back, "the emperor wants you. He sends for you."

"What, now?"

"Of course, now! Come with us, come at once . . ."

Old Yen bowed in lamplight to the imperial summons, and hurried across the bridge of boats between this and the wharf. A step up here, a leap down there; a long stretch from rail to rail; a tug on one cable, to draw the next boat closer. Strewn timber and coils of rope to be stepped over or around, tricky footing in the gloom.

And so to shore, wet and filthy and obedient. Here were his summoners, a party of soldiers. Some were women, but soldiers none the less: which made them the emperor's personal guard, who had sailed here on Old Yen's own boat.

He said, "Why should the emperor want me?"—but they only shook their heads and hurried him, faster than old tired feet wanted to go over wet stones in the dark.

He might have believed this back in Taishu-port, where *the emperor* could sometimes mean *Mei Feng*. She might send for him just to see him, to be reassured about his health and safety; or to ask about the mute child and its welfare; or about the dragon, or the goddess. Or to be angry with him, about any of those or for any reason else.

But Mei Feng was on Taishu and he was not. This city was not that city. His girl was beyond his reach.

HERE WAS an end at last, the gate to the governor's palace; and oh he was weary now, and still bewildered. All the more so when his escorts took him through one courtyard and through another, into a room that was too small and too private for his deserving, and here was the emperor indeed.

Also, here was Mei Feng. Where she could not be, where she was not, here in Santung. It wasn't possible. This was a dream.

Except that she was scowling up at him from a luxurious heap of cushions, she was tumbling a cat out of her lap and scattering cushions and coverlets all over as she came at him like a pocket typhoon, an invasion of one, furious and irresistible.

Small hard body, cable-tight and whippy as bamboo. Her hug threatened to squeeze all the surviving breath out of him. Then she lifted her face, still frowning. "Why are you so wet?"

"Wet? Mei Feng, it's *raining* . . ." Had she perhaps not noticed the typhoon, here inside palace walls? Had she been conjured here from Taishu, and never passed through open air between?

"Still?" She glanced from one escort to another. Mute and treacherous, they shook their heads. Old Yen thought back: oh. Perhaps it had in fact stopped raining, a little while back.

"Well, but it has been; and there was work to do . . ."

"And you didn't think to stop work, to change your wet clothes and maybe eat a meal, maybe sleep till morning? And you," his escorts again, "you didn't think to find him something dry to wear, before you dragged an old man up a steep hill after he's been up and working hard all last night and all day since?"

"Mei Feng, that's not fair! The emperor said—"

"Oh, the *emperor, he* said, did he? And that makes it all right, does it?"

She was swiveling around now to bring her fury to bear on his imperial majesty, except that he forestalled her. He was right there, his hands were on her hips and his chin in her hair, his smile must be resonating through her bones as he said, "Of course it is all right, if the emperor says so. The emperor is a god," with his long godly arms wrapping themselves around her now, and it was good to see them so kind with each other again. "And besides," the emperor went on, "Old Yen would have been just as wet if we had left him undisturbed. He would have worked just as late or later, he might still have forgotten to eat supper. And now we have him here under our eyes, you have his company and can make sure that he eats a good meal and dries his beard and sleeps until you wake him in the morning."

"You might have sent someone down," she growled, refusing to be placated, "to do all that without dragging his poor tired soaked self all the way up here. I would have sent Chung, if you hadn't stolen him away to make a soldier of him."

"He made a soldier of himself," the emperor crooned, rocking her gently, "or else Shen did that for him. Not me. Do you want him back?"

"Not particularly. Not if he doesn't want to come, if he'd rather camp out in the rain and be mysterious. Leave him to Shen. And don't change the subject," which was blatantly, magnificently unfair. "Look at my grandfather, see the state of him? I'm ashamed of you, all of you," with a glower for his escorts, lumped in with the emperor, "treating an old man this way. You, go and find him some dry clothes. You, fetch food. Hot food, he needs heat. Will someone, anyone," addressed to the room at large, "bring him a cup of tea at least? Oh, never mind. I'll do it myself . . ."

Old Yen stood quiet. This really wasn't about him, it all lay between Mei Feng and the emperor. Who quieted her with his fingers on her lips, who spoke into her silence: "Hush, you will not. You will lie down and speak to your grandfather, tell him the news you have. I thought you might like to do that, which is really why I sent for him tonight."

Disarmed, she was utterly ungracious, unrelenting. "He still wants a cup of tea."

"And he shall have one. I will make it myself."

"You? Do you know how?"

He laughed, and kissed her at last. "I do. Yu Shan has taught me."

Mention of Yu Shan brought another fleeting shadow to her face. But she held her hand out to Old Yen and settled him among her cushions, curled herself up beside him. *News,* the emperor had said, but she didn't share it yet. She seemed to cast about rather for something else, anything else that she could say instead.

"I am sorry that you had to make that climb, Grandfather. We weren't up here for the storm, we took shelter in the jade store and that would have been an easier walk for you, only the river wouldn't stop rising and the emperor wouldn't let us stay," *he wouldn't let me stay* she seemed to mean, "so we all had to troop up here where even he could be absolutely sure the water would never reach us . . ."

She was hiding something. It might be how she had contrived to come here from Taishu: had she begged a ride from the dragon, perhaps? A ride on the typhoon? Or it might be why she had contrived to come, what absurdity had brought her in chase of her man. If she was so keen not to tell, Old Yen was at least as keen not to hear it; but the emperor was frowning over his kettle and his teapot, which was nothing to do with the complications of making tea, and he would preempt her if she didn't hurry up.

The scruffy cat had come back to her and she was fussing with his fur, unteasing mats with her fingers. "Grandfather. I'm, I'm going to have a baby."

Which made him a very old man indeed, he realized with a rush of delight. Very Old Yen: a *great*-grandfather. And part of the imperial family, great-grandfather to a dynasty . . .

He was still absorbing that when the emperor brought him a cup of tea. Imperial tea, fine and extraordinary, not at all the harsh brew he drank himself; and the emperor was sitting at his feet all unexpectedly, for all the world like a son-in-law looking for advice.

"Grandfather, you know more about the goddess than anyone except perhaps her priestesses. And you know the dragon too, you believed in the dragon when perhaps nobody else did."

Well, of course: the one implied the other, you couldn't have the goddess unless you had the dragon too, her prisoner.

Her escaped prisoner.

The emperor said, "We need to know how to fight the dragon, how to chain her again."

TWO

A Tiger's Lost Song

one

$\mathcal{M}$a Lin had her daughters back.

Those two who were still living, at least, she had those. The third in a way had never left her. Little Meuti's body might lie unmarked and overlooked between the paddy and the road, in some bare scrabble of soil that even Ma Lin could not find for certain; her ghost was a presence intermittently, *tug-tug* at Ma Lin's trousers.

For a while she'd been all that Ma Lin had of daughters, and welcome so.

But now the girls were back, the living girls, Jin and Shola. Insofar as Jin ever could come back, which was not very far, perhaps, not far enough. Sometimes she was not there at all, and the goddess lived through her. Which might be Jin's own choice, but Ma Lin didn't think so.

She didn't like to think about her elder daughter's choices, nor her life.

Still, this life or any was better than what Meuti had, *tug-tug* from somewhere forgotten under earth. And Ma Lin's own life was better with her girls. Even given the company they came with: women of the emperor's court—only servants, they insisted, but they seemed terribly grand to Ma Lin—and soldiers too, guards to watch her daughters. Actually she thought they watched her more, to be sure she didn't steal the girls away.

Even given the women and the soldiers and the emperor's own

message, written on a paper that she could not read and was obliged to treasure.

There was no need to read it. Ma Lin had understood it from the first, just from the weight of it in her hand, the self-importance of the imperial seal. It said that her girls belonged now to the throne—the Throne Victorious, a battle fought and a city won, and all thanks to her daughter—and were returned to her only as a gesture, as a kindness, for a time. She should hold herself ready, the letter said, to say goodbye again.

The emperor's words might be holy; she still thought they were wrong.

He might be divine, but he was not alone in that.

If her girls belonged to anyone, she thought it was to the Li-goddess whose temple this was.

SOMETIMES THEY could still just be girls, no meaning else. As now, when she sat on the height of the temple steps with Shola, shelling walnuts. Making a game of it, trying to split the shells evenly so that Jin on the step below could float them like little boats in a bowl of water, fill them with dry rice and make a fleet of them, coffle them together with fine-woven ropes of her own hair and tow them like barges from one side of the bowl to the other, as a great fleet of ships might fill itself with men and sail from Taishu to the mainland and back again if it only had Jin to play goddess, to keep the dragon at a distance.

For now there were no ships, no fleets. The biggest boat Ma Lin had seen since the invasion was a sampan on the beach below. The soldiers used that to ferry back and forth across the creek. They brought food over daily, paused to pray, went back to their tents and fires on the beach. They were building huts.

If anyone was bold enough to sail the strait, they didn't do it under Jin's guard; she was here.

If anyone tried to keep the dragon at bay, Ma Lin didn't think that it was working. They saw her often from the headland here.

This little boat didn't bother her, apparently, or else the river was not hers to claim. Sometimes she seemed to pause, to hang like a fortress in the sky, to peer down in what might be curiosity, might be discontent. There was no saying what she might be looking at: the sampan, the temple. Jin.

Ma Lin looked back, sometimes. *I am a mother; I too can be a dragon.* It was all bluff, of course, but that was easy with the temple at her back and her daughters in the temple. She could be ferocious, when she didn't need to be.

She had been ferocious actually, physically, at need—but not against a dragon. Nor against the emperor, nor the goddess, though they took her children from her. Ma Lin knew her limits, and they were men.

THE DRAGON was up there now, drifting against the wind, an idle undulation, a livid scar in the sky.

Ma Lin and Shola had watched for a while, but she was almost commonplace at this distance. They turned back to the nuts.

Until there was shouting on the beach across the creek, voices thinned by distance. Other sounds too, scratching jarring sounds that would be worse if they were closer, steel on steel. Ma Lin knew.

Men rose up from where they had been squatting on the headland or drowsing in the sun. Women clustered in the temple doorway.

Ma Lin told Shola to take her sister in. Yes, yes, the nuts too; the rice, the bowl of water; everything, if Jin wanted it. Just, go *in* . . .

Then she joined the guards at the cliff-edge, where they could look over the water to the beach.

Where men were fighting, but she knew that already. The sounds were bitterly familiar.

She couldn't tell, they all looked alike to her; she had to ask, "Who is it, who has attacked the camp?"

This was what the camp was for, of course, to guard the temple and its approaches, its treasures, herself and her daughters. Jin.

The man beside her shrugged. "Rebels."

She might have said as much herself. Any man with a blade in his hand and not an imperial soldier, he was a rebel by definition. Those men down there might be loyal followers of Tunghai Wang, acting under orders. Or they might have no orders; they might have lost their officers and turned bandit for lack of any other way to live. They might just be hungry.

It didn't seem to matter. They were men; they were fighting. Ma Lin felt tired more than frightened now. Perhaps they would win, perhaps not. Either way, she thought she would trust herself and her daughters to the goddess, rather than to men. They all looked alike to her. Looked and felt and smelled alike, blood-washed and grim and monstrous. She wanted none of them anywhere near her daughters.

She could be grim herself, if she had to be. She too had smelled of blood.

Her eyes were good enough to pick out the bodies sprawled on sand, the men still standing. Still fighting. And falling, the emperor's men, one by one under just too many blades.

When the last of them had fallen, then came the aftermath: rebels went among the wounded with knives, and left none living.

The soldier beside her grunted. His captain swore. Then started calling orders, as he saw the rebels head purposefully for the sampan. "You, you and you—down the path, delay them any way you can. Catch them in the boat, as soon as they come to land. Go!"

It was death, surely, three men to delay a dozen. The word itself was a giveaway, delay. None the less, the three he picked went pitching down the treacherous footing of the path, blades in hand already.

"You and you, halfway down, that place I showed you. Dig out the rocks we loosened before. Use poles, and stay above them; the path will collapse. Then you can defend the point, as the rebels try to climb. The rest of you, stand ready at the top here. Any who come this far, we are enough for them."

Perhaps they were. If there weren't just as many rebels or more sneaking through the woods this side of the creek. The captain did send a couple of men to the trees, to cry a warning. They were all he could spare; that was all they could do.

It lay in the goddess's hands to defend Ma Lin and her daughters. The soldiers could look after themselves, or die. Most likely die. She thought she would be safe, though, with her girls. She would join them in the temple, when it came necessary. In the meantime she stood with the captain, just to see.

The rebels heaved the sampan into the river's flow, piled aboard—and left the paddles alone, ignored the punting-poles, drew up the sail and steered with wind and current, out past the headland and into the breakers of the strait.

"Are they . . . Do they think they can take that out to *sea*?"

That was the captain, his voice almost querulous with shock.

Apparently they did. Likely it had made at least one journey across the strait, from Taishu in the emperor's fleet. Perhaps under a former master it had been back and forth like a silk-weaver's shuttle. These little boats did that, she knew, fishermen with a catch to trade. They used to do it all the time.

Perhaps they would again—but not under the dragon's eye. Ma Lin would not have taken any boat to sea just now without her daughter aboard, big Jin with the voice of the goddess in her throat.

She cast an eye upward, and there was the dragon indeed. Hanging like a banner in the air, like a long tail of bright silk that defied the wind—or controlled it, summoned it perhaps, her wind, her own—to hold her just exactly there beyond the surf, above the strait.

Her strait, her own.

If that wasn't true, the dragon surely thought it was.

She looked like a cat, Ma Lin thought, patient for the inevitability of a mouse.

The sampan beat straight out to sea, as the men did snatch up paddles now to drive it through the awkward waters where surf and tide met current. Ma Lin spared them an occasional, incredulous glance. Mostly, she watched the dragon.

Where she hung in the air, where she turned as though the wind had shifted, as though the wind could shift her.

WHERE THERE was something to be seen on her neck, a lumpen strangeness that broke the smooth sleek lines of her, jutting crudely upward.

WHERE IT looked almost—almost!—like a man, a rider on the dragon's back.

WHERE THE dragon was moving now, but not toward the sampan. It looked almost, almost as though she were coming to the temple.

BEING RIDDEN to the temple, as though the man on her back meant to pray here and needed her to bring him in.

ALMOST, SHE almost did. Not quite.

The temple sat with its feet in a hollow. Beyond that was a rising grassy lip, and then the bare rocks of the crag thrusting through like teeth above the drop, above the crashing sea.

The dragon settled on those teeth, right on the edge there, the claws of all four feet biting deep. Ma Lin couldn't possibly have felt the deep rock of the headland tremble under that sudden weight, no, not possibly—but she thought she had. She thought those teeth had almost broken loose.

Soldiers ran for the temple, which she thought was wise. Others plunged off down the cliff path. That she thought was stupid; there was nowhere to go down there. Perhaps they were swimmers, perhaps they had in mind a swift splash across the river—but she doubted it. She doubted they were thinking at all.

She and the captain were simply standing, watching. She thought that was admirable in him, stupid in herself. She should have gone to the temple. She still could. The dragon was only sitting there, Ma Lin was out of reach and could yet make a run for it . . .

Except that none of that was true, not quite. The dragon wasn't only sitting there; she had turned her head to look at them. And her neck, her long neck was coiled back, poised, like a snake on the verge of striking. Ma Lin wasn't at all sure that she stood out of reach. Or that her legs could run. There was something captivating about the undersea glow of the dragon's eyes, much that was terrifying about the mouth and claws and the simple dreadful size of her. Between the one and the other, Ma Lin wasn't actually sure that she could move at all.

The figure on the dragon's back hoisted his leg across the spiky ridges of her spine and slid down over her extraordinary scaled hide. Using her leg and foot as steps, he came to ground; then staggered a little and had to stand for a moment with one hand clinging to her iron claw, catching his balance, like a sailor come to port.

She just crouched there, monumentally impatient, moving not at all.

At last, he walked away from her. Ma Lin almost thought he pushed himself away, determined but a little reluctant, still a little wanting to cling.

Something about him puzzled Ma Lin. He'd just stepped off a dragon, but not that. Not just that. He didn't seem big enough, somehow. To be riding a dragon.

Not a legend, not a hero, not a god.

Not a man, not that either, now that she could see him clearly in the sunlight.

Just a boy. That was it: just a frail, bony boy with wild hair and ragged trousers, no shirt, no older than her Jin. He looked like he was made of paper, stretched over a frame of green bamboo.

Then he turned to face the dragon, and now he really did look like he was made of paper, used paper, because all his back was written on, deep black characters that Ma Lin couldn't read.

SHE'D THOUGHT—no, she'd *assumed* that he was coming to one or the other of them, the priestess or the soldier. She did look like a priestess these days, she knew that. It was in her stance perhaps, the way she walked in the world, the goddess at her side.

This boy who rode the dragon, he seemed quite uninterested in her and the captain. Neglectful of them. He faced the dragon, rather; and one arm lifted, and without seeing his face Ma Lin couldn't tell whether that was a wave of farewell or a gesture of dismissal, *go now,* such as a man might make to a servant, or a mount.

Not, surely not to a dragon.

But the dragon rose, lifting effortlessly from the headland as though she only willed the world to fall away and so it did.

The boy tipped his head back to watch her. She apparently tipped her head down, to look at him.

Ma Lin couldn't imagine how he bore it, the intensity of that stare, both eyes blazing.

Perhaps he couldn't turn away, perhaps he was snared entirely in the tangle of her thoughts. Crushed under the simple weight of her attention. But he seemed—well, almost easy. Hands loose at his sides, one foot poised on its toe in the grass, head cocked like a boy caught in conversation.

He might almost have been smiling. She couldn't see his face, but something in his body said so.

Then the dragon rose farther, turned and was swiftly gone, out across the water.

A great wash of air came from her whipping tail, and Ma Lin could have choked on the stink of it, all sea-mud and rot.

THE BOY, it seemed, meant to stand where he was and watch her. Watch over her, perhaps.

The captain moved no more than his eyes, from boy to dragon and back to boy again. For a competent man, he seemed helpless to do anything but watch.

Someone had to move, to speak. That would be Ma Lin, then. Apparently.

She stepped forward, a little hesitantly. The boy wasn't the only one whose world had rocked beneath him.

She was a short woman, but her head still came up higher than his shoulder. Not a big boy, not a strong boy; scrawny, she would have called him, accustomed as she was to heavy men.

She wanted to say, *who are you?*—but questions are invidious and answers unreliable. She wasn't even sure who her own daughter was, from one moment to the next.

She said, "I am called Ma Lin." That at least was a certainty.

He glanced sideways at her, distracted. His mouth moved, and for a little while no sound came from it. He scowled; she thought, *you have been too long talking to the dragon, little one. In your head. You have forgotten how real people need to speak.*

He cleared his throat, shook his head, tried again. This time he found his voice, or a thin unready scrape of it. It was good enough for her; she had heard far worse a voice from one she loved.

He said, "My name is Han. She," his eyes turned back to the sea, to the dragon, finding her instantly even against the glare of sunlight on water, "I don't believe she has a name. Or none that she will share."

"No." It would be beyond imagining, for a dragon to bear any name a human mouth could pronounce or a human mind encompass. Now she had seen, she understood that exactly. Perhaps it was a kindness in the dragon, not to share. Perhaps a dragon name would break a human mind entirely. "Are you her slave?"

He said, "No. Or yes, perhaps. Sometimes, if she would let me. I have been her master too. Sometimes, when she will let me."

"I don't understand."

"No. Nor does she."

For a moment, Ma Lin thought she had fallen in with a magician. But he smiled and shrugged and shook his head—*how can I possibly understand what baffles her?*—and something in her warmed unscrupulously to this unscrupulous, unsettling boy.

For want of any other question, she said, "Tell me."

He said, "She likes to kill. She has been a prisoner, our prisoner, chained by our magic; she says she has drowned in human voices for too long. She wants her waters back, the rule of them, but even more she wants to see men die. I can . . . prevent her, a little. I can prevent her killing me, and others too. Does that make me her slave? Perhaps. I don't know. The most I ever was before was a pirate's boy, and the most I ever stopped him doing was killing me." He stopped and smiled, rubbed his nose, perhaps realizing that some might see that as a gift he had. Survival was a place to start, perhaps.

His face changed as perhaps he remembered someone else, whom the pirate had killed regardless.

She said, "Not everyone would think it was a slave's place to keep his mistress from what she wanted most."

"No—but some of us, we have to. Sometimes." He stared out to sea. "Someone else," he said, "can stop her killing, on the water. It makes her furious, but some boats, some fleets she cannot touch."

Ma Lin confessed, a little. "The Li-goddess," she said, nodding. "This is her temple."

"Ah. Is that why she brought me here?" It was a question without an answer; he didn't wait. "She thinks that only some boats are protected. Someone holds her back, she says. Like I can."

"Yes." Ma Lin was boastful suddenly, stupidly. "My daughter: she speaks for the goddess. I have her here now," with a jerk of her head back toward the temple, the crowded temple steps, where soldiers and women together were staring at this priestess who dared speak to the boy who rode a dragon.

"You do? Well, keep her close. The dragon does not love her.

Nor those like her. I think there is more than one. She has been waiting for a boat that had no protection." His eyes found it, and hers followed: the sampan, a speck now on the water. He knew where it was because the dragon knew, she thought. The dragon hung above it, pendulous, a rock in air.

"You could protect them. You said it."

"Perhaps. Yes. But she has my promise. She needs to know whether she can still do this."

"You mean she plans to kill those men? And you will let her . . . ?"

"Will you argue for their lives?"

For any lives, she meant to say, she wanted to. But her eyes moved willy-nilly to the beach across the creek, where men lay dead because those in the sampan had slaughtered them.

"They are rebels," she said, as if that mattered, as if it could. As if one lord's service was different from another's. And then, "They are men too. Like your pirates, like you. Has your dragon not killed enough rebels?"

Apparently not. He shrugged. "Your emperor would want them dead, because they killed his men. You might want them dead, because they would have killed you too if they had come up here. She wants them dead, because they are abroad on her waters; and because she really, really needs to know. Keep your daughter in the temple there, don't let her interfere."

She said, "I will," thinking *Shola will;* and, "Can you not . . . ?"

"I can," he said, with a faraway look in his eye, "but I promised."

Ma Lin turned back to the glimmering strait. Without his sure gaze for guide she had to scan for the speck that was the sampan, and the darker larger speck above it that was the dragon.

Almost, she wanted to turn around: as if she expected or dreaded to see her daughter stride forth, shrugging off little Shola and fearsome with purpose, inhabited, ridden. If the goddess stood

here and watched, Ma Lin thought, in Jin's body, she could prevent it.

But she didn't know, or didn't care, or else Ma Lin was wrong.
Or those men out there were not her people, or else they were beyond her reach.

She didn't appear, at least, here on the headland or out on the
water. Surely she could have shaped herself a body of water, if she
had chosen to? She could have risen up to defy the dragon and protect the sampan, *these are my seas . . .*

But she did not, and perhaps they were not.

Ma Lin didn't exactly see the dragon strike. She saw her fall,
spear-straight, a dark rip in the sky; but she lost her against the
water, where she had already lost the boat, in the scatter of light
and confusion of the waves.

What she saw was the splash of it, a great eruptive rising hurl
of sea.

The dragon, she was sure, could cleave the waves as neatly as a
blade. This was a statement, a declaration, *I can!*

A shout, a fling in the face of the goddess.

Men died, so that one immortal might make her mark against
another.

Nothing changes.

"I wonder what they wanted," she said. "Who they were, where
they were going."

The boy shrugged. "Wherever they went it would have been the
same, fire and death." And then, "No. Whatever they wanted it
would have been the same, water and death, their deaths. Whatever they thought, this was always where they were going: to the
belly of the dragon, or the belly of the sea."

"It is not only their deaths," Ma Lin said. "The people will
starve if they cannot fish, if they dare not go to sea." She felt like
a priestess, negotiating. The Li-goddess had always looked kindly
on fishermen, and they on her; her temple in Santung used sometimes to smell more strongly of her worshippers than it did of joss.

"Taishu will starve altogether, if her people lose touch with the sea."

"She may not always be this angry," Han said. "I don't know. She must have let boats sail once, before she was chained. Perhaps she will allow it again, later. But she has been in chains a long time," *chained by men, held prisoner by your goddess,* "and she is very angry now."

She was, yes. Angry, and exultant also. At least, that was what Ma Lin saw, as the dragon breached again: bursting from the water to climb in giddy spirals, high and high. Food in her belly, if dragons needed food; freedom in her waters, freedom in the air. Freedom to strike, where men disregarded her and dared to sail unprotected. Death in her eye. She had much to celebrate.

Also, she had a boy. A strange boy, but anyone would be strange, the dragon's voice abroad, her plenipotentiary.

Food in her belly if she wanted it, but not in his; he was dreadfully thin. And half naked, barefoot, alone . . .

Ma Lin said, "Will she come back for you?"

He smiled. "When she wants me, when she thinks I might be useful. Or when she is angry again, when something goads her temper and she needs someone to hiss at."

"Well. While you wait, come inside and I will feed you. Find you a shirt too, and a decent pair of trousers."

He shook his head, strange boy. Starveling creature saying no to food, which should have been his first thing. "I won't wait for her," he said. "Not here. She can find me when she wants me; she'll know where I am." As he knew, always, where she was. Ma Lin had seen that, how his eyes found her irrevocably, exactly. She wondered what it must be like inside his head.

"Where will you go, then?" In his place she thought she might go far from the sea, far and far, hope to go so far that the dragon would lose touch.

He said, "I have . . . someone in the city, if I can find her. She did this to me," and his hand addressed the skin of his back, the tattooed characters he couldn't see himself. *She gave the dragon to me,* Ma Lin thought he meant, or else *she gave me to the dragon.*

"They have had typhoon in Santung, as well as war. She may not be there." *She may not be living.*

A shrug; she would not be as easily found as the dragon, perhaps. Nevertheless, he meant to look.

"It is no good place for a boy to be wandering on his own." She wasn't actually sure that she wanted to keep him here, or why that would be, if it was so; she seemed to be arguing for it none the less.

"No one will trouble me," he said. "The dragon would not allow it."

"The dragon may not be near enough to prevent it." A sudden blade in a back alley: what could the dragon do? If she were undersea, or soaring to the sun, or guarding her precious strait against another boat's incursion?

She expected another shrug, and won another smile: an expression of confidence, rather than carelessness. He thought the dragon would dance at his tail to keep him safe. Strange, strange boy. Or a strange life, to teach him such lessons.

Her own life had been strange enough, this summer. Perhaps that was why she wanted to keep him. Perhaps it was only for herself, for the man he would grow into, for the sake of the man she had lost and the son she never had. She was surrounded by women here and all the men were soldiers, nothing that she wanted. She would have liked a boy.

It seemed that she could not have this one. She said, "Stay," and he laughed aloud.

He said, "I must find Tien," though it wasn't clear to Ma Lin what he meant for her when he found her. She had done this, apparently, to him and to the dragon both: with whose consent and at whose command, there was no telling.

"Well," she said, "I will give you food for the road, because you have to eat. And a shirt. The captain might want to send a man or two with you; that would make the way easier, and help your search perhaps. He might think you need watching over." He might think that he would lose his place, if he let the dragon's boy wander unsupervised into Santung. He might think that he would lose his head.

He might be right.

two

This sudden hurry was apparently all Mei Feng's fault.

She liked that, rather.

Left to himself—as if he ever was!—the emperor would surely have stayed in Santung for weeks, perhaps for months: rebuilding, raising fortifications, scattering Tunghai Wang's defeated forces to the winds.

In his head, at least, that's how it would have been. In fact, if Tunghai Wang had been quicker to organize after the typhoon, the emperor might have found himself leading another desperate defense of the indefensible city. More likely, he would have found himself once again on the first boat to Taishu, sent away to safety like a child while his generals tried to save something of his army and his empire.

But Mei Feng had come, had chased him across the strait and across the city with her pregnancy like a banner held aloft, and now everything was different. Now he was eager to take her home, to see her safe and show her off, bragging young father, *see what I did.*

It was a blessing, in almost every way.

For once this morning he had gotten up before her, even. She wasn't sure that he had slept at all. He had kept her awake with talking, with touching, his long hand covering all the breadth of her belly, wondering how long he would be able to do that before she swelled. And how should he tell his mother, what would the old woman say, how immeasurably much would she welcome this? And . . .

And Mei Feng had fallen asleep at last to the onrunning murmur of his voice; and had roused this morning to the clatter of his trying to find the way out of an unfamiliar room in unfamiliar darkness, he who never rose before the sun was high. His substitute in bed was much smaller, softer to the touch, not necessarily less demanding: the little cat, Jiao's gift, who had been told to sleep in his basket but had manifested himself somehow beneath the covers, in a tight little curl against her flank.

Lacking the emperor—and not wishing to spoil the emperor's fun, by waking before he was ready for her—she reached down to stroke the cat good-morning. Her fingers spread through warm fur and felt a gratifying vibration; this cat purred with his bones, seemingly, silent and contained.

Then he uncurled himself beside her, stretched luxuriously—like a puddle of molten steel stretching itself into a tao, she thought, all edge and purpose—and sank little needle-claws into the flesh of her armpit.

She hissed, and squirmed away. He emerged from beneath the quilt to make first vociferous inquiry about his breakfast.

Happily, by then the emperor had finally found the door and sidled out. So she could tuck her hands behind her head and discuss matters openly with the cat where he perched on her chest, agree that service was shoddy in these times of war, that armies might come and go and typhoons too but there was never any excuse for delay in bringing breakfast. A scratch behind the ears was a good thing, to be sure; a stroke beneath the chin might well be welcome; but still, these were not and must never be first order of the day . . .

The door banged open again, allowing the emperor to discover her legitimately and cheerfully awake. He fetched in lamps and servants; blessedly, they brought trays with them. The traitor cat abandoned her for their greater allure, while the emperor settled himself on the bed and cupped her face with those fingers that could set all her skin atingle even before he kissed her.

Perhaps she could take lessons from the cat. Too much praise and wonder wasn't good for a boy, but he did deserve his own reward. If he could only feel it in her body, the way she felt the living tingle of the jade in his, that would be perfect.

Slipping her hand inside his robe, she scratched experimentally at his skin with one fingernail, and watched him twitch. Saw him smile. When she had him home, she still meant to borrow a needle and prick him all over to see where it would penetrate, where it blunted, where it bent and broke. She couldn't understand quite how his body worked anymore. He felt human enough, magnificently human. It was hard to imagine how a steel knife would snap sooner than penetrate imperial flesh, though she had the haft of it in her own keeping now, just as Ai Guo had the would-be assassin, the trusted eunuch in his.

She didn't quite like to think about that.

Perhaps she should set the cat to scratch the emperor. That little demon could make even a jade man bleed.

BREAKFAST WAS eaten on the bed that morning, a treat for all three of them. The cat had the best of it, she thought, a whole array of leftovers: chicken in basil, pork in a hot pepper sauce that made him sneeze but not stop eating.

Herself, she was happy enough to share eggs and rice with the emperor. If he dropped occasional jewels into her bowl— a shred of ham, a water-chestnut, a prawn filched from under the nose of the cat—that was undoubtedly his privilege. When he tried for a second prawn and found the cat alert this time, snatching it back with ferocious accuracy, then of course it must become a game, clacking chopsticks against batting paws. She watched and smiled and felt unbearably grown-up until someone else—not her!—coughed and murmured something about the sun and the tide, inexorable things somehow not quite subject to imperial whimsy.

So then he must hustle into his clothes and chase the day, leaving her simply to sit on the bed and carry on eating, as placid as an old goat. The cat might have the tidbits; bulk was enough. And she knew about time and tide, better than anyone in the palace here . . .

By the time they paraded down to the wharf—the cat complaining in his closed basket, which she wasn't allowed to carry herself—half the fleet was ready to sail, fit escort for an emperor in his pomp. Bright banners flapped at mastheads. Even Old Yen's bashful boat had been brought in to the wharf and vividly decked out in yellow.

If Old Yen had been offered any decoration himself, he had refused it. The mute temple child, though, was there in yellow bands. He would have been fetched down early, no doubt, to be certain sure the dragon didn't attack the fleet in harbor. Grandfather would be certain sure that she could not, because the goddess had a temple right there on the front and would protect it. Mei Feng thought that perhaps the dragon would not because the strait was hers but the river not, and this harbor was uncertain ground. Uncertain waters.

Someone would have weighed doubts and certainties and questions, and sent the child ahead anyway.

A woman had him today: a temple-woman, shaven-headed and drably dressed. No yellow. The child might belong to the emperor, but she did not. She belonged to the goddess.

Even the child's status was debatable. He was a eunuch, and so the emperor's own, by all law and custom—but he had been claimed and possessed by the goddess. He had spoken in her voice. How to choose, between rival divinities? Mei Feng was only glad she didn't have to. She knew where she belonged; that was enough.

He held his hand out, to help her up the gangplank. Which was . . . just delightful, when she had been running up and down this same gangplank all her life. One of her earliest memories was of running and falling, shrieking as she plunged, gurgling far down into the water and rising irresistibly to the surface again like a bubble, like the bubble of baby-fat she was. And then shrieking again, shrieking entirely with laughter when she saw a long array of faces peering anxiously down.

He was all caution and awkwardness, making it actually quite difficult for both of them on the narrow bouncing plank. Still, they reached the deck without mishap. Old Yen was there at the rail to bow them aboard, for all the world as though he had not sat up late with them last night, plotting the downfall of dragons.

The emperor must stand with the master of the boat, to welcome his other passengers aboard. Mei Feng had no such obligation. She could skip forward to the bows, greet the silent staring child with more solemnity than she quite liked, the nun perhaps with less than was proper. She eyed the masthead with a transitory yearning: it would offer the best view of crowded docks and empty sea, the sky as it waited for the dragon. And she would of course take no harm, no harm at all from a scramble up the mast and a squat on the crosstrees, she had lived half her life up there. But some people would worry about her now, and other people would just be outraged. Word would get back to the dowager empress, how she had been cavorting, how the emperor had allowed her to risk his unborn child. None of that would go well, for her or for the emperor.

So no, she would keep both feet firmly on the deck. She would settle here on the peak, as decorous as she could manage, and watch who else came aboard; and nobody could conceivably complain. It wasn't even raining anymore.

OF COURSE they could complain, of course they did. The boy Pao had swabbed the deck, and it was still wet beneath her; and the emperor's pregnant consort should certainly not be sitting on a rough deck anyway, out here in the open under the common gaze; and there was really nowhere suitable aboard, but they had done the best they could in the cabin there, for her and for the emperor too, if she would only come now and approve it . . .

She made a rude noise, and offered to sit on a fish-basket if they really thought that would be an improvement over the deck.

She could feel the magisterial weight of the emperor's frown all the length of the boat. She knew that he wanted to come and scold, come and fuss at her until she moved. Of course he would believe a damp deck to be a threat, if they told him so. He'd never seen the women of her childhood, working in the boats and the fields, gutting fish on the beach until the very day they birthed. He'd probably never seen a birth. Never even seen a cat give birth . . .

She scratched at the basket where it sat on the deck beside her, provoking a discontented yowl in response.

"Pity you're not a girl-cat, you. Find yourself a girl, when we get to Taishu. Bring home some dainty beauty, then we can show him how it works . . ."

Meantime, here came people to distract him: generals in plenty, hurrying, ashamed to lag behind the emperor. Soldiers caught sleeping, they would hate that. And would pack out the cabin, and so gift her the perfect excuse not to be chased in there even by the emperor. He wouldn't try now, he'd come and join her on the peak instead. She could teach him about ropes and knots, first lessons in how to sail, he'd like that. She could tell him how they'd bring up their children on the water, in and out of boats, in and out of the sea as she had been herself, salt-blooded and fishtailed and—

Oh. The dragon, she supposed, would be a difficulty there. She'd forgotten about the dragon.

The emperor hadn't forgotten about the dragon. He was plotting with her grandfather to find some way of plotting with the goddess. Perhaps they really could see the dragon chained again, and then the children could tumble in the surf without a care, little princes and princesses sailing little boats in line behind their father's . . .

Here came the medical girl, Tien. It was hard to see her as a proper doctor, but she was sovereign against Mei Feng's uncertainty; Tien had no doubts, and so was to be treasured. It was her voice that pinned hope down and made it real.

Mei Feng wanted to take her back to Taishu. Bizarrely, Tien wouldn't come. Mei Feng wasn't quite clear whether she'd refused a direct order from the emperor, which was unthinkable; or whether he'd seen the refusal coming and so ducked the order, which was perhaps just unlikely. Either way, the emperor and Mei Feng both wanted her, and yet she wasn't coming.

She'd come this far this morning with her own parade, a string of patients who were very definitely coming. Some were walking wounded, some on stretchers. Grandfather's boat wasn't the biggest, but it was the one they came to anyway, in Tien's determined wake.

Perhaps that was Yu Shan's wake. He was immediately behind Tien, his poor clan-cousin in his arms. Siew Ren was like an emblem of the day, a counterbalance, a reminder that shadow underlay the sun. When she was conscious she clung to Yu Shan, didn't want to speak to other people—or perhaps didn't want other people to look at her—for which Mei Feng was profoundly and shamefully grateful.

Tien came striding up the gangplank, all purpose, signing those behind her to wait on the wharf there.

Yu Shan ignored her signal and followed her aboard.

Tien had a bow for the boat's master, a deeper for the emperor. No one was kowtowing this morning: not with a war behind them, a deck beneath them, a celebration ahead. Familiarity and experience together had changed things. It would be different again back on Taishu, back in the formal court, but for now everyone shared just a little in the emperor's victory, they stood just a little closer.

Yu Shan walked straight by the emperor with no more than a nod of recognition as though they were brothers, close brothers.

He might be right. It was the spirit of the day that gave him license, Siew Ren in his arms who licensed the emperor to take no offense, to lift his hand in an unspoken greeting and turn his attention back to Tien.

Tien, she thought, was negotiating. *Those who have given most have the best claim.* Any boat in convoy with her grandfather's should stand under the same protection, but the wind lay in the dragon's charge. Another typhoon would scatter any boats it did not sink: and what then? Grandfather's would be the only one known safe, with the goddess's own adopted babe aboard. The babe and all of Tien's patients, if she had her way . . .

Yu Shan had carried Siew Ren directly into the cabin. He would have kicked the door open, except that someone ducked ahead to open it for him. What was that man's name, Biao? He had been with Tien; now he seemed to be with Yu Shan. People needed to be fluid, in these fluid times.

Yu Shan went in; very shortly afterward, the first of the generals came stumbling out. He recovered his balance first and then his dignity, pulling his dress straight in a trembling fury, exactly as though he had been manhandled. His brother-generals followed, all more or less unwillingly. She really wished she'd been inside to see what happened.

Whatever it was, the emperor didn't want to hear it. He gave them short shrift, visible from distance: they could stay aboard unsheltered, or they could go to another boat. Some gathered in the mainsail's shadow; some trooped down the gangplank, scowling ferociously at the stretcher-bearers, who waited with a finite patience for these grand men to get out of their way.

Stretchers were passed upward from wharf to deck, between many willing hands. One by one they went into the cabin. How so many men and women might be packed into that narrow space, Mei Feng couldn't quite imagine. She thought they must almost be lying on top of each other, so tightly wedged that not even a storm could toss them about.

If a storm came, if the dragon came.

It was madness, to want to fight the dragon. But it was a kind of joyful madness, something else to celebrate. The emperor had looked at his new-won city of Santung, his first victory, and wanted more; he had looked at her, his first girl pregnant with his first child, and wanted more. Some women might resent that, but Mei Feng welcomed it. She wanted him to be bigger than he was, not to let war and circumstance force him back like a tortoise into the shell of Taishu, defensible and passive, going nowhere.

Before, she had wanted him to be content—with Taishu, with her—as she was with him, building a palace and learning how to be together, how to survive his mother. Now—well, now she had looked beyond herself and beyond him too. She'd seen the world, and she wanted to see him in it, making a space for their child. Their children. She wasn't enough for him anymore, not in her own eyes.

The last of the patients came aboard, and she thought that might be all; but here, late, just as the boy Pao leaped ashore to cast off the bow-rope, here came one person more. Here came Jiao.

Mei Feng had not quite forgotten about Jiao, but put her out of her mind, yes, that. If she'd been looking for anyone more, it might have been Dandan. Who had closeted herself somewhere, according to rumor, with the old pirate and his torturer. It sounded strange; sometimes it sounded unbelievable. Mei Feng missed her friend, but apparently not enough. She hadn't made time to ferret the woman out and learn the truth of it.

There would be other boats, back and forth. Minds could be changed; orders could be sent, if necessary. Meantime, here came Jiao. Who was no substitute, no easy friend. Nothing easy about her at all, these days.

No point the emperor looking for a bow from her. She wouldn't even think about it. Probably, neither would he. A word or two passed between them: Mei Feng saw her glance at the closed cabin door, and turn away.

Whether she came forward with purpose or blindly or just unheedingly, Mei Feng couldn't guess, but Jiao didn't stop until she had to, which put her right here beside Mei Feng.

Who said, "I didn't think you'd come."

"Didn't you?"

"Not on this boat. Maybe not at all." In truth she hadn't thought about it, but seeing the tall woman here now was a deep surprise, and Mei Feng was hurrying inside to work out why, and this was it. "With Yu Shan taking his clan-cousin back to the mountains, I thought you would stay in Santung. I thought you might prefer it."

"Nothing to come back for, you mean?"

"Well. It wasn't the emperor that brought you to Taishu, nor him that kept you there. It wasn't even him that drew you to his service. It was wonderful to have you in the forest, but you weren't there for him."

"No. Smart girl, aren't you?" Her voice was oddly dead, as though she half wanted to suggest that a smart girl might like to stop talking right about now, but that she really couldn't be troubled to say it, and it really didn't matter anyway because she couldn't be troubled to make any trouble about it either. All of which was so unlike Jiao, who would trouble the stars if she could reach them, only to see what happened next.

"So," Mei Feng went on anyway, relentless in pursuit of something she couldn't quite see and wasn't at all sure that she wanted, "it's likely to be quite hard going to and fro, there won't be many boats," *until the emperor can chain the dragon, anyway.* "I'd have thought maybe you'd want to stay in Santung for a while . . ."

There may be another battle for you to fight, she thought, *you might like that.* For sure there'd be nothing on Taishu that she might like. Nothing but the sea like a wall all around and no going anywhere, no leaving; and the boy she loved pent up in the mountains with his hurt girl and no place for Jiao, and the emperor distracted by imminent fatherhood, no one to fight and nothing to steal and what in the world would a pirate do?

The lean woman shrugged. "I expect something will turn up that looks like work for Jiao. If not, well. So long as there are soldiers with money to lose, I won't be lonely. Maybe I'll enjoy doing nothing for a while. It's a gift, and I used to have it. I could try to rediscover that."

It was thoroughly plausible, and utterly unconvincing. Mei Feng had seen Jiao working and gambling and idling in the sun—but none of those had been what she was there for. She was there for Yu Shan, and without him there would be a hollowness at the core. Maybe she'd find herself a crew and a task that would engage her; maybe Mei Feng could find one for her.

Maybe Grandfather and the emperor had found one already. Pirate could turn dragonfighter and be glad of the change. They might yet all be glad to have her.

They'd need to find the right weapon to use, though, and the ground to stand on. Fighting the dragon was a dream at the moment. Grandfather was sure to involve the goddess, but Mei Feng couldn't see Jiao spending much time in a temple, unless she was looting it.

Come to that, Mei Feng didn't think she'd ever seen Jiao spend any time in a temple: not even stepping in to offer a handful of moon-cakes and a stick of joss for luck. Even in the forest they'd kept a light burning on a little shrine of stones and most people would leave the last bite of their breakfast in the smoke, but not Jiao.

That might make a difficulty, in any plan to enlist Jiao as a dragonfighter. Grandfather wouldn't expect others to match his own devotion, but he might resist someone who disparaged the gods entirely.

And the goddess, of course, she might have her own views on the matter.

Mei Feng really wasn't sure what they were getting into; nor at all sure that they should bring the pirate in with them. Only that Jiao needed something, and this seemed to be what they had.

three

There was no going back to the tent.

There was no going back to anything.

Tien knew that; she had always known it. Life was a river, not a road. It carried you onward always, into the dark.

The tent had been her uncle's all the time. Even when she thought to claim it, even when she found that Master Biao had done that thing already: it was still truly her uncle's. They only inhabited it for a while, Biao and she. They stood in for him, poor shadows. It was never theirs, never either of theirs.

Which didn't matter now, though it might have before. Before the emperor came, before the dragon.

THE EMPEROR offered an alternative; the dragon wrecked the tent.

TIEN COULDN'T blame the dragon. She was only surprised at how small, how almost human the gesture was.

How pathetic, almost.

Han had already left, running either to the dragon or away from the dragon, Tien couldn't tell, only that he was running away from her.

By the time the dragon came—in Han's wake or at his incitement or in spite of him, again she couldn't tell—Tien had left the tent herself. She was following Biao down into the city, because she had nowhere else to go. She felt the dragon's coming, like a temper blotting out the sun; she looked back to see her, rain-shadow made manifest, up on the ridge there tearing the tent apart.

Raging and helpless, hopeless.

Pathetic.

TIEN CAME down into the city and found Biao, found people in need, was a doctor.

Found her way at last to the jade store and the emperor, a pregnant girl and a line of wounded soldiers. Was a doctor.

Mei Feng wanted Tien to go back to Taishu with her, with all the wounded who were fit to travel. But some were not fit and some would not go, and besides, this was Tien's practice now: here in Santung, this side of the water. She said no.

It was hard to say and hard to keep to, once said, but she stood by it. Even in the face of imperial demand. The need was here. Mei Feng did not need her, she only wanted.

Need was contingent, always. After the typhoon, Tien needed somewhere to take her patients as the river rose. In the rain she'd found a temple, ransacked and abandoned. Her practice lay now in its galleries, nursed by Mu Gao and a random, shifting population of the hungry and the lost.

Tien was there and not there, called back and forth across the city a dozen times a day. She had attended the emperor's favorite, pronounced the imperial pregnancy, joyful news. She was suddenly famous, the only doctor anyone wanted: what could she be but lucky? And never mind the wounds of war, there was sickness in the city already, those diseases that rode on the back of hunger and fear and filth. She was busy. Even Biao had been a help, when he could be drawn away from Siew Ren for a while, when Yu Shan would let him go.

No longer. They were all gone now. The good doctor sees her departing patients to the door; of course Tien had gone down to the dockside, to watch them all away. Yu Shan carried Siew Ren in his arms; Biao followed like a servant. Tien had dosed the girl so deeply she was only half conscious, but that half was all pain. She groaned and tossed her head despite the drugs, and Yu Shan sweated as pale as the dawn; Tien thought she should have dosed him too.

The emperor was there already on the boat, with his entourage. Tien tried to persuade him that her patients needed the cabin-space more than his generals did; Yu Shan was more direct. Generals were evicted, stretchers installed. She smiled beatifically upon the emperor, bowed and turned away.

Went to turn away, at least, her mind already on where she meant to go next. He actually had to reach out a hand to touch her, to detain her.

"Majesty?"

"Mei Feng," he said, with an anxious glance forward to where his woman sat in the bows. "Can she really carry this baby safely? She's so small . . ."

That wasn't quite what she thought he'd say, and she liked him better for it. "Majesty. Mei Feng isn't one of your pampered delicate beauties," the kind of court women that he didn't actually seem to have or want, "she's peasant stock, tough as a root."

"She said that. Even so, she should have her doctor with her. She should have you."

"Women have been bearing babies for a long time now, and most of them without sight of a doctor from beginning to end. You will find Taishu full of women much wiser than I am, who have helped one another give birth to half the island."

"She wants you," he said stubbornly, meaning *I want you, I want her to have you,* and he was a little baffled by the fact that she was not in fact coming with them.

Tien said, "That is flattering, majesty, but ill-advised. You have your own doctors, if a doctor be needed. Truly, I have small experience in this."

"You think my doctors have more?"

"I think they know more about the difficulties that surround an emperor, yes. Trust them, before you trust me. And your own mother, of course," the only woman living who had borne a child to an emperor.

This time he let her go. She bowed and turned and balanced down the gangplank, reached the wharf and walked away: feeling eyes, perhaps more than one pair of eyes burning into the back of her neck.

Still not looking around.

Not looking up, either. Not looking for the dragon, no.

RETRACING NOT her own steps of this morning but the emperor's: going not to her hospital but farther, up to the governor's palace.

Tien wanted her library back.

She was anxious, but only a little, that Tunghai Wang might have taken it. If he had actually valued it, if he had understood it, he wouldn't have given her such free rein. It should have been full of scholars and the wise; Tunghai Wang should have wanted it extremely, but she didn't believe that he knew what it was.

She was anxious again, but again only a little, that it might have been pillaged for the simple convenience of paper. Or for no reason at all, only because these things happen in times of war. If it had survived Tunghai Wang's occupation, though, it should have survived the emperor's. Especially with the emperor himself actually camped out in the palace, unconsciously protecting what was as valuable to him as to his enemy. If he had only known.

She should, perhaps, have told him what he had. How she had used it, how she thought it could still be used. Military men might see the dragon as a weapon, though, they might be that bold. Someone was sure to see Han only as an instrument. She had been ruthless herself, she knew, but only in conscience. She was kinder, she would be stronger and more careful. She and the dragon would fight over him, and she intended to win. She thought she could, if only she still had the library.

Through the gate, then, and across the public courtyard, in at her familiar doorway. No lamp left burning for her today; she made her own light and carried it down to the library.

Here were all the books and scrolls, *her* books and scrolls, untouched. Here was the niche of polished stone where she could safely set her lamp. Because one worry would always rush in to replace another, she was already wondering how she could keep both access and privacy when the emperor appointed a new governor. With that filling her head, she needed a moment to register a movement in the gleaming mirror of the stone. That was not the lamp's flame, neither her own self reflected. She stood still and saw it more clearly, saw him rise behind her shoulder where he must have been crouched patiently in the dark of the room, waiting. Waiting for her.

Here now, she turned; and here was Han.

Still shirtless, as she had seen him last. The better perhaps to flaunt what she had done to him, to cry it like a betrayal to the world. Or else to flaunt it at the dragon, to hurl it like a banner in her eyes, *see me, I have the measure of you. I am the measure of you.*

That was not true, but some control he did have, and Tien could give him more. He could be fearsome, he could matter more than emperors.

If he would allow it. He had a feral, half-mad look in his eyes, unless that was the dragon looking out of them. She was feral and half mad, and with reason.

He had a blade in his hand. Not a tao, just a knife: a short knife, long enough.

Tien said, "Doesn't the dragon feed you?" He had always been bone-bare; now he looked starved, all gaunt ribs and glare. There was something else about him, something more startlingly new, but what she saw first was the hunger.

He was confused, momentarily. He blinked and said, "She . . . doesn't think. To do that."

"And neither do you, I suppose. Here, I have food," cold rice and bean paste, good enough for a hollow belly. "Sit and eat, before you fall over."

He shook his head, quite slowly. He hadn't come for food. Nor for her, or not in the way he used to. Quickly, then, she came up with other questions. "Who let you run around loose? And how did you know where to come?" Both elements in that seemed monumentally unlikely, but Han's life always seemed to shade from the unlikely to the impossible. With the dragon at one end of the chain, anything might happen at the other.

He shrugged. "There were soldiers watching me, but they got caught up at the harbor," which meant he'd given them the slip in all the fuss, while his escort was entangled with military protocols: explaining themselves to an officer, perhaps, turning to produce their prisoner as justification, finding him suddenly not there. It sounded very Han. "After that, I just asked people where I could find you. Everybody knows Tien the doctor."

And apparently everyone knew that if she wasn't at her hospital, she'd be here; and demonstrably Han had no trouble inveigling himself into the palace, with the emperor leaving and everyone down at the dockside to see him away. She was willing to bet that he'd had a shirt, though, not to scare the servants with his dreadful written skin.

He was trying to scare her, or else accuse her. Maybe both. He said, "She wants to kill you, Tien. For what you did," a flex of his shoulders to speak of it, and of course that was the new thing, the strangeness: she had never seen him before without his chains. Here he was free, body-free, and more tied to the dragon than ever, or she to him.

"I'm sure she does," Tien said. It was almost not frightening now. The dragon wanted to kill everyone, more or less.

"I won't let her, though. She knows that."

Of course she did; she must know everything that was in his head. Tien had made her a gift of it. The girl almost thought the dragon should be grateful.

"And you?" she said.

"Oh, I could kill you. I could let myself do that."

Tien had nothing to offer him but the truth. She said, "I am sorry, Han, but I did have to do it. For everyone's sake."

"Everyone's sake but mine," he said, that much self-aware at least; he did still remember why he might want to kill her.

"Yes. Of course." That was what betrayal meant, that you hurt the one you loved. Not him alone, perhaps—him and herself and the dragon too—but him most of all. It was the right thing to do, and she had done it. He might even agree with her if he was sane, if he didn't have that cold weight of dragon in his head. It was still betrayal. Her hand it was that tattooed him, that bonded him and dragon lifelong; there was sense, perhaps, in letting it be his hand that slew her for it. Sooner him than the dragon.

He might not forgive himself after, when he remembered that he loved her. There was nothing she could do about that.

She said, "I couldn't let you free the dragon, whatever you promised her. I still can't. But what I can do," *I think I can,* "I can find a way to put her back where she was, beneath the strait. I can make her sleep again. That'll be easier for you, Han. She'll be quiet in your head. You help me here, help me find what I need, we can work together . . ."

We can be together. That used to be enough, but he was mad now. He shook his head, almost frantic. "That's not, she couldn't bear it, don't you even *threaten* that . . ."

And the knife was lifting his hand again, that was how it looked, that the intent was in the blade and not in him.

Perhaps the intent was in the dragon, and he was just a puppet.

Perhaps they both were, puppets to the moment. Apparently she was going to stand here and let his knife kill her, whether or not he had any will in the matter. Not going to move, not going to resist or cower or try to run away.

Not going to call out, even, to whoever they were whose voices she could hear in the hall, whose slow shuffling footsteps rang so loud.

Figures shadowed the doorway, two old hurt men who couldn't conceivably stop Han if he really meant to do this. One was bent and leaning on a crutch, while the other stood too carefully erect. She knew severe pain when she saw it, and she was seeing it twice here, two contrasting patterns of pain.

The straight man said, "You again, is it, lad? Has nobody killed you yet?" Meaning *even yet,* measuring just how astonishing this was.

And that man, his voice was all it took, apparently, to stop Han.

To have him turn away from Tien, suddenly purposeless, hanging like weed in water, mindless drift.

To have him stare at the man in a blanching terror, as though all the ghosts of his past had risen up at once.

Tien wanted to go to him, when she saw him so suddenly scared. And was too slow, because the man with the crutch moved first. Haltingly, effortfully, he dragged and swung his twisted body across the floor. Han just stood and watched him come. So did Tien, so did his companion in the doorway.

Finally close enough to touch, the crippled man reached out with his free arm and seemed to do no more than that, a touch on Han's elbow, barely so strong as a grip.

Han gasped, and the knife fell from the fingers of his one good hand as though all the strings of his arm had been cut.

The bent man balanced awkwardly on unsupported legs for a moment, to flick at the knife with his crutch. Sent it skittering across the floor, almost to the straight man's feet.

Who bent over—very straightly, very slowly—to retrieve it, and came up smiling, sure that all the power in the room now was where it ought to be, where it belonged, in his hands and his friend's.

Nobody seemed to be saying anything. Nobody felt the need. Tien was negligible for now, she felt that herself. What she had to offer here was slow and long-term and dependent. Dependent on this room, more than anything.

Han had lost most, here and beforehand. Even before he had been reduced by madness and reduced again by fear and now again by losing the little other thing he had, the little knife. Still, he looked from one old man to the other—and not at Tien at all, because she was negligible, or for whatever other reason he might hold closer to his heart—and didn't speak, didn't need to.

In response apparently to his silence, the palace seemed to grow abruptly darker, abruptly colder, cast into deep shadow, as though a cloud hung directly overhead to obscure the sun.

If so, it was a cloud with purpose. She couldn't quite tell if it was actually Han's purpose, or if he had just called into a void, *do what you will*—but there came a terrible clatter of falling tiles and breaking masonry, the snapping of ancient beams, a distant scream shrill enough to cut through steel, a groaning sound that welled up beneath their feet and might well be the complaint of the earth itself at too great a weight descending.

The library had no windows, which was probably just as well. Nobody wanted to look out to see the dragon looking back at them.

Han looked back at the old men, which might almost be the same thing: not frightened now, not cowed, not possible to bully. No one spoke, no one had any suggestions. It wasn't quite an impasse, only that not one of them quite knew where this would lead, where they could possibly go from here.

four

*P*ing Wen would often go walking in the rain.

Sometimes he said that he liked to do this because it reminded him of other days, harder, better, when he was young and on campaign, a simple soldier for his emperor.

Sometimes he said that the rain made a cloak, to isolate him from the intrusions of the world. A palace wall might do that but not well, not well enough. A palace was a world to itself, and full of intrusion. A garden within a palace wall was better; rain in a garden within a palace wall was better yet, worth waiting for. It gave him space and time, quite undisturbed.

He had other reasons too. One of those—never confessed— was the pleasure he took from stepping indoors again, having his women strip away sodden clothing and rub him dry, fetch him tea and whatever other comforts he might demand, the intimate services due to his rank and power.

The typhoon and its sodden tail had kept even him indoors. Today's rain, though, was only a shower. With much to think about, Ping Wen welcomed the chance to step out. Later there would be petitioners seeking an audience, and he must needs sit on his little stool below the empty throne and dispense what he could from almost-empty hands. There would be a council meeting, no doubt, where he could be no better than first among equals. There would most certainly be an argument with the dowager empress, the Widow of the World he liked to call her, who would need reminding—again!—that she had no right to what she tried so very hard to seize. Even her son was not hers to keep. He belonged to the empire, if he could hold it. He had almost lost it already, all but this small island, or she had lost it for him. Now he was abroad and trying his strength, his own strength.

Ping Wen did not think it would prove to be enough.

Was betting against it, indeed, but cautiously.

Helping to tip the scales, indeed, but not in outright rebellion, never that. He had seen justice meted out to rebels; he had been the man who did that, on occasion. He did believe profoundly in the empire, in the sacred right of the emperor to rule. Only not perhaps this emperor, nor his mother through him puppetwise. Ping Wen would do what little he could—what very little, the least he could—to bring about a change. Which meant a change of dynasty, necessarily, as there was no heir to support. Which meant that he must give some aid at least—or at least some opportunity— to Tunghai Wang.

And then perhaps strike himself, in his own interest, unless Tunghai Wang's position was manifestly stronger.

Ping Wen did after all have the Jade Throne within his own compass, even if he sat at its feet. It would be the work of a moment to shift from the stool to the throne above, if he only dared to do it.

The emperor had gone to make war, and there was no news. There could be no news while the dragon soared above the strait, until one victor or the other contrived to send a boat protected from her temper.

Ping Wen had been secretly delighted to see the emperor off in such a boat. If no news came back—which seemed all too miraculously likely—then he would make that shift indeed, in his own and the island's interests. The greater empire could wait, for now.

It was much to think about, and he was grateful to be doing that in the air, in the rain, in the privacy of air and rain together.

· · ·

HERE WAS a bridge above a lily pond. He had always loved lily pads in a garden in the rain. He leaned on the curve of the parapet and watched the ripples for a while, how their pure concentric circles were checked by a sudden wall of green, how they were reflected away, how they came together in other and more complex patterns. And were interrupted by a fresh fall of rain, breaking those patterns and making new again.

Forces of wind and water played on the pond, and were absorbed. Things changed constantly, but only on the surface. Below, fish fed on undisturbed.

Ping Wen looked at the pond and saw the empire, of course. How could he not? The empire that endured, that absorbed all its petty people and their squabbles, their comings and goings, their dynastic shifts. The emperor and his mother, Tunghai Wang, Ping Wen himself—drops of water falling, sending their ripples out, seeing them bounce back or shatter or die away.

Voices in history, lost as suddenly as one raindrop's fall is obscured by another, by ten thousand more, that constant patter that will blur and drown any individual, no matter how weighty . . .

That constant patter that will mask the sound of soft and careful footsteps behind a man, footsteps that are blurred already, irregular, pattern-free. Ping Wen never heard his killer coming, barely saw the black silk cord as it dropped down over his head and found his throat and tightened there with a jerk.

He was perhaps remembering his old campaigns, his soldier-days.

He reacted, at any rate, like a soldier. Sly and simple, vicious and unthinking and immediate.

His elbow slammed backward, seeking the solid body that must be somewhere there. At the same time he was ducking and twisting into that choking tug, not to let the assassin set a knee in the small of his back for a good clean draw. Ping Wen had seen men strangled, had ordered it on a battlefield and afterward, men and women too. Had strangled some few himself, at need. He knew how swiftly dangerous that cord could be.

The pressure on his neck was bad already, squeezing, dizzying. His elbow found nothing; he could feel the man's straining weight but only through the noose, not physically on his back, not reachable. His fingers clawed at the cord and couldn't grip it, couldn't slip inside, it bit so deep into spare flesh. There was a darkness threatening at the corners of his sight, a flickering like glowflies, there and gone and there again.

Like raindrops falling into a pond, there and gone, swallowed . . .

Ping Wen fought for breath, what breath he could; and forced his hands from his throat and groped behind him till he found sodden cloth and flesh, man as rain-wet as he was, from crouching long hours in this ambush. Gripped what he could and plunged forward, over the parapet and down into the water.

THERE WAS a terrible wrench on his neck, but the assassin was off-balance already, couldn't take all his weight all unexpectedly. That man was coming with him, down and down.

Down to the surface of the pond, where the lily pads lay like scales; and through that shattering skin and down again, down deep to scare the fishes.

Ping Wen had what breath he had, not much. He had what strength was left him, the slow temper of a firepot, the sudden blaze of bamboo.

He was an old man half strangled, and his enemy was half his age. He saw that, turning in the murk of the water, abruptly face to face with the man who meant to kill him.

The man who had lost his chance when he lost his grip on his deadly cord, when they hit the lilies. He had a blade in his belt, and was reaching for it even as he kicked for the surface. Ping Wen saw that too, and had no notion of a sword-fight underwater.

He wrapped his arms around the other man's legs, and drew him down.

. . .

PING WEN'S feet touched bottom, but the pond was deep. The man above him could see the air, perhaps, but couldn't reach it. Clawed for it, kicked for it, snatched at it in handfuls, but his hands could do him no good up there above his head and his legs could not kick free of Ping Wen's grip.

They were shadows within shadow, fighting a shadow-war. Even flesh felt slow and cool and different, differently solid, here below. Ping Wen watched the man in silhouette above him, black against the dapple of the light; the man must see him less, or not at all.

Desperate, the man did drag his hands down from where they clutched at air. Did draw his tao and try to slash beneath him, tried to cut Ping Wen away like gripping weed.

Ping Wen could follow the line of the blade as it came down, could slide aside and still stay underneath the man, give him no chance to wrestle, just hold his ankles and wait.

Wait for that last bubble of used air to leak from desperate lips, wait for the flailing arms to fail and fall limp, wait for the last shudder of effort to waste itself in water and be lost.

And then, then, he could almost not remember what he ought to do himself: let go those ankles, push against the silt and rock beneath him, rise.

Let his own body rise and his enemy's too.

Break surface.

Tear the floating lily pads aside and breathe.

One gasping, sodden, painful breath, and then another.

More, more air; more air than all there was, he wanted that. Shuddering, hacking at the hurt of it, he wanted more. All the pain there was, he'd take that too, just to remind himself of what he had that the dead did not. This floating bulk beside him, the dead man was still dead: hanging from the curve of his shoulders, face down in the water as if he would drink and drink, drink all the pond and so not drown in it after all.

. . .

Ping Wen was slow to swim to land, leaden and unhurried. Slow to haul himself out of the pond, that too: no strength in him but a dawning wonder, that he had survived.

It would be the old woman, the dowager empress who had sent her man to kill him. No doubt of that. She had given up on poisons, evidently, and tried a bolder way. And he had survived it, but not by men's precautions, the wisdom of a long life lived at court.

Not by a soldier's strength either, or not wholly so. It was the soldier's fighting mind, his instinct that had dragged them both over the parapet, yes—but not a soldier's patience that had simply held the man underwater until he drowned. Soldiers could be patient, sure, but even soldiers need to breathe.

Old soldiers, old half-strangled soldiers need to breathe sooner than their assassins.

They do not squat on the bed of a pond and wait for death to take other people and not to touch themselves.

Inside himself, Ping Wen felt like a man rising out of water, brushing obscuring leaves aside, drawing himself into a new light and seeing differently. Forgotten by death, it seemed he could remember himself. Or understand himself, and the path he trod now.

Immortals had no need to breathe. The dragon had spent centuries beneath the sea, untroubled. He was no dragon, and no immortal either; but the emperor, the old emperor who had died at last was divine despite that, and could very likely have walked the sea-bed from Santung to Taishu and never needed air along the way. His boy the young emperor could take a blade-thrust to the body and survive it, heal without a scar.

And was abroad just now, and had left the throne quite empty with Ping Wen's mind upon it, Ping Wen's body at its feet. Perhaps the jade had reached out that far already. Perhaps his ambition had reached out to the jade.

He rose from the pond on unsteady legs, feeling some touch of godhood in him, and a new determination. The old woman would die, when he was ready; her son too, when he was in reach. Ping Wen would rise from the stool and sit the throne. This day had been a sign.

HALFWAY TO the palace, he met with frantic servants come in search.

The boat, the emperor's boat was in the mouth of the bay, riding the late tide into harbor with the dragon overhead.

THERE WAS a fleet, a small fleet at the emperor's tail, but he had to send runners to establish that. Some facts are so big they eclipse anything else. The first lookouts had seen only the emperor, in the dragon's shadow.

WHILE HE learned the truth of it—no, the emperor's boat was not the sole survivor; no, this was not anything like the whole war-fleet returning; yes, every boat was decked in yellow and yes, the empress knew it and was already on her way to the dockside to greet her son returning, despite the rain—Ping Wen was dried and dressed, and had taken no pleasure in it at all.

Hurriedly, anxiously, with his hair and beard still damp, he gave certain orders and then went out into the rain again: in pomp this time, nothing he could enjoy or profit from, processing from palace to harbor humiliatingly late, slow, in the old woman's wake.

On the way, he realized that he had forgotten entirely to tell anyone about the would-be assassin. Perhaps the empress's people would have discovered and removed his body by the time Ping Wen could return. Best to wait, and check later. Better to say nothing than to send men on a fool's errand to a corpse no longer there. Servants would whisper, and laugh behind their hands: *the old*

*man took a soaking, and tried to pretend he had a hero's fight with
a killer. Vanished killer. A killer who could come and go unseen,
even dead . . .*

He found the empress and her entourage already on the quay,
the emperor's boat just docking. There was, apparently, no room
for him. He must stand in the rain-shadow of a warehouse, because this wretched fishing port had no space for ceremonial; he
must watch from a distance while the emperor and his mother
greeted each other, while her trivial clerks kowtowed to the imperial triumph before ever they made room enough for him.

When at last he was allowed close to the returning warlord in
his victory, that warlord was more concerned with his woman,
who had somehow spirited herself across the water in his shadow.
The emperor had brought her back, but in something opposite to
disgrace, another kind of triumph, seemingly: only that she was
seemingly ill, seasick and needing help even on the short plank
down from deck to quay. He insisted on giving her that help himself, which was added disgrace to her because of course it could
not be disgrace to him, no commoner could disgrace an emperor.

At last he could be persuaded to hand her over to another, because Ping Wen was all too visibly, all too impatiently waiting.
And for some reason it wasn't her grandfather who took her, because that old man was still aboard the boat, waiting for something else altogether.

Waiting on imperial orders for Ping Wen, apparently.

So said the emperor: "Ping Wen, good. The man I want. I want
you to go to Santung in my place, be my voice there as you have
been my voice here: be governor in my name."

"Majesty, you do me too much honor . . ." Be a sea away from
the Jade Throne, a stone's throw from Tunghai Wang? There was
an end to his ambition, death to his new resolution, death perhaps
to himself. In Santung there was nothing that he wanted, or could
use.

"No, no," said the emperor. "You deserve this and more. I

would keep you at my side, except that I most especially need a man I can trust in Santung. Go, go now: this boat is waiting."

"Majesty, I am not ready, I am not packed . . ."

"All your servants, all your things can be fetched over later. The fisherman has orders to come straight back again for those. I am leaving a squad of soldiers on his boat, to ensure that he does. I have departed the city all too soon, in too much of a hurry, but I had to see Mei Feng home, I had to bring her myself. She bears the hope of us all." He meant that she was pregnant, which was another blow to Ping Wen's heart, another problem. Another death, at least, to be arranged from the wrong side of the strait. "Go you, go now. I need you there, and they are ready for you. I have left you an army; you have a city to fortify."

Ping Wen had no choice. He went.

five

Yu Shan couldn't carry Siew Ren all the way to the mountains. That was a loss, a hollowness, a failure every time he looked at her and every time he looked away.

Physically, of course he could have done it. He could have swept her up and run all the way and never felt the weight of her, except on his mind and heart.

Practically, it wasn't possible. Biao couldn't have kept up, with all his bags and packs, and it was no use telling him to follow. He needed to keep with her, she actually needed him more than she did Yu Shan. Which was another failure, another loss. Several times a day her weeping skin must be bathed and anointed with Biao's preparations. Yu Shan wanted to take that duty to himself, but was never allowed to. The mixtures must be made up fresh every time, Biao said, in different proportions as her condition changed. Only he could do that, and only he had the skills to apply them properly, with the proper charms and blessings.

Biao was a dragging weight, then, a land-anchor on Yu Shan's urgency. More than all his words and fussiness, though, more than his fat puffing slowness when he walked, more than anything was Siew Ren's pain.

Yu Shan couldn't carry her because she hurt too much, he hurt her when he did that.

Failure, loss, something to live with.

Siew Ren rode, then, in a padded cart-bed behind slow oxen.

Biao of course rode with her most of the way. Between his bags and his bulk, he left small room for anyone else. Yu Shan walked.

Not alone. Other clansfolk had been hurt, burned as Siew Ren was or hacked with blades, crushed by stones or pierced with arrows. They too wanted to go home, in search of family or jade-magic or else just in despair. The emperor's victory had been too easy won, and all too terribly expensive.

Because Yu Shan was making that same slow journey, of course they came along. It only made sense to go together—and besides, he was Yu Shan. Grim as he was, distressed as he was, they did still want to be with him. Clouded as he was, he saw that and resented it as he resented Biao: something needful and obstructive, coming inevitably between himself and Siew Ren. He wanted to be the one at her side night and day, always there when she reached out, when her eyes opened, when she spoke. He couldn't have that. And understood all the reasons why, and resented them all even while he saw to the doctor's little comforts, while he ran up and down the caravan keeping the other wagons to the same careful pace, speaking to everyone, smiling where a smile was most needed. He had a limited ration of smiles these days, and he kept them for these others, friends and comrades. Siew Ren had no use for them, so he might as well spend them elsewhere.

THE ROAD ended—at last!—in a broad open area of stamped grass and mud, where generations of wagoneers had driven their beasts and made camp and traded simple goods for raw jade, watched all the time by generations of wary guardsmen. Here began the mountain paths, climbing to the high valleys. Here the oxen and their wagons could go no farther.

From here on up it was donkeys or feet—and the sick or badly injured could not sit a donkey if they had one. There were few anyway, in the hills. Clansfolk were walkers by nature and by long tradition. Donkeys were a luxury, not to be depended on. Strong legs were better. If their legs failed through age or accident, most people stayed at home. What was there to travel for? Most people stayed home anyway. This campsite was the closest they ever willingly came to the road away, before the emperor changed everything.

Now the road was bringing people back, and some couldn't climb the mountains. Some couldn't even walk.

Yu Shan was still not allowed to carry Siew Ren, although she did need carrying.

The clans had come down from their valleys as they did for the jade-wagons, tough folk used to carrying great weights of stone. Forewarned, prepared, they had improvised litters from lengths of bamboo with hammocks slung beneath them.

Those who had devised and made the litters of course insisted on bearing them. It was their right. And Biao of course would walk beside Siew Ren, in case she wanted him. On narrow mountain paths, there would barely be room for him: none at all for Yu Shan too. All he could do was get in the way.

He had hurt Siew Ren enough, too much already. He would not risk a stumble. He could walk in front, perhaps, lead the march home—but there was no need for him or anyone to do that, and this was far from a triumph, and it would be hard then to say goodbye as one litter after another peeled off as the path divided, as they took their own ways to their separate valleys.

No: Yu Shan saw each of the wounded away with those friends who had come to fetch them, made his farewells here and then followed in deep evening shadows, last of all on the steep path home.

Last except for the one who came behind him: distantly, quietly, not distant or quiet enough. Not by a distance. Of course he heard, of course he saw shadow move through shadow. He used not to be so alert, but he was wiser now.

And stronger, quicker, not so kind.

For a while he thought he might just walk on, keep with his people. Keep at their tail, between them and what came after.

Then he thought the other thing.

He let the others get ahead, and farther ahead. Once the last of them was out of sight, he sat on a damp rock and waited.

For what, quite, he wasn't sure. What he would do, what say—he was trying not to think about it. Nothing in his life was what he wanted now.

It used to make him happy when he saw her. And her, the other way around. No longer so. He saw that as his failure, her loss.

Tonight, he saw her before she could possibly have seen him, the dark of himself entirely still beneath the dark of the trees against the looming dark of the mountain.

He watched her come and felt nothing but guilt and sorrow.

Oh, but she was good, though. She couldn't have seen him when she first came into his jade-enhanced sight; by the time she was twenty paces short of him, she couldn't possibly have missed him; even knowing her as he did, he had no idea where in the intervening climb she had finally noticed that he was there. She didn't pause, she didn't jerk or lift her head or want to turn away, she gave no sign at all. She only kept on coming. At first she was following him, and then she was coming to him, and that made all the difference in the world but she was too proud to show it.

He stood up, which was not really a gesture of respect, not quite: only that staying sat on the rock would have been the other thing, a gesture almost of contempt; and he did want to meet her eye to eye. Whatever he was going to say, whatever she was.

She said, "Last time we met in a forest, it was me who surprised you."

He said, "You're not surprised to find me here."

She said, "No."

And that was it for a little while, as though it had all been said already.

Into their silence came a noise from somewhere else, impossible to locate: a long low rumble that swelled into a reverberative flood as though rocks of sound were being tumbled over and over one another, crashing and grinding together. It echoed between one slope and the other, it climbed under its own impetus or fell beneath its own weight, it might have been higher or lower than them or in another valley altogether. It was like the wind, slipshadow and potent, irretrievable as it died away.

She said, "What," and swallowed, and tried again: "These are your mountains. What was that?"

He said, "I've never heard it before." And then, more honestly, reluctantly, "It was a stone tiger, I think, but—"

"But you've never heard it."

But he had seen one, when she had not; and he had been with Siew Ren at the time, and not with her; and none of that was good, and none of it was any help right now. He had wanted all his life to hear the jade tiger sing. Some nights he and Siew Ren had sat together in the dark and waited for it, feeling almost that they deserved it, that it would be the mountain's recognition of themselves.

He really, really wished that it had not happened now.

It came again, filling the valley entirely, a deep-throated claim of possession. Yu Shan had seen the dragon more often now than he could reasonably count; it felt almost like heresy that the tiger seemed somehow more wonderful. If only because it was closer, smaller, more immediate. An achievable astonishment, like jade.

Perhaps the tiger was welcoming Siew Ren and the other wounded back to the mountains and valleys of their birth, to their place of restoration.

Perhaps it was welcoming him.

One thing for sure, it was excluding Jiao, or that was how she heard it: as a warning-off, a curtain drawn between them. A claim on him, a rejection of her.

She stood there, upright and waiting, expectant. More than

twice his age, immeasurably more experienced, a dark soul who had been his delight: she stood there, waiting for him to hurt her one more time.

This path only led one way. He said, "I'm sorry, Jiao. I need to be with Siew Ren now, because that's what she needs. You know, you've seen. Go back to the emperor, be his long right arm, someone he can lean on. Mei Feng's just a distraction now. He needs someone fierce, or he'll be all swallowed up by the baby and everything else will fall back into his mother's hands, and you know how well that works."

She looked at him, she listened with scrupulous care; she said, "You keep talking about what you need, what Siew Ren needs, what the emperor needs. You don't think, you don't even wonder what I might need. For me."

He stopped, he thought about that for a minute; he said, "No. No, you're right, I don't. I can't. I'm sorry, Jiao. I said that already. I am sorry, but there's nothing I can do. There isn't space in my head now to worry about you too. Or the emperor, Mei Feng, anyone. You'll have to do it without me for a while, all of you."

"All of us. Yes. Even now, I'm just one of them, aren't I? One of the people you're leaving behind."

"I think it's the other way around, I'm asking you all to leave me behind. You're the ones with the exciting lives. I'm just going to sit in the valley here and help Siew Ren get better. But—yes. Please, Jiao. Make me happy one last time, go and be with them, help them all. Yes."

She stood straight in her sorrow, and—although he stood higher than her on the path, and although he was tall for Taishu, jade-eater tall, and how much easier had his life been when he had nothing on his back to worry him bar a weight of stolen jade, and nothing ahead to worry him bar a journey to find the emperor, and nothing at his side to worry him bar a pirate holding steel at his throat?—she seemed almost to grow, almost to rise above him as though she were a goddess slipping out of human form as she said, "No. What you're forgetting, Yu Shan, is that I never was one of them. I was only ever with you."

And then she turned and stepped off the path and was gone like a goddess into the forest and the night; and there was absolutely nothing he could do, not even cry a warning after her. She was a stranger here, and she knew already how dangerous that was.

The clans weren't the only risk, it wasn't only men who walked these hills at night, and she knew that too. The tiger didn't really need to call again.

When it did, Yu Shan closed his eyes to hear better, to see the black-barred green of its fur again, the vivid green of its eyes so like the emperor's, so like his own; and when the long liquid song subsided, he shivered—not in tribute, exactly, and exactly not in conclusion, *there, that's finished, done with,* no—and hurried on up the path again, chasing his companions, chasing Siew Ren, never looking back.

six

If there was one thing worse than riding a horse, General Ma thought—and of course there was, there were many things worse than riding horses, and for some men he himself was one of those worse things—but if there was one thing more immediately uncomfortable than riding a horse, it must be riding a mule.

General Ma was a fat man who had contrived to stay that way down all the many miles of the long pursuit, across half the width of empire, and not by and large by riding horses. Or mules. He was a man who loved his comforts, and one of those was food and another was his carriage, drawn by whatever beasts he could muster, which usually meant the best in any province.

Now, after half a day astride, he did not dismount so much as roll out of the saddle and tumble groundward. He was fortunate to land on his feet and remarkable only for keeping them, for not staggering, not falling flat onto the flags of the courtyard.

He grunted and peered about him at the torches and the lamps and the dark pooling shadows between, looking for another of his comforts, his boy Yueh.

And saw quite another figure advancing at him, and contrived almost to make it look, almost to make himself believe that of course he was not looking for his boy, not looking for comfort, no, not yet. Of course he had been looking for the generalissimo.

"My lord," he said, with a low and careful bow.

"Ma." Tunghai Wang still had this disconcerting habit of presence, of being where he was not looked for, even with his army spread impossibly wide across the country. With that, apparently, came the habit of knowing: where one had been, what doing. "What have you learned?"

"Little enough, my lord. Little that we did not know already. It would be easier to interrogate prisoners, easier far to compare what they say one with another, if we could bring them all together in the same place."

"You mean in the same city, in Santung."

"Yes, my lord. It would be easier to see your men fed too and kept in order," which was General Ma's other task and had been hard enough in all conscience when they were in Santung before, harder on the long road there, was proving harder yet in this chaotic scattering.

Tunghai waved a hand. "This is an old song, old friend."

"I know it. But songs get to be old by being repeatedly sung; and truths do not become untrue through overtelling. If you could take Santung again," said that way just to goad him; of course he could, everyone knew he could, "then I could serve you and the army better. And we would have more prisoners, and far better information."

"And the boy-emperor could come from Taishu again, whenever he chose, and take the city back once more. We can both of us take Santung, and neither one of us can hold it."

"Perhaps—though the longer you wait, the longer you let him inhabit it, the better chance he has of holding it. They are already building fortifications. You would do well to interrupt."

"Fortifications, yes. I know this, I have seen. What more?"

"If you wanted more, you should have kept Ai Guo. I have plans of the works; each man draws them differently," with a shudder at the memories: the stink and the noise of them, those prisoners snatched in raids or trying to raid on their own account, venturing incautiously beyond the city; the garbled speech and ruined fingers struggling to draw, "but you may be able to make some composite sense from them. It may even resemble what they are actually doing," though he at least would not willingly gamble anything on that, not money nor hope nor certainly his life. Not willingly even other people's lives.

Tunghai Wang looked at him carefully, spoke thoughtfully, said, "Perhaps you are not the right man to organize my intelligence for me?"

There was so much threat in that, for all that they were old friends, for all its bland consideration. Ma flinched physically, and felt himself do it, and knew that Tunghai would have seen.

"No, no," he said, trying not to gabble, not to plead; and then—spotting the boy Yueh in the shadows, and desperately recovering some little poise because some things were after all possible under a great compulsion—"you will still not find anyone better than me. Only, I could do better work in Santung. And you should not let the emperor sit there too long undisturbed."

"Is the emperor still there?"

"No." Another thing learned today, something to give up. Relief. "The emperor has gone back to Taishu, and will send a governor. We don't know who, not yet."

"If the emperor can go with such confidence, he can come back. And bring his army back, and take the city."

"Perhaps—but how many times? He has taken some soldiers with him, and may take more—but he must leave a garrison. He must spend more men every time you come against him."

"And so must I."

"Indeed. But you have an empire at your back, and he has nothing but the sea."

"And the dragon," Tunghai Wang said gloomily. "She may not fight for him, but she does not work against him. That is almost as good. If she brings another typhoon—"

"It will impact his men as much as yours. And if she lets his army cross the water again and again, that only helps us whittle it away." It was no easy task to recruit new men for Tunghai Wang; Ma was stretching ever farther for ever-thinner drafts. Still, what was not easy was at least possible this side of the water. For the emperor, not.

"Even so, we need to address the dragon. Ma, if the legends are true, the mage-smith who chained her originally came from the north. I want you to send—"

It was a habit, apparently, to interrupt an old comrade. Perhaps it would be a good habit to break, if Tunghai Wang won through to emperor. For the while, though, he was only generalissimo, and so: "I have already sent," Ma said. "More than one party, on more than one route." *This is what I do,* in case it had been forgotten in this muddy aftermath where all Ma seemed to do was grumble to and fro on a mule.

The north was a long way, of course, and there was a great deal of it. Who knew that better than Ma, who had measured that distance in his wheel tracks, whose task it had been to shepherd an entire army all the way? Tunghai Wang might have led it, the head of the comet, bright and demanding; Ma's task had been to sweep up the tail, to keep myriad men fed and clothed and shod and fit to fight. And to marshal scouts and spies ahead, to marry their reports to Ai Guo's interrogations, to track the emperor as he fled. No one knew the country better than Ma, who had mapped it and pillaged it from the Hidden City to Santung.

Which being true, he had his own notions and his own experience to marry to the legend. The stories might speak only of a monksmith mage from the north, but Ma was not sending out his men at random. Ma did not believe in random.

"Ah," said Tunghai Wang, hearing perhaps the gentle reminders in Ma's words. "Good. Well then, come in and eat with me," for all the world as if this were his own house, as if he were emperor already and all houses were his own.

As if Yueh were not waiting in the shadows there, with the promise of a bath, a private meal, other pleasures.

Well. Yueh would wait. The generalissimo, he was not so good at waiting. And the more chance Ma had to speak to him, the more chance to change his mind, to take him back to Santung in force and speedily, as soon as might be. As soon as next month if it could be managed, and it would fall on Ma's shoulders to manage it.

seven

*A*h, Jiao.

In the forest, in the dark, in all her pain and fury.

What she most wants, honest above all, she wants to point that fury at herself: for being here, for allowing this to happen. For making herself helpless in the clumsy, unhappy hands of a boy who had no idea what to do with her.

Too late: she cannot find herself. She is lost, somewhere between love and rage and rejection. In the forest, in the dark. Like the tiger's roar, she seems to be everywhere and nowhere, immaterial, dissolved. Her body she is sure of, as ever: it stands just here on the valley slope, that way is east and that way back to the road, that the shortest way to the city, that to the sea. But her body is not her self, and never less like it.

She should have known, she did know. Of course she did. None of this is Yu Shan's fault. What else could he say? She would have said the same, only less kindly. She was . . . not kind. No. She could be generous, but that was another thing.

She should never have followed him here; she should never, never have let him catch her on the path. She was better than that.

She used to be better than that. When she was herself, before she lost herself in a pair of green eyes and a touch of the unworldly, the tingling touch of jade.

Well. She had learned; she would not follow him again. With those eyes of his and those broader senses that the stone in him enhanced, here in his own hills too—no. She would not. Let him go. She was lost; he was lost to her. She could live with that. She could recover herself, and be content. As she used to be, self-sufficient, pirate of the road . . .

LOST SHE was, but not in body, no. This was his own valley, just opening up before her: a good place to be leaving, swift as might be. Her legs took her upslope, far from the path, to where great rocks and crags thrust out among the trees.

She wanted to be angry at herself, but couldn't pin it down. Yu Shan was immune, invulnerable; he had done the right thing and she couldn't fault him for it.

She might have blamed the emperor, because that kind of anger can be as unfair as it chooses, but he was too distant and his responsibility too diffuse.

The voice of the jade tiger sounded again, unnervingly close, except that Jiao had no nerves tonight: or else she was all nerve, a one-string instrument, resonating high and clear and hurtful.

All of that and vicious too, the sharpest edge, cutting where it touches, wherever it is touched.

IF SHE was not, if she could not be warrior or lover tonight, if pirate was out of her compass, well. This body could always hunt.

She had hunted men and women in her time. Most of her life she had hunted for her food.

One lean winter, before she made a pirate of herself—or perhaps it was that winter's work that did it, that turned her feet to the road and her soul to the wild—she had lived by hunting, selling skins and bones and horn in a rough market. Wearing what she couldn't sell, wearing it and sleeping on it, learning to tan and work leather and to carve. Cutting and drying and keeping, keeping above all, wasting nothing. Sewing with sinew, chewing jerky, hide boots on her feet and bone tips to her arrows.

She'd never hunted tiger. She'd had more sense than that, but not tonight. Tonight her sense was lost with the rest of herself, or she would not be here.

THE TIGER called, and Jiao responded. With no bow, no spear and no help, she licked her fingers to wet her nose, climbed the nearest outcrop to rise above the confusing scents of trees and under-growth, lifted her head into the cleaner higher air and sniffed for tiger.

It was easy to blame the tiger. It had shown itself in one night to the emperor and Mei Feng, which mattered not at all, and to Yu Shan and Siew Ren together, when she was not there. That mat-tered cruelly much at the time, and all the more tonight. Its every roar was a goad, if not a gloat. Whatever it meant, it had chosen them and not her. Tonight it rubbed salt into that open sore.

Very well, then. She would be the one who made a choice. She owed nothing to the tiger, or the mountains; nothing to Taishu, nothing to the emperor. What she owed the boy, he had refused.

Very well, then . . .

THE CALL was deceptive, deliberately so: what better for a hunter than to confuse its prey past reason, so that it knows not which way to flee? The tiger's voice echoes and swells, it hunts on its own terms, uses fear as a whip to drive its victims this way and that.

Beyond fear, beyond caring, Jiao was too canny to believe the seductions of the tiger's voice. Her nose had been spoiled in the years since she lived truly wild, but not ruined by joss or perfume or the sewer stinks of low-town life. Piracy had its benefits, and some came unexpected.

There: there was the breath of it on the breeze, the dense musk of cat woven through with the dusty weight of stone. It smelled a little like a wet rock on a hot day, a little like the rain-soaked kitten-cat she had relinquished to Mei Feng, just a little like Yu Shan.

Jiao dropped back to the forest floor, turned her face into the wind and ran upslope, light-footed and long-legged, lean and fatal and fatalistic, hunter on the trail, all else left to pool behind her in the muddy valley.

SHE RAN, she sniffed the air, she followed game-paths and sought out pools among the rocks where the high beasts came to water.

She thought this tiger was leading her a dance, it left her so much sign. Here was a pug-mark in the mud, in the moonlight; here was a twist of fur caught around a thorn, stiff between her fingers, so pungent to her nose that she didn't need her eyes to find it out.

Above all, here and everywhere was the tiger's song, close enough now that it could not fool her, high on the hill with no encroaching walls to catch an echo.

AT THE last, up toward the ridge, the trees failed altogether. Here was open rock and scrub, bright moon; here was Jiao; and here, yes, here was the tiger.

Vast it was, still as the mountain, loud as storm. Upslope from her, it stood heraldic against the sky and took her breath away, stole her own movement and made no use of it.

UNTIL IT turned, turned its head to look at her.

Eyes like Yu Shan's, vivid and unreadable.

Was it growling, or purring? And did that, could that make a difference, when either one could make the rock shake beneath her uncertain feet?

AND WHY did cats always, always come to her, as though she would always be a friend?

HER TAO was less than steel tonight, almost a weapon of wind: a whisper as she drew it from her belt, a hiss through the air, barely a glimmer of moonlight.

. . .

MEN TALLER and heavier-built had complained at the weight of her long blade, swinging it in practice. Yu Shan had not complained, but even he had noticed. Tonight it was nothing, it had no weight, only balance as it swung: perfect balance, herself and the blade in a pure ideal of motion and achievement.

THE TIGER was grace itself, ideally adapted. They met, beast and blade, in the exactness of the moment. Jiao hardly even felt the impact in her arms. All the weight was in the tiger, all the shock was in her head, and that was too much hurt already.

ALL THE awkwardness, all the ugliness came after. Hot blood spraying and the chaos of the tiger's fall, its body all unstrung, ungainly, uncat. The brute separate thud of its head, falling onto rock.

AND THEN herself, doing the ugly things.

Breathing, living, she who had unstrung it in her anger.

Heaving up the hot head and setting it on a rock to stare out her anger for her, all across the valley.

Cleaning her tao on the fur of its flank because that's what you do, it is expected, if only by yourself. Perhaps by yourself and the thing dead at your feet, its ghost needing the contempt of that dismissal.

Setting that blade aside and drawing another, a knife fit for skinning.

Spreading out the body for the first needful cut, noticing it was female and still in milk.

NO MATTER. Too late.

SKINNING IS a method, a process: once learned, easily adapted. It was only effortful because of the brute weight of death in a creature so long, so massive.

. . .

JIAO WORKED and sweated, peeling the skin free of its carcass; then lifted her head, hearing the sudden second music, the sound of another tiger.

THIS WAS a youngster come in prowl, in prowling search of its mother.

EYES IN the darkness, a stiff moment's staring, sniffing, scenting blood and human; and then the tension, the crouch, the vicious startle of the great leap forward.

HER TAO was out of reach, she was out of time, all she had was this useless little knife; and why, oh, why did they always come to her . . . ?

THREE

Too Wide a Sea

one

The good doctor sees her patients to the door.

The wise doctor greets her sponsor, the master of her house at his open gateway, with his other servants.

If he is an unknown quantity, where he is to be master of a city and all the lands around, when there is war in the land and a dragon in the sky—then and there the thoughtful doctor goes down to the harbor, to greet him as he sets first foot ashore.

Half the city had the same idea, but Tien was known and cherished now. Simple soldiers made room for her, elbowed her a path through to the wharf, glowered down their own officers when those men objected.

No one knew who the new governor would be. The emperor had departed in a flotilla, promising to send; one single boat, the old man's fishing boat was returning, still decked haphazardly in yellow. Blessed by the emperor's own person, it might never net for fish again. Not the emperor aboard this time—he would still be crooning over his pregnant girl, which was sweet, but wearing— but someone high enough, bold enough not to see the boat stripped of decoration before he stepped aboard it.

Tien didn't particularly care. It would be one man or another. It might be the former governor returned, who had fled to Taishu with the emperor before the rebel army ever reached here. It might be him, but the speculating soldiery around her thought not. Hoped not. They wanted a man who would fight before he fled. It might be one of the generals who had fought alongside the emperor to win the city back; that was what the soldiers wanted, though some wanted one man and some another, and they were sure to fall out over the choice.

It might be no one they knew: one of the emperor's civilian entourage, an official from the Hidden City. A eunuch clerk, more used to ink than blood. No one here would welcome that.

"Or his mother," a voice said, grimly jocular. "Put the strait between him and her, he'd love that."

"Hush." Jokes were always dangerous, close to the circles of power. Jokes about the empress could prove lethal. Whoever owned that voice was right, though, the emperor would appreciate the sea's separation between himself and his mother. Briefly, Tien wondered if Mei Feng—*pregnant* Mei Feng—might have influence enough to make it happen.

Pregnant, though, she might not want it. She might be glad of a strong woman's presence in the palace, a cushion of experience in a frame of iron will.

Besides, the most fickle of emperors would not send a woman—any woman—to rule a city in a time of war. Nor a clerk, no. It would be a soldier, that was sure.

All that mattered to Tien was that he listen to her, whoever he was: that he give her what she needed, and let her care for her charges in her own way.

All her charges . . .

THE BOAT came nosing gently alongside the wharf. Two men stood in the stern. One was grandly dressed and stiffly upright; the other older, more bent, as darkly windburned as the wood of his boat.

He called out from the steering oar, and a boy stood up in the bows with a rope in his hand. There were men ready below, but he ignored them all to make a wild leap over the rail, landing on the wharf with a barefoot stagger that had Tien wincing.

All boys are made of leather and bamboo—it was her uncle's phrase, and the memory of it made her smile. *Sometimes they rip, sometimes they break, but you have to be rougher than you'd think.*

Quite unhurt, this boy looped the bow-rope swiftly through an iron ring and tied it off, then ran to take another as it was tossed down from the stern. She watched him, thinking of a different boy altogether. And shook her head, strict with herself, and waited until the old man above and the boy below had set the gangplank in place from deck to wharf.

By then more men were appearing from the boat's cabin. Before any of them could get in her way, before the new governor came to shore or any of these waiting officers went aboard to smooth his way, she marched herself up the flexing gangplank and onto the boat, all unexpected and out of proper order.

It was a day to be surprising, to be impertinent if necessary; and she had her best excuse to hand, in open sight. Those men weren't the only folk aboard. In the bows of the boat, a woman sat with her arms curled protectively around a child who ought to be too old to be so coddled.

"General." Tien had his name now, from the whispers up and down the wharf—*Ping Wen, he's sent Ping Wen*—but soldiers and great men like their titles better than their names. Even Tien quite liked to be called *Doctor*. She bowed low, and read his confusion as she straightened. "General, you have a child aboard, who has been my patient. I am anxious for his welfare, as I think the emperor must be also."

That was, if only just, enough. The tall man seemed to consider each one of her words, test their weight and substance, their meanings and implications. Then he considered her again, in the light of them. "You are a doctor?" It wasn't—quite—incredulous, but it might have been.

"By imperial decree and service. I am my late uncle's heir. I had the honor to attend the Lady Mei Feng before she sailed with the emperor; and as I say, my lord, I have had your escort-child in my care."

"Very well." She was no more than a child herself, in his eyes. He said so with no more than a blink, less than that. But he was willing to be astonished, ready for it, he had that in his favor. He even held up two fingers to keep the shore-officers back as they came sweeping up in outrage at her cheek. "If you wish to examine the child, do so now. I would say *take him, keep him for me, take your time,* but I am forestalled, I find. Old Yen will sail again immediately, and the boy of course must go with him."

"It is the emperor's own order," the fisherman said.

She thought Ping Wen should resent it more, because that order said *you are stranded here,* without recourse, without retreat; but the general seemed almost complacent.

She bowed to him once more, genuinely grateful, and went forward to the boy and his nurse.

The woman was a stranger, a nun, competent enough. The child was clean and fed and seemed content. It would be as well, perhaps, to have him gone again, never properly here. Let him leave before Mu Gao could come in search of her son, before she upset both of them again.

In any case, the boy was Tien's excuse and not her reason. She wanted to come close to the new governor, to make herself known to him, to win his favor.

What she hadn't expected was to look up and find him at her shoulder.

He said, "I must endure an hour of ceremonial with these," one of those delicate little gestures, that didn't even point toward the cluster of men around the gangplank but nevertheless included them all, "and others like them; but do you come to the palace when you are done here, and wait for me. I will send when I am free. I have a task for you."

"General, I will. I would value time to talk."

That was another startlement for him, that she had interests beyond his unnamed task. He took it well, though, just a quirk and a nod before he walked away.

. . .

SHE DIDN'T know why the emperor was quite so urgent to have the fisherman back so soon. "So that I can come again," the old man said to her, as they watched formal greetings happen on the wharf, "with the general's people and his properties. The governor's, I should say."

Tien didn't think even the emperor could be quite that heedless of others' weakness. The old man looked exhausted already.

"Don't you dare," she said, laying fingers on his wrist to count the pulse of his liver, the pulse of his heart. "Go back if you must, if he has ordered it—but rest on the way, let your boy take the tiller. You do *let* your boy take the tiller . . . ?" with a frowning scowl because she knew the answer before she asked the question.

"Well," he said, equivocating, "the boy is new to the strait and the boat, new to sailing, and the oar is hard to work . . ."

" . . . And he will learn far quicker for working it himself, rather than watching you. You are to tell the emperor, if you please: a full day's rest, a day and a night at least, before you cross the water again. Or shall I send a man back with you, to say so?"

"No need. The governor is sending men enough, with messages of his own; he has been writing all the way across."

She might not have let him leave, despite the imperial order. She might at least have made him stay one night on this side of the water, except that she thought it would be better, so much better if Mu Gao did not see the child. Let him turn and go, then, weary as he was. His boy understood her orders; so did the men he carried. Let him go now, as soon as Tien had scurried off the boat . . .

SHE FOLLOWED Ping Wen up to the palace. Court politics and army politics and all the needs of a city under siege, and one man to negotiate among them: one man that she must negotiate herself, a stranger needing to be read and learned and swiftly understood.

He would need to feel the same about her. It was a pity, really, that he was not hurt or sick himself; people grow close to their doctors. And generals close to those who doctor their troops, the sentimentality never leaves a soldier—but the men here were only Ping Wen's troops by appointment, he hadn't fought with them, there was no shed blood shared. That was a pity too.

He might find himself sharing their hunger, as time passed with the dragon on sea-watch and Tunghai Wang's army in the hills all around. There had been little enough to eat in Santung all summer, but there could be less hereafter.

She wasn't sure that she could wait that long.

So. Up the hill and she caught him up; processions are slow, ceremonials slower yet. He and his entourage were standing in the public courtyard, just within the palace gate. She wasn't sure about that entourage. It looked makeshift to her, a hurried assemblage rather than the considered team he would need to bring order and security to Santung. No doubt the old man would fetch more help when he returned, but she still didn't understand the hurry.

The palace staff was just as makeshift. Soldiers and clerks and servants almost at random, those whom the emperor had gathered up and then abandoned here. And herself, of course, she ought really to be among them. She was a divided creature of uncertain loyalties, serving Tunghai Wang before the emperor came; even now she split her time between the palace and the hospital; but she did most definitely have one foot firmly in the palace, and was determined to keep it there.

That was one of the matters she needed to explain to Ping Wen.

Meantime, around the palace wall she went. Running now, suddenly urgent, and there was little of the respected doctor to be seen in the bedraggled, sweaty, mud-splashed girl who finally wheezed and panted in the shadow of a minor gatehouse.

The guards there knew her anyway. It seemed that all the army knew her by this time. She was fussed at, for running in the heat; she was offered water, dried fruits, a seat here in the shade and all the company, all the gossip she might want.

"No time," she said, laughing, gasping, batting them off, "no *time*! But thank you. Later. I will hear all your news, but later . . ."

She did offer them the name of their new lord governor, but they had it already. Palace whispers ran faster than she did herself, which was no news at all.

Still hot, then, she hurried through the damp rock-and-moss pathways of the garden, under overhanging branches, past pools of gaping fish to a door into a back wing of the palace. Familiar corridors beyond, wood and stone and not a breath of air. Here was a room where she could strip off her dress and wash with cool and perfumed water. Here were fresh clothes to choose among, all of them in solemn grays and blues, the neutral thoughtful dress of a doctor. Soft slippers on her feet and she was ready.

Ready to wait, but not here. Ping Wen had said that he would send for her; whoever he sent, anyone who knew her would know where to look first.

To the library, then: and finding it more brightly lit than she was used to, still not used to this, other people among her books.

Offered a cup of tea from an iron pot that was not quite hot, she apologized for not having thought to bring fresh. And turned on the word and left them, went to the little stone porch where they kept a charcoal-pot smoldering. Fed it tinder, blew it into life. Boiled water.

Made tea.

Good tea, palace tea, not the rough brew that soldiers favored, that she had learned to drink but never relish. Her old men would make faces, perhaps, but they would drink this just the same. It was one of her acquired skills, to induce sour old men to swallow what they would rather not.

BACK IN the library, the darkly green perfume of the tea overlay the dry dusty smells of old paper and old unpolished wood. Old men had their perfumes too, but these were clean old men, she saw to that.

The text she worked on was difficult, almost too artful to be legible, even where she knew all of the characters. More than once she had to ask for help, for two other pairs of eyes to pick at strokes of ink, minds to pick at meaning. It all ate time. She knew nevertheless that time was passing, some quiet aspect of her mind was still consciously waiting for a summons; she couldn't lose herself entirely in her work or in her company.

Nevertheless. When the interruption did come it was potent, it was unexpected for all that it was waited for.

She had missed the sound of footsteps in the passage, she had somehow missed the sudden sense of presence in the doorway, coming in. What she saw was shadow, fallen across her page.

And lifted her head half ready to protest, half willing to say *he'll have to wait, I can't leave this now, I almost have it clear in my mind*—but he was enough to drive that and all else clear out of her mind for a moment, because she had never anticipated this. *I will send,* he had said, not *I will come.*

Here he was nevertheless, Ping Wen himself, in her library. She was not daunted, of course, oh no. She was accustomed to consorting with rebel lords, with Tunghai Wang, more recently with the emperor himself. What had she to fear from an administrator-soldier, one who did not even fight . . . ?

Even so. Startled first, she was swiftly in hand again, and making herself as pleasant as she knew how. Bowing low—well, there was simply no room to kowtow, precious little floor at all in between all these racks and shelves, these chests and desks and lampstands, chairs and men—and calling him lord general, saying, "I had not thought to welcome you in here . . ."

"I am sure not," he said. "I was . . . curious, when I had barely begun to ask for you and it was so immediately known where you would be found, and what doing. And with whom."

"Ah, my lord general, let me introduce—"

"There is no need. General Chu Lin and I are . . . old friends.

Ai Guo I know too. Though I have never known either of them as a scholar."

"Ah. That would be my doing," with a smile, and never mind all the currents in the room, all that hidden knowledge that might be threat or promise. Sail the surface and see what comes, treat with storms when you have to. "They are my patients, and I was always taught that the mind's health matters equally alongside the health of the body. That the one indeed will feed the other. And there is so much to do here, and it matters so much, I have conscripted them both."

"Indeed. And what exactly are you all looking for in all these books?"

"Um. If my lord general would come with me . . . ?"

Perhaps she should be calling him *my lord governor general*? But he seemed content enough, and that would be a terrible mouthful; and she did rather like that sense of holding back, of treating him with respect but not kowtowing, not filling her mouth or his ears with meaningless flattery. Treating with him as someone also worthy of respect.

She took him down the passage to their tea-porch, and so out into the courtyard. Stood back, stood quiet, let him look.

Let him see the damage left by the dragon's landing, that no one had quite dared yet to clear up: all the fallen tiles and the slabs of broken masonry, the wrecked roof across the way, the great indentations filled with rain and seepwater where her feet had rested, where the stone flagging and the ground itself had simply yielded beneath her weight.

Of course he couldn't see what had followed her coming, that long breathless time that had been not quite a negotiation, almost a conversation, except that no one actually spoke.

Sometimes Tien thought they had a pact, almost, she and Han and the old men and the dragon.

Every time she caught herself thinking that way, she came here, like this, to see what the dragon left behind her when she took her boy away.

The tree, the ancient ebony that might have stood for centuries just there, slightly off-center in the courtyard: that now lay in splinters where her belly had descended. Ebony was one of the hardest woods Tien knew, even still on the tree it only grew harder with the years; and in all the stories Tien had heard, the dragon's belly was supposed to be her weakest spot, her vulnerability; and yet . . .

She said, "We are not the first to have had trouble with the dragon. Someone wise has collected this whole library. We are reading through it now, in hopes of finding some way to control her."

Not a pact, no. A promise of resistance, perhaps, each to each. And Han caught between them, not to be forgotten.

Ping Wen said, "Good. I . . . had not realized that she came to land here," *in my palace* he was saying, and his pallor was stressing that. Almost, she thought he meant to reach a hand out and lean upon the doorpost. "I had thought her limited to the strait; I thought the city safe."

"I think we all thought that, my lord. Or else that the goddess would protect us all along the coast here, where her temples are."

"Well. Apparently we were wrong. Ask what you want, then, it is yours. Find what you can in the books here, if you cannot find a way to chain her to my will."

I am ahead of you, general my lord governor. I have done that already, chained her to another's will: only that I did not put you on the other end of her chain, and I am not sure that it has helped. And then, aloud, "You said you had a task for me, my lord general, another?"

"Yes. If this can spare you for the day?" Good; he was making concessions already, his own demands contingent on her choices.

"My lord, my friends here are more experienced with old texts," odd though that was in soldiers, pirates, torturers. Most of what she knew had come from her uncle, not from books. Most of what she knew about dragons had come from Han. This hasty summer's reading had given her enough, just, to do what she had done; the consequences of that they would be living with for a while yet. She was happy to leave the reading to others for a time. "They both still need my care, and I have a temple full of other patients, but—yes, of course, my time is yours if you desire it."

"Good," he said. "You have experience in caring for these mutes of the goddess."

He knew that, he had seen; but what he had seen was all there was. "That one boy, my lord. He was my uncle's patient and in a way my own. I was never sure how much we did for him," except to save his life, perhaps, and what was that? "If the goddess has a use for him, it's beyond my skills to meddle with. If there are others, I have not seen them."

"One more," he said, "there is one more that we know of. The emperor sent her to a temple outside the city, but I want her here. She will be safer here."

"Yes, my lord." That was inarguable, if it was safer to be in imperial hands. There were rebels all around Santung. Also, if this girl were the promise of security at sea, then Ping Wen would feel very much safer if he held her close. Especially now he knew that the dragon had come to the palace. That news had shaken him, when he had seemed less than secure already. He couldn't speak against the emperor's command, but he had not been happy to see the old man sail away. He wanted such freedom under his own command, and who could blame him?

"I am sending a troop," he said, "to fetch her in—but I would like you to go with them. There should be someone with experience. Who better than a doctor, and a woman too? It will not take half a day."

"Of course, my lord." This was how to treat with the great: give way entirely, and then bargain your way back to strength. Lay a burden of generosity upon them, and take full advantage while it was fresh. "My assistant Dandan will see to these men's needs while I am gone."

"Yes, yes. Come." He wanted to see her gone; he would usher her himself to the palace gate if he had to. That was all to the good, embedding her more deeply, setting her more firmly at his side in his own eyes and those of the court, the palace staff, everyone who mattered here. Tien was being seen to matter herself, which was ideal.

Better yet, here *was* Dandan, coming down the passage. She would have kowtowed by instinct, by long palace training, except that she was burdened with a tray. Instead she pressed to the side and tried to efface herself entirely, until Tien ruined that entirely by stopping dead and addressing her by name.

"My lord, here she is! What have you here, Dandan, nutriments for our patients? Soup, warming ginger soup for their healing tissues, good. And seaweed to strengthen their bones, yes . . ." Whatever she had must be whatever she had been able to beg, steal or scrape together from a far-depleted kitchen in a city close to starving. Tien knew. Probably Ping Wen knew also. But it was easy to make it all sound like medicine, so sparse it was and so particular. "We are short on good things, my lord," *we are short on everything,* "so if you could allow Dandan her run of the kitchens and storerooms, as the emperor did . . . ?"

"I am sure we can spare a bowl of ginger soup and some boiled seaweed. As I am sure that any assistant trained by you will be, shall we say, scrupulous in her depradations?"

"Indeed, my lord. And then," taking the lead, walking on down the passage as she spoke, on his errand so that he had to hustle to catch up with her, "there is my hospital, so many of the emperor's troops so badly hurt; their needs are greater. I need food, my lord, as well as medicine . . ."

BY THE time they came to the great courtyard and its gateway above the city, she had named everything she wanted, everything she could think of wanting. She thought perhaps he would have granted her the moon too if she had only thought to demand it, if she would only go on his commanded errand, go *now* . . .

Here was the governor's own carriage for her to ride in, for her to fetch back the one girl he wanted and her sister who would apparently come too. Before ever he set foot in it, Tien did. And here was an escort of soldiers, mounted and on foot, before and behind the carriage. It was no way that she had ever traveled. Her uncle's tent would pack down onto an ox-cart, and she used to ride atop the folded silk, when she wasn't driving the oxen or another wagon laden with patients too ill to walk.

She had thought that was freedom, exhilarating, the life of the road. She had thought that closed carriages were its opposite, like traveling in cages, like the condemned.

She had been wrong, she learned. Even for an hour, this was still the road; that was still the world that rolled by outside the windows. Everything changed, every minute. Just sitting here in unaccustomed luxury, she herself was changing. For one thing, she was learning that luxury did not necessarily equal comfort. Every rut in the road jolted her extremely, from her tailbone to the base of her skull, despite the cushions beneath her and the padded silk on every side. The ox-cart had been a better ride, where her own steel-spring legs absorbed the jouncing. Still, she could curl up and fold her legs beneath her, cling to the sill of the unscreened window and put her head out into the air, watch the sky and the trees and the paddy, the sea when she could see it. She could listen to the soldiers laughing as they rode, as they ran: laughing at her perhaps, but that did her no harm and them some good. It was always good to get away for a while, and to laugh.

And now this was as far as she could go in the carriage, and these men would escort her through the trees till they came to the temple where she had to take two girls away from their mother.

Which was the opposite of easy, and she understood exactly why Ping Wen had chosen her to do it. She could hate him for that, perhaps, except that in his place she would have done the exact same thing herself.

Here was the headland, here the temple, and a boat out at sea beyond. That was bold, or else it was stupid. Both. No dragon in the sky overhead—she'd checked already, first thing, as they came out from the trees; she did that as a matter of course now, almost without needing to raise her eyes, she thought she was developing an extra sense that simply knew when the dragon was there, and when Han was with her—but the dragon could be there at any moment, swifter than wind. Or she could strike up from undersea, tear the heart from the boat before the crew ever knew it.

Or—looking more carefully, squinting through the dazzle of sun on water—that might almost be safe, that boat. It might almost be the old man's fishing boat, that had sailed from Santung with the child to protect it. Tien wasn't confident to tell one boat from another, even close up, even tied to the wharf, but she had been aboard that one for a while, and this was surely like it.

There was no reason for a boat headed for Taishu to be here now, as though it had crept along the coast for hours and only just turned out to sea—but she wondered, she did wonder.

Here was the temple, and she wasn't near ready to do what she had come for; and here was a woman standing on the temple steps, staring out at that boat on the water as if waiting for catastrophe, wondering at the delay.

Or, no. Not her, not that. Tien took another look as she came closer: at the body of her, that rigid pose that said she meant to stand there watching the boat until it was entirely gone from her sight, and then maybe stand some more. Until the night came, maybe, and maybe later.

At the face of her, set as rigid as any muscle, as pale and stiff as a sun-bleached bone. A face that showed nothing, that told everything.

This was a woman not waiting, a woman to whom her catastrophe had already occurred.

Tien was wise enough to see that. She saw it daily. Wise enough also to bring the boat and the woman together in her head—two solitudes, like two characters each written on a separate page, making a third if they were only read together—and so to guess at the nature of that catastrophe.

Still, she did have to ask. "Forgive me, but where are your children?"

There should have been soldiers too, a troop sent by the emperor to protect the most precious, most valuable of all his subjects. It was astonishing to Tien that he had been willing to return the children to their mother even under guard, this far from the city and so exposed, with rebels all around.

There was no immediate sign of the soldiers either, nor the women who had accompanied them. Tien did not think they were all in the temple praying.

The woman turned her head, a slow eventual process, as though her mind were a paddy and Tien's words had to wade through it, the weight of water and the cling of mud beneath.

She turned as though there were pain in movement, pain in every muscle; more in the shift of her eyes, that moment when she was no longer looking at the boat.

As though pain were what she expected, a natural consequence, woven entirely into the fabric of her life.

As though it were dreadful, but didn't really matter anymore.

She spoke in a voice dulled by too much, one hurt too many. Still a mother, though, still asking questions. "My children? Have you come for them too?"

"Yes," Tien said, more forthright than she had meant to be. "Yes, we have. By order of the governor in Santung, we are to take them to the city. You too, if you will come."

"You are too late," the woman said. "He is too late in sending you. And only a governor, not enough. He could not call them back, even if he had the voice to do it. See there, see the boat? They are on the boat. The old man came for them first."

"The fisherman?"

She shrugged. "Perhaps."

Tien was sure now. Sure of this too, though again she did still ask it: "And the soldiers?"

"Yes. They went too. Everyone went."

"They didn't argue?" He was only one old man, with a boy for crew.

"How could they? It was the emperor's order. He had it, he showed it, written and sealed and tied with yellow ribbon . . ."

two

A soldier's loyalty is not always given to his country, or to his commander.

It can be rooted deep in land or family, community or cause. It can be swift and sentimental, given to an officer, a squad, a comrade; it can be purely and pragmatically for himself, for his own survival.

Shen was born to the old emperor's service, trained to it. Soldiering was what he did, and he was the emperor's soldier because all men belonged to the emperor. It was easy, and always would be.

But the old emperor died, of all the impossible things. Shen had thought that he would live forever. Bequeathed to the service of his son, Shen found himself in the middle of a war and losing it. Running away from it, rather, making an endless retreat all across the empire; and wondering often and often how it would feel to be on the other side, a rebel in chase. Wondering often and often why he was not a rebel, why fortune had shaped him so unlucky; and—of course!—why he did not simply slip away one night to find the rebels, to join them, swinging a head or two in one hand as proof of his good faith.

What it was that kept him loyal to a boy he had no reason to believe in.

A man can wonder and wonder inside himself, find no answers, and still not shift. He was the emperor's man regardless, across the empire and across the sea, in all that great defeat.

Then fortune played with him all unexpectedly, so that he met the emperor and others too, found people to believe in. The emperor, and others too.

And now—well, now he was across the sea again, without orders or permission, the emperor left behind him on Taishu. Shen was still loyal, or he thought so. It was only that there were other loyalties, which seemed to matter more.

The boy who had come to fetch him was possibly more confused than he was. He had been a rebel, almost by default: sucked up by Tunghai Wang's army somewhere on the march, made into some kind of a soldier. Not a good soldier, perhaps, no fighter, but fit to carry a load or haul a wagon.

Haul a rope, apparently, on some dreadful fire-flinging machine, he and his squad together.

But the emperor came up out of the impossible river and stole their hearts or their courage or their loyalty, whatever it was that had made them rebels before; and he left them with Chung, the boy said.

Shen heard that the other way around, *he left Chung with them,* with some uncounted number of frightened and dangerous men.

And now the boy wore an imperial sash, Chung's own; and had come to find Shen and fetch him back across the water to Santung. On Chung's own initiative, apparently. And yes, that sounded like Chung, and it sat like a warm promise in Shen's belly.

THEY CROSSED the strait with Ping Wen, unquestioned because anyone who might have the right didn't have the time to wonder about two random soldiers, in all the urgency and ill temper of that crossing. Disembarking behind the new governor and his scant entourage, Shen followed the boy past wharfs and docks and godowns, all along the river path until it was lost beneath a ruin of stones and mud, where steep paddy terraces had collapsed in the typhoon.

And still on, farther on, scrambling almost on hands and knees over the worst of it with their feet sinking deep into soft sticky mud at every step and their hands finding holds that turned treacherous, that slipped away and left them sprawled and filthy and hauling each other out of sucking traps. Shen almost wanted to suggest it might be easier to swim, except that the river was roaring high.

He did say, "Perhaps we should have brought a boat?"

The boy grinned, smeared a muddy hand across his muddy brow, glanced at the water and shrugged. "Could you row? Against that?"

"We could have waited for the tide to turn." Tide and current meeting, fighting each other; perhaps they might fight each other to a standstill, as he and Chung could, almost. Shen always won in the end. But Shen's shoulder was not mended yet; like this, he thought perhaps Chung would defeat him. He was sure he could not row a boat even one mile, even on the quietest water.

ON, THEN. Not too much farther on: just to a bridge, where the guards greeted the boy by name and Shen with guarded nods.

Over the bridge to an island in mid-river, where someone not entirely competent had set up a crude camp. It might have been any army bivouac if it had only used the space more sensibly, reaching all the length of the island instead of crowding down at this end, awkwardly squeezed between the footings of this bridge and another. That other bridge was gone, but its stone remnants made the campsite even more cramped and uncomfortable, while the farther end of the island was open and empty and ridiculously unused.

Half a dozen men sat around a smoky smudge of a fire, toasting something indeterminate on bamboo skewers. Shen didn't look too closely. After a year on the road and months on starveling Taishu, he knew too well that some questions are better left unanswered.

Some questions, though, still demand to be asked. His guide-companion looked almost as helpless as he was himself, blinking around at the makeshift tents. "Um, where's . . . ?"

If he hesitated, it might have been because he didn't quite know whether to ask for Chung or Master Chung, or even Captain Chung: what respect does a boy owe—among his own comrades—to the man that they've surrendered to? When that man is in no way a soldier?

But it might only have been because he saw a tent-flap fall aside, a figure coming out, an answer as the question died away. Or he heard the voice, perhaps, as Shen did.

"Shen! There you are already, I never dared to hope for you so soon!"

And then there was nothing for the boy to do but fall back, join his friends around the fire and hope for a share of whatever was on those skewers, because boys are always hungry. Shen was still mostly hungry himself, though ware betide anyone who thought to call him a boy. Right now, though, he could be satisfied with this, with the hurtle of Chung's body into his and his own yelp, "Careful! Mind my shoulder . . . !"

"If your shoulder was a worry," Chung laughed into his ear, "you should not have brought it here."

His hands were more careful than his words, gentling Shen into an embrace that left that healing shoulder free, that was still more intimate than Shen would have been by choice in front of strangers.

No matter. Shen could endure it all, the jolt of pain and the curious stares, for the sake of this: a live lithe laughing body in his arms, a certainty where there had been doubt before.

He said, "How do you come to be in charge of . . . these?" *These enemies,* he meant, *these prisoners,* who were seemingly quite free and unwatched, given license even to cross the strait and back. He had heard one version of that tale already; he wanted another, Chung's own, in case that came out easier to understand.

He wasn't hopeful.

Chung said, "Who says I'm in charge?"

"I say it. I took one look at your camp here, and I knew. Who else would choose so badly? And house and feed his men so ill, so close to all this city?"

"Well, but it's hard here." Chung was still laughing, but he was defensive too. And practical too: "And you're here now, and your soldiering is better than mine, you can help."

"I can take charge," Shen said unequivocally, "when I know what you're about. But any of these men will be a better soldier than you; they should have scavenged better tents than these, and better food too."

"They've been busy. We found the godown where Tunghai Wang stored all his firepots and their makings, there's been a lot to carry. And no road. We towed it in the end, a barge on the river and a rope to shore. We're still storing most of it on the barge, just to be safe. But it was work, and there's not been time to do much else."

"That's why you're not a soldier. The men's comfort is the first thing. Whatever you're here for, the work, that comes after. What *are* you here for?" *And why are we all crowded down this tight little end of the island?*

"I'll show you. If you'll just let go of me, enough that I can walk . . ."

It was, of course, Chung who was holding on too tight to let them walk. Disentangling themselves from each other took a little time, thanks entirely to his stubbornness; but soon they were picking their way through the camp and into that wasted open space, the bare bleak rock of this islet.

"The water came right up over here, when the river rose," Chung said. "We were crowded up on the bridge there, the highest point of the arch and we still got our feet wet. There was nothing left of anything, except one barrel I managed to save . . ."

That explained why it was all so clean underfoot, scrubbed free of soil and ash and weeds, all the litter of life. It wasn't as empty as he'd thought, though: there was a line of pots, like storage vessels, and a line of barrels opposite. At the far tip of the island was a structure of sorts, an improvised bamboo frame.

"Why didn't you build your camp at this end, and keep your stores down among the footings of the bridge, where you could pile them up and not worry?"

"We'd worry," Chung answered, smiling. "No one wants to let the fire anywhere near the bridge. None of this is any safe at all. What's in those barrels will burn just on its own, if a flame touches it. Mixed together—well. I'll show you. That's better than trying to explain."

He called back over his shoulder. Men came, eager but careful: handling the barrels with a nervous respect as they filled a pot with this and that, mixed the ingredients with a long and cautious stick, sealed the pot and carried it forward.

The bamboo frame overhung the river, to let them lower a platform down almost to the rushing water.

"This is the only safe way we can do it," Chung said. "You can't really watch, but—well, you'll see."

Shen frowned at the frail platform. "Can't you build it better than that?"

"No point. It won't survive, however well we make it. It just has to hold the pot, just for a minute. Watch."

The pot stood on the platform and hung against the vertical face of the island, a man's height or more below where they stood, out of sight to anyone not leaning over. A long wick came back up to Chung's hand.

"It wouldn't be this long, of course, if we were using it in war. Just, this is as careful as we can be."

Here came a man with a smoking firepot. A lidded pot, and he was still wary. Shen had never seen men so scared of what they did themselves.

Here came two men, carrying a construction of bamboo and rope and padding. It might have looked almost like the body of a man beneath a quilt. A wet man, a drowned man; it was dripping, from rain or river or both.

"We call that the dragon," Chung said. "They wouldn't let me call it Tunghai Wang, and I wouldn't let them call it anyone else. So it's the dragon, which we can all agree about."

Shen was worried, if these men still held even that much loyalty to their former commander. Still, he was here now. That at least reduced the worry. It was being apart, being helpless that drove him frantic, not knowing what madness Chung was at now.

He said, "Nothing's going to set that alight, it's all water."

"Like the dragon. You wait. You watch."

The mock-dragon—though it still looked to him a lot more like a man—was hung out from the frame, as high as a man might jump above the pot. Then, bizarrely, everyone lay down flat on the rock. Chung pulled Shen down too beside him, before ever he touched wick to glowing coal and set it aflame.

It burned down below eye-level, below the level of the rock they lay on, and then there was nothing: interminably nothing, a long dragging wait. Bored and restless, Shen pulled himself forward to peer over the edge, see how close the flame was to the pot—

—AND CHUNG screamed, literally screamed as he scrabbled at Shen's bad shoulder to drag him back again.

"Don't you *understand*? It's going to—"

No, he didn't understand—or he hadn't, until that moment.

Chung's voice was cut off by a vicious flare of light and a brief and dreadful roar, as though Chung had bottled up a fraction of storm in that pot, thunder and lightning both. The frame swayed above them, a rope snapped and flailed wickedly in the air, the mock-dragon bucked and twisted amid a hail of bright flaming points flung from below.

The river hissed like a nest of snakes, smoke billowed slowly up to follow the sparks, but Shen was watching those as they rose, as they faded, as . . .

. . .

ALL AROUND him, men were covering their heads with their arms. Shen was slow still; Chung had to reach out and pull him in tight, wrap his own arms around both their heads together.

Even the dragon when she flew, she came back eventually to earth.

There was a patter of little impacts all around them. Something stung Shen's leg, even through his trousers: stung first, and then burned.

When Chung would let him, he sat up and reached to rub at the soreness, then to find what had bitten him: a hard sharp hot little shard of blackened pot.

Bewildered, he turned and saw the mock-dragon.

Splintered, shredded, torn half apart by a blizzard of those little vicious impossibly burning things—and impossibly set aflame too, although its ripped innards were still running with water. Steaming as they smoked.

"Chung. What have you *done* . . . ?"

"Oh, I didn't really do much. It was Tunghai Wang who set his machines here and gave them the firepots to fling. I just happened to be here with Yu Shan and the emperor when one of the pots rolled into a flame and exploded. See, if you just throw them, they break open and the mixture inside catches fire from a fuse, and that's what burned our friends so badly; but if you light the fire inside an unbroken pot—well. This. They erupt. Every little shard is lethal. And they're hot enough to spread the fire too . . ."

They were. The frame too was aflame, and men were hurling water to douse it.

"Chung, that's—that's *wicked* . . ."

"Yes." He beamed at Shen, like a man who has finally learned to soldier. "Let me practice more, let me build a machine to throw them with and learn how short to cut the wicks, so that they explode before they strike, and then we can give the emperor a weapon to win any war . . ."

three

*B*iao liked these people, these clansfolk.

He wasn't so sure about their home, a closed valley among re-mote hills; this was far and far from any life he knew. Anything he valued.

For jade, though: the chance of jade was worth a sacrifice. And there were other compensations, more immediate, a full belly and an easy day; and the respect they showed him, all unforced. He knew himself to be an idiot here in the forest, and nevertheless they called him Master Biao and deferred to him as though his lit-tle wisdoms were worth far more than theirs, even in their own country.

He loved that.

And this, he loved this, that they came to him to say, "We are walking the bounds of our clan claim today. We will meet our neighbors on the heights, and not fight, because they are doing the same. It will be a good thing if you are there." This was more than a welcome, almost a demand. *Be one of us, be one with us.*

Well. He would do that.

First, he did need to be a doctor. This was Yu Shan's family compound, but Siew Ren was here. That was inappropriate, Biao understood. Yu Shan's mother had not spoken for her at the last clanmoot, had not been able to speak for her because the boy him-self wasn't there to be presented and approved. Ancient customs might be no more than token when the young people had known each other all their lives, but still: by clan law he had no claim on her, and she should have gone back to her own family, higher up the valley.

Yu Shan had brought her here regardless. It seemed as though, in his guilt—too late, in every way that mattered—he needed to claim her any way he could. Which meant physically, her presence in his home; and physically again, his presence at her side, by her bed, hour by hour and day by day.

Biao thought he would drive her demented, and wondered what the treatment was for that.

So far, she didn't seem to care. He wasn't quite sure that she'd noticed. She was caught up in the immediacy of pain, wrapped entirely in her ruined flesh and skin; she paid no heed to the world even a breath beyond. Or perhaps she hid from it. Better to hurt, perhaps, and not worry how to live beyond that, crippled and scarred. She hated to be touched now. Yu Shan thought that was because any touch hurt her, even his, even the most gentle; Biao thought it was because any touch was a reminder of the world, *all of this is waiting for you,* the rest of her life, hard and unremitting and worse perhaps than pain.

Biao was the only one whose touch she would allow. Not even Yu Shan was let doctor her.

This was his morning, then: that he woke in the little hut he slept in all alone, rather to the scandal of his hosts; he washed with the family at the well, and spoke of this and that, and today they invited him to walk the bounds with them; and then he made a brew and cooled it and went in to his patient.

Siew Ren too had a hut to herself, because her cries and moans kept people wakeful. There was a handful of children in the compound, but children sleep through anything; it was the adults who lay disturbed and restless in the common house because Siew Ren was far beyond sleep, beyond caring. Pain was a knife, whittling at her, fining her down. Sometimes what it cut away fell out as sound.

She was quiet this morning. Quiet so far. Yu Shan was there as ever, crouched at that little distance that he'd learned: close enough that he could reach her in a moment, far enough away that she didn't feel loomed over, about to be touched. If she opened her eyes and saw him there, she wouldn't flinch away.

Probably.

Biao bustled straight past Yu Shan and dropped onto the dry earth floor beside her pallet.

Her eyes opened, her face twisted in the dim door-light. Lips turned back from teeth: it was her new version of a smile. At least, Biao had decided to read it so. He beamed back down at her, and lifted the lid from the bowl he carried.

This was the hard thing, night and morning and through the day. All her burns, which meant half her body, must be bathed with this. She must be lifted and turned and touched all over, most particularly where she hurt the most, where her skin was gone and her flesh was raw and weeping.

She didn't trouble to try not to scream.

Every time they did this, Yu Shan would try to help, to hold her; and she would bat him away with vague terrible gestures, wild awkward arms and flopping hands. She would lean sobbing into Biao's grip, though he found it almost impossibly difficult to hold her and turn her and dab at her all at once. He was sure that he hurt her more than necessary, just through having it all to do himself. But she couldn't be persuaded, she would not have Yu Shan touch her.

Today, when it was done, when she was lying back and lying still, settling into the steady embrace of her pain again, Biao felt an unaccustomed twist of sympathy for Yu Shan, like a knife in the gut. He did not ordinarily rate himself a kind man, or a generous one; perhaps he was being a doctor, thinking as Tien would, seeing the world her way. *At last,* Tien would say. Seeing two patients, both in need.

Biao said, "Yu Shan. When Siew Ren has drunk her tea and eaten what she can," another brew and a bowl of congee with certain herbs in it, which he would prepare and Yu Shan feed to her spoon by spoonful, a duty she allowed, "come walk the bounds with your clan, with me."

He shook his head, but Biao was ready for that. His voice rolled on almost without pause. "For her sake, Yu Shan, not for yours. Let Siew Ren rest an hour or two without you hovering above her. Your desperation is an obstacle to her recovery."

It was cruel, which worked well with his new sympathy: balance over all, this way and that. Yu Shan gazed up at him for a moment, then unfolded his limbs and stood slowly, towered above him, nodded with a brutal care. No words: he seldom had anything to say anymore. That nod was effort enough, almost praiseworthy.

Biao stepped back to let the young man blunder out into the day. One last glance at Siew Ren, who didn't move, he didn't expect her to: pain enclosed her like a shell its nut and she lay utterly still, encompassed within it, but her eyes were on Biao. *See what I do for you, how I work for your comfort?* Even in this dimness she could read that, even though he stood against the dazzle of the door-light. Her gratitude might be useful to him yet.

Not all the clan would come to walk the bounds. Biao had known cities where this would be a fair-day: ceremonies and games, dragon boat races on the river, food and music and other pleasures outside the walls all day and half the night. Not here. In the mountains borders were worth fighting for. This was not even a way to keep peace with the neighbors, only to establish where the fights would happen.

Ordinarily, at least, that was true. Things were . . . no longer ordinary. Even a stranger to the island, even Biao could tell. He knew the reputation of the clans, from legends of the imperium and soldiers' gossip together; and he knew too that they were aware of change. Their children had gone away to fight for the emperor, to fight *together* for the emperor. Some had come back hurt, blood-bonded each to each in a way no clansfolk ever were before.

Inevitably, some had not come back. Some of their own, some

of their neighbors' children. Not many, but in a way that only made it easier to mourn, knowing that everyone held the same few missing faces, the same names in their minds and memories.

Some of the clansfolk were not even carrying weapons as they made the slow march up to the traditional mootpoint, high, where the trees failed and the rock grew more barren and debatable.

Their neighbor-clan was waiting there already by the time Biao arrived, blowing hard and almost grateful to Yu Shan for staying with him. *Almost* was *not quite,* and he wasn't really sure that the boy was there in fact. Only the shell, perhaps, the simple physicality of him, empty and mute. Even that was a comfort when he walked barely faster than you wanted to, a slow trudge up the endless slope and you could actually seize hold of his arm and find an inexhaustible strength in it, the strength of stone if only stone could climb.

The mootpoint was flat rock, an unexpected platform here on the forest's edge. Of those who made the climb, half were young and hurt; and it seemed that the young ones had come up largely to see their blood-kin from the next valley, whom they had fought beside just days before. After so much hugging and whispering and showing scars, it would have been hard for their elders to glower and snarl at one another with any conviction.

At first they stood in two groups, while the young folk mingled. Then one individual recognized another across the gap, with a nod and a grunt; someone took a step forward and saw it matched, and was committed because stopping now, stepping back now would be ridiculous; soon the two clans were so mixed that they set out to walk the bounds in a single band.

A single band and Yu Shan, perhaps. Even he walked with others, though, and not all of his own clan. Biao wasn't actually sure this would do him any good, but he could see no harm in it. No possibility of harm.

"Master Biao."

She was not quite a stranger: one of those who had traveled

with them on the road, slipping away to her own people where the path divided. He had advised her how to treat the wound she carried, a deep gash to the shoulder. He hoped it had been good advice. He thought he'd said what Tien would have said, more or less. That was the best he could do.

She seemed fit enough, at least, arm in a sling but healthy otherwise, a good color and keeping pace.

It was a pity that he couldn't remember her name, but she expected that, or she read it in his face.

"I am Chia."

". . . And we were together in the jade store, you helped us with your good arm when we had to move to higher ground, although the effort left you bleeding. I remember perfectly. How is the shoulder now?"

"It's good, thank you." She raised it in the sling, higher and more easily than perhaps she should have done, so soon with such an injury. Perhaps it was just youth and health; or perhaps they were right, these youngsters, that they would heal faster and better if they only came home.

Tien might have known if that was true. Biao was out of his depth but hiding it, riding it, as he had done all his life. Using it.

"Keep using the herbs as I have shown you," he said, "and work the flesh there, work the arm if you don't want the scar to stiffen it."

"I will, Master Biao."

"Good. Come to show me, in another week. You know where I am staying."

"With Yu Shan, yes. With Siew Ren . . . If I am allowed to, I will come."

"I'll tell the watchmen to expect you. You and your clan-cousins, I'll say you're under my care. They respect me, I think."

"Of course. You may need to come to us, even so. Though after today . . ." She looked forward, she looked behind, to where two clans walked almost as one; she shook her head, smiling, bewildered. "It isn't usually like this, you know. It isn't *meant* to be like this. We walk our side of the ridge, they walk theirs, and it's a lucky day if we only throw hard words at each other. A rare day. Usually it's stones. Maybe your coming will be good for all the valleys, Master Biao. Maybe they will let us all come to you."

A voice called her name, a young man's voice, and she skipped ahead. Biao felt almost benevolent, watching her: almost as he thought he ought to feel.

There were others to talk to, other hurts to ask after, other healings to marvel at privately and nod over in public as though they were to be expected, as though they were all his own work. There was perhaps even the far distant dawn of hope for Siew Ren. These others had not been so badly hurt, not by a long way, but even so . . .

He might say that to Yu Shan. He might not. Better perhaps to let the boy build his own hopes from what he saw about him, so that if those hopes failed he would at least not blame Biao.

There were ridge paths through the forest, breaks where rock thrust high and the trees fell away and they walked under cloud and sunlight, under a sudden warm shower of rain.

The elders were talking about jade: how thin the old seams were, how hard it was to find fresh. "They say jade is the tears of the dragon. Well, she is free now, what does she have to weep over . . . ?"

Biao was already used to such talk, already bored by it. His eyes moved to follow a couple of youngsters straying high up the mountainside, beyond clan territory: two lads easy together, out adventuring . . .

Lads caught in a sudden stillness, staring down into a hollow.

Lads turning, waving madly; their voices following a little later, as though it took time even for sound to tumble over these stony slopes.

Voices calling, long broken wordless cries. They might have meaning, clan-talk, some tongue of the valleys, but Biao could not distinguish it.

The healing young had to help one another, in a sudden upslope scramble; it was their elders who reached the lads first, saw what they saw, stood in the same still place, somewhere dreadful.

Biao came up last, puffing and gasping, snatching at a hand when it was held out to him and only realizing after he'd grasped it that it had been meant to hold him back, to say *no, don't look, you don't want to see this.*

By then he was expecting bodies, death. What else?

He used that resistant arm just to haul himself up those last few steps, against the hot ache in his legs. Frowned at its owner, *I am Master Biao the doctor, don't try to deny me;* and pushed his way through to the hollow's rim.

And looked down, and saw death indeed, and not at all what he was expecting.

IT WAS wet down there, darkly wet, and that was more than rain. There was blood in it, which the rain wouldn't allow to dry. Biao could smell it.

So could the gathered flies, in all their number.

There was a body, yes. Just the one, and that was dark too, wet too, strange. Too long and skinless, skinned: not human, something animal, but what animal here grew to such a potent size . . . ?

There. On a rock beside, another dark wet thing, a head: intact and terrible, tongue lolling between vicious teeth where the jaw hung slackly open.

"I didn't . . ." His voice sounded wrong, all manner of wrong against their silence. But someone had to speak, and it might be the right of the stranger. He swallowed, and tried again. "I didn't know you hunted tigers, in these hills."

"Stone tigers," someone answered him. "And no, we do not hunt them."

Now he saw, yes, the banded fur was green between the black, the pure color of imperial jade. No doubt the eyes too, no doubt they would match the eyes of these people around him, these shocked people, some of them weeping now, some raging in their silence.

Rare beasts become mystical: meaningful to those who live among them, almost mythical to those who live elsewhere. Biao had never expected to see a jade tiger, had barely ever imagined they were real. An adjunct to tales of the emperor: why would they need to exist, outside the stories? What would sustain them, more than the credulity of peasants?

What would they need to sustain them, more than that?

Here it was, though, dead and skinned, and of course the clansfolk were appalled. Yu Shan was trembling visibly. Biao remembered some story that he and Siew Ren had seen a jade tiger, somewhere in these forests. The emperor too, but that mattered less; the emperor was not here.

Of course Yu Shan must see this as an omen. So did everyone, no doubt.

Perhaps they were right. Perhaps they were all right. If it was an omen, though, no one there knew what it meant.

Biao did what he had always done, stole the moment. Took it to himself.

Stepped down into the hollow, where none of the clansfolk had quite dared to tread.

Blood in the mud that soaked his shoes, but they were wet already. Flies and stink in the air; breathe shallowly through the mouth, try not to swallow anything.

He turned his back to the body, to the head. Lifted his eyes to the people grouped above him, lifted his voice and said, "This, now, this is a horrible thing. You will want to know who has done it, man or monster, demon maybe." If jade tigers prowled these hills and there was a dragon in the strait, who knew what other creature might not rise from stories and be true?

Someone, he thought, ought to find out. In case it came down from the high hills and wanted to hunt in the valleys.

Voices rose, not directly against him, not directly in response but stirred by him—*not us, not any of us, not your clan or ours, we would not, could not . . .*

They must have their own stories of tiger-killers, dangers to the beasts. Nothing lives that does not die, except immortals and even they face dangers. Even the dragon could be chained. There would be stories.

Biao sent these people away, into their own story. "Go you, all of you now. It is a horrible thing, but I am a doctor and good can come of this. There are organs I can harvest here, to make medicines; this magnificent creature can be as generous in death as she was in life." He was guessing at everything: what kind of stories they would tell one another about the tiger, what gender the tiger was. Skinned, it was hard to know what was missing. The way the carcass lay, sprawled on its back with the legs fallen open, he should have been able to tell but there was only a hollow there, a dark gathered pool.

It was a pity not to have the penis, if the beast had once been male. A jade tiger's member, guaranteed by the creature's head: the value would have been incalculable. If he had been allowed to take it, if he had been allowed to sell it, if he could have found his way to the proper marketplace and spread the word that he had such a thing.

On this stranded island, among these stranded people, that was a long chain of doubt. More likely someone would have claimed it for the emperor. Who else could own the harvest of a stone tiger, than he who owns the stone?

There was no penis that he could see, and he was reluctant to dip his hand into that pool and feel for it, at least while anyone was watching. It was still possible that there would be no harvest at all, that they would let Biao take nothing. People were muttering among themselves, eyeing him askance. Stranded, he thought: without tradition, because who would ever kill a jade tiger? It was unknown, unknowable.

Being a doctor worked in his favor, if it was a favor to be left in a pit with a stinking fly-blown corpse. Even these people knew that tigers were a great source of health and strength. Being a stranger should have worked against him, except that it set him apart from clan obligations. Two clans watched him here, and they watched each other too; joined in outrage, still neither one would let the other take possession of the carcass.

Which left it for him in the end, as it had to, as they could not conceivably leave it to rot. It was rotten enough already; the reek of it was almost tangible. Perhaps it was too late for harvest now. If he had been a true doctor, he would have known. Tien would know.

Tien was not here. He was; and he was the best they had, these frantic clans. Yes, he could take what he wanted of the tiger's parts. And no, they would not linger here to watch him at his harvest. They could not abide that. They would scour the forest for strangers, each clan to its own valley, no more marching together. Already they were pulling apart, each inclined to blame the other for allowing some intruder through, some monster, human or otherwise.

They would warn their farther neighbors too. The mountains would be closed. No one would get through, who had not fled already.

They would leave Biao to his work.

He wanted nothing else just now, than that they should leave him.

In a pit, with a stinking fly-blown corpse.

He took what he could, always, whatever came in reach. There was power here, influence. Opportunity. They would know him now to be the man with the tiger's parts. What he actually took—unwatched, unsupervised—would matter far less than what he was believed to have taken.

He had a knife, he had pockets and a pouch. The forest was full of leaves that could be folded, creepers to bind one parcel with another. Above all he had time and solitude and his own wily craft, his long history of making do.

He turned to the head first, because whiskers were easy: easy to name, easy to harvest, easy to prescribe.

A jade tiger's whiskers were stiff as bamboo splinters, stiff and sharp. He could blunt his knife, just trying to hack them off. Perhaps they could be plucked more easily than cut, if the flesh that held them was as rotten as it smelled . . . ?

He gripped one as tight as he could manage in the wet, and tugged. Felt resistance, and wrenched at it—and felt his fingers slide along the slippery length of the wire-fine whisker, and felt the pain that followed, and looked down to see bright blood welling where fingers and palm together had been sliced open.

And cursed, and danced a little against the pain; and might have kicked the corpse if it weren't so foul, might have kicked the head rolling into the blood-sodden mud if it hadn't been set so high on its separate rock, if it hadn't been blind and glaring at him.

Was sensible instead, fumbling in his pockets for something that might make a bandage. He couldn't go back to the compound oozing blood.

And could find nothing on him, and of course the tiger had nothing to offer; so he lifted his eyes to the lip of the hollow, thinking to try the forest, and so found that he was not after all alone.

YU SHAN had not gone with his clansfolk, or else he had come back.

He crouched up there on his own, unbearable company even to himself. Discovered, he stepped down into the mud with a bitter reluctance, shuddering at the touch of it on bare feet.

He stared at Biao, eye to eye. That was high strategy, Biao knew, all the boy had. Look at something, one thing, not to see what else was there, that he could not bear to look at. Biao had done the same thing often and often, with the reverse intent: hold their eyes, not to let them see what he could not bear to have them discover.

Yu Shan had discovered the worst thing already, which was not Biao's incompetence any more than it was the carcass itself, though that was what his eyes avoided. The worst thing was not here.

"She did this."

"What? Who—?" *And why tell me? Tell your clan, they're on fire to know.*

"Jiao, of course. She was here, she followed me. I *spoke* to her, I sent her away . . ."

It's my fault, he was saying, *I did this.* Which might even be true by his own harsh reading. Biao thought people were both more simple and more complicated than that, but boys tended to feel what they wanted to feel, and guilt was always high on that list.

Biao said, "Well. Your people will find her, if she's still—"

Yu Shan shook his head. "She will be that way," a jerk of his chin, up the mountain. "She will go up. She will be hurt."

"How can you . . . ?"

"There is blood here, blood and blood," though he still wasn't looking at it. "The tiger's blood, and yours. There must be hers too. I could smell it, if yours wasn't fresh and the tiger's so rank. She will have been hurt here." It was an article of faith, apparently, *you don't kill a jade tiger and walk away unharmed.* "She will have gone up high. I could follow, I could track," *I could sniff her out,* "but I need to go back to the compound, to be with Siew Ren when she hears. She will hate this. Hate it."

Biao looked at Yu Shan, looked up the steep bare wet rock of the mountain. "I am no tracker, and no hunter either."

Yu Shan shrugged. "She will be up there." *My people will not go,* he seemed to be saying, *and someone should.*

"She will have to come down. Eventually." No one could live up there for long; Biao didn't see the urgency. She would come down, and the clans would find her in the forest.

Yu Shan's eyes were jade-hard, all glitter and depth. "She will be hurt, and you are a doctor."

"You want me to *heal* her?"

A shrug. "Perhaps. I want you to find her, and do what you do. Me, if I found her, I would kill her, I think. I can't look," for her or at the tiger. "I have to go to Siew Ren."

"Your people will kill her anyway. When she comes down." *Let her die up there if she's hurt as badly as you think, as you want her to be.*

"Perhaps," but his eyes were compelling. Lethal. "You go, Biao. You find her."

If Biao understood anything, if he had learned only one thing in all his life, it was to recognize when a man had no choice.

Himself, or any man.

IN THE end, it was easy.

Terror attracts.

Sometimes, it does.

On the barren slopes of a strange mountain, where you can see nothing but rocks and sky and the threat of eventual night, when you dare not go back down without what you were sent for, which you have no hope of finding; when you hear a woman's voice in the clear air, and are afraid; when you hear a tiger's rumble in that same air, and cannot tell where on the mountain it might be coming from, and are mortally afraid.

That kind of terror, yes, can draw you on.

Biao scrambled over scree and rough tussock-grass toward the sound he heard, one of the sounds, the woman's low murmur.

The other sound, the tiger, he really had no idea. Was it behind him, hunting? Was it ahead, alluring? He couldn't tell; he couldn't stop. All he could do was hurry on and hope to find Jiao, and hope to help her, such that she would not kill him.

Such that she would kill the tiger for him, if that was necessary, if it was coming after him. His little knife would be no help, no hope at all, even if he had the courage to fight a tiger on its own mountain. Which . . . Well. He thought not, probably.

HERE, SOMEWHERE here: the sound rolled down this slope. The sound that he was following, her voice. She seemed perhaps to be crooning. Perhaps she had run mad.

Mad might be better, almost. No sane woman would tackle a tiger.

Tackle and kill it, kill and skin it and then hide up on its own mountain, where its own kin stalked.

Perhaps he should hope that she was mad, that she might do it again.

THERE WAS an overhang, a great scarp of rock above; between that and this sliding, cruel slope, there was a darkness.

It could be a cave of sorts, at least a shelter from sun and rain. If not from tigers.

Yu Shan might look at unstable scree and see blood-traces, where she'd scrambled up. Or smell them.

Biao's own hand bled again as he scrambled on all fours up a slope that slithered away beneath him as he went.

Nothing was solid, there was nothing to grip, it wanted technique and speed and he had neither. What he had was the persistence of terror, just a little more frightened of what might lie behind him than he was of what might lie ahead. And besides, fear itself had become irresistible now, like a toothache to the tongue, he had to probe it.

Up he went, then, cursingly, scrabble and kick and slide and scrabble again; and eventually—quite a long time after the woman's

voice had fallen silent, though the tiger's still sang somewhere—
he did come up far enough to seize a hold that didn't give beneath
his weight, solid rock that did indeed bring him into a sheltered
space that a desperate woman might just think a cave.

IF SHE were desperate, she didn't show it.

Her face showed nothing, it was only a blank in shadow. Her
blade was just as dull, with no source of light to reflect as it waited,
as she did.

The blade she held in one hand. The other lay on the neck of
the tiger.

WAS THAT growling, or purring? Did tigers purr?

Whatever the noise was, it resonated dreadfully beneath the
rock of the overhang. It rolled out and down the mountain like a
threat, the fearful sound that he had been bold to climb into, except when he thought it was behind him; in here, under here, it
was not a threat at all. It was worse, far worse than that. It was a
statement, an inevitability: as certain a promise as the edge of that
blade.

More certain, perhaps, than the blade. Biao was a man who noticed such things. Jiao was a right-handed woman, and it was her
right hand that lay on the tiger's scruff. The long blade of the tao
looked less dangerous, in her left. He thought it drooped rather,
toward the floor of the cave.

It was the blade, nevertheless, that made him certain this was
Jiao. That was Jiao's blade. The rest . . . Well. Her face was hidden,
and her body too, largely. Something was wrapped around her,
more than the lightless quality of the cave. With her long legs also
drawn up out of sight, there were only her arms to announce her.

One that held a tiger, and one that held a blade. Droopingly, unconvincingly, not like Jiao at all. Even left-handed, she should have
been more compelling than that, and simply stronger.

Nevertheless, it was Jiao's blade.

He said, "Jiao, come out into the light and let me see how you are hurt."

For a long time, too long, she didn't respond. Perhaps the point of the tao dipped lower, but he didn't think that was at her choosing, or under the influence of his voice.

When there was movement, it was the tiger that moved, unless some little pressure from her hand had moved it. It rose to fill that cramped space between rock above and rock below; its voice rolled on like thunder appallingly contained, so that Biao had to shout shrilly through it: "Leave the tiger, let it stay within . . ."

Now at last Jiao answered him. With a laugh first, a savage broken thing; and then her voice, all scorn, all Jiao. "What, do you take him for a trained dog? Kitten in a basket? If he chooses, he will come."

"Is he . . . is he safe?"

"Safe from you, I think," and that laugh again, harsh and horrible. "Safe in the world? Perhaps not. The world is a cruel place, it killed his mother. I try to keep him safe, but do not promise. Is the world safe from him? No, not at all. It killed his mother. But will he eat you? Perhaps not. I do not promise; I think he must be hungry now. Back away."

Biao was doing that already, edging to the limit of the cave-mouth and beyond, out into the fall of light, onto the scree again.

The tiger followed him.

And stood sure-footed on the shifting slope, vast paws spread wide. Too wide, Biao thought, too vast for the size of cat above; gods and demons, was this thing only a *cub* yet? It was a monster already, longer in the body than Biao was tall. Longer than Jiao, perhaps. Heavier than both of them together. And young, yes: ferocious because it was afraid, perhaps, still growling deep in its magnificent throat, staring at Biao with hot jade eyes, its body set like a trap to snap and fling at a moment. At a move, at a word— and the move might come from Biao, but he thought perhaps Jiao would have the word ready on her tongue in case she needed it.

The tiger's eyes shifted to look back into the cave. Here she came now. Biao didn't relax. The creature might be less dangerous in her presence, but only because she was more so. On its own, it was unpredictable, unknown; with her, he thought it was another weapon to her hand. One that she could handle more easily just now than the tao.

Here she came, bent over and moving more awkwardly than the overhang could justify, not just crouching to avoid a cracked head. And she was still wrapped in, wrapped in—

The sun struck at her, and he saw what she was wrapped in.

He should have known, of course. He could not possibly have forgotten: only that a jade tiger in the hot distrustful flesh was a little distracting, and Jiao in this mood was almost more so.

It was, of course, the skin of the tiger's mother.

Jiao clutched it around her like a blanket, and it trailed in the dust behind her like a gown. She seemed almost bowed under the weight of it. It was hard even to look at her, except in revulsion: she was weak and broken, she was *human,* and wearing— wearing!—this extraordinary object that should have clothed a living wonder.

On the cub, light ran like rippling water between the shadows of his stripes.

On Jiao, on a dead tiger's fur, the sun could only show its proper colors, green and black. And the dark spill of blood, dried in spots and streaks and patches everywhere, breaking all the vivid patterns of the hide, telling a wrongful, woeful story. And it was stiff to fold and difficult to handle, and frankly it smelled of days-old blood and inadequate cleaning; and still it was strong and brilliant, still it spoke to the power and the glory of the living beast, the shame of this woman who had taken it.

This woman who was shrugging it off now in the sunlight, letting it fall anyhow onto the scree.

This woman who was naked underneath and slicked with

sweat, grimy with dried blood and mud, but the filth of her was only another coat, another covering.

Underneath was the truth of her, the torn ruin of a warrior.

Spare flesh and muscles like cables, tendons like wires, skin that had been cut and burned and scarred a hundred times, a hundred different ways, and patched indifferently together to heal as it would.

And now, new damage that should probably not have healed at all.

Biao had seen a thousand soldiers' bodies, he was intimately familiar with the damages of war, of steel and wood and stone. Flame too, now, flame above all.

He had never seen anything like this.

Jiao had been mauled, of course, ripped open by the tiger. Ripped apart, almost, from neck to hip, all down her left side: deep and terrible gashes, through skin and flesh and bone together. The shoulder—well. He could see how she would have trouble holding up the tip of her heavy blade. He couldn't actually see how she managed to use that arm at all, with the muscle shredded and the joint misshapen, the bone past any hope of true alignment.

And yet, and yet . . .

All this horror had been wreaked on her bare days before, she'd had no treatment and no care. Biao thought she should probably, almost certainly be dead. Surely feverish, racked with pain, dying. Surely that.

And yet. Here she was, walking, standing, albeit not very straightly. There was a glitter of strangeness in her eyes, but that was not fever. Pain, perhaps, but if so it was a pain that she could manage.

All those open wounds, that should be scabby and wetly ripe with infection, gleaming with pus—they looked all to be skinned over already, far too soon. She might never be rightly shaped again, but the shape she was, something was preserving.

She looked at him, at his astonishment, and laughed again. The croak turned into a cough, and she wheezed at him. "Have you water? Little fat bewildered man?"

"Yes, yes, that I do . . ." He thrust the skin at her and she snatched at it one-handed, tipped it, drank with a clumsy greed that spilled as much over her skin as down her throat.

"Ahhh . . ."

The tiger cub came to her, and licked that runoff from her skin. Her smile was savage, as she took one more swallow for herself and then pushed the spout roughly into the cub's mouth as it if were a nipple.

As if it were a nipple, the tiger sucked and swallowed.

Drained the skin entirely in two swallows and then closed its jaws more finally, bit off the spout, pierced the bag, played with it, shredded it with claws and a shake of its head.

"That's what he would have done with me," Jiao murmured. "Nearly did."

"Wait, what? The *cub* did that . . . ?"

"Yes, oh yes. Did you think his mother? She wouldn't have been so uncertain. Have you food? I could use food. So could he."

Dried fruit, Biao carried. He had nothing else to offer, and she didn't offer any to the cub. She ate with a dreadful earnestness, her one hand letting the tao dangle utterly while the other filled and filled her mouth; then, smiling through stained teeth, "Need more water now."

"Sorry, I haven't . . ."

"No, of course not. Perhaps I can chance the forest."

"They are looking for you, the clans. The word is spreading already, valley to valley."

"Of course."

Surprising himself, he said, "Wait one more day, and I will bring you food, and water-skins. Medicine too, something for the pain. You do have pain?"

"Oh, yes," she said. "Yes, doctor, I have pain. It is . . . extraordinary."

He was pleased, almost, to hear that not all the laws of nature were revoked here. She should have pain; the state of her body demanded it, and so perhaps did justice also.

He said, "How did this *happen*?"

He didn't say that information was the price of his help, but perhaps she heard it anyway. The glance she gave him was amused, in a terrible way. Terribly amused.

She sat, slowly, and drew the skin up again around her shoulders. He helped, on the left side, where she couldn't manage with any grace or comfort. The skin side of it felt raw and stiff, nothing like leather; it smelled and was sticky like aging meat. He wiped his fingers on the fur, which was coarse, almost harsh to the touch, but still set a tingle in his flesh.

She said, "I killed his mother," which was not starting the story in the right place, but Biao was—just—too wise to interrupt. "Killed her and skinned her before he smelled me out, before he came. Perhaps it was her that he smelled. He came . . . It was dark, and I heard him coming, he's a noisy brute," with a glance that might almost be affectionate, if this spare, bare creature could remember affection. Biao wasn't sure, and would never want to trust it. "All I saw was the eyes, though, and the—the *intent* of him, the purpose.

"And I couldn't reach my tao, all I had was a skinning-knife and that would do nothing but prick at him like a goad.

"So I did the other thing, all I could think of to do.

"I dropped the knife, grabbed his mother's hide and wrapped it around myself."

A pause, a long pause, while she gazed at the cub and remembered, while Biao watched her and tried to imagine; then she shook her head, took a breath, carried on.

"I was too slow, of course. Who can move faster than a tiger? A jade tiger, in his own hills and frantic for his mother . . . ?

"But."

That seemed to be enough, or she thought it was, that and a gesture: to the tiger-skin, to the tiger.

It wasn't enough for Biao. "But?"

She sighed, rolled her eyes perhaps, said, "*But*, once he'd hurt me, once I fell, once we were tumbling downslope and we were all rolled up in her skin together, he was surrounded by the smell of her, which was what he knew and trusted; and it was all mixed up with the smell of me, my blood and her blood together in her fur, and . . .

"Well. He's young, he's not very bright. I think he thinks I'm his mother."

THAT WAS something, an explanation, not enough.

Nowhere near enough.

Biao said, "Your wounds, your damage . . . You cannot, you can *not* have recovered this much, this quickly."

"No," she said. "I think he should have killed me. Even after he stopped wanting to, the hurt he'd done, I should have died. I've seen men die enough, I know dead when I see it. I crawled up here to do that, to die. Like a cat, high and alone. Except that he came with me, so of course I brought the skin. And wrapped myself in it, because he was there, and because I was cold and wanted the comfort. And, well. Like that.

"And then, like this. I am . . . healing. If you want to call it so. Not dying, that at least."

"Let me see."

"For what?" Her expression said *there is nothing you can do, this is out of your hands.* Perhaps it also said *I know what you are, Biao, you are a pirate and a thief like me.* Perhaps that was just his conscience.

He shrugged. "Curiosity."

Honesty won through, where he thought a bluff would not. She shrugged off the skin again, to let him look more closely in the light. Flesh was knitting itself together wherever tooth or claw had torn it, skin was forming over the raw. It was happening too quickly for sense, and too quickly for her body too. Broken bones were marrying all askew, in whatever splintered pattern they now lay. Her shoulder was twisted, savaged out of all repair. He was surprised that it could take even the weight of her arm, let alone a blade in it, however unconvincingly.

She said, "Like Mei Feng and the emperor, I've been too close to Yu Shan all summer, I have a little of his jade in me. Enough that it won't let me die that easily. That's on the inside. The rest? I think it's the skin. Like sleeping in jade, swimming in it . . ."

He touched her here and there, and felt the flinching that she would not show. She might always hurt, he thought, this badly. "If I had Tien's needles here," he said, "I might do something for your pain."

"If you had Tien's skill," she snorted.

He nodded. "That too. That first, perhaps." He had the tiger's whiskers in his sleeve, and did not offer to use them. "She is the wrong side of the water now, but you should seek a doctor out. Not me."

"Not you, no." She said it like a promise. And then, "Not any-one, perhaps. I might just stay here with the tiger." *And the pain.*

"You can't. How would you live? And the forests won't be safe for you. I said, the clans are looking. You need to move quickly, get ahead of the word." *If you can.* He wasn't sure it was possible, only that the opposite was not.

Why did he want to help her, why see her survive? He wasn't sure of that either. Only of the one thing, that even a token assis-tance had its price. That was fair, it was honest. It was how he dealt with the world. She would understand. She of all people, she who likely understood him better than anyone on this island.

He said, "Stay here today, and I will bring you food in the morning."

She eyed him sardonically. "The tiger needs to eat too."

"For the tiger too. I will bring meat," though it would likely be dried, and he would have to steal it from the compound's wind-house. "Milk I cannot manage."

"Well. I think he is old enough now to live without his mother's milk. He will need to be." Still she eyed him, still she waited.

He said, "I will tell them that I saw you heading westerly. They'll think you are trying for the coast, and a boat away. With luck," and the skills he had, the frauds his life was built on, "they will chase that way."

She said, "They must know there are no boats, with the dragon watching."

"Jiao, these are mountain people. They dig stone, they live in the forest, they never look at the sky. They never leave the valleys. They don't think about the dragon. Yes, they've heard that, but they don't know it, it's not—"

"Yu Shan knows it."

"And Yu Shan says that he will kill you, if he finds you—but he told me where to look, he didn't come. He doesn't want to find you. He'll lead them that way, if I tell him to. Which would let you slip away easterly. If you're quick, if you're careful. If you're lucky. That's as much as I can do."

She looked at him assessingly, and shook her head. "Not yet. If you can do it now, you can do it in a week, when they're less hot, when they think I've gone already. Bring me food and let me rest, let me heal . . ." *Leave me with this,* as her good hand pulled the tiger's hide up again, over her crippled shoulder.

"No," he said. "Now, tomorrow, or not at all. Now, or I tell them where to find you. Tell them true."

Her fingers clenched in the fur, but her eyes showed no surprise. "What do you *want*, Biao?"

"That. The tiger-skin. Tomorrow."

"I'm not ready. Another week . . ."

He eyed her flatly. "Tomorrow. I'd take it now, but the clan would backtrack me and find you. Tomorrow, in exchange for food. Before I send them westward. I'll say I had it from you, in exchange for your life. It'll be true, more or less."

Her gaze moved to the cub. "He might follow you, if you take the skin."

Biao managed, with a blinding effort, just to shrug. "That's the risk I take." He'd bring a tao, but only for his own soul's comfort, not for use. He wasn't Jiao, to slay a pouncing tiger.

"He might not follow me."

"No. You're not his mother. That's the risk you take. Is your life worth it?"

She just looked at him.

four

The Forge was almost starting to feel like home.

Han liked it—almost—for the solitude, for the security. At the moment, he thought, there was only one person he cared about, and he didn't want to be with her. He'd rather be here, on a rock with no jetty, where neither she nor anyone else could come. The solitude was all for him.

The security was for the dragon. Again because nobody—no magician, no priest, no army—could come to land here. This was a place of safety for her, and he thought she needed that.

Every time he thought that, he laughed at himself for the rank impertinence of it. What safety did she need, from anyone except perhaps the Li-goddess? And all the goddess ever did was protect people—her own people, perhaps: not everyone—from the dragon's attacks. Either she had no aggressive intent, or else she would need to work through people to achieve it, and she had not mustered them yet.

And yet the dragon did keep coming back to the Forge. She had her own reasons, which she would not share or else he could not understand. When he saw her land once more on the peak, when he saw her turn and turn like a dog making its bed in the rushes, when at last he saw her settle, what came to mind every time was security, for her. Not solitude: solitude was for him, who had lived all his life with other humans on every hand. She was alone all the time, except for him sometimes, who did not count.

He wasn't fool enough to think that she came back for him.

The first time, he'd thought that she might never come back at all, that he was stranded again, marooned again. Doomed again.

That first time, he'd felt relief at the first sense of her returning.

Now he took her coming for granted, but was still sure that it was not for him.

She wanted to feel safe, he thought, and so she came here, where no one could come at her. Except himself, of course, but she knew that she was safe from him.

Safe with him: he would protect her, if he could.

Which was another absurdity, and almost worse.

She could go to the sky, or to the sea, where she would be safe from anyone who could neither fly high nor swim deep and deep.

That might not include the goddess. Han didn't know. He did know that someone, somehow, had chained the dragon once, and that she dreaded its happening again, and that she kept coming back to the Forge.

Sometimes she lay curled at the peak there and watched the water, like a guard at her duty.

Sometimes she watched Han, like someone intrigued by another's little life: the bathing, the digging, the gathering and gleaning. The cooking. He always wanted to show Tien, when he cooked. And found himself showing the dragon instead, which wasn't quite the same.

Sometimes she watched him from the inside, which was worse.

Sometimes she slept. He was fairly sure that whenever she wanted to sleep, she came back to the Forge. For her safety.

Once, just once he had slipped into her mind while she slept, to watch her from the inside. He had walked deliberately in her dreams.

Never again.

It surprised him sometimes that she would want to sleep at all, after centuries on the sea floor, trapped in dreaming.

Perhaps she had no choice. *Sleep* was one of the words on his back, and he could compel her into a slumped somnolence; that was only a mockery, another way to take her freedom from her. This was something else, a genuine dream-filled slumber. He had been astonished the first time, and he could still be astonished now. Why in the world should she need sleep? She was an immortal, wild as the wind and as restless, shifting as the tides and as relentless . . .

She had mocked him for his physical weakness, threatened to do dreadful things while he slept.

And yet here she was, curled like a snake on a mountain peak. Raising the height of the mountain, making a new peak in herself, of herself. Not snoring, no—not conspicuously breathing, even—and yet apparently asleep. Decidedly asleep. Perhaps her great body demanded it, perhaps that was the price of such tremendous physicality, that she must obey at least a few of the laws that bound mortals to their flesh—but he was still surprised. Astonished, when he thought about it.

ASTONISHED ALSO at himself, that he would choose to sit here and watch her sleeping. So close to her head, snapping-distance if she should wake, if she could snap, if she would choose to do it.

He didn't, now, think that she would. They had come to . . . an accommodation. Yes. Call it that.

He sat beside her head and watched her, almost watched over her while she slept.

When he slept himself, often he woke to find her wakeful on the peak, or in the air just overhead, or thrusting head-up from the sea.

Often and often, while he slept, he was aware of her lightly in his head, in his dreams, curious and watchful.

Even now he was aware of an open door that he could step through, into her mind.

If he chose not, if he found her dreams appalling—well. At least it was his choice, his opportunity.

. . .

SHE MIGHT sleep, but she stayed alert. She was never, ever, sleepy.

Now her eye, the one great eye that he could see snapped open. Briefly it surveyed him, considered him, engulfed him almost except that she had swallowed him long and long ago; this out here—this body—was only a shadow, a messenger, a husk.

Her head lifted and swung: out to look over the sea, back to look at him. Both eyes now, the focus of her attention, of her glare.

What is it, great one?

There is a boat on the water. On the strait.

Again?

Again. Her head turned again, like a needle seeking north. Seeking, finding. She was right, of course: a dot of black against the shifting patterns of green and gray and blue, between Taishu and here. He could pick it out exactly, following her lead. And, *This carries one of her cursed children, I can feel it from here. I cannot touch this one. I will not try.*

No.

He wanted almost to shift his seat, to sit on the height of her leg and throw his arm across the ridges of her neck, just to be physically with her in her shame as they watched the boat go by . . .

No.

As they watched it come.

he human body," Ai Guo said, "is a fascinating artefact, a fascinating study."

He was lying on his back, naked. His groin was draped in a scrap of silk for an absurd and ineffectual decency; his head was propped up on a silk-bound wooden block to allow him the very study of which he spoke, his own body the exemplar—the rather disgusting exemplar, though none the less fascinating for that disgust—and Tien the student-master with her silver needles to make her points for her.

She grunted, not listening, laying hands on his twisted leg. Tapping lightly, feeling out the bones beneath the skin and the run of muscle, judging where her next needle ought to go. In its misshapen state the limb was an artefact indeed, manufacture of another man's intent. He flinched when she found a point of consistent pain, perhaps unwittingly.

Perhaps not. She was another article of his study, and her own body spoke against her. Tien was a believer, and one of the tenets of her belief was justice. Something in her thought it right that he should hurt so much. She was a doctor, and would try whatever she could to relieve his hurts; and in doing so she worked against that instinct, and all her body betrayed her. He found the whole process fascinating.

Like a person under interrogation, she had a story to tell the world and a story to tell herself, and they were different. He could read them both, because that was his profession; and just now his mind was very much on his profession, as those fingers of hers—those doctorly, judicial fingers—tapped out pathways of pain within himself.

This was instructional in the most useful way, learning from the inside just what could be achieved by pressure applied to old damage. He could look down the length of his body and see the external evidence, what had been done to him, how long ago; he could watch what Tien did now and measure that directly against what he felt, how his body responded.

Never mind that she was seeking to ease his hurts, however much she felt that he deserved them. There was a lesson in every seeking fingertip. He watched, felt, learned.

And if all this ruthless self-examination, all this uncharitable consideration of a young girl doing her best to help, all this *study* was a device to separate himself from the actuality of his pain, well. He did know that. It was an element in his study.

So was talking about it.

He said, "We see the mean mechanics of it, laid out here," with an airy wave at himself as though he were a diagram exhibited, as though the simple lifting and wafting of a hand could cost him nothing, nothing at all, "but the meat is not the man, I think. Where does the spirit, where does the soul reside?"

"Where does it hide, you mean," Tien countered, no fool she, "when the body is unbearable?"

"That too. Like the emperor, fled to Taishu because the empire is untenable for him at the moment. There is a tether, clearly, but one can achieve at least a little distance. Even without benefit of your teas and needles."

"Oh? And did you allow your prisoners the benefit of a little distance, ever?"

"The art is . . . not to do that. To keep them absolutely within their bodies, within the pain. Unh," as her tapping fingers drove a needle in, perhaps a little sharply. "But you and I together, Tien, you with your knowledge and I with mine, with our very different practices, we could combine our skills and experience, and—"

"There is nothing," she said harshly, "that I want to do, that your—*skills and experience*—could possibly contribute to."

"Except perhaps to chain the dragon?" he murmured.

She stood very still, the tip of one needle resting against his skin there, too light to scratch. He knew just where to drive that needle, to extract the utmost pain and the thinnest, most urgent gasp of confession. So, he suspected, did she.

She only waited, and the needle wasn't any kind of threat in her hand: only relief withheld. If he pointed that out she would correct it at once, setting the needle just where she meant it to go. He had only distracted her mind, not driven her from her duty.

He held his silence, enjoying the tremble of waiting in her, the determination not to ask, the absolute expression of patience at its absolute limits.

Until she broke, as she had to, because he would not: until she drew a tremulous breath and turned her head to face him and said, "Explain?"

She had dropped her precious needle.

He thought she hadn't noticed.

A cruel man would have pointed it out, perhaps, tormenting her with further delay while she scrabbled about on hands and knees to find it. But Ai Guo never had been cruel; he thought cruelty inefficient, and not interesting. He said, "We know that one spirit may stretch to subdue another, even in its own body. You have seen the goddess do that in her chosen children."

Tien twitched as though the memory were a needle unkindly placed, unkindly tapped at now to drive the point a fraction deeper in her flesh. "An immortal," she muttered, "what they can do . . ."

"What they can do, we can discover how to do it. A tether runs both ways. In large, we know already. We know it can be done, from a mortal to an immortal. It has been done; the connection is there, and you yourself helped to make it stronger."

No flinching now. This was a pain she was accustomed to carrying, long and deep. She said, "Han."

"Han, yes, who is already a check upon the dragon when he chooses to be. Whose predecessors were the means by which she was kept asleep through centuries."

She was beginning to understand him, reluctantly. She shook her head regardless. "I don't think Han will do more than he does already, to keep her from harming us. I don't think he'd be willing, even if we could ask him. He is . . . not necessarily given to the emperor. Or even to the people."

"No." Was it cruel to make her wait for this, until she could say it for herself? Ai Guo didn't think so; he thought it was necessary.

Delaying, she said, "It's no use, though, we don't know what magics were used on his chains before. I did as much as I could manage, with what I found in the library, but . . ."

"You did magnificently," he said, "for a girl working on her own, in a hurry, with no help. I am here now, and we can plan. With what you and I have read in the books collected here, with what you know about the body and how it resurges, what I know about the spirit and how it retreats, what we both know about truth and ease and silence—well. I think we could between us find ways to work on Han in his body, ways that would reflect back on the dragon. Ways to make her sleep again."

In chains, he was saying; which meant, necessarily . . .

"I don't," she said, "I don't think I can chain Han again. I couldn't."

"I could," said another voice; and that was Li Ton, who had been a party to this conversation all the time, sitting in a corner waiting his turn to lie beneath her silver needles.

six

Young people stand as witness to their elders' lives, to carry memory as lessons to the future.

Sometimes Old Yen thought that age-old principle had been perversely turned about, to make him stand as witness to Mei Feng.

To *allow* him to stand as witness to Mei Feng.

Sometimes to learn from her, and carry those lessons on into his own life.

HE HAD been summoned to the palace today, to help plan a way by which the Li-goddess could be used or manipulated or induced to put the dragon in chains again. Hale her down to the sea-bed again and keep her there, for the convenience of empire and the privilege of boats.

Caught somewhere between rage and outrage, he had only stayed because of Mei Feng, because in these days he would seize any chance to be with her. And what else did he have to do, where else to be? His instinct was to go to sea; when he was in the grip of a fever—often, when he was younger, when he could be angry or bored or appalled at any moment, with barely a flying cloud beforehand to warn of storm ahead—there was always this call to take it out into deep waters, to lose it in wind and tide and the toss of salt wood beneath his feet.

Even he could hardly go out in these days, just to cool his tem-

per. He had license—some said an extraordinary license—but his
own notions of honor and right wouldn't allow it. When any trip
beyond the shallows meant taking one of the children, how could
he do that for simply selfish reasons? How could he dare?

He would do it for a fishing trip, but fishing was about survival
now. His duty was to lead a fleet, because he could always find
where the fish were shoaling; and to protect it, because the goddess would stretch her hand out to encompass every boat that
sailed with his.

Gathering so many independent captains and masters without
warning was as hard as herding cats. If he went to the dockside
now, it could take half a day; by which time the tide would have
turned and the wind shifted, those who were ready early would
have changed their minds while those who came late would be impatient to go now. And then someone would come running at the
last minute with another summons from the palace, another meeting where Old Yen's presence was required, somehow impera-
tive . . .

It could still astonish him, how much his life had changed since
one fog-bound night on the water. He could look around at
Taishu, at everything he knew—his own village and Taishu-port,
the coastline and the strait, the Forge, Santung beyond the strait,
the goddess's temples and precious little else—and see how very
much had changed all over, everything perhaps except the coastline. He could look on a world of change and yet be astonished by
how much had changed for him.

The more things changed, the less it seemed to matter. People
were still idiots; the goddess was still remote. Even in the high
houses and the palaces, people were still idiots, particularly that.

Here in this palace, now, he bottled up his fury and sat quiet,
listening to priests and generals plotting how they might inveigle
or bully or even dare compel the goddess into doing what they
could not, snaring the dragon back into her captivity.

At the risk of feeling disloyal, he might at any time have said, *How do you know that she can do this thing?* There seemed to him small point in plotting the impossible.

Or he might have said, *If she can indeed do this thing, if she wanted to do it, do you not think she would have done it before this?*

Or he might just have said, *If she does not want to do this thing, how in the world do you imagine that you can persuade her?*

Any of those or all of them, one after another—but none of them, as it happened, because Mei Feng knew his thoughts as soon as he did, and frowned mightily at him across the broad space of the throne room, and so he sat in silence and was no help to anyone on either side of any argument at all.

He stayed for Mei Feng, for no reason else, because it made him happy simply to be with her. Which was just as well, because where the emperor had commanded him he had no right to leave. He was aware of that, vaguely. Nevertheless, it was only Mei Feng's presence that kept him in increasing discomfort on the polished floor. Old legs were not made for kneeling long. He was used to standing, he could stand all night and into morning with the give of an unsteady deck beneath his feet, and his knees would take that and take it and never an ache or twinge. Here, though, these boards might be magnificent in their dark polished luster, but they were cruelly hard beneath old bones; and he was tired of listening to fools. The priestess from the temple was the only one who spoke sense, and of course they would not listen to her because she was a woman and a native and saying no to all their grand plans and propositions, saying *No, that will not work; this is a goddess you would treat with, and you cannot treat her so.*

Which was what he wanted to say himself, all he really wanted to say. So he held his tongue and his temper both, with a most extraordinary patience; he kept his place until at last the emperor dismissed all these idiots to further study and confabulation, against better ideas on a better day.

Old Yen might have hobbled out of the grand hall in pursuit of the priestess, only to tell her how glad he was of her wisdom, how grateful to hear it. He was painfully aware, though, that he should have supported her and had not. It would seem dishonest to make an ally of her now, walking out the two of them together, where he had done nothing when it mattered to deserve that alliance.

Besides, he wanted to spend more time, real time with his granddaughter.

Besides, his knees had stiffened up abominably, and the priestess was too limber. She was at the door and away before he had contrived to reach his feet.

So he looked instead for Mei Feng to appear at his elbow, dutiful granddaughter skipping across the hall floor as soon as she saw he was in difficulty—but she was unexpectedly slow, slower than he was even, using the willing anxious emperor for leverage as she pulled herself to her feet and shuffled over.

Predictably, she was scolding as she came: "And what, has age stolen your wit along with your tongue, that you didn't think to ask for a cushion? The goddess herself could testify that we have enough of them here, enough to sit you in luxury all across this floor and halfway back to harbor; but you would first need to ask . . ."

What she meant, of course, was that she should have seen his discomfort sooner and had not, and was feeling guilty. What she ignored, of course, because it did not suit her, was that it was quite impossible for him or any man to call for a cushion in the emperor's presence, in the emperor's throne room yet, where the emperor himself sat uncushioned on the cold hard throne of jade.

The emperor was apparently feeling guilty on his own account. "You too, Mei Feng, you could have had a cushion. I could have thought. And you could have stayed where you were, I could have helped Grandfather come to you . . ."

She tilted her head back against his shoulder, to scowl up cat-like into his face. She'd had her little cat in her lap before, but her slow rise from the stool had dislodged it. "Twenty steps! That's hardly going to upset the baby. I'm not *ill*, Chien Hua. Only carrying my lord's child . . ."

She wanted, Old Yen saw, to be petted like the cat, to have her two men chirrup at her. The trouble was, she was conspicuously ill: not carrying her lord's child well, not well at all.

The emperor said a little of that, as much perhaps as he dared admit. "You were ill this morning."

"I'm ill every morning now. Ever since that day coming back across the strait, when I was sick on the boat." She shuddered at the memory, or else at the disgrace of being sick at sea, she who had been practically born there. "It means nothing. If I'm sick on the floor here, someone will clean it up."

"No doubt. But I would rather not have you sick at all. You can't afford it," his long fingers tracing her body beneath her clothes, her bones beneath her skin. Old Yen knew that body, too well for heavy silks to disguise it. She had been work-thin before, all muscle and sinew and not a pad of fat; now he thought the emperor was right, she was too thin suddenly, except where her belly was just showing a bulge. Perhaps there too, perhaps she should be bigger by now. "And all this excitement," the emperor went on, "all this froth in your head can't be good for the child either. I think you should go to the Autumn Palace with my mother. We've kept men working out there, so you won't have to camp. That was your idea, remember? It's really quite comfortable now. And you'll be safe, and separate from all of this, and my mother will take her doctors so I know you'll be looked after, and . . ."

She said, "Separate from all this. Yes. *All this* being the dragon, and the war, and the goddess, and my friends, and my *man*, and . . ." *That's you, fool*—she didn't quite say the words but her voice did, and her hands most certainly did, clenching in the silk of his robe; her eyes too, lifting to glare at him.

"You never wanted anything to do with the war," he muttered, increasingly defensive, increasingly lost.

"I never wanted *you* to have anything to do with the war. With Ping Wen's stupid war. But you went ahead and did it anyway. And I was *pregnant,* and I knew Ping Wen was a traitor, so I just had to come after you—and now you want to send me *away*? With your *mother*?"

"I thought you and she were better friends now?"

"Only because we were both fighting Ping Wen, when we'd given up on fighting you. You can't send me away with her, Chien Hua."

"I don't want to. I just think it'll be better for you and for the baby if you go somewhere quiet. And you've no hope of leaving my mother behind, that's her baby as much as it is mine, so . . ."

"I said you *can't* send me. Because I *won't go*."

"Mei Feng. You hate these meetings, the endless wrangling; you're just like your grandfather, you hate it when we even talk about the Li-goddess, because we're not from Taishu and you think we don't understand her. You don't need to worry about me anymore, we've isolated Ping Wen on the mainland—your idea!—without any boat that he can use to send any kind of trouble after us. You've a baby to build inside you, and you need to build yourself up at the same time, and you'll never do that while you're here being sick and worrying about everything. Nothing's going to be any easier for a long time yet, you're not doing yourself or the baby any good; there's just no reason for you to stay in the palace and be ill and unhappy and—"

"Oh, what, you mean I'd be better away in the hills there, being ill and unhappy and out of your sight? No wonder they call it your Hidden City, if you're just going to hide me away there. With your *mother,* and everyone else you don't want to deal with."

"Mei Feng, I don't know what you *want* . . ."

They were both of them missing their cues here. If she could just say *I want to be with you,* which was the blunt truth of it, he would be utterly disarmed and the fight would be over. But she wouldn't say that now, she was too busy throwing stones and watching him duck, making him angry.

Old Yen couldn't interfere, and didn't want to watch.

Instead, he did what he had wanted to do all morning, what had been impossible till now: he turned his back on the emperor, and on his granddaughter, and walked out of there.

IT WAS Mei Feng's privilege to abuse the emperor, to argue with him, to call him names and tell him he was wrong. She had immunity. With his child in her belly she had an absolute immunity, she was practically sacred in herself.

It was Old Yen's privilege, it always had been, to take his boat to sea. He had immunity, in the eye of the goddess's favor.

With one of her chosen children in the belly of his boat, that immunity was absolute. Not even the dragon could touch him.

He stole a little of Mei Feng's immunity, then, to walk out of the imperial presence and out of the imperial palace, grandfather of the beloved concubine, untouchable, untouched.

Then he walked down to the harbor, to his beloved bastard boat, to claim his own.

"PAO!"

"Master?"

His voice called the boy tumbling out of the cabin before Old Yen had set so much as a foot on deck, he was that keen suddenly to be at sea.

"Run up to the temple and ask for one of the children to be fetched down." It would be the castrated one, most likely, with his nurse. Old Yen didn't care. "Say that we won't be long gone, only that we must go now."

The boy was learning ocean ways. He cast an eye at the water to double-check himself, and found that the tide had shifted not a fraction from where he thought it ought to be at this time, this day; he lifted his head to sniff the wind; and frowned, and turned back to Old Yen with an argument half formed already, the apprentice ready to instruct his master.

He was a good boy, but this wasn't the time. Old Yen was in a hurry. "Yes," he said snappishly. "Nevertheless, we will bring her out into open water, despite tide and wind together. I will show you. *When* we are free to leave, which will be when you have run to the temple as I told you."

Pao's shifty glance toward the cabin door was something else altogether, a confession writ large, for anyone who could read the script of boy. Old Yen had fathered sons, raised them on and in and around this very boat; he knew.

He said, "You may see your—friend—off my boat at the same time. Now." He wasn't angry, only impatient. He might have expected this, coming back so precipitately; certainly he should have expected it sometime. Should not have forgotten that a boy was a boy above all, even in times like these. Especially, perhaps, in times like these.

"Master," Pao said, almost desperately, "I don't . . . If we shan't be long at sea, I don't need to go to the temple, I've got . . ."

His voice and his wits had both failed him, apparently, he needed rescue; and found it in the sudden opening of the cabin door, the little girl looking brightly out.

Little, little girl. If he tried, no doubt Old Yen would remember her name. Her face he was in no danger of forgetting.

He said, "Hullo. Have you been visiting my boat?"

She nodded cheerfully.

"And your sister too?"

Another nod, a little more wary, that came with a glance up at Pao. A boy is still a boy, and her sister was a pretty creature. Pretty and vacant, too easy a conquest perhaps, except that one little girl stood between her pretty helpless sister and the world.

One little girl and the goddess too. There was no telling when the big girl would be vacant and when she would be possessed. Pao might be a boy, but he was no fool; Old Yen thought he could be trusted.

Aloud, still talking to the girl, he said, "We were about to take the boat out for a sail. Just until sundown. You can help if you like, while your sister sits up in the bows. I know she enjoys that. Pao will show you what to do. Later, you can give me a hand on the steering oar."

She was no fool either, this sharp little thing; she knew there was no choice being offered here, *would you like to come to sea?* Old Yen had been very careful about that.

Besides, she was used to this, she knew about her sister's borrowed authority. She went to Pao and took his hand, led him back into the cabin to help tell her sister. Old Yen was glad to see that, not to see trust dismayed.

IT WAS work with rope and oar and prayer together, to bring the boat out of harbor at such a time. Without the prayer, he still thought he might have done it. He knew all the workings of the boat intimately, and the waters here too: where the secret currents lay deep to grip the keel, which sail would bring her by the head so that she seemed to dance out against the run of wind and tide together. Prayer gave him confidence, though. What he might or might not manage, the goddess would guarantee.

Unless she knew where he was headed and why, unless she could read his heart. Apparently not. He'd not been certain of that.

Pray and betray. He had served her and observed her, respected and been grateful to her all his days, and never more so than now; and now he went to beg a favor if he could from the very power that opposed her, that he and Mei Feng and the emperor should all oppose.

He supposed that made him a traitor to the emperor too, but it was his goddess that troubled him more.

.   .   .

THE DRAGON might have been anywhere, in the strait or in the sky or somewhere else entirely. Nothing that he knew of kept her here, except her own sense of possession or her own abiding anger. Both. This was—or had been—her territory, and her prison too; something made her reluctant yet to leave it.

Not the boy, surely. Just a boy, after all. Boys got everywhere, it was true, in the heart not excluded; and a-dragonback not excluded either. Old Yen had seen that for himself. It seemed impossible, but this new world was full of impossibility.

And the boy was—in Old Yen's mind, at least—irrevocably attached to the Forge; and if he wanted to speak to the dragon then he had to speak to the boy, which meant . . .

Well, it meant this: the trip he had meant not to take. The kick of the deck beneath his feet and the tug of the tide against the oar as he worked their course northerly, pure solace to be in such direct communion with his goddess except that her welcome was a deception and his acceptance of it a betrayal. The jagged tooth of the Forge on the swift horizon, more jagged than he was accustomed to, and Pao's cry of warning from the bows as that sharp outline resolved itself into the outline of the dragon, lying curled on the island's peak where the forge-fire used to gleam like a great eye across the strait.

The dragon who stirred now, as they sailed in closer.

Who lifted her head and looked down directly at them.

Old Yen was glad, more than glad to have the girl aboard, who could keep the dragon away. Even though he betrayed the goddess whose legitimate power it was, who used the girl only as her instrument.

Even though he hated the way that she did that, and had been appalled each time he heard her speak through one of her chosen children.

THE DRAGON didn't lift into the air, nor dive into the sea. She didn't open her impossible mouth, stretch down an impossible distance and swallow them all, boat and all. She stayed just there as he sailed toward her; as he made his wretched, trusting, treacherous maneuver, depending on the high surf and the goddess in her ambiguity—he used to think it a kindness—to lift the hull over the rocks that waited, to drop himself and his passengers and his precious bastard boat safely into the quiet pool behind.

"PAO."

"Master?"

"I am going ashore. You will stay here, with the girls."

"Of course, master." That wasn't *of course I will do as you say*. By the boy's voice, by his manner, no other notion had entered his head.

Old Yen grunted. Shouldn't boys be more adventurous? Perhaps he had listened to too many stories in his own boyhood; perhaps he had told himself too many. Still, he didn't think he or any of his sons would have stayed meekly aboard when it was only a short swim ashore and a dragon waited on the island.

Himself, he did not intend to swim. He told Pao to prepare the sampan. Ordinarily he wouldn't care. He'd get wet anyway scrambling over the rocks that fringed this narrow lagoon, so why worry?

Today, that question had an answer.

There was another boy, a very different boy waiting on the rocks by the water's edge, and Old Yen wanted to greet him eye to eye and not with seaweed in his beard.

HE HAD Pao row him across, then, while he stood tall in the bows as though he were somebody important, as though the boards of the sampan didn't leak and he didn't have water lapping at his bare feet. Of all the changes of this summer gone, he thought perhaps the change in himself might be most shocking. Everything that had happened made a kind of sense to him, except this: that he had become a man who spoke to emperors. A man who would take it upon himself to speak to dragons.

WELL, ONE dragon.

One at a time, at least. He supposed there must be others, elsewhere in the empire. This might become a profession for a younger man, He-who-speaks-to-dragons. It might already be a known profession, elsewhere in the empire. Not here where it would suddenly be useful, now that they had a dragon and needed—Old Yen thought—someone to speak to her.

PAO STOOD in the stern and worked his oars with the careful art of a newling determined not to disgrace himself.

The sampan's bow nudged rock, and the boy who stood there stretched out an arm to help Old Yen ashore.

He did it unthinkingly, perhaps: his natural arm, his right.

As Old Yen reached to take that open hand, he saw how the boy had a rough raw scar where a thumb ought to be.

Without it—well. He had no grip to mention.

And he was stick-thin, no weight to him, nothing to balance with. Sooner than have them both end up in the water, Old Yen frog-hopped urgently out of the boat, the way he used to sometimes when he was a boy himself.

For a moment he was tied to ground only by that insubstantial grip on his wrist, that unreliable boy.

His feet found rock, wet and slippery. They might have gone either way, the boy and he; they hung either side of a point of unbalance, and could only stare desperately at each other and wonder who would fall first, who would drag the other down.

If Old Yen let go, he could save himself. He had wise bones; he could trust his legs to find a better balance, his feet to find a grip.

If he let go, the boy would fall, no question.

Old Yen had wise bones but a foolish head, apparently. He hung on. A fall into water was no catastrophe, but there were rocks down there and a broken head wouldn't dry out in the sunshine, a broken boy was not replaceable.

Not this boy, at least. He was the one who truly spoke to dragons.

IT WAS Pao who saved Old Yen, saved them both.

Pao who thrust a sudden dripping oar at him, something to hold on to. Old Yen's free and wheeling arm snapped down, to clamp the blade of it in his armpit. Pao was just strong enough to hold him, just long enough to let him save the other boy that fall.

They stood there, teetering a little, laughing a little now, all three of them. Over the water, shrill cheering said they had an audience. That would be the little girl making all the noise—but Old Yen glanced across, and there was the big girl waving.

He lifted his elbow, to free the oar. Pao hoisted it high in both hands and waved back with cheerful idiocy, while the sampan rocked dangerously beneath him.

"Pao!"

"Master . . . ?"

Fool of a boy, he tried to turn and unbalanced himself, flung the oar about wildly just to make things worse, toppled one way as the boat beneath him tipped the other . . .

The end was inevitable. The splash of it made a thorough job of soaking Old Yen and the dragon's boy together, where they stood hand-fasted on the rock.

"WHAT ARE you called, boy?"

The ghost of a smile in response, as they climbed the path to the peak. The boy was almost a ghost in himself, pale and thin and distant.

"She calls me *little thing*, largely. I . . . have been called Han, by people."

"Han. Good. Yes. The pirate called you Han, and so did the girl you had with you. I remember." He was, he realized, only talking: filling his mouth with words, empty words, to keep back the one thought in his head. With an effort, he stilled his tongue. Took a breath, spoke again. Said, "She speaks to you. You can . . . speak to her?"

"Yes."

"Good." Now that he was here—he could smell her on the air already, he almost thought he could feel the weight of her on the rock beneath his feet, pressing down—he found that he absolutely did not want to be He-who-speaks-to-dragons.

Now that he was here, indeed, he found his feet lagging on the path, the air harder to push his body through, harder to breathe. These were not his skills; he was not a man of the dry land, of the climb, any more than he was a diplomat or a clerk. He had no authority, from his emperor or anyone. Only the pressure of his people, his island at his back and the call of the sea before him.

Besides, why should the dragon listen? He had nothing to offer her. And no defense, unless the goddess stretched her hand this far from the boat, this far above the sea.

He wondered if the boy would literally be the dragon's mouthpiece, speak in her voice, all silt and savagery. And if he did, whether the dragon would sound any different from his mouth to the way the goddess sounded from the girl.

He hated this, he hated all of this. He hated the way his legs faltered abruptly, remembering perhaps how this path turned just one more time around that crag of rock and there it would be, the peak, the forge itself, there she'd be . . .

There she was, indeed, that ridge above the crag: that wasn't rock, that was dragon-flesh, the curved ridge of her spine where she lay coiled and waiting.

He didn't have to do this, but someone did. And he was here, where perhaps no one else could come. Which meant that yes, he did have to do this after all. He hated that too, that it had to be him, when he was so very uncertain and afraid.

Perhaps he should have brought someone else, a courtier, a diplomat, a general—but he didn't know how, or how he would have persuaded them to come without the emperor's consent. Against the emperor's intentions, indeed.

The boy was smiling again, fractional and absent. "You shouldn't worry," he said, "I won't let her eat you."

Just for a moment, that had been almost the least of Old Yen's worries. Reminded, he nodded his thanks. And thought it was fitting, probably, that he should give himself over from one side to the other, from the protection of the goddess to the protection of the dragon's boy. So go all traitors, from hand to hand and weaker all the way, more lost, less hopeful. Less to be hoped for.

And so he came, up the steepness of the path and around the final spur of rock to the summit, to the dragon.

And the boy went past Old Yen and sat himself on her clawed foot, as though it were a footstool before the throne of her; and curled his arm around her leg in a way that seemed almost protective of her, ridiculous as that might seem; and cocked his head at Old Yen in invitation, *tell us why you're here.*

He could barely remember, for the moment, why he was here. She was . . . impossible to measure, in her simple impact. And she was *looking* at him. That was why he watched the boy so closely, because he dared not look at her. He dared not meet her eyes.

The boy's feet were dirty. There was an obscure comfort in that, that her hand-servant should come to her with dirty feet. And set those feet on her own foot, and neither one of them care.

And Old Yen's seeing that, drawing comfort from it, showed him that he wasn't even meeting the boy's eyes, let alone the dragon's.

So he lifted his head with an effort, reached for some power of words that he'd never actually possessed, said, "Tell her she is killing my people."

Han looked at the dragon, and for a moment Old Yen saw them both in profile: the scrawny fine-drawn boy and the legend risen from the sea, immortal, unchanging. The one whose temper he had come to change.

There were to be no dreadful voices, from either the dragon or the boy. They looked at each other, that was all; and then the boy turned back to Old Yen. With a shrug.

The shrug might have been enough on its own, but neither one of them was sure. The boy said, "Yes. She doesn't care. You don't matter to her. Only when you come out on the water, on *her* water. Then she gets angry." Twice angry, he meant: once for the trespass, and once again when she couldn't come at them, when they sailed under the goddess's protection. The boy hesitated for a moment, then spoke again, said it again another way; he was speaking for himself this time, Old Yen thought, defending her. "She leaves you all alone on land, but you shouldn't come out on the water."

"We have to," Old Yen said simply. "Taishu cannot live without the sea. Even before the emperor came with all his army, Taishu could not live without the sea. Now—well. She will starve the whole island, if she does not let us fish. She used to allow that, I know. There are stories told in our villages, how we used to sail out in her shadow. We had a special agreement; the fishermen of Taishu were safe from her, that was understood."

We were her people, he seemed to be saying. He whose whole life had been devoted to the goddess in her waters. The words were like foul mud in his mouth, but that did not keep them from being true.

Han consulted the dragon, in silent interchange. "She says it was not she who broke that agreement, but it was broken. When the people of Taishu cooperated with the mastersmith to chain her, and with the Li-goddess to keep her chained."

He said, "I do not know that history," but he was prepared to believe it none the less. Perhaps the people of Taishu had been ashamed at the time, or afterward, and so chose not to make it into a story.

Han said, "She . . . does not tell stories easily, or I do not understand them when she tries. Her mind is too big for me. But I think there was a ship filled with jade, which tried to sail to the mainland. For an emperor, long ago. And that was *not* a part of your agreement, and so she ate the jade, she says. I think she means she sank it. The boat. Perhaps she did eat the jade. And the emperor was angry and sent a man, a mage, a mastersmith; and he worked with your priests, and built the forge here and chained her. And your goddess held her prisoner beneath the strait, and you and all your people sailed back and forth above her head, and . . . Well. She is still very angry."

"She hasn't tried to eat me."

"No."

They looked at each other, each perhaps guessing what the other might be thinking, that she did not seem actually so angry anymore.

Old Yen was a fisherman and not a diplomat, but that only meant he had spent half his life in bargaining ashore. He said, "Han, what does she *want*?"

"Oh, gods, I don't know," Han said, laughing, hurting at the hard of it. "She doesn't tell me that."

"Perhaps, do you think, we might *ask*?"

FOUR

Walls of Water

one

Things change.

That was the lesson of Pao's life, his recent life.

He had been in swift succession a peasant boy, a soldier and a sailor. He still felt the same inside, he still recognized himself every morning: the body he woke into, the feel and stretch of it, the face he saw reflected in a bucket of wash-water. He needed someone else to tell him he was different now, and there was no one.

That was one of the changes. All his life before, he had seen the same people about him every day: his family, their neighbors, the village down the way. Wagoners on the road and boatmen on the river. Until the emperor's men came and took him to be a soldier. Then he was alone, no one to witness to the life he'd had before. No one to care. A peasant boy, what was that, why would it matter?

So then he was a soldier, one in a crowd, almost invisible even to himself until a sergeant picked him out and sent him to Old Yen to be a deckhand.

Sometimes it seemed that his own name was the only thing he kept, from one shift to the next. Even that didn't seem to mean him any longer, when he no longer knew quite what he meant.

Things change, and not always for the worse. Perhaps his name was learning a new meaning, as Pao became more and more the sailor. He had his sea-legs and a little sea-sense now. When he was frightened now, it was always of something that came from the land.

Almost always. The dragon frightened him, more than he could say. That was just good sense, no shame, though she was entirely a creature of the sea, storm and wind and water. Even Old Yen, he thought, was a little afraid of the dragon.

Fear hadn't stopped the old man bargaining with her while Pao clung to the boat. Pao might have been ashamed of that, except that someone had to stay with the girls. Even to himself, they were excuse enough.

THINGS CHANGE, but not everything changes.

This boat, this bastard boat: she didn't change. Her master might replace every timber in her frame, he might fit new masts and new sails and rig her all anew and she would still be the same wilful, wayward creature, tricky in any weather, responsive only to him. Pao was learning to handle her, but mostly what he learned was that she would not be handled except by Old Yen. Her own choice of master, he thought sometimes, as though she really were the stubborn living thing they all liked to pretend.

Renew every plank and every rope, she'd still smell the same, of salt and fish and bilgewater below. She'd still kick beneath bare feet in a following wind, still wallow in the troughs of a high sea, still try to turn side-on to the swell and so broach. Still be slow and sluggardly against the steering oar, almost too heavy to be hauled across the wind.

She'd still respond to Old Yen's wise old hand, and not to Pao's. He was sure of that.

THINGS CHANGE.

A week ago, this was the only boat that dared go to sea alone. A fleet might cluster around her, too close for comfort in a boat that liked her sea-room, but no one else would sail in the dragon's shadow. Even with an escort child aboard, there was not a sailing-master on Taishu prepared to venture out unless he followed Old Yen's wake. A week ago.

Now?

Now all the fleet was gone from Taishu-port, and Old Yen's boat rocked here against the quay alone. Old Yen was ashore, at the palace, where he preferred suddenly to spend his time. The fleet sailed without him and without the magic children too, because he had struck a bargain with the dragon; which left Pao here, on the boat because he had nowhere else to be.

Not alone, though, because things change.

PAO STOOD on deck and gazed around at the empty harbor; then he turned aft to where the little girl stood with her arms stretched high above her head, small hands clinging as best they could to the steering oar.

"Where are we going, Captain Shola?"

"Home," she said. Of course. "We're going home."

Home meant her mother and the temple on the cliff, above the creek. Twice now, Pao had taken her and her sister away from there. Or Old Yen had done it, rather, and at the emperor's order, but Pao had helped.

Shola didn't seem to bear a grudge. Her sister, Jin—well, it was hard to know what Jin might want, but she bore no grudges either. He was sure of that.

Things change; Jin smiled when she saw him. That was all for now, but it was enough. For now.

"How's the weather?"

"Easy sailing," she said, gazing about with a faraway look, as a sailor might, as she thought Old Yen did exactly. "Wind's in the west, south and west; he'll take us home."

He was and he would, if they were going. The little girl might only be at play, but she was playing with what she truly had to hand. Pao liked that, and admired it, and wished that he could offer her something better.

"Soon now, perhaps," he said, the best he had, a hope that she had already and did not need from him. "Soon, they'll let you go, perhaps." Why not, when the children weren't needed anymore, now there was a pact with the dragon?

She just looked at him, a little more cynical than he was. "Where's Jin?"

"In the cabin."

A mighty frown. "You shouldn't leave her."

"She sent me to fetch you. We have made tea."

"You shouldn't leave her with the *kettle* . . . !"

And Shola was already bustling past him, on her way to save big sister from herself. Pao grinned as he followed in that small determined wake, because things change but Shola was too young yet to understand that, quite.

THEY CAME into the cabin and there was the kettle, yes, steaming over a charcoal pot; and there was Jin, yes, close enough that Shola might well worry.

Not Pao. He had seen the slow change in her big raw hollow sister, seen it and treasured it and said not a word about it, not to alarm or excite the little girl, not to alarm or excite himself.

Pao had grown up with sisters on all sides, older and younger than himself. He had missed them in the army, on the road. There were women, there was a great deal of talk about women and some of it excited him, some excited even as it appalled, but none of it was a substitute for what he'd lost. He liked having girls about him, at ease, at play.

It didn't happen, couldn't happen: not on the road, not in Santung what short time they were there, and not on Taishu either. The local girls were frightened, or else they were taken and claimed by older men, or both.

And then there was Old Yen and no possibility of girls, until this: these two, back and forth across the strait, a charm against the dragon.

When they weren't at sea, they were just girls, one tough and one troubled. The tough one was willing to play little sister to him, willing to let him play brother to them both; the troubled one—well, she was pretty in her heedless awkward way, and he liked to look at her, but she was like another sister in his head.

Sister growing back into herself, he thought. Perhaps. Now that the goddess didn't need her.

He was curious and hopeful and wanted to help, but mostly he just liked to be among them. Playmate, brother. That would do. He was making himself a family that he wouldn't have to leave.

His soldier-friends would have been mocking, incredulous, if they had seen him like this: drinking tea with a girl who was empty-headed and ripe for the taking, the only obstacle her baby sister who could be easily tossed out, tossed overboard if necessary, if she made a fuss. Some of the men he'd known—not friends, no—would have tossed her overboard for fun, and only then gone in to her sister.

Pao had been made a man so many ways this summer, every time the world changed. There was a simple pleasure in being allowed to be a boy again, laughing with sisters.

At times like this he thought Shola was the elder sister, oldest of them all.

She was the one who worried, and that was an adult thing to do. Jin had no worries in her head, and Pao worried so little at times like this, his fool mind was so determined to believe the world would do no harm to three children playing families on a boat, he hadn't even thought to draw the gangplank up.

If he had thought, he still wouldn't have done it—Old Yen would be angry, coming back at whatever unpredictable hour to find himself cut off from his own boat; and there were always soldiers on watch on the wharf in any case, so why worry, what need?—but he hadn't even *thought*.

NOT UNTIL he heard the plank creak under an unexpected weight, felt the boat tip in response. Someone had come aboard, and not Old Yen. He knew that man's light tread, the almost imperceptible burden of him, the sense of the whole boat sighing, resettling into herself as her true master came back to her.

This was something else. Some*one* else, or more than one; the boat had seriously listed under the gangplank's pressure. If it was just one person, it was a fat one, or else heavily burdened. And few people were fat on Taishu anymore, and who would be bringing cargoes onto Old Yen's boat in his absence . . . ?

There were noises too, a sort of coughing grunt, a clink of chain. He didn't know.

Pao picked himself up from the cabin floor, too late and too slow, seeing Shola ahead of him in her worry. He signed to her, *hush, I'll go see; you keep your sister here, keep her quiet.*

The little girl nodded. Pao opened the cabin door, slipped out and closed it again at his back.

AND ALMOST wished he hadn't, finding himself face to face with a tiger. Wished he'd left it wide and could cry to the girls to flee, swift and surprising, out the other way and over the side, down to the wharf and away. A door was no protection, the creature would sniff them out regardless, however quiet they held themselves within.

And no, of course they couldn't outrun a tiger if it chose to give chase; but this was a tiger on a chain, which might delay it at least a little, maybe long enough . . .

TOO LATE now. Too late, too slow.

THE TIGER was green and black, like a creature risen out of myth.

Its eyes shone like wet polished stone, like jade, flat and deep together.

Its mouth hung open, a little; its black lips were drawn back, a little; its teeth seemed very close and very sharp, the chain quite thin.

A little, a very little part of him thought that perhaps he ought to look the other way, look ashore to see help coming, guards, soldiers, men with bows and blades.

Most of him, the best of him knew that was nonsense. There was no help, no sound from the wharf at all. The world changed, and no one ever came to stop it.

Besides, it was hard enough to look away from the tiger at all. Impossible to look back at the world unchanged, untiger'd.

All he could do now was see who held the chain.

He lifted his head with a great effort, very great.

Saw her, knew her. She was famous, almost. Besides, she'd been aboard before.

She might almost know him.

For sure she knew the emperor, and Mei Feng too. Why did he not feel reassured, at all?

Because she had a tiger on a chain, perhaps. And because there was no sound from the wharf, nothing at all, when a woman with a chained tiger should have attracted a noisy chain of followers. This woman particularly, who was always in company and seemed somehow more dangerous yet, positively lethal on her own. Even without her tiger.

And because she had a smile on her face that he did not like at all, that said *I have a tiger on a chain;* and because she stood strangely hunched and twisted, as though something unimaginable had broken her, unimaginably badly; and because he simply knew, he always knew when the world had changed again and things had gotten worse.

He thought perhaps she scared him more than the tiger did, which meant perhaps more than the dragon too.

He stood on the deck there with his back to the cabin door, and never even thought till later that he might have made a reckless run himself, down the gangplank and away.

Jiao smiled that terrible smile and said, "You have the children aboard with you, I know. I have been watching. Where have all the other boats gone?"

Watching, she said: not *listening*, not *talking to people round about*. He supposed it would be hard to ask questions, with a bright shining tiger on a chain. Or at least it would be hard to find answers of any value.

She could ask him anything, alone as they were in this shifting world, with the girls behind a flimsy door behind him.

He said, "Fishing."

She frowned. "Without the children?"

There was the other child, the castrated boy—but he was safe ashore, and Jiao might know that. She'd been watching.

He said, "We don't need the children any longer, just to go fishing."

"How not?" She hadn't expected this; he could almost feel the world changing for her too, sliding into a new configuration.

He said, "Old Yen came to . . . an agreement, with the dragon." Stood face to face with the dragon, as Pao now stood face to face with a tiger. "She allows us to fish, if every boat flies a green banner to say it is from Taishu and only fishing, not out to cross the strait."

"He came to an agreement." She had to repeat it, he thought, in order to believe it. Even then her voice was full of doubt and question. "What in the world did he have to offer to a dragon?"

"I don't know, he didn't say." Not to Pao, at least. Privately, Pao thought that even Old Yen didn't know actually why the dragon had agreed. What he might himself have conceded. Pao thought the old man was a little scared of that. "All we have to do is fly the banner."

"And yet you are tied up here, no banner," with a glance at the mastheads, "and no fishing with the fleet, although Taishu is still hungry and everyone knows Old Yen would sooner fish than breathe. Why so?"

"Old Yen is at the palace. Mei Feng . . . has not been well."

"Ah." Her face would have told no one anything, except that Pao had seen her in other moods and knew how expressive that face could be. What this stillness meant, he wasn't certain: only that it must mean something. "Well. Girls with babies growing are often not well, and imperial babies are said to be hard work. Also, old men can be fretful, and young men just the same. When the young man in question is the emperor, well . . ."

She shrugged quite carefully, quite unconvincingly, with her dreadful twisted shoulder. Pao said nothing. He was both male and young; what did he know, what could he tell her about pregnancies and sickness? He knew that Old Yen was not a fusser, and was sick himself with worry. It wasn't enough. It wouldn't have been enough in the face of Jiao alone; under the eye of the tiger, it was nothing.

She said, "Well. Lacking Old Yen, we must make shift. Can you sail the boat by yourself?"

Absolutely not. He said so. "It takes two," two at least, two who knew her temper.

Comfortably, Jiao said, "Well then, it's lucky you have me to help. I've been on boats enough. Tell me which ropes to haul, and I will haul them. And we have the girls, if we should need them, if there's anything they can do."

Urgently, he said, "You don't need the girls. I told you, we can fly a banner and sail freely . . ."

She said, as he had dreaded, "Not if the dragon's watching. She would see we are not fishing, and not coming back to Taishu. Did you think I wanted to go out for a pleasure-jaunt, idiot boy? Or to fish, to feed the emperor's soldiers another day? Or to feed my tiger?" with a little tug on the chain that brought a sidelong glance of jade-green eyes, a low grumble in the collared throat. "He might like fish, I expect he would, but he can wait. We'll cross the strait to Santung. I think you can bring me there, with the girl to speak for us against the dragon. Unless the goddess abandons us, of course. In which case the dragon can eat us all, and be damned to her."

two

I don't know what you're doing here, anyway. What, has the sea run out of fish all of a sudden? Or have you finally decided to trust Pao out in your boat alone, unwatched . . . ?"

Old Yen smiled, a little thinly. "There are men and boats enough, to fish for me."

"Grandfather, you are twice ten thousand years old and you have never said that in your life before! You have never *believed* it in your life, and you don't believe it now. You think you're the only man on Taishu who can find where the yellowtails are shoaling, and all the other boats just bob along in your wake and grow fat on your cleverness. And you," reacting to a snort from the other side of the bed, turning her head to glower at him though even so much effort was a real strain, she was so *tired* and her neck did ache abominably, she'd never realized just how heavy her head was, "don't you have, oh, I don't know, an empire to rule? A war to fight? Go plot the downfall of your enemies . . ."

Feed my people she might have said, to both of them together. It was all she really meant to say, apart from *go away*. But that would have frightened them, it would sound so valedictory, last message of a dying girl: which would only have made them linger longer at her bedside, even more reluctant to move.

She thought she was dying, probably, and her baby with her. She thought perhaps the baby was dead already, and killing her from the inside. She had bled, a little, two days ago: just enough she thought for a barely begun baby to be bleeding out.

The pain had come before, brute stabbing pains as if the baby were a blade in her own gut and slashing, slashing. There had been days of that. And then she had bled, that little bit, and now the pain was entirely different in kind. Now it was a slow rotting kind of pain, as if she carried a dead thing inside her to poison her blood and bile. She thought she stank on the inside, she was turning putrid and foul from within.

She did think this would kill her, tomorrow if not today.

So did the emperor, perhaps. So did Old Yen. Whatever they said. They sat one on either side and held her hands when she would let them, and said stupid hopeful things when she would hear them, when she could. Sometimes she drifted on a dreary tide, their voices would fade to nothing and she could be blessedly somewhere else for a while; but those same shifting treacherous tides would bring her back again, strand her on this bitter shore, this bed. She would rouse and hear one voice or the other, the two men she had loved most and best in this world, and wish one more time that they would go away.

This evening she was more sharply here than she had been for a while. She knew it was evening, because the useless doctors had brought her a draft of tea that must be drunk at sunset, they said, before the moon could rise. When the world hung poised, they said, between one power and another. *Slack water,* she wanted to say, and she knew the same thought was in her grandfather's head; and she said nothing, because any sailor knew that seafolk die at slack water.

The doctors were fools, but she forced herself to drink their tea, just to make her menfolk happy.

And so was sick, brutally stabbingly sobbingly sick, so messily sick that the little cat ran off and the emperor had to lift Mei Feng out of bed so that all her quilts and bedding could be changed.

Now she was clean and settled again, and her men were sat again on either side of her, and she was stranded high and dry, no hope of drifting off with her insides feeling ripped apart. And so she was grumbling at them, as much like herself as she could manage, in the faint failing hope of sending them away with argument if she couldn't drive them off with curses.

Her arguments weren't working either, her sharp thin nagging little voice had no power to it. The emperor squeezed her hand too lightly and smiled and said, "No wars now. Thanks to you, little one, and your devious mind, and the game you used to play with Grandfather. If Tunghai Wang fights anyone now, if he still has an army, it will be Ping Wen. The rebel and the traitor, let them fight each other. I don't care."

"You should care," she said frowningly. "When they have killed each other, you need to be ready. Go back and reclaim your empire, march all across it, let everyone see you. All the way to the Hidden City. Take the throne with you, you could have another coronation, you'd like that. Your mother would love it."

"It's a terrible long way, and I like being here with you. I'll wait till you're fit to come with me. You and our child, our boy, let the empire see him and know I have an heir . . ."

"Stupid. You shouldn't wait so long." *We will have no boy,* she meant, *and no girl neither; our baby is dead and so will I be, and what will you have waited for then?*

He only smiled again with a terrible sorrow, squeezed her hand again with that terrible gentleness, didn't shift. Didn't go away.

She might have turned her scowl back on her grandfather, but that would be just as useless. She knew why he was always here now, and never at sea. Oh, he was just as caught in sorrow and anxiety over her, of course he was; but there was more than that. He didn't want to sail under the dragon's banner. He had negotiated with the creature himself, and she was still awestruck that he could do that, her own beloved old man, that he could find the courage and the wit to confront an immortal and come away again whole and unharmed and victorious; but at what cost? His own victory was a terrible thing to him. He felt it as a betrayal of the Li-goddess, after serving her all his life and now making a deal with her fled prisoner, her enemy. The best he could manage was to present that deal to the emperor, make him a gift of it, and step away. Not fly the dragon's green himself.

Which meant not go to sea, because he wouldn't willingly use the goddess's children either. He had always hated that.

Poor grandfather: in his age, when he should be most easy with himself and the world too, he had lost all his contentment. First his goddess, now his purpose.

Soon his granddaughter, her too.

Me too.

He held her hand, and she really wished he wouldn't.

She could feel every one of his years in its hard lean fleshlessness, in the swollen knuckles and the ridged calluses. She'd never minded that, except that she knew his knuckles pained him sometimes. But now she could feel his hesitancy too, all his losses building up, and she couldn't bear it. It was her fault, she thought, perhaps. If not for her . . .

Well. He would be without her soon enough.

And here was a sudden welcome weight on her feet, the little cat come back to her, assured of warm clean bedding and a comfortable welcome. He walked all up her body and thrust his nose at hers in a self-contented greeting. There were crumbs in his whiskers. Nobody could feed themselves enough, even here in the palace, but everybody fed her cat.

He was her excuse to slip her hand free of Grandfather's, to stroke the small round brow and scratch beneath the jaw, feel his purring. He was really all the company she wanted, though of course she could never say so. *Go away* was the same as *let me go,* and of them all, only the cat was selfish enough to allow that. Human beings were differently selfish: wanting to keep her, only to spare themselves grief.

It was too late, she thought, for that. Their grief was inexorably coming, however hard they refused to see it.

The cat would come, inexorably in search of her; and find the bed empty, and fuss a little perhaps, and then nest in the quilts anyway, before he went off in search of better warmth and someone else to fuss him.

They could all learn from the cat, she thought, though none of them would do so.

Perhaps she had learned from him herself. There was something ineluctably cat-like in her own wanting to creep away, to find a hole and a silence, a solitude to wrap herself around. Much though she loved her men, she would so like them to leave her alone now, and they would not.

Not for the first time, the emperor said, "We should have brought your doctor, mine are useless. Grandfather, will you go——?"

And not for the first time, before Old Yen could say yes, Mei Feng said, "No, lord. Chien Hua," just because he liked to hear her say his name. "No. She is *not* my doctor, just the one who told me I was pregnant. Which I knew already, all but having someone say so. And she doesn't want to come, and Old Yen doesn't want to go," however much she'd like to have him gone. She would willingly send him away, but not to sea. "I will do well enough under your doctors," but there she lost him because even he could see that she wasn't doing well enough, not well at all under his doctors.

"She should be here," he said, and Mei Feng wasn't sure whether that was sulking or determination.

"She wouldn't come," she said. "It would be folly to send. Folly twice. First because she wouldn't come, and second because you would gift Ping Wen a boat and one of the children. The dragon's truce won't take anyone to Santung, you'd need to send a child. Which would anger the dragon and break the truce, give a weapon to the traitor and not help me. Don't do that, lord. For all our sakes, don't do it."

"Well, but you need . . ."

He didn't know what she needed. Any minute now he'd fetch his mother in again, in case the old woman had remembered some miracle cure between yesterday and today. Probably her honest best advice would be to find himself another woman. Many more. Create the harem that was his birthright; this was why, Mei Feng was the perfect argument for it. Even the empress had tact enough not to say that, though. Not yet. Perhaps she was waiting for Mei Feng to say it for her.

Not yet. Not now. The little cat curled up on the quilt, tight against her side; Mei Feng sank her fingers into thick warm fur, and waited.

three

*P*oor General Ma was on a mule again, and had been so for hours. His comfortable carriage could never have made this climb.

His comfortable body was not built for mountains, for mules, for adventures. His boy Yueh liked sometimes to call him a man-mountain, but that was another matter, and a boy of course could be tenderly squashed if he grew too mocking. There was nothing tender in Ma just now, except his nether parts.

He had Yueh at his bridle, leading the accursed mule. That was a comfort. And he had men enough, blades enough to discourage any pirates of the road. If there were bandits fool enough to cling to these slopes in hopes of a living. There must of course be traffic up and down the road; food must rise this way and no doubt treasures, gifts. If Ma had the management of it, he would manage it in caravans, occasional and massive, too great to challenge. Bandits would be first daunted and then starved. Even before they were hunted.

The road had climbed through forest and scrub, out onto bare rock. It clung now to slopes of stone, that must be terrible in winter; they were terrible now, Ma thought, in the encroaching dark. The sun kept sneaking away around an outcrop, only to show itself again as the road turned in pursuit. Every time they caught up it had sunk lower, growing fat and red as it fell.

He was fat and red himself, and had a terror of falling. Mules were said to be sure-footed, and this one had not stumbled yet, even where the road was most broken. He could, he supposed, trust the mule. And his boy at its head. Yueh had been with him a long time now, many months, and never put a foot wrong. Ma approved a careful boy.

The road led them abruptly into a cleft. That was better, with rock rising on either side: no fear of falling here. Ma looked up instead of down and saw a narrow sky above, purple and full of stars. His men called to one another, forward and back, not alarmed quite but discomfited. Sun could be seen ahead, waiting to greet them as they emerged; yet here was night lingering, as though it had been trapped from yesterday or longer. That last of the light was too far for comfort, when they must walk and shiver in this soul-stealing shadow where the night gods lurked.

Ma might not be comfortable himself, but the men's comforts were his daily task. He spoke to his boy, and Yueh's bright song rose about them. The rock walls caught it strangely, tossed it about and held it hanging in the air in fading echoes as though it had met its own ghost on the way. But, oh but: Yueh's voice had an uplifting magic to it, dispelling fears. It raised feet and spirits both, that had been inclined to drag. It gave the men a beat to march to, and—wise boy!—it was a song of the north he gave them, all unprompted. These might be the strange mountains of the far south, almost as far as it was possible to be; they were all northmen yet, and their faces were turned that way, the way this road was tending. Home lay somewhere far ahead, but this was a taste of it, and welcome.

CLOSER THAN home, they found what they had climbed for, why they had come all this way, why Ma had sat his mule and his blisters when he should have been safe below and plotting warfare with Tunghai Wang. Ping Wen the traitor was in Santung; that was all the news that mattered. Great events were afoot, plans were laid but could not be realized without Ma—and yet here he was, miles and leagues and days away, too far to glimpse the sea however dreadfully high he climbed.

And here, here at last was the reason for it: a high wall, a locked gate, a lone lamp shining in the dark.

Someone had already knocked a thunder on the heavy timbers of the gate. By the time Ma's mule reached it, there was a rattling of chains beyond, and a slow swing open. No questions asked, even of strangers who had made this climb unannounced and with such chancy timing.

Here was a tunnel of stone, the gates drawn back against the walls and still no men, no questions. Another lamp burned in the tunnel; at the other end were gates again, closed again.

They led the way now, Yueh and Ma and the mule. His men packed in behind them, muttering and anxious. More so, when the first gates closed themselves at their backs. There was an arrangement of chains, Ma saw, vanishing into the wall. Let the men fear ghosts again; for him, this was a good beginning. He believed, he chose to believe devoutly in human hands at work on those chains.

The gates ahead swung open, and here at last were people, men with shaven heads and dull robes, bowing them through into a courtyard. Yueh clicked his tongue to draw the mule on, and here was what Ma needed, what his good boy brought him to: a stone block where he could dismount with some degree of dignity, if no grace. And here was a man come to meet him, a man who carried dignity in his own person. One among many, but Ma could still tell the abbot, even in the dark.

"Sir, you are welcome here, you and all your party." The depth of the bow that proved the welcome, the abbot's head on a level with his feet reminded Ma that he was still standing on the block like a prisoner in shame, like a slave for sale, like an arrogant man asserting his own importance. He stepped down hastily—a little farther down than was comfortable for a heavy man with short legs; it forced a grunt from him, but his boy was there to catch his arm and save him an ungainly stagger—and bowed in his turn.

"My lord abbot, I am sorry to have come so late, and unannounced."

The abbot smiled. "Most of our guests come late. The only way to be early up here is to spend the night on the mountain. We may close the gate at sunset, but we leave a light burning to help you find us. Come, you have sat that abominable beast for hours, frightened half the way and wretchedly uncomfortable for all of it. *I* know. What you want now is somewhere for the outer man to sit that neither sways nor teeters above calamitous drops nor rubs its wooden cheeks at your more tender skin. For the inner man, you want tea and hot food. Then the promise of a wash and a soft bed, and you will be contented till the morning. Am I right?"

"Yes, yes." He was disturbingly exact; no man should see so well in such a darkness. But, "The needs and comforts of my men . . ." Ma knew those to be the first duty of an officer. He was accustomed to arranging them, but only on a grand scale, for a regiment, an army. Faced with his own small squad and far from his proper station—his desk and inks and brushes, dispatch-runners and riders waiting, his web of contacts and communications that made him feel all spider, all in control—he felt as much at a loss as they were. He knew his duty, though: however sore his buttocks, whatever the griping ache in his legs or the different gripe in his belly.

The abbot's smile was unshiftable. "There is no need. My brothers will take care of all. See . . ."

Indeed, his tired soldiers were being led away, almost by the hand some few of them, those who stumbled or shivered where they stood. Ma's boy too, who had attached himself again to the mule's bridle: a monk was urging him another way, presumably to where a stable stood ready. Stall and straw, grains and water for a weary beast. Yueh gave one last glance back, looking suddenly so weary himself; Ma's guilty heart stirred in his chest, and he took one instinctive pace toward the boy.

The abbot's hand on his sleeve checked him, light and absolute.

"Let them go." The voice was just the same, light and absolute. Ma couldn't move against it. "Let them all go. You have done what you had to do, you have brought them here safely. They are mine now, until I give them back to you. Let them go, and see to yourself; allow me to see to you. Come," again, irresistibly.

His hand on Ma's elbow, his gentlest of touches gripped as a veil of ice will grip a stone in winter, unshiftable again. He could shift all of Ma's stubborn, reluctant bulk as a breeze will shift a feather, no effort, no strain at all. Ma found himself walking in quite another direction: through an archway and up a staircase and stone walls rising all around him, lamplight and no windows.

It was hard, he found, to tell monastery from mountain. Perhaps that was as it should be; perhaps endurance was the prime quality of both. Ma had cause to hope so.

At the head of the stairs were the abbot's own apartments, richness and austerity bound curiously together, like a plain meal highly spiced. The abbot guided Ma to a chair, and he sank into its cushions with a gasp of relief. The abbot himself perched on a simple stool, such as he might have made himself in his novice days and used daily since. His long fingers gestured, *look your fill;* himself, he was looking at Ma.

Self-conscious under scrutiny, knowing himself fat and greasy and a little ridiculous, Ma nevertheless carried on looking. There was a fireplace, cold now in a mountain summer; an idol occupied the ashpit, a bright and gilded god with jeweled eyes, hung with costly silks and wreaths of fresh-picked flowers. A single thread of smoke climbed from a censer at its feet, wrapped itself about the idol like another scarf, like a prayer-flag, and slid away up the chimney.

The floor was as ruthless stone as the walls, but there were rugs beneath Ma's feet, if none for the abbot. The man's cot was as rude as his stool; the painted landscape that overhung it was as fine as any Ma had seen.

There were treasures in profusion, on walls and chests and shelves, wealth in gold and wealth in art and craft. If he had been another man—if he had been Tunghai Wang, say—Ma might have looked for jade somewhere in the shadows of the room, and might he thought have found it.

Footsteps on the stairs presaged a scurry of monks with trays. The abbot had eaten already, or else he did not eat supper, or else he did not eat with guests. The heavy tray—all brass and lacquer-work, heavy in itself but a burden mostly because of what it bore, bowls and lidded pots alive with steam—was all for Ma, set down at his elbow on a table of ivory and ebon.

Another monk, another tray, and this one did go to the abbot. This one held the tea: a pot of iron and cups of celadon, lovely in themselves and strange together, a basket of thick white butter. Ma was not sure that he had seen butter since he left the north, the true north, in the spring of the previous year.

"Alas, it is only brick-tea," the abbot said with a gesture of apology as honest as it was needless. He had perhaps seen where Ma's eyes lay, on that shallow basket. "We brought the custom with us long ago, and keep it still. I can sweeten it with butter, if that is to your taste?"

"Oh, absolutely, please, yes. Please . . ."

And so there was the hot and coarse and bitter tea, shot through and through with clinging sweet rich oily butter. Ma drank, and sighed, and drank again. The abbot refilled his cup.

And then there was food: no meat, but vegetables and rice and dried fungus, hot pastes and bitter sauces, salt pickles and sweet fruit. Ma ate with busy chopsticks, only marginally disconcerted by the abbot's watching him. He was used to eating alone: with Yueh to serve him, with clerks and messengers waiting for orders, eyes on every mouthful.

The abbot waited until Ma had finished—too long a time, per-haps, with no expression of impatience, sipping like a man who took pleasure in the little things, the daily tasks, the tea—before he spoke again. And then he said nothing to the purpose, he showed no hint of curiosity why this heavy man had hauled him-self so far above the world with a squad of soldiers to protect him and a boy to serve him and a balky mule to carry him where he so very evidently would very much prefer not to be.

Instead it was all a smooth crisp shell of conversation, deliberately hollow, a blown egg. It was a way to say *We have the manners of the world here, and the time of the gods. There never will be any hurry, so long as you are our guest. Tomorrow or the next day or when you will, when you are ready we shall talk about why you have come. Till then, we shall talk about anything else, anything but.*

The abbot spoke of the monastery and its people, of a long chain of daughter-houses reaching all across the empire, over a long long chain of years. How they had brought their gods, their crafts, their customs and, yes, even their curious shaggy cattle all this way, like children playing hopping-games from point to point. From one peak to the next, for they were a mountain people serving mountain gods and the mountain-chain ran all this way, though these hills were nothing, nothing like the high plateau of home.

That long history was in fact exactly why Ma had come, and he thought the abbot ought to know it. He thought he did know it. Why else would they both be here, why else the monastery? Here?

Food in his belly, exhaustion in his head: it was satisfaction, perhaps, that closed his eyes one time too often, for a moment too long. The abbot laughed softly and struck a small gong in an embrasure. There was a scurry of sandals on stone, a young monk in the open doorway.

"Go with Kampong Fen," the abbot said. "He will take you to your bath and bed."

It was an effort just to heave himself up, but the monk's hand was at his elbow, a whippy strength he could lean into. Which reminded him: he paused, a little dizzy in his mind but solid on his feet there, still on the abbot's rugs. "Where's . . . ? I ought—"

"Your men are settled and content," the abbot said, "even your mule is fed and sleeping now. Go, go. There is nothing to interrupt your own needs and pleasures, insofar as we can serve them."

That wasn't quite right, but Ma seemed to lack the impetus to contest it.

The monk picked up a lamp and Ma followed him, down stairs and along a corridor, through an archway to a suite of rooms more comfortable than the abbot's.

And here was his boy Yueh waiting in a pool of steamy light, and all was well after all. Here were warm water and clean cloths, sweet oil—butter-oil, he thought, with an inward smile—for his sorenesses and blisters. A teasing, familiar gentleness in the boy's familiar, long-familiar hands; which turned rough once he was washed, a hard rubbing with coarse towels; which brought him to bed at last, tingling and refreshed, to lie among soft quilts and feel soft warm skin, a slight and wonderful body settle obediently against his own.

And then those hands again, impertinent, precise. He had no resistance, none. One last bone-bare stir of conscience, just enough to ask, "Did they feed you?"—but it seemed that he must be satisfied with no more than a chuckle in response before the tender mouth it came from found other, more determined purpose on his skin.

MA WOKE to the sound of hammering, the sound of his own contentment written in the air.

Knowledge is power; and power does not die, it cannot be killed, only suppressed in one quarter to rise again in another. An emperor can be killed—with difficulty, if he can be caught: even this one, Ma thought, this runaway boy with his extraordinary luck, extraordinary tales beginning to attach to him—but the empire abides, another man always rises to seize the Hidden City and the throne.

That would be Tunghai Wang if the generalissimo had his way, if Ma laid it out for him.

If he could keep the dragon from interfering, more than she had already.

He was in the place to do that, the right place, sure.

A high place, and the sound of hammering.

THERE WAS a window, small and square and shuttered. A finger of pale mountain sunlight had poked through a knothole in the wood. Ma judged the angle of that acutely, flung back his quilts and tumbled his boy out of bed.

"Master?" Yueh lay sprawled on rugs, laughing up at him, naked and beautiful and his own.

"Washing-water," Ma grunted, "and food, whatever these monks are used to eat in the mornings." *Tsampas,* he guessed, and more butter tea: great churned pipes of it for the monastery at large, more delicate pots for the abbot's guests and the butter to mix themselves. That would do him admirably. The men he'd brought might struggle, perhaps—but food was food and they should be grateful. Something hot in their bellies and no dragon in the sky, no imperial soldiers hunting: they should be glad enough. They should be settling here, anticipating days of this. Barrack walls against the weather, barrack food and barrack beds, no work, no fear, no worry. Nowhere to go, nowhere to be but here.

He hoped to disappoint them, sooner than they imagined. For now, though, let them lie, let them snore and scoff and squabble . . .

With his boy gone trotting off, Ma rolled himself out of bed and hobbled to the window, sore it seemed in every part that moved. Well, he would hope to disappoint himself also, if his self had hopes of rest and recovery here. Butter tea.

The shutter swung inward, to show a broad stone ledge—or was it rock, the actual rock of the mountain? Was the monastery a blown egg, a mine dug from the living hill?

He leaned out foolishly and tried to see, and couldn't quite. Built or otherwise, the monastery presented one flat face to the wind, like a cliff that clung to the mountain at its back. He could go down and out into the yard below, peer up at it and look for the

marks of man, try to guess if it were one or the other or both together, half built and half dug out.

Or he could ask the abbot. He needed to speak to the abbot, as
soon as might be.

As he leaned out like this, perilous above the fall of it, the sound
of hammering rose up to meet him, hard and metallic and per-
functory.

The sound of his boy's laughter at his back was less clear, muf-
fled by his own naked bulk wedged in the window frame.

He heaved himself back in, helped somewhat by Yueh's hands
but only somewhat, as the boy was seized by giggles. Ma cuffed
him equably—he had seen his master's vast buttocks before, after
all—and only then spotted the parade of monks behind him, bearing bowls and towels and a tray, none of them wreathed in steam
enough to have disguised the view.

No matter. Ma wrapped himself in a quilt and thought himself
magnificent enough.

LATER, WASHED and fed and dressed, he left the boy in the room—
he would sleep, of course, if he was given nothing more to do; Ma
gave him nothing bar a clip on the ear and a handful of dried fruit
to munch on—and stopped the first monk he found, asked to be
taken to the abbot.

And was taken down and out, into the hard stone yards and
then along, through one and then another. They were ordered almost like the courtyards of a house. Here was the entrance yard
beyond the gate, that he had seen already by lamplight, roofed
with stars. Here next the stable yard, where his own cursed mule
was stalled alongside rugged ponies, where there was room also
for all the monastery cattle to be housed and fed come winter,
though the beasts were out on a lower pasture now. Here next—

Here was the hammering like a wall, like a gate closed against
them. Stepping through the arch, Ma felt as though he stepped
through a solid fall of water, though it was only sound.

Here were broad-chested men, monks with shaven heads, stripped to the waist as they worked: as they bent over anvils with great hammers in their hands, as they stood back to let wiry novices—stripped even further, some of those, stripped to a twist of cloth, scrawny buttocks and gangling limbs showing burn-scars everywhere—take their work and thrust it back into a furnace or else quench it in an iron trough of water, in a sudden scalding gout of steam.

Here were half a dozen furnaces, fed and stoked by those same sweating novices; here were a dozen anvils, all of them in use; here was no noise except the hammers, but the hammers were noise enough for this mountain. Too much noise for Ma, he couldn't bear it.

He stood just within the arch, saw the abbot an impossible distance ahead, almost at the far side of the yard, beyond the anvils. Beyond the noise, unreachable.

Ma looked a mute appeal at his guide—no point in speaking under this heaviness of sound, this brute iron rain of blows—and gestured, pleadingly. *Would you fetch him to me? Would he come? You will find me back there, if he will. In the stables. Doing my duty by my mule . . .*

THE MULE took Ma's arrival as a matter of course, only to be expected. Ma felt that perhaps he was owed a little more, that someone somewhere ought to be acknowledging the surprise of it, and really there was only the mule.

And then the abbot came, and Ma struggled a little under the surprise of that, and struggled a little not to show it. He was used to ordering the comings and goings of a thousand men at a time, but only on paper, with brush and ink. In the flesh, he had trouble sometimes giving orders to his boy. The notion that the abbot of a high establishment should come to him—to fat and comical General Ma, who was only made general because he was useful and convenient, not because he was any kind of soldier—and only because he asked it . . . Well. Yueh would take it for granted, but Ma was taken aback.

"What," the abbot murmured, "you have come all this way and climbed my mountain at the last, you have suffered pains and discomforts and a thousand inconveniences on the way, and shall I not walk across a courtyard?"

"My lord abbot, you were busy among your brothers; it ill befits a guest to interrupt the work of the house, let alone the work of its master."

"My first work is to take care of our guests. And all my brothers know their own work, and get on very well without me." He was a brisker man in daylight than he had seemed last night. If they stayed any longer in the mule's stall, Ma was afraid that he would cast about for a brush and start to groom the beast. Or find a broom and sweep dung out of the stall.

To spare them both, Ma walked out into the yard again. It was a bright day, a pleasure to enjoy a clear sky with no equivocation, no anxious peering for the dragon.

He said, "The work of your house is in iron, I find."

"Indeed. I think it a useful discipline, to remind us of the iron grip the gods take on our world. We are born in chains, General Ma; freedom is as much an illusion as wealth and power and achievement. The wheel of life has an iron rim, and we are bound upon it. Up here, we sit above the world and its fogs, we see more clearly—and what we see is a rigid order, discipline beyond the mortal. Our own life of ritual and labor is a shadow, an expression to the gods of what we see below. We account for every hour, we bind ourselves about with prayer and smoke and custom—and we work in iron, we make axles and wheel-rims and chains."

That was an invitation, and Ma was not slow to seize it. He said, "There was another house, a sister-house of yours I guess, that was famous for its chains."

The abbot nodded, smiled. "The world called it the Forge, I know. Sometimes when the wind blows I call this valley of ours the Bellows."

Was that another invitation, was the abbot laying out a path of stones for him, *step here, and now step here* . . . ? Ma was unsure, but swift to step regardless. He said, "Does the typhoon reach this far inland, this high into the mountains?"

"We have our own storms," the abbot said judiciously, "mountain-storms. The typhoon is a tale here, rather than a trouble to us. Still, we look down on the world and see how much it is troubled. We do know of the typhoon."

He could look down on the dragon, Ma thought, from the height of this cliff-house: look down on her as she flew. He was glad to have a wall around the yard here, to hide him from the edge. It was a great wrong to find himself standing higher than birds in flight, higher than clouds. Higher than the dragon. That was why he feared heights so much, he thought; it was an impertinence, to lift himself above his proper place.

Some men were not afraid, apparently. He looked down at the abbot, surprised as he always was by courage and by size, the incompatibles. "You may know how much we have been troubled recently along the coast, since your sister-house came to its unhappy end?"

"Indeed. Pirates, we hear, slew our brothers at their work. So of course the dragon rose, and brought storm with her from the depths. Storm and war."

Actually it was Tunghai Wang who had brought the war. Which meant that it was Ma, largely, because it was his work that allowed the army to move. "Yes. The dragon has been a dreadful trial to us all, who live beside the sea. As she was before she was chained, as she always will be unless she can be chained again."

There, he had said it; and the abbot did not laugh. Nor curse, nor scold him. Yueh was apparently right, as so often: *You are not a man to be laughed at, or easily dismissed. Or scolded. You should learn that. You have great weight in the world,* a cool hand laid upon the matter of his belly, addressing the substance within. *You should learn to see yourself dressed in your own importance, as we all see you. Lord.*

Ma saw himself dressed in his boy's care, no more than that. And was grateful for it, now especially, something to depend on as he waited. It was a breathless wait, for the abbot would not be hurried and this thin air did Ma no good when he was nervous and hopeful.

The abbot turned to address two young novices who dragged a hand-cart across the yard, pigs of crude iron making the wheels—iron-bound, yes, and iron-spoked too against the weight on the bed above—clatter and spark on the stones. Their shaven heads gleamed with sweat, their eyes gleamed with mischief as he spoke to them, but not perhaps so much as his own did. They ducked their heads respectfully to him, bowed more deeply to Ma, hauled their load away.

The abbot said, "I have told them to fetch your boy, take him higher up the mountain and teach him to fly kites. I hope you have no objection?"

Ma blinked. "No, no, none at all, my lord abbot"—they would find the boy sleeping, and he might as well play as sleep—"but I don't understand." There seemed to be little in kite-flying to express the harsh rule boasted of, the strict devotion that accounted for every hour, iron in the soul.

"No. Our kites are flags, our flags are prayers, we lift them to the gods—but you didn't bring your boy up here to have him learn our ways. Nor did you come yourself to exercise your mule."

"No." Let it be direct, then. "My lord abbot, I need a monk-smith."

"Not even that, I think: you need *the* monksmith." And that same chastening smile, and, "I am your man."

four

They were Dandan's patients, her two old men, her particular care. That was understood.

Tien might have adopted them into her library and taken charge of their treatments, because she could doctor them properly, where Dandan could only ever nurse. Nevertheless they were Dandan's old men, no question.

The boy Gieh might have appointed himself their servant, which meant he could spend half the day sitting at their feet while they talked dangerous nonsense at him, and the other half nosing through their things while they were with Tien. Nevertheless, they were still Dandan's old men. Yes.

She didn't have to heal their broken bodies, or ease their many pains. Tien would do that, as much as could be done. She didn't have to bathe them, wash their clothes or clean their room. Gieh did that, as much as he saw the need and they would allow. She didn't have to fetch them food, the boy did that too, along with far more potent spirits than she thought good for them. Or good for him, because they certainly shared, those wicked old men, they delighted in corrupting the boy. She was growing used to his shrill ramshackle laugh echoing down the passage late at night, his pale sweating silence in the mornings.

On the face of it, perhaps she had no duties now. And yet, they were still her men. She had nothing else that was hers. Mei Feng, Dandan's mistress and also perhaps her friend, was gone back to Taishu. Dandan had stayed by her own choice: which was in no way the act of a friend, and almost entirely the fault of the old men. Which really only confirmed how tied they were now, each to each, Li Ton and Ai Guo and she.

Which was entirely sufficient to explain why she was out here on the beach now, some miles from the city. She had a basket on her arm and she was gathering.

She didn't have the coast to herself. These hungry days, there were scavengers on every beach: digging for whelks and razor-shells, netting shrimps in the shallows, stranding themselves on tidal islands to fish the surf. Eyeing strangers with something close to loathing, as something close to thieves.

Dandan came from the palace, and was in no danger of starv-ing. Nor were her old men. Still, she came from the palace and might have brought trouble with her, and did not. She was toler-ated, largely because she never did bring trouble. Tolerated and still watched, muttered over, isolated. *Take what you want but not too much, nothing that we might want ourselves . . .*

Day by day she did that, free and distrusted and begrudged. Let them dig and wade, let them swim far out to distant rocks, let them guard their precious waters and take what they could struggle for. Dandan scrambled, rather, and took only what the sea offered up to the sun.

She went out as the tide sank, to ruin hands and feet and clothes together, finger-fishing in revealed pools and gleaning from the sharp-edged rocks around.

Mostly, she collected seaweeds. Kelp drying in tangles on the sand, bubbleweed floating in a shadowed pool; blackweed and threadweed and saltgrass, she knew a dozen and could find them all. One would strengthen the blood, another nourish the liver. Threadweed strangled diseases of the belly, while saltgrass en-couraged a healthy flow of urine. She prepared them as needed, soups and teas for her old men. To the boy Gieh they were medi-cines and not food, and hence no part of his province; to the girl Tien they were foods and not medicine.

It was all that Dandan had just now, and she clung to it tenaciously. Most days would find her out along the shoreline, east or west. If some days she carried her basket home empty, small blame to her for that. Some days, there was nothing worth the bringing back.

Some days, her life seemed barely worth the living. She would gaze across the water toward distant Taishu and wonder if she should have gone when she could have gone, left her old men and been a better friend to Mei Feng. Who was pregnant, after all, and had few friends else.

Dandan could persuade herself, often and often, that she'd done the wrong thing. Trapped herself the wrong side of the strait, among people who didn't know they needed her. Old men could be obtuse, and boys were worse. Boys could be *obnoxious*.

When she thought of the old men, how she had first seen them, there was reassurance in that. Her anger stirred to life again, and her determination. They were her special cause, and she could still raise them from the pit they'd fallen into. Tortured and torturer together, she could save them both. She could find them a place to be and a way to live, unfettered by their long and dreadful histories.

She was quite certain of that.

And even so, some days she ended up out here on the rocks, empty-handed and helpless, hopeless, almost in despair for herself. Staring at the sea and wondering, rebuilding her own story in her own imagination, telling it otherwise, putting herself otherwhere, seeing herself happy . . .

SEEING A sail break the horizon, today, here, now.

AT FIRST she thought it wasn't a sail at all, she thought it was only the very tip of the Forge, strangely visible today where it hadn't been before.

But she watched it, she scrambled higher up the slew of rocks to give herself a better vantage, and it was definitely a boat. Not a small boat, but flying only a single sail.

She thought, she really thought it ought to hurry more.

Her eyes checked the sky and saw no dragon, but that was no guarantee. The dragon was as likely to erupt from beneath, the sea her element.

There must surely be one of the goddess's children aboard, or they could never be so casual. Even so, Dandan thought they ought to hurry. She thought one sail was idling, almost insulting, certainly tempting fate.

Watching, she saw the boat edge closer to the coast. She could see a tall figure at the steering oar, a shorter—a boy, she thought—running between the stern and the foremast, where the sail hung.

She thought it was the fisherman's old boat. It had a distinctive shape and an uncommon size, too large for a sampan but yet not quite a junk. That wasn't him, though, steering it. And it didn't seem to be quite sailing where they wanted it to go. There was a sense almost of panic in the boy's restless skittering forward and back; there was . . . something else, inexperience or injury at the stern there.

Dandan was almost sure now that the tall figure on the oar was a woman: which meant that it really ought to be Jiao. The woman stood tall but twisted, though, hunched over to one side, not like Jiao at all. She worked the oar one-handed, as best she could, which was only a little short of hopeless. Sometimes it dug in too deep, trying to stir more water than one hand could possibly shift; sometimes the blade lifted suddenly free so that she staggered at the lack of resistance, once almost pitched herself entirely over the side, barely managed to save herself with a rail-grab from her other hand, her bad arm, with results that put her on her knees for a minute there while the oar swung free and the boy had to come pounding back to take it.

Slowly, uncertainly, Dandan understood they were in trouble. She knew nothing about boats, but surely the boat shouldn't be standing side-on to the waves as it came, carried in crabwise like flotsam?

This close to the shore, it shouldn't be a killing kind of trouble. She knew nothing about the sea either, but this beach shelved gently even beyond the tideline. If they were trying to keep the boat out at sea and making too poor a job of it, they should just run aground and have to splash ashore, no worse than that. She thought. No unseen rocks to rip the hull apart, not depth enough to sink it.

Even so, Dandan did make her way down to the water's edge, to where sodden sand oozed up around her toes. There was a deadly attraction to imminent catastrophe. She wasn't the only one drawn down here; the beach was littered now with dark still figures watching. She might be the only one with even the vaguest hopes of helping. She thought these others saw only hopes of salvage.

The boat came on in its inevitable beauty, helplessly bound in the laws of tide and wind and current, like a fish dragged in by a net. Its side loomed, suddenly broad and high in the shallow curve of the bay, as inappropriate as a stranded whale. Perhaps it would destroy itself for very shame, tear itself apart when it struck . . .

It turned at the last moment in shallow water to strike bow-first, almost to look intentional. It sounded like the dragon come to land: hissing and snapping, a slow rending groaning crunch. The boat seemed to shiver from stem to stern. Ropes flew loose and the sail fell. One voice—one child's voice—screamed briefly. Then it was still and quiet, caught upright on the keel, startling and perverse in not enough water to sustain it.

The incoming tide would float it off, Dandan thought, and more skilled hands would come to sail it up the coast to Santung, to a proper harbor. No great harm, to sit here for a few awkward hours . . .

· · ·

EXCEPT THAT there was a rush suddenly across the sand, and this was no family scavenging for shellfish in the rock-pools, or seeking profit from a wreck. They came from the rocks, where they must have been lurking; but these were men, too many and too rough. Men who seized her up as incidental profit, herself and other women from the beach as they charged into the breaking waves.

Men who had fought the emperor, rebels. If she hadn't guessed it already—struggling, kicking, terrified, seeing a new and brief and terrible life emerge like a boat from fog, all too clear—they confessed it, boasted about it as they called up the stranded vessel's steep dark dripping flank.

"Ohé there, the boat! Let ropes down, let us aboard!"

"Who are you, and what can you do to help?" The voice was Jiao's, no question, for all that she stood like a cripple and moved like one now.

Would fight like one too, surely, if she could fight at all. If she would try to.

Even healthy, even Jiao could not have fought this many men alone. If she had wanted to. "We are Tunghai's men," their captain called. "Tunghai Wang, who will be emperor. We want this boat, and everything you carry. Everyone you carry," making it obvious that they knew about the escort-children. "You can come with us, or else we will set you ashore here, if you let down ropes right now."

Dandan didn't believe him. Neither did Jiao; that woman was twice her age, and many times as sharp in the ways of men and war. "Oh yes," she said, laughing harshly. "I'm sure you'll be very kind to me, you and all your men in turn. And then toss me overboard after, me with my useless arm and all. It's a pity; I might have come willingly to your Tunghai Wang, and told him whatever I know about the emperor's plans. But I don't think I can trust you now, can I?"

"I don't think you have a choice," the captain called back, while his men hooted and laughed in their turn. One of them leaped to seize a dangling rope-end, to haul himself up hand over hand. Dandan tried to cry a warning, but the man who held her closed his great foul hand across her mouth so thoroughly she could barely even breathe. She tried to bite, but he only tightened his grip and growled in her ear, a slow exploration of everything he meant to do with her later, when they were afloat.

In any case, Jiao was watching, leaning over the side to see the man as he climbed. Reaching out with her good arm, her heavy tao to cut the rope he hung from.

The man splashed down eruptively. Jiao laughed from above, and all his colleagues were laughing too, but their captain had a thoughtful expression on his face. He wouldn't be stalled for long. One man standing on another's shoulders could reach the boat's railing. Or an hour's work ashore would bring back ladders. One minor mocking victory for Jiao was a goad to the rebels, not a defeat.

She vanished from the side. Above the men's muttering, Dandan heard the rattle of a chain released, Jiao's voice sharply raised. Looking up, she saw a shadow spring from the boat's deck, loom above the men, impossibly overleap them.

For that little moment, staring up at an ominous dark body, something deep-rooted in her said *dragon*.

She was already afraid, then—twice afraid, once of the rebels who had snatched her and once again of this flying thing, this creature—when it came splashing down mightily and twisted around in the water there to face them, lifted its magnificent head and roared, a guttural world-shaking noise, malign and directed and intent.

Not a dragon, no, of course not. Dragons didn't ride on boats, nor fly on a human's say-so.

Nor did tigers, jade tigers, that she had ever heard.

DANDAN HADN'T realized that a tiger, any tiger could be so big.

Or so close to her.

Or that a jade tiger would be so vicious-seeming. The stories she'd heard, Taishu stories were all about the beasts' benevolence, unexpected rescue, guidance. Meaning. That above all. It was always significant, if you glimpsed a jade tiger in the forest. They were the gods' messengers, some said, fetching truth from heaven. Leading the chosen. Even Mei Feng, after her night on the mountain, her encounter, she had said—

NEVER MIND Mei Feng, and never mind the stories. This was real, present, now. This was a tiger in the flesh, a hot wet fury. Some of the men were running already, and their captives too, the women they'd taken from the shore. Dandan thought that was probably a good idea.

Actually they were floundering more than running in water that came thigh-high, waves that washed higher. Dandan's own captor was one of them, abandoning her unheeded.

She thought probably she ought to follow. It was only good sense, to choose him over the tiger.

Only, well, the sea was waist-deep on her, and the swell covered her breasts as it came in; she couldn't hope to keep up. If the tiger came bounding after them, it would reach her first. She wasn't sure she wanted to be the sacrifice that let the others get away.

The tiger crouched low, like a cat at play, except that it crouched in the sea. And had such a rage in it: its mouth agape, its wicked teeth like white jade, just that hint of green. Even its stripes were like forest shadow, black in a green light. Its eyes shone, ferocious.

Dandan wasn't sure she could have run, even if there had been sense in it. She wasn't sure she could move, against such a glare.

Also it was Jiao's tiger, seemingly. She shouldn't forget that. That had to be worth something, didn't it? The men had threatened the boat, and Jiao had unleashed the tiger. There had been that rattle of chain, that command.

Jiao wouldn't let it hurt Dandan. They were on the same side. Weren't they . . . ?

Remembering what Jiao had said to the rebel captain, Dandan was suddenly not so sure.

Still didn't start to run, though. Couldn't move against the hot stone glitter of those eyes, the coiled tension in its sleek wet dreadful body.

Also, it was beautiful. That counted for something too. Apparently it was hard to turn your back on beauty, even where it was terrible.

SHE WASN'T the only one not running.

A handful of men had stood their ground, rallying behind their captain. They stared back at the tiger, equally tense, moving no more than it was.

Perhaps, Dandan thought, they could let terror and tension wash through them and ebb away. Perhaps if none of them was stupid, if none drew a weapon, there needn't be any kind of fight at all. Perhaps the men could just wade slowly back to shore after their fleeing companions; the tiger could leap up onto the stranded boat again and drip all over its deck while Jiao fastened it to its chain again; and Dandan, Dandan could . . .

SHE WASN'T sure, quite, what she could do. What she should.

AND THEN it didn't matter anyway, because Jiao spoke a word from above and the tiger leaped.

FOR A moment, in the air again, it almost blotted out the sun. Eclipsed in its shadow, the men drew blades. Did they really think their simple taos could make any difference to *that*?

Dandan shrank back against the dank timbers of the boat's exposed hull. She thought the tiger would slay the rebels, and then turn to her. She did just want that little pause, that little space between them. To say *no, I did not stand with them, I was not one with them, no,* if the question ever arose in the afterlife. She didn't quite see how it would matter then, but *I was faithful, loyal to the emperor*—it mattered to her, it mattered now.

THE MEN were fighters, trained and tested. They knew their lives were in the balance here, they fought to save themselves; they used blades and brains together, they worked with one another, they made a deadly team.

The tiger had none of that. It was a creature alone, magnificent but lethal only in itself. And still an animal, however splendid. It fought because that was its nature. Almost, it might have been playing. Seeing it so closely—seeing how lean it was in its slicked-down fur and how supple, twisting and rolling in air and water— Dandan was beginning to think it very young. Still monstrous, still vicious, but young. Not quite a kitten but still a cub, a youngling. Almost, she could have pitied it.

IT LEAPED, and fell among the gathered men and their raised blades. In that little moment she thought she would see a slaughter here, the swift death of something lovely.

And then the tiger was in the midst of the men, rolling and kicking in the water, yowling when it had air. With a ring of armed men around it, Dandan still thought it should be doomed, dying already, bleeding out into the sea.

But it was still a tiger, jade tiger, immensely more than any man. Where it kicked, a man was hurled back, brutally bleeding; where it rolled, it rolled with a man between its paws, pierced and pierced, his head in its teeth.

It could break a man with simple impact, the stone strength of the thing. One long raking kick with a hind leg could gut him, open him from throat to groin and spill out all his innards.

Why didn't the men—the surviving men, so few—have sense now to run away?

Why didn't she?

· · ·

PERHAPS, LIKE her, they still couldn't turn their backs. Even though it meant their deaths, separate and dreadful.

The captain was the last to die. She thought perhaps he might have welcomed that. He seemed the type: first to meet the enemy, last to fall.

Last of the men, at least.

There was still herself.

The tiger was sea-washed, still green in all its aspects, only its appalling teeth and jaw stained red as it tossed aside the ruin of that last man and turned its head, unsatisfied.

Turned to her.

DANDAN MIGHT have cowered there against the hull until it leaped again. She might have died, her body ripped asunder beneath the tiger's claws, her lost ghost to haunt the weed-wracked shore.

She was too afraid of that: so much afraid that she did the other thing, she stepped forward into the tiger's stare, lifted her head, found her voice.

Found at least a thin and tremulous memory of her voice, a shadow. Enough—barely—to call up to the deck there, "Jiao . . . ?"

The pirate presumably could see her. Dandan couldn't actually look up, she still couldn't take her eyes from the tiger, but she heard Jiao bark with laughter and then say, "No, you leave her. Leave her be. Get after those who ran away, save me one of those men."

The tiger seemed impossibly to understand. Its gaze lingered on Dandan one little moment longer, and she thought it would still like to kill her. Then it turned, almost more liquid than the water, and plunged away in a series of leaps and splashes, bounding high above the breaking waves.

Jiao watched it go, and pitied the men it chased, and hoped it could distinguish soldiers from civilians, or at least men from women.

She was still watching that distant racing shadow when a ladder of rope and bamboo clattered down to swing in the air beside her.

SHE MADE the perilous climb, and at the top she found not Jiao but a boy, pale and anxious as he helped her over the side.

The two girls she expected to see were in the bows; at this distance she couldn't tell if they were upset at having run aground, if they were oblivious to the slaughter below.

Jiao was in the boatmaster's place, by the stern oar. Dandan didn't need the jerk of the boy's head to send her aft. There was never any question who was in charge.

There were so many other questions—*Jiao, what happened to your arm, your shoulder? Where is the old man whose boat this is? Why did you come ashore here? What did you mean, when you said about going to Tunghai Wang? Where, how, why did you find yourself a tiger, a jade tiger . . . ?*—that she could apparently ask none of them, they clogged her throat and left her speechless.

That last especially. The tiger filled her mouth and mind, it left her trembling so hard that she could barely stand. She had to cling to the rail. And could only stare up at Jiao, bewildered and not feeling very rescued after all, still afraid.

"Well. You're Mei Feng's little friend, aren't you? The one she left behind?"

It seemed that there were words after all, perhaps there was just a hint of pride. She said, "I stayed, yes." To take care of her old men, and she would give anything to have them with her now, quiet and experienced and potent at her back.

"What were you doing here?"

"Gathering seaweed. There is not much to eat, even in the palace."

"Ah. If you're still in the palace, you can help me to Ping Wen."

She could, perhaps. At least, she could take Jiao past the guards on the gate. But, "Your tiger would do that," half joking, half hoping for a smile. Not seeing it, and plunging on doubtfully, "So would this," the boat itself; and then, a more specific gesture, "so would they," the girls in the bows. So, most emphatically, would they.

"Yes," Jiao said, "I thought that. Something to bring, a gift. Only polite, I thought. But he can't have my tiger."

With immaculate timing, a low and terrible howling came rolling out across the water. Jiao glanced ashore, and her mouth did twist now into a smile, utterly humorless. "I think he's done what I asked. Good tiger. That may be another way to buy my way into Ping Wen's good graces, if I bring him a prisoner."

"Jiao, I don't understand." In honesty she understood none of this; here was a question she could ask at last. "Why should you need to do that? If you come from the emperor . . ."

Her voice died away, in the face of that smile again. It looked worse every time it appeared.

Not from the emperor, then. Dandan wondered briefly if she herself stood in any danger here. Perhaps she should stop arguing how much Jiao really didn't need her.

But there seemed to be no way back from here, for either of them. Once Jiao had made that implicit declaration, *I am not here from the emperor,* which was to say *I am not loyal to the emperor,* it didn't really matter what else was said between them. There were no secrets left, only things that had not yet been said. Dandan said, "You told that man, you might have gone to Tunghai Wang . . ."

"Why, so I might. A gift for one will do as well for another. I was fairly sure of my welcome, if I could only find him," with an awkward one-armed gesture that mocked Dandan's own, encompassing the boat, the girls in the bows. Not the tiger. "But his people found me first, and I didn't like them. Did you? So I think perhaps I'll go to Ping Wen after all. I find I like his people better." That smile again, meaning Dandan, *I mean you.*

Dandan shivered, and knew that Jiao had seen it. She wanted to rub her arms, where her skin was prickling. She said, "But, but

Tunghai Wang, he's a *traitor*," and how could she go from one to the other, how could she not care?

"Yes, of course, you little fool. So is Ping Wen. Didn't you know?"

Dandan shook her head slowly, meticulously. She did know that Mei Feng believed that, of course; it was impossible to spend any time with the girl, to be close with her at all and not to know it. Dandan had never believed it, though, a traitor so near to the throne. And if it were true, why on earth would the emperor have appointed him governor of Santung . . . ?

Ideas, revelations came slowly this morning, it seemed, but they did come. Jiao only stood there, while Dandan worked things through on her fingers. The governor of Santung sat in exile from Taishu, from the throne. The strait lay between them, and the dragon ruled the strait. It could not be crossed except in those vessels protected by the goddess, which carried her chosen children— which Jiao had apparently stolen, in a stolen boat. Brought as a gift to Ping Wen, or else to Tunghai Wang. Two traitors in stranded opposition, and yes, Dandan could see why the emperor would leave them so. And why the girls would be so potent a gift, to either one: how this one boat's one journey could turn the war.

"Come," Jiao said, watching all that parade of thoughts as it tumbled slowly through Dandan's reeling head. "Let's go and see what my tiger's caught me. If he's left any of them alive."

JIAO HAD the boy—Pao was his name—drag a line above the high-water mark and anchor it among the rocks, in case the beached boat should float free on the rising tide. The big girl Jin had to carry little Shola ashore, through water that was breast-high already; Dandan needed to let the waves lift her as they came, or she would have been mouth-under.

Dripping wet on dry land, Jiao set them in marching order, the girls and the boy and Dandan too. She put herself last, where she could overwatch the line. At her word the two girls set off, firmly hand in hand and it was hard to tell which one led which, though Dandan thought she knew.

She thought that between them, she and the boy Pao might have overpowered this new Jiao who sounded so brash but walked so tentative, who had struggled to climb down on the ladder.

But this new Jiao had her tiger, which was out of sight but had probably not gone beyond earshot. It had left a trail. Here was a body on the beach, some fool rebel who had lingered to watch the slaughter in the boat's shadow, thinking himself safe away. Finding himself wrong. He must have turned to run again, too late, seeing the tiger bound toward him; he lay on his belly, in the bloody rags of his clothing, with the spine torn out of his body.

The tiger hadn't lingered, it had killed and run on. There were dark marks in the sand, bloody pawprints on the rocks. Jiao waved them on, but Dandan balked, just for a moment. If they must encounter more bodies, at least the girls needn't be first in line, the ones who found the dead.

Besides, there was the tiger. Jiao might trust it; she might not care. Neither of those was true of Dandan.

Swiftly, trying to seem indomitable, she set the girls behind her, in Pao's care, and took the lead herself. Jiao only watched with flat black eyes and an ominous silence.

On, then. On over the rocks, where she had come to gather seaweed. She had had a purpose then, her old men; she had had a basket. Almost she looked around to find it, somewhere on the tideline at their backs. Almost, she thought she ought to fetch it. Almost.

But she could hear the tiger somewhere ahead, beyond the rocks; with the girls at her back, she really had no choice. Someone had to show them how to face tigers.

Like this: up over the rocky margin to the dunes and broken land behind, where men might think—for a minute, for a little minute—that they had room and time to run.

Until the tiger ran them down, one by one, to leave bodies like footprints sprawled all in a line.

Cats will defend their kill. It was standing four-square astride the last in line, and the salt air rumbled with its growling.

As they came closer, Dandan saw that the man was moving, if only a little, while the tiger's belly-hair dripped seawater on his body.

She seemed to be walking more slowly. Well, she had reason for that. It wasn't the fear—or no, of course it was the fear, she was terrified entirely, she had seen nothing of this animal except its willingness to kill, but it was more than that. What was she meant to *do* . . . ?

In her mind, perhaps she could walk up to a tiger where it stood above its prey. Her legs might not manage it, but her imagination could. After that, though, even her imagination failed, came to a dead stop, as her legs did when the tiger lifted its head to look at her.

Still growling.

It still had blood on its teeth. Its tongue licked suddenly, threateningly at its lips as it looked at her.

She didn't turn away, she couldn't move. She heard Pao muster the girls to one side, so that Jiao had a clear path forward; she heard the woman's boots on rock and sand and weed, she heard the woman's breath at her ear with that little catch in it that spoke of pain, constant and endurable and foul.

Dandan couldn't even lift her eyes, apparently, not take them from the tiger's.

She could speak. Apparently. She said, "Will it do what you want?"

"If he wants to."

Dandan meant, of course, *can you keep it from attacking us?* Jiao's answer was not reassuring. The woman had maybe meant it that way. There was a bitter amusement in her voice. Everything in her seemed bitter now, and everything that came out of her: a broken stem that oozed an acrid sap.

The tiger had leaped down from the boat and attacked the rebels, just at her word. It had left Dandan alone and chased the survivors, which was even more extraordinary, again at her instruction. More and somehow worse, *save me one of those men* she had called down from the deck, and apparently it had done exactly that. In honesty, Dandan thought that Jiao could tell it to step away, lie down, be quiet; she thought it would do those things. Not like a dog, not in obedience, but she thought it would do them anyway. Jiao might not admit it—wanting to feel better about herself, perhaps, or else wanting to be more cruel than she seemed—but the tiger wasn't in control here. It was pure and deadly with a lust to kill, and it was entirely an aspect of Jiao's unfathomable will.

She thought.

Even when she was afraid, Dandan could be angry. Even when she was angry, she could still want other people's lives to be better. She said, "How does it know? What you want?" meaning *I know that you're in charge. You should know it too.*

Jiao laughed shortly. "He sits in my head and listens. I think. I don't know why he does that. His choice, not mine. He's not *trained,*" for all the world as if she sat in Dandan's head and had listened to her own thought about a dog's obedience. "I don't take him for granted."

Yes, you do, Dandan thought. Even if what she took ultimately for granted was that sooner or later it would make the other choice, and turn on her. Jiao wouldn't care. Or thought she wouldn't.

For now, Dandan said, "You told it to save you one," *and it knew, just exactly what you wanted,* which the more she thought about that, the more frightened she could be. They said the dragon had a boy now, but this woman had a tiger and she thought that was worse. "It did that, but if you want that man to live you should probably let me look at him. Which means you have to make the tiger step away."

Jiao laughed. "Are you frightened of my tiger, little one?" It sounded forced, and entirely false. Jiao was not as easy as she pretended, though it was not the tiger that concerned her. She was having trouble dealing with people, Dandan thought, in this new incarnation, unless it was herself she couldn't deal with.

Dandan said, "Yes, of course I am, how not? And so are the children," with a jerk of her head to encompass the girls and Pao too. He would be angry if he heard that. "And that man between its paws will die of fear, if he doesn't die of his hurts first."

"If my tiger doesn't eat him first." Jiao gave Dandan a wintry smile, then unwrapped a chain from where it lay coiled above her bony hips. She swung it casually one-handed and strolled forward, into the tiger's complaint.

And spoke to the beast as a woman might to a recalcitrant youth who was sulking and dangerous and still susceptible to bullying. Dandan couldn't hear the words but she knew the tone exactly, she used it herself: on the boy Gieh, often and often on her two old men.

The tiger kept up that rolling roil of a growl, but there seemed to be no great intent behind it. Not enough, at any rate, to challenge Jiao. Who fastened one end of the chain to a leather collar around the tiger's heavy neck, doubled the other about her fist and heaved unhurriedly, until at last the tiger moved away at her side. Unless it was the other way around, that she paced the tiger as it went padding slowly over the rocks, all weight and purpose until it lay down abruptly in the sunlight and began to wash, all cat.

Dandan was no doctor, but she had learned to be a nurse. She gave the injured rebel as much attention as she could manage, with half an eye still on the tiger and half on Jiao, half again on the girls and their watchful boy. She thought, most likely, the man would survive. She used his ruined clothes to tie up the worst of his wounds, as he groaned and sweated and lacked the strength to yell aloud.

He was another gift that Ping Wen would no doubt be glad of, a man from Tunghai Wang's camp to be interrogated; which meant that if he was stubborn, if he wouldn't talk—well.

It would mean work, another kind of work for Ai Guo, and she was helping.

five

Siew Ren was sitting up and talking when the soldiers came.

Not sitting up and laughing, no. Never that, never yet. Not sitting in the sunshine either; she wouldn't leave the gloom of her little hut, didn't want to join her clan-cousins in the world again. Not ready for that. Whether it was the scars that held her back or the abiding weakness, Biao wasn't sure and she wouldn't say. Couldn't say, perhaps. Something kept her clinging to the shadows.

Still, though: sitting up. Talking. In the softest, thinnest voice, but talking in any sort was progress. Sitting up was a triumph.

Biao wished, he really wished that he could claim its credit for himself.

He would have done so if only the truth weren't so widely known, so vividly on display about her shoulders, beneath Yu Shan's possessive arm.

She sat up with the tiger-skin wrapped around her, the only brightness in the dark of the hut; she spoke from its embrace.

Biao had brought it to her, his little inspiration. He had tucked it around her in the bed, despite her tears and protests, despite her pain; and that same night she had started to improve, and now—

Well. Now she sat up in bed and nestled into Yu Shan's side, and spoke to him.

Now there was a succession of the injured, making their slow negotiated way from neighbor-valleys, neighbor-clans. Some came daily. Some came in litters, and stayed.

Biao was almost not a doctor now, as he almost never had been. Now he was more or less the Keeper of the Skin. Something like a palace eunuch, organizing and arranging: who would be treated when, how long each might claim the skin each day.

Some days he even took it out of the valley. He went under guard, and was never sure if the guards were there to protect him or to contain him, to prevent his running off with it; but still, he was allowed to go, to treat those too hurt to come to him.

Siew Ren was always reluctant to let him go, though really that only meant the skin. She was reluctant even to see it set around someone else's shoulders, even here in her own hut, even just for an hour. Biao and Yu Shan both told her and told her that it was not hers, she couldn't claim it, she couldn't keep it to herself. It was a gift, they said, from the mountain gods who watched over all the clans at once, or else from the jade tigers, from the tiger herself who gave it up; it was a gift to everyone who needed it, and she must share.

She had cried when Biao first wrapped her in it, but she cried again when he first took it away. That time, Yu Shan had moved to stop him. He had to argue against the determined passion of a young man distraught and hopeful both at once, furious and physically daunting.

Biao had no chance ever of wresting the skin away from Siew Ren's frantic clutch, let alone Yu Shan's. He only had his words to rely on, as ever—except that this time he had common justice too. Even truth, perhaps. That was something new.

He didn't actually know how to deal with the truth, so he simply treated it as another lie, familiar territory, fuel for his insinuating tongue.

He left the girl and the skin together in their shadows, drew the young man outside.

Said, "Yu Shan, she has to give it up."

"No. She needs it. You *brought* it to her, and she needs it. You said that. You can't take it away now."

"She needs it, yes. She is not the only one."

"She is worst. Worst hurt," which still bit at Yu Shan like a deliberate cruelty, that it should be his girl who suffered most. "She needs it most."

"And has had it for a full day and a night together and is better already, you know that. You can see." That morning there had been a procession of clan elders through the hut, specifically to see. There had been much muttering and stroking of beards, stroking of the tiger-skin. Plans hatched, no doubt, possession to be disputed. Biao needed to establish his own authority quickly. "Even now, you can't call her worst hurt any longer. You could call her fastest mending."

"But if you take it away from her—"

"Only for an hour at a time. She won't get worse again, Yu Shan. I promise you that. It might even be good for her. What's happening now is magical, the influence of jade or, or the gods," he had nearly said *the immortals* but that was so obviously, so spectacularly the wrong word, he bit it back unformed. If this was a miracle, it was wrought in death. "You know yourself," *jade-eater,* "too much exposure to the stone will change a man; and stone is cold and dead, long dead. How much more may change, how much *must* change, when one is wrapped around by what was freshly living, jade in the tiger? Here on Taishu you say that jade is the dragon's tears, but I think you are wrong, or else that is an old story retold with a new ending. Here, now, I think jade is the tiger's blood, and I think we should be careful with it. Too much of any magic can be . . . well, too much. Too much for a mortal to sustain. We should give Siew Ren's body a chance to begin its own healing."

Yu Shan looked at him for a moment, said, "You don't know that. You don't know *any* of that."

"No," Biao said regretfully, uncomfortable outside his proper

ground, trapped in truth. "No, I don't. I'm . . . not exactly guessing, but the next best thing," remembering Jiao and how she
looked, how she moved, caught in the snare of too-hasty healing.
And again with the truth, open honesty, "I saw Jiao and you didn't.
I may be wrong, of course—but do you want to make that experiment on Siew Ren?"

No. No, he didn't. Biao talked more, a lot more, about potent medicines and sensible dilution, strong sun and the need
for shade, rest after food, all the examples he could think of; but he
had won already. He just had to give Yu Shan time to realize it.

At first the other patients all came to Siew Ren's hut, so that
the skin could be taken from her shoulders—by Yu Shan, his gentle fingers working against hers, irresistibly—and immediately
wrapped around another's. Where she could see it, where she
could still grip the edge of it, make believe that she was only loan-
ing out, not quite relinquishing. Keeping hold.

At first they came only from this valley, their own clan. As word
spread, others began to make their difficult, painful way through
the mountains to bargain for their own miracle, a little time in
touch with the tiger's hide. Which might have been refused, should
have been impossible if these hadn't been friends, comrades hurt
in common battle, blood-kin. Might still have been refused if Biao
hadn't been there, detached and respected, to put the case for sharing: to say, at the last, "Do you truly want a war? There will be
war, if you try to keep this thing to yourselves."

Scarred men shrugged; there always had been war, between one
clan and the next. What difference?

"The difference is that you used to fight for land. This would be
for life itself. And it would go on and on. Whoever took it, they
would be the next attacked. There would be more and more hurt
for the skin to heal, too much. It is a wonder, but you would destroy yourselves over it. No one clan can claim this thing, or the
clans will be dead in a generation."

It was his skill to be glib and persuasive, more of a wonder than the miracles he peddled. This time he had a legitimate miracle, and still needed to outshine it.

"How can we manage it, then?" one old man asked. When they turned to him for the answer, he knew that he'd won. Like Yu Shan, they laid themselves in his hands, and were barely aware of it.

"Leave it with me," he said, just that one little step short of *it is mine*. They would come to accept that slowly, as he handled it, as he made the decisions and they did not.

They had done so, even to the point of letting him take it out of the valley. He allowed guards to come with him, for the clan's own comfort. Never as many as the elders would have sent: "I welcome your protection," he said, "but I do not need an army massed about me. I am just one man alone with a skin, in the end. Everyone knows me, everyone knows what I bring. No one will harm me, no one will steal what I carry."

His best guarantee of that lay in the fact that what he said was not quite true. He could send all the guards away and it would still not be true, that he was just one man alone.

There was one, not quite a guard, who would never leave him.

Would never leave the skin, rather, not let it out of his sight.

"Yu Shan," Biao said, quite mildly, "I thought it was Siew Ren you loved?"

The tall young man said nothing, only reached to touch the wonder-skin with tentative, expressive fingers.

"And yet you leave her," Biao went on relentlessly, "overnight and longer, we'll be two days on the road together this time . . ."

For once they were on their own, or at least their escort was asleep. Biao and the boy were sitting up over a late low fire. Biao had trouble sleeping, such a treasure in his grasp; Yu Shan seemed to need no sleep at all.

Biao was talking nonsense and he knew it. Goading Yu Shan was like goading jade. He sat there smooth and silent and only said, "I need to be sure."

"Sure of what?"

"That the skin comes back."

Not *that you bring it back,* not quite. Biao still had work to do.

AND WAS doing it, in a manner of speaking, back in Siew Ren's hut, when the soldiers came.

They were in the doorway suddenly, blocking what little light there was: soldiers as Biao knew them best, veterans, road-scarred. Set these men among Tunghai Wang's and they would have been indistinguishable.

Soldiers can go anywhere, can be found anywhere; and yet they seemed out of place here, suddenly in the mountains, in the valley, at the door. It was remarkable that they had been let come this far. Mountain folk are jealous of what little they have, their land, their lives. They do not suffer strangers gladly or often.

These strangers wore yellow sashes in their uniforms, which said they came from the emperor. He was a friend known and welcome; even so, Biao thought he should have sent a runner from the clans, some green-eyed youngster who would know the ways of the hills. He still had plenty such among his guard. And he would have thought of that, or if he had not Mei Feng would have reminded him, and when did the emperor ever do anything without Mei Feng's blessing?

Which meant that sashes or no sashes, these men were not from the emperor; which meant . . .

Which meant that Biao needed to be careful, but that was his common condition. He needn't worry for his own skin, not here. The clansfolk would protect that for him. No matter how good these soldiers were, jade-soaked valley warriors would be faster and stronger and very much more vicious.

There would be warriors all around these now, hands openly on tao-hilts, distrust openly on their faces. Arrows nocked to bowstrings. Biao need only concern himself with what the men brought:

news, a request, a summons perhaps except that he would not go. The people here—his people now, he liked to think, he wanted them to think—would not let the soldiers take him.

Biao rose to his feet, went out, left his patient with Yu Shan.

Said, "Well, what? The swifter you name your errand, the swifter you can be away again."

From the shifting unease on their faces, they wanted nothing more. The clansfolk around them were standing very close, and there were naked blades playing with the sunlight. But the soldiers were stubborn, they were dutiful. Their captain said, "Master Biao, we have been sent to fetch you back to Taishu-port, to the palace."

That was more or less what he had expected. Their disappointment could wait a little; let them gather slowly that he wasn't coming. He said, "Who sent you?"

"The dowager empress." That was honest, and should make it easier to refuse. The empress had no particular authority on Taishu. Of course she had the weight of years and experience, widow of one emperor and mother of another; of course her words mattered and her wishes commanded men—but not in opposition to her son's words and wishes, not anymore. And not so much in the mountains here. The clans were independent-minded. They knew the emperor, some of their own had fought with him. He had both their allegiance and their loyalty. His mother might be twice an empress, might have jade in her own blood to make her so tough and let her live so long; she was still a stranger from far and far away, they knew nothing of her, they owed her nothing.

They would not let soldiers take their doctor.

Biao was confident of that.

He said, "I cannot come, these people need me here; but why does the empress want me? Is she ill? She has doctors of her own," whom she had haled with her all the way from the far north. She would have better reasons to trust them than him.

"The empress is eternal." Which was obviously not true, not even emperors were eternal. Though the boy Chien Hua was doing his best to perpetuate the myth, surviving wars and assassins, recovering from lethal wounds, having knife blades break against his imperial green hide.

A captain of the military must know that his old woman would not live forever. His meaning was plain; he meant *the empress is well, and does not need your doctoring.* So, then . . . ?

Biao waited. Soon enough the man went on. "She doesn't want you for herself, and it isn't you she wants. You have a thing of magic, she has heard, a tiger-skin that heals . . ."

Of course she had heard. Biao had sent messages himself, to alert the palace to this wonderful thing, and whose hands held it safe. He wanted it written and known. "In the right hands," he said gruffly, "it will heal, yes." That was nonsense too, his hands held no gift. But the skin was his, he felt somehow that he had earned it; he would not part with it. Nor would the clansfolk. He and the skin were one. The soldiers would not be let leave with either one of them. Already he could see blades being raised with purpose.

He made a little sign with his hands, *gently now, gently.* "If not for herself, what use does the empress have for my tiger-skin, or me? It is not a trophy, to hang unused in a palace hall."

"The emperor's favorite, Mei Feng, is sick. Sick to death, most likely; and likely to lose the emperor's baby, if it has not already died inside her. The empress will do anything to save that child."

Naturally. And the emperor would do anything to save Mei Feng, only that he hadn't thought of this. Or else thought of it and dismissed it. That seemed less than likely, except . . .

Biao said, "There is a skin in the palace already. Yu Shan told me he had seen it there."

"That has been tried. Mei Feng has lain beneath it for two days, two nights together, and she only grows worse."

The emperor would be despairing, surrendering to fate, watching his beloved die and believing in nothing anymore. The empress would be despairing and clutching at straws. Sending for anyone, anything that might promise hope. It was the difference between youth and age; Biao recognized it intimately.

A blade had broken on the emperor's back, and still he doubted. He was all boy yet; it was a weakness, open to exploit. Biao was talking already, and somehow not bluffing for a wonder, speaking perfect truth. "I don't know why the palace skin would not be effective, unless it is simply too old. Or not genuine, perhaps that, not a true stone tiger." No bluff now about the needed hands of a healer. He was on safe ground, and meant to stay there. "Mine is . . . assured. And people rise up better than they were. I cannot promise that it will heal Mei Feng, or her baby; it may be too late already. You should have come to me sooner. Still, I am willing to make the attempt." He was surprising no one, gratifying no one. Of course he would go, for the emperor's favorite. He must go. There was no choice in the world.

"No," said a voice at his back.

That was Yu Shan: risen from Siew Ren's bedside—*like the emperor*, Biao thought, *rising from Mei Feng's bedside, that must be as rare as this*—to stand four-square in the doorway of the hut behind them, blinking at the sun, his arms spread across the open entrance and his immaculate strong body like a locked gate, *you shall not pass.*

"No," he said again, "you can't take it. Not to the city. Siew Ren needs it here."

It was true. And so were the soldiers' hands on their weapons true, and so were the clansfolk's blades rising again, the glitter of arrowheads in the sun. So was the foretelling stink of blood in the air, that was very true.

Biao said, "I will come back. A day's journey to the palace, a night's sleep for Mei Feng beneath the skin, a day's journey back here again," he had almost said *back home.* "I've been gone that long between one valley and the next. Siew Ren will be fine until tomorrow night."

It was true, not a word of a lie; but Yu Shan saw too truly. He said, "What, you think one night will cure her? And her baby too? There is magic in your tiger-skin, but not that much, Master Biao. I think perhaps less with every day, I think it's fading. Failing." And then again, "No. Do you think they will let you go, if you can help Mei Feng? They will keep you there however long it takes: days, weeks. Until the baby's born, and later too. You know they will."

True, and true again. Yu Shan gave him nothing to deny. Until right at the last, the boy overran himself in his enthusiasm. He said, "I won't let you take the skin. I won't let you go."

"Oh, and what, will you outspeak the emperor? These men speak for him," even if he didn't know it yet, if his mother hadn't told him. "Is your voice stronger?"

A momentary hesitation, then Yu Shan said, "My voice is nearer. My voice is *here.*"

"And so is the emperor's, through these men."

"If they try to take you away . . ."

"What, will you kill them all? You could, of course. And what will the emperor do then?"

"These come from his mother."

"They do," and they were looking frightened in that dangerous way that reaches for weapons. Biao tried to still them with the same gesture he had used before to the clansfolk, *gently, gently, let the wise solve this with words.* "And do you not think perhaps his mother will speak to him about it, if her men don't return to her with the skin—and the doctor, yes—who might cure his beloved? If they don't return at all? Yu Shan, be sensible. I have to go; you have to let me go," as though he had any voice in this at all.

"No . . ." But he was weakening, he was ready to be persuaded.

"I will go; I will come back. I will bring the skin back. I have promised."

"How?"

"I will bring Mei Feng back too." It was that easy, in the end. "She was happier anyway, when she lived out here with you. I will wrap her in the skin and fetch her back to the mountains, and then everybody will do well," and he would have one more coin to bargain with, a golden coin, jade-bright as a tiger's eye.

six

There needn't be trumpets. Nor fireworks, though there were in fact fireworks almost every night now. They were gaudy and welcome and superfluous.

Triumph could be a quiet thing, Chung had learned. It could be what came after the fireworks, in the absence of trumpets. Slipping into his bed, into his heart; a whisper in his ear, a hidden touch in the dark, contentment. Contentment could be triumph, indistinguishable.

Shen had come to him—across a dragon-guarded sea, through a war-shattered city, along a typhoon-wreaked valley: Chung could make that a march of heroes, privately in his head, if he wanted to—and it might have been triumph enough, something to be treasured.

More than that, though, Shen had stayed with him. The battle might be over, but not the war; there were still two armies in the land. There was Santung-city to be made strong, to be defended. There was a new governor in need of good advice, good soldiers. There were daily patrols and nightly raiding-parties sneaking out to confront Tunghai's rebels: to harry, to drive off, to destroy.

That above all, actual fighting. Chung had not realized how much fighting there would still be, between two armies caught in an inglorious deadlock. The one not quite besieged, the other not quite defeated, loyalties uncertain on both sides. Every day there were lines of men on either bank, heading out beyond known perimeters, dragging wearily back with wounded and with prisoners, reports.

Shen could be a part of that, rising into fame. He should be, for reasons that were as obvious to Chung as they were to him, even before he spelled them out in brutal, painful detail. Fighting was what he did, it made the definition of the man he was; his shoulder was healed well enough to be disregarded, if not quite depended on; his skills and temper would make him genuinely useful to the governor and hence to the emperor. In his own mind he was wasted here, useless to anyone but Chung.

And yet, he chose to stay. Here on this little river island, isolated from the real army and the real war. Avoided, indeed, by everyone outside their own small band of artificers. Condemned as crazy, dangerous, likely to explode at any moment.

Food and other supplies were left on the bank by the footings of the bridge. If there was a message, it was a bold soul who would cross the water to deliver it. Messages were few, in any case, and mostly variations on *Please don't do that.*

Which made Chung smile when Shen laughed raspingly, before he rolled the paper into a twist around black powder to make another fuse.

Isolation draws men tight together, where it doesn't tear them apart. No one had to stay, but few were leaving; the core of Chung's little team was still those rebels who had surrendered to the emperor, unless it was to Yu Shan, unless it was to him.

Santung could not be defended, that was known. It was Chung's task, almost his self-appointed task, to prove it untrue.

This steep-sided valley was his proving-ground. Water and mud and stone, river and rain and ruined paddy, broken walls and crumbling terraces: it was his entirely, while he learned the possibilities of what he had to play with.

If he succeeded, the world would call that his triumph, and be wrong.

This was his triumph, this man at his side who shared his hopes and ideas, his failures and losses, his meals and his bedroll and his dreams.

WHAT WAS coming up the river now, that was a procession, almost a circus. Not a triumph.

Chung stood on the island's downstream peak, below the bridge, with Shen beside him and his men packed close behind, all their attention on the succession of boats that rowed blazingly, blaringly against the current to come to them.

Chung had fireworks; the boats had trumpets. Again and again they sounded across the water, proclaiming all the yellow in the canopies and pennants, in the costumes of the men who rowed and the soldiers who stood on guard at prow and stern.

Privately, Chung thought there was perhaps a little too much yellow. After spending time at court, time with the emperor himself, a lot of time squatting in corners waiting for Mei Feng's summons, he had some sense of propriety. A governor was the emperor's representative, speaking with his voice and authority—but yellow was the emperor's own color, which made it some kind of sacred, and a mortal man ought to be more careful.

A mortal man with only half an army, especially so, when he had enemies in the country all around.

Unless Chung could compensate for those absent soldiers and more. Rewrite the rules of war, almost. In his bleak times, untriumphant, he felt he was being asked to do just that.

And here came Ping Wen now, to review his progress.

He didn't feel ready at all.

"You're ready," Shen murmured at his elbow. "We will show him wonders, you and I."

"Well, not that," Chung said. At the second attempt, touching dry lips with a dry tongue. "Something, though, at least we have something to show him."

.   .   .

PING WEN stepped ashore on the river's bank, not on the island. Landing directly from a boat was always awkward, always graceless. All the traffic came and went by river now that the road was so chewed up and the slope above so dangerous, but almost always with this little hiatus, a step aside onto the bank and so over the bridge.

Or not. For most traffic, the step ashore was already too close to the foolhardy with their flashes and bangs and fires. Bundles and barrels could be left there on the bank, moorings hurriedly slipped and boats away on the rapid current.

Not today. Drums and trumpets and flags, and a slow assembly; Chung sent his men to their places, while he and Shen climbed to the high arch of the bridge.

They had discussed this, of course: how to greet the governor, what the protocols should be. Whether a governor ranked higher than a general, when both ranks dwelled in the same body.

They had discussed it and not agreed, could not agree. In the end Shen wouldn't talk about it anymore, so Chung was stranded in his uncertainty.

In the end, now, he realized that he was going to do exactly as Shen did: which was no doubt exactly what Shen had wanted all along.

PING WEN saw them waiting, and understood that to be for him; understood the ground they met on, the narrow span of it and all the uncertainty beneath; chose to leave his retinue and come alone up the steep boards of the bridge, to that apex where they stood.

Possibly he expected them to greet him on their knees, kowtowing, striking their heads off those same boards.

Possibly, then, he was disappointed. Shen stood erect and greeted him with a low and soldierly bow, an officer to his commander, no more than that. Chung had been a little distracted, thinking that Ping Wen was quite definitely wearing too much yellow; there was hardly room for any color else.

But the emperor was far away, and this man held all the power of his office. Chung was only a fraction late in bowing; and then, wondering what next, he was delighted by his joy, his triumph, Shen.

Who paced slowly backward before the governor down the difficult slope of the bridge, drawing Chung along with him with not a touch, not a glance, only a perfect trust. So they became Ping Wen's forerunners, his bannermen, while they remained still utterly in possession of what was theirs, like a gate closed against him: a gate that opened only at their own choosing, at the foot of the bridge, as they stepped one either side and bowed again, scrupulously low, not so much soldiers now as hosts welcoming a guest. At their invitation, on their sufferance.

PING WEN must have hated that, and could speak not a word against it.

IN HIS train came functionaries and guards, but Ping Wen was all that mattered here. Ping Wen and his satisfaction. However much they might play with protocol and take advantage of any ambiguity, Chung really did want to keep what he had here. His little platoon, his machinery, his island. His fireworks. His Shen. His entire triumph, he wanted to preserve it all intact, and Ping Wen's favor was his only means to do that.

Shen was ahead of him, literally at least: gesturing the governor toward the new machines, cautioning him away from black oil and powder, showing him prepared pots with their fuses. Explaining how the machines worked, with all their ropes and tethers. Wafting a hand at the men standing by, crews eager to work.

Casting a swift glance back at Chung, *this is your triumph, do you want me to steal it all?*

It wasn't stealing, if he made a gift of it.

Even so, Chung stepped forward to join them, to stand at Ping Wen's other elbow and say, "We are ready to demonstrate what we've achieved, my lord governor." Shen was calling him *my lord general;* it was almost wonderful how they made a matched pair, how they divided duties naturally between them. "Um, the process is not entirely without risk," indeed the lord governor's lordly yellow slippers were standing in a black stain on the rock that even scrubbing had not been able to shift, where an early experiment had gone catastrophically wrong and nearly killed them all. Who knew that a half-filled pot, a leaking pot would be more deadly than a full one? There seemed no reason to it. "It might be wiser for your excellence to remove to the farther end of the island," beyond the stone bridge-footings, where his entourage awaited. "Or even perhaps to view from the bank?" Send him over the bridge, remove this tall watchful terrifying man from Chung's territory altogether, let him not threaten the triumph . . .

"I am a soldier," Ping Wen said, mildly aligning himself with Shen instead of Chung. "Where my men stand in danger, so do I." Chung felt an urge to say *they are my men, or else we are all the emperor's men, you too*—but fortunately he was not quite such a fool as that. Besides, Shen knew, and was frowning at him mightily. "I will watch from here, if I am not in the way of your work."

No, no, they assured him, not in the way at all, if he would only take two paces backward, not to stand so exactly between the stack of projectiles and the flinging-arm of the first machine. They were only sorry, they said, that they couldn't offer him a chair to sit on. As he could see, they were very barely furnished here. There were boxes, there were chests, there was perhaps a ridge of rock . . . ?

A sharp clap of his hands summoned a functionary at an urgent anxious trot. A word sent the man back to the bridge. His own word had two soldiers racing over the water and back again in very short order, with a heavy ornate chair in gold and red lacquer slung between them.

A servant from the boat followed, with a cushion in his hands. That was . . . well, Chung supposed that the fabric could be said to be gold, though when the man set it down for Ping Wen it did look very yellow next to the actual gold of the chair's embellishments.

If Ping Wen had ordered it made for himself—well. It was almost a declaration.

He directed the positioning of his chair, had it moved once because it was unsteady and a second time because he feared an obstructed view. Shen was the very image of respectful patience, a rock carved standing with his hands behind his back. Chung twitched and fidgeted, felt himself doing it, could do nothing to stop it. Not by himself. It needed Shen's arm to reach out—a rock that moved, a miracle!—to take his wrist and grip it wordlessly. Shen's own stillness crept into Chung from that touch, and lingered even after Shen's hand retreated behind his back again.

They waited, then, side by side until the governor was settled and content. At his nod, Shen released Chung with a glance—*this is yours now, your achievement; show it off now, be triumphant*—and went himself to stand behind Ping Wen's chair while Chung joined his men around the machine.

He didn't really need to be there. The men had drilled and drilled for this, they knew exactly what they were to do. He wanted, though, to lay his own hands to the work. More, he wanted Shen—whose shoulder would not bear the weight of the work—to be the one who explained things to the governor, that soft insidious voice speaking soldier to soldier.

He couldn't have that, it seemed. Shen stood mute: of malice, he was sure. Ping Wen waited inquiringly until Chung had to lift his head, lift his voice, almost shout to be sure his words would carry:

"Tunghai Wang built machines like this, and set them here. They flung pots across the water, filled with a liquid that caught fire when they struck and broke. Like this . . ."

A nod to his men and they went into action, drawing down the flinging-arm and loading its basket, standing to the ropes when all was ready. Chung himself touched the smoking end of a slow-match to the pot's fuse. "Fling!"

Ping Wen already knew everything that Chung had told him; and he knew most of what was to come, or else he himself would not have come this far to see it. One did not surprise the great. Besides, Ping Wen had no doubt seen such war-machines before. Used them, very likely. He had been a genuine soldier under the old emperor.

The men heaved, the long arm hurled upward, the pot flew from its basket and seemed almost to hang in the air for a moment at the top of its arc, black and strange, before it crashed down to earth. They always did that.

They didn't always land quite where Chung intended. It was nothing but relief to see the projectile strike rock, rather than splash into the water; relief again when it functioned perfectly, breaking apart and giving Ping Wen a moment's clear view of its viscous black contents before the eruption of bright flame.

Chung let the governor watch for a minute how the flame clung, how it burned rock and mud together.

Then he explained—swiftly and concisely, because he had practiced this as much as the men had practiced pulling ropes—how he revised the missiles to make them explode in mid-air. For demonstration, they loaded the same machine and shifted its aim farther along the riverbank, to where a makeshift cluster of head-high poles and taut-stretched banners stood in for enemy soldiers.

"Fling!"

Nothing could go wrong today. It was his triumph. The projectile rose, and hung, and fell; the flame ate down the shorter fuse and licked in through the touch-hole; there was a flash too bright—too yellow, they were all usurping the emperor's prerogative today—for the sun to drown it, a bang that was frightening even at this distance, even to those who were waiting for it.

When the smoke cleared, Ping Wen could see exactly what Chung had hoped for, poles ripped from the ground and banners shredded, everything on fire.

"That was a lucky shot," he called to the governor, disarmingly confessional. "They don't always explode at exactly the right time; they don't always reach the distance. But if an army marched along this road, we could sit here in safety and promise to destroy it."

That was an opening, an obvious flaw. He left it open deliberately, like a gate; the governor obligingly stepped through it.

"This valley is not the only way to approach the city; that road—what is left of that road—is not the only way to pass this valley."

"Indeed, your excellence. If the army marched along the ridge up there, we could not fling our pots that high. If we stood on the same ground as the enemy, we could destroy the front ranks of a charge, but the reach of this machine is just too short; by the time we had reloaded, the ranks behind would have swamped us. What we needed was greater range.

"A pot that rose higher would fall farther off, but the oil used by Tunghai Wang," picking up a little jar of it and tipping, pouring a thin stream carefully into another jar, treating it with due respect even while he disparaged it, "is too heavy for a machine like this to fling high or far. In the same warehouse, though, we found many of the powders used for fireworks; and in your service in Santung we found artificers who used to design and make fireworks for imperial celebrations. We brought them here," the last crucial ingredient in his little team, "and they worked on the canisters while we, Shen and I worked on the machine itself." While they made one entirely new, indeed, with a longer arm and longer ropes, and no simple basket at the flinging-end but a complex sling of rope and net to extend its reach farther yet, to flick like a whip and so send the missile hurtling on its way.

First—purely for comparative purposes, and not at all because he was a showman, no—he demonstrated how far the old machine could throw a powder-projectile: not really halfway up the steep slope of the valley's side, but close enough that he could call it so. And the blessed thing exploded just as it ought, in a fierce sheet of flame: did he have the Li-goddess at his back, had he fetched her here from Taishu on the wings of his wishing, to have this perfect day fall into place about him . . . ?

While Ping Wen must still have been considering what such a weapon could do to the massed ranks of Tunghai Wang's army, on any road or across any field, Chung moved his men to the new machine. And loaded its net, set its aim, had them fling.

The projectile soared, a high black dot against the blue of the sky; it fell to earth up on the ridge there, exploded there, phenomenal.

Ping Wen perhaps didn't realize it but he was beaming behind his mustaches.

"With some few of these machines around the city, excellency, you could put an army to rout from such a distance your own men would never be in danger."

"Yes," was the answer. "Yes . . ." And then, because of course no one in authority is ever truly satisfied, "Can you make the, the missile go higher?"

"Higher, excellency, yes." They had done that; but, "If it goes higher, it does not go so far." Trial and error had taught them the perfect trajectory. Which he had just demonstrated, and for some reason Ping Wen wanted more, he wanted something other.

"Work on that. Oh, I will send men to you, and you will teach them how to make these machines, and the . . . missiles . . . they fling. And how to use them, of course. Pass on your skills. But you, particularly: I want you to work on this. Make a machine that will fling a canister high, high. And have it explode high too. At the height of its arc. Work on that."

seven

Old age is all about loss, measurements of loss. He knew that: he had seen it in his grandfather, in his father, in himself.

BUT OLD Yen had lost his boat, and that was immeasurable.

FOR A while, for a little while it had almost been supportable. It had almost not mattered, when he thought he would lose his granddaughter. When all he could see was Mei Feng shrinking in the too-big bed, shrinking into her too-small self, and someone came to tell him that his bastard boat was missing from the quay. Was it the emperor, looking back? No, surely not, he surely would have noticed that . . .

Whoever it was, he had barely understood them at the time. Had let the words wash by him, almost unregarded. Might have grunted, perhaps, some kind of acknowledgment. Perhaps.

Then the doctor came from the mountains, with his tiger-skin. That was a bad thing, a jade tiger slain. There had been talk of a jade tiger on the quay, on a chain; he hadn't troubled himself over that. This, though, this skin was right here under his eyes, vivid green and black, as though some distant forest sunlight fell on it still, even in the shadows of the sickroom.

Out of great evil, a good could come. Perhaps. So said Master Biao. He wasn't like the other doctors, the emperor's, the old woman's. Not haughty, not a courtier, not palace-trained at all. Old Yen trusted him not at all, but in a totally different way from

how he didn't trust the palace doctors. This one he thought perhaps might make a difference.

And perhaps he did, or at least his tiger-skin. Old Yen was
afraid of any good that might come from such an evil, he feared
some taint might creep into Mei Feng from the naked contact of
the skin, the raw rotten ill-cured leather that showed where a knife
had hacked it from the carcass and scraped it clean, not clean
enough.

Still, tainted was better than dead. He thought it was, he hoped
it was; and he did have reason to hope. Master Biao wrapped Mei
Feng in the skin, and she seemed to breathe easier from that moment. After an hour, she opened her eyes. After another, she was
trying to speak. Even trying to withdraw an arm from the skin, to
reach for a goblet of water.

The emperor lifted her and Old Yen held that goblet to her lips,
as he had many and many a potion that the imperial doctors
would have had her drink. This she did drink, she gulped it down
and asked for more; and wriggled into the arms that held her, and
gazed down at her stripe-swaddled self and said, "Oh."

Said, "Oh!"

Said, "Is it, is it meant to, to, to move . . . ?"

Just for a moment, Old Yen thought she meant the tiger-skin.

Then he understood, and his heart twisted inside him.

AFTER THAT she wept, a little. The doctor had her washed and
swaddled her again, and she fell cleanly asleep with her two men
sitting over her. And in a way that was the night that she came
back to her grandfather, and in another way it was the night that
he lost her once again. When she woke Master Biao had become
the man that she would listen to, and he was quite determined to
take her away from Taishu-port, which meant taking her away
from Old Yen.

"She should come to the Autumn Palace," Master Biao said,
meaning the emperor's new Hidden City in the hills. "It will be

quiet there, for her recovery and her baby's growth; and I have other patients, people who were badly hurt to protect the emperor. She cannot have the skin whole to herself, it must be shared."

Nobody could argue with him now, with Mei Feng entirely his, nodding in weak agreement to everything he said, even when he proposed that the dowager empress go with her. "The emperor must stay, of course," *he must let you go*, "he has a world to govern; but you, my lady, you need to rest and restore your strength. Let your baby grow. Away from the world and worry, with eyes to watch you when I cannot, hands to make a home around you. Who better than your child's grandmother? Let her take charge; let her build the palace while you build the baby, while his majesty builds the empire anew. Put yourself in her hands, hers and mine . . ."

In the doctor's vision, there was apparently no place for Old Yen. Nor should there be, of course. He was a fisherman, and the Autumn Palace was as far as you could come on Taishu from the sea.

It was then, sitting there, hearing his granddaughter being taken away from him again, that Old Yen remembered about his boat.

He slipped out of the bedchamber without a word. Found his way out of the palace eventually, blunderingly. Through the courtyards, past the guards: they all knew him, they were all probably surprised to see him leave at last. He was surprised to find it in himself, the strength of leg, the strength of purpose.

Then he thought no, this was the opposite of strength: he was broken and falling away, a dead branch snapped from its stem.

A fisherman without a boat: could anything be sadder or less use?

An old man without his family, perhaps. But granddaughters come and then go: it was only proper. The boat, though—Old Yen had come to it, not it to him. It had been the fixed point all his life, older than the house he lived in. He had built the house he lived in.

He thought the boat had more or less built him, and he had never thought to lose it. Pass it on, yes, when he was too old at last, Too Old Yen—but not lose it, even then. He expected to sit on the headland and watch it out and back again. Possibly with a grand-daughter aboard, he used to imagine that, Mei Feng steering while her strong young man worked the sails and the nets. Or the other way around, perhaps. She liked hauling ropes, she liked to fish; she liked, he thought, to glance astern and see someone she loved with the boat in his charge and her too.

But then her strong young man, the someone she loved turned out to be the emperor. He took her away, and Old Yen had to look for someone else to take the boat.

Pao, he had been thinking.

HE CAME down to the quay like a stranger, shuffling from berth to berth like an old fool who couldn't remember where he had moored, couldn't tell his own boat from a stranger's.

There were boats and boats, the harbor overflowed with boats, and none of them was his. Uselessly, knowing she was gone—yes, and Pao too, stolen with the boat—he still went all along the quay and back, all along the harbor front and everywhere. Every-one saw him, everyone knew. No one spoke to him. What was there to say? They were a gruff community; they left the talking to others.

Something to be glad of.

SOMETHING TO be sorry for: a voice, speaking to him.

Saying, "They took our girls, as well as your boy."

He looked around, and found the temple priestess there: a tiny woman, barely so high as his elbow, like a small fierce coal he had always thought her, incense-sprinkled in a censer. Her own pas-sion raised smoke to the goddess.

He said, "They?"

She said, "The woman. And her tiger."

"Did she fly the dragon's banner?"

She might have lied, of course. A boat can lie.

"The men say not, or not while they could watch her."

A woman with a tiger on a chain, she can certainly lie if she chooses to, but she probably has no need to.

If she had the temple girls, she certainly had no need to. She could sail wherever she chose, and the dragon would not touch her.

OLD YEN wanted to go to sea urgently, and not to fish.

No boat, but he had friends, old friends and a life's legend at his back. He had courage, unless he was confusing that with pride. Above all, he was prepared to lie for what he wanted. Lie a little, and on land. Not on the water. What, to the dragon? Or to the goddess? While his life hung between them . . . ?

Still, he was bold enough to exploit his friends and his legend; to toss courage and pride and faith and skill into the hull of another man's boat, and take it away from him without a qualm.

"HUANG LI, I need the use of your sampan."

Huang Li's sampan had a legend of her own. Right at this moment her master was bailing her, where she bobbed at the end of a long chained line of better boats. When she didn't leak, she swamped; the fleet was all too used to seeing Huang Li pass his fish-baskets up for another boat to carry, while he slipped overboard and turned her entirely turtle, just to empty her of water.

Startled, he said, "You? Need my . . . ?" like an echo that broke somewhere in that little distance between them, that great gulf. Old Yen was unofficial master of the fleet, could have any other boat for the asking and would be better off with any of them, and must know it.

Did know it. Old Yen would face down an old friend with dishonesty; he would not willingly do more harm than he could help, and this was the boat the fleet could best afford to lose.

He might be the man the fleet could least afford to lose, but there was no help for that. Not now.

"You want to fish?"

"Yes." There it was, the first lie: such a little word to take a man's livelihood from him.

"We are just returned from fishing." Obviously they were; there was flurry all around the harbor, baskets and carts and strings of fish. There was a journey's-worth of water in the belly of Huang Li's boat, and he was bailing.

"I know it."

"Well, then . . ."

"Huang Li, you are tired but your boat is not. And I, I have not been to sea for . . . many days," *lost days, irrecoverable; and I have lost my boat, and near enough my granddaughter too,* "and my soul needs it. You have fetched in many fish, but we can never have too many," an appeal to Huang Li's understanding, following the appeal to his heart. Old Yen was learning tricks he didn't like.

Like a boy, he was saying, *like we were boys again, do you remember? I need to row my heart out of its pain, I need to get wet and weary under a hot wet sun, perhaps I need to shout or scream or weep aloud where no one but the sea can hear me. We will not mention the dragon, or the goddess. We will pretend that we are men, and concerned only with fish.*

"Well then," said Huang Li, seeing only the lie of it, the appeal to the boy he used to be, "you will fly the dragon's flag, yes?"

"Of course," Old Yen said, lying entirely.

"Well, then." That was all it took. Huang Li forsook his bailing and stepped up; Old Yen stepped down, picked up the bucket and bailed.

Even the bucket had a leak.

At last, there seemed less water in the sampan than there was in the harbor. Old Yen cast off the lines, stepped up to the oars and worked the long boat slowly out into the shift of the sea.

Droning his prayers already, which felt like an impertinence. He wasn't sure he had the right.

Even so, he did need to be praying. He was doing two foolish, dangerous things at once: taking a bad boat into difficult waters; and challenging the dragon for no reason except that his goddess had betrayed him and betrayed him, she had frightened and bereft him, and she was surely the only power that could keep him afloat in this boat and in the face of the dragon. If he believed anything, he had to believe that.

He was testing her, he supposed.

No, he was sure.

He didn't have the right.

Nevertheless, he needed to be praying.

OUT, THEN: and farther out than Huang Li would dare without a fleet for shelter, for rescue at need. His sampan did have a keel, she was fitted for sea, but the open sea outfaced her. Spume broke over her sides, and all her seams worked to keep the water oozing in.

Old Yen kept his head high, his voice low, his arms working the oars. If the sea should swallow him, well. It was no doubt better than being swallowed by the dragon.

Between the dragon and the goddess, though, he didn't think the sea would stand a chance.

The sampan was actually fitted for a mast, though Huang Li never dared to raise one. He'd put a pole up now, purely to fly the dragon's flag.

Old Yen made no move to do so. He thought perhaps there had been a voice—a scandalized voice, shrill with panic—calling after him as he left harbor, "The flag! The flag!" but he ignored it. He left the fabric folded at the pole's foot, as wet as everything as water slopped up and down the narrow hull as the sampan met the first swell of the sea, pitched her bows skyward and then plunged into the trough beyond.

. . .

OLD YEN rowed until Taishu-port was invisible at his back, until Taishu-island was a dark line and a smudge, until the Forge was a prominence, a mountain peak jutting from the sea.

He had no intention of landing. A visit to the Forge was a visit to the dragon, and he expected to have the dragon visit him. Best to have it out here on open water, utterly within reach of the goddess.

If she chose to stretch forth her hand and save him, only because he was himself, and her devotee, and in need of her.

A test, yes. And an impertinence, and a gesture flung in the teeth of all the gods. And a lament, a bitter cry of outrage, inexpressible loss.

OLD YEN rowed, and, yes: here came the dragon.

She lifted from the Forge, where he had looked to find her. At least she came through the air, where he could watch her all the way. Sooner that than have her hunt submerged and rise only at the last to swallow him all unseen, unready.

She flew to him, and stooped down to the water—but not the fierce falling stoop of a raptor to its prey. This was almost a gentle descent, almost a graceless landing: a great splashing belly-flop too close, that had the sampan tossing wildly beneath Old Yen's feet, shipping water from bow and stern and both sides all at once.

In that same moment, he thought he heard a frantic spluttering cry, a great whoop of protest and exhilaration. When the waters were calm enough that he could afford to lift his head to look— and when he had found his courage again, because this was after all a dragon—the source of that cry was right there to be seen.

And an explanation for the dragon's approach and her ungainly landing, that too, because a boy—the boy, her boy—was clinging to her neck.

Half naked and thoroughly soaked, he had a mad grin on his face and a chancy, unstable-looking seat astride her neck-ridge. A man might try to ride a dragon, Old Yen supposed—the way he'd ride a mule, clinging with both legs and whatever his hands could grab at—but he'd only stay aboard if she allowed it.

If she was going to eat Old Yen, she'd need to do it more delicately than her custom was. Stretch over, turn her head to nip him lightly out of the boat rather than diving, snatching, plunging, a dragon in all her expressive fury. She'd spill her rider else, and make a waste of that humiliating landing.

SHE HUNG in the water by an effort of will, he thought, much as she could hang in the air. She didn't float, she didn't bob on the surface like a duck. Rather the water flowed about her, struck and swirled against her flanks as though she were rooted stone, an islet.

Her head was poised like a risen snake's, the moment before it struck. Even so, it wasn't the strike that Old Yen feared. Not yet.

It was her eye, rather, her vivid gaze more than her gape: that brutal cold intelligence, the weight of ages, something else . . .

The need.

She needed something, or she would not have come like this. Like a supplicant. Bringing her boy to be a voice for her.

That was terrifying, that the dragon might want something of him.

THE BOY called out to him, across the water:

"She says, you aren't flying the flag."

"I am not."

"She says, she might have killed you."

"That she might."

"Don't you care?"

That wasn't the dragon asking. Old Yen was glad that the boy could keep at least something of himself, his curiosity. Not like the children of the goddess, who had to lose themselves, it seemed, before her voice could find them.

He shrugged.

The dragon . . . leaned over. Her vast head stretched toward him, tilting; the great mouth opened; apparently she was going to eat him after all.

It seemed that he did care after all. Nothing in his body moved, not even his tongue, not even the air that was caught suddenly in his throat. He didn't call out to her, or try to. But his mind, yes, his mind reached out to the Li-goddess—*oh, save me now, if you would save me ever!*—and she was there.

There in his head, reaching to batter him aside as a tidal surge will bat a boat aside however well anchored she may be. Reaching to possess him, to take his body to her own use as she did the bodies and voices of her children.

Rising inside him like something old and foul and rotten, an effusion, a bubble of gas from the filthy black mud below the harbor-pool.

Oozing all through him, seizing control, taking everything that was his; leaving almost no space for Old Yen himself . . .

No, he thought. *No, not that. I won't, you shan't. I do not give you that.*

Then it was a struggle, a still chill wrestling-match, his body the ground and the prize together. He had expected to face the dragon and to test the goddess today; he found himself fighting the wrong one for what little he still valued, his own self.

Fighting and, astonishingly, winning. He would not yield, he clung like weed where he did not cling like limpets; she forced her way in like the tide, passing through and about him, unable to wash him away. Her last clutch was almost feeble, almost desperate, a dead fling of spray that could not reach to the heights of him. And then she ebbed as the tide must, she all but rushed out of him.

He opened his eyes, not realizing that he had closed them. Saw the dragon poised and waiting, interested, apparently not eating him quite yet; and saw the boy leaning dangerously over the dragon's neck, fascinated, wanting to be closer; and saw the water sloshing in the belly of the sampan, saw how it seemed to move against the rhythm of the boat.

At first it was almost nothing, just odd enough to catch his eye, who had seen so much bilgewater in so many, many boats through all his years of life. This was . . . slow water: not rushing quite as it ought to, not quite so fast or quite so far.

Less far with every pitch and roll, it seemed. So much water, but it wasn't reaching the side-planks of the sampan. Rather it was heaping itself up amid the thwarts there, massing, drawing itself together around that strew of nets and baskets . . .

Drawing together and rising up, making a figure of weave and water, rope and bamboo and the sea and the silk of the dragon's banner too, all tangled together into something that hauled itself up the pole to gain height and coherence, as though even water-flesh needed a spine to hang from, to cling to.

Something that was not quite like a human figure but like enough: it had the height of the pole and as much breadth as it could hold in a frame of broken basket; it had weight and almost solidity; it seemed at least to have two arms and a head above, although there was nothing below that might suggest legs, only a thick twist of rope-and-water about the pole.

The head shaped itself a mouth, and tried to speak—and couldn't do it.

Old Yen knew her, ached for her a little, unless he ached for what he'd lost, herself as he had known her; thought, *I did that*. If she had lost her voice, it was because he denied her his own.

She was like a ghost, he thought, adrift without a body. She needed to borrow. Without a human body to work with, she lacked more than voice. Potency, impact. Effect.

She had been his goddess all his life, and now she was—well. Not so deep as a well. A wisp of water clinging to a pole.

Children who had lost themselves in horror, their bodies she could seize and use. Not a whole man's, who was ready to resist.

If he had yielded to her, perhaps she could have held the dragon off through him. She needed human strength, it seemed. Lacking anything but seawater to work with, she was mute and ineffectual. The dragon peered, closer yet, and there was nothing she could do, his goddess.

Which meant nothing he could do, Old Yen, but stand there waiting in this three-plank shell of a boat. Waiting to be sunk by the dragon or sunk by the goddess in her helpless disintegration, swallowed by the dragon or swallowed by the sea . . .

HE'D FORGOTTEN. The dragon *wanted* something.

THE BOY might almost have been sniggering as he looked at what the goddess wrought, what a small thing she made of herself.

He sobered quickly, though, as if the dragon had touched his mind with cold reality. He called across the narrow water. "I will not let her hurt you. Despite the flag. She needs . . . *we* need someone to go to Santung. Because no one there will come to us, as you did."

It was absurd, a conversation with a dragon through her boy; but Old Yen said what was obvious, what was absurd. "You could go to them."

"We have been. We break things," and it was clear that he didn't only mean the dragon. "We need someone else to go. We need you. You will talk to us; you can talk for us."

"What to say? And to whom? I know no one." That wasn't true, and the lie died on his lips. He had ferried Ping Wen across the strait; he knew the governor himself. Not perhaps to speak to, not on his own authority—but any man sailing the strait these days carried an authority he didn't own himself. Ping Wen would listen, if he went. Again, then, "To say what?"

"To say . . . to say that we need to talk to them. As we talked to you. To make an agreement, how they may use her waters."

The goddess, the water-creature on the mast, she seethed and writhed; she wanted to cry *my waters!* and could not.

Why the dragon should want such an agreement, when she had no need of it—well, that was a matter for her. He would meddle in the affairs of dragons as little as he must, strictly where they collided with his own. The great pressed against the lesser, and something had to be exchanged between them.

He said, "With which side?" There were two armies on the mainland, two commanders. Himself, he would trust neither— but again, that was a matter for her.

"With either. Both. Whoever holds Santung." The boy shook his head, helpless. The dragon would have small concept of human politics, or war. Why should she care? He said, "Go to Tien, the doctor; she will know who you should speak to. Who you should bring to speak with us."

"You want me to . . . ?"

"Yes. Bring them to the Forge. Or, if they will not come, have them fly a flag outside the city, somewhere there is room enough." *Where we will not break things,* he meant. "We will come."

THAT WAS IT, apparently. The dragon lifted from the water and bore the boy away: back to the Forge, to whatever strange life they inhabited there.

Old Yen stared at what clung to the pole before him, dizzy with revelation, with disappointment. *Old age is a measurement of loss.*

At last he did what Huang Li did, often and often: he slid over the side into the warm lifting embrace of the sea, reached above his head to grip the sampan's side, sank and kicked.

Tugged her past her precarious point of balance, overturned her entirely.

Swam beneath her for a moment, and saw nothing; climbed up onto her inverted hull and gripped the keel, heaved, let her toss him off as she righted herself again.

When he slithered back aboard he found her entirely vacated, wet wood and nothing more, except that the dragon's banner had tangled itself so thoroughly about the pole that it clung there still.

Old Yen spent some time sitting in the sun untangling it, until he could fly it loose and free from the pole like an ambassador's credentials as he sailed across the strait toward Santung.

He had a mission from the dragon, apparently, which would serve as his excuse. In fact he had, he had always had a mission of his own.

Old Yen wanted his boat back.

FIVE

Cities of the Heart

one

It was, Mei Feng thought, like a compact between cities.

There was the empress, the mother-city: a stronghold bleak and dark and weathered, walled all around. Demanding, untrusting, unyielding.

And then there was herself, open and broken, frightened and hopeful and alone. Too small for the world, needing an alliance.

The empress might have swallowed her whole. Certainly she had intended that. Perhaps she still did intend exactly that. But Mei Feng had proved not quite swallowable so far, more than a mouthful; and she sat as it were at the mouth of a valley, where the empress held the heights. If the dowager meant to come at the world at all, if she was not content—and she was not!—to squat in splendid isolation and scowl down and be ignored, then she had to come through Mei Feng.

Through my child, Mei Feng thought, hugging the small hard roundness of her belly. To the empress, of course, it was her son's child, nothing of Mei Feng's. Even so, Mei Feng was the gatekeeper.

They could never be equals, she and the indomitable old woman; they might never be friends. Little by little, Mei Feng was inheriting what used to be the dowager's own. Her son's loyalty, her claim to be mother of empire, everything. Except her rank and title, because Chien Hua might love his little island fisher-girl but he would never marry her. That was understood.

For now, the empress could be counsel and mentor, the only woman living who had borne an imperial child. She knew better than her own doctors, how this would go. "I have seen normal women," she said, "give normal birth. It is not like that for us."

Us, she said, often and often now. Making an alliance of them, two women against the world: strength in shared secrets, sharing secret strengths. "Imperial seed makes us sick," she said, "even as it makes us strong. What grows in your womb, what grew in mine, they are not quite human, these sons of empire."

Mine might be a daughter, Mei Feng thought, secretly rebellious: her strength, not for sharing.

"Mortal flesh, of course, conceived in mortal passion—but still they have jade in them from the start, at the heart. That's what makes them so heavy to carry, so hard to us. But we, we women, we have something of the stone in us too, from lying close with emperors. That's what gives us the strength to carry them, and to endure. It is . . . always bad for the woman, to bear an emperor's child. You now, you are having it worse than I did. You are too young, I think. It wants a woman, where you are still a girl. I let slip a dozen, before I could bring the one to term. Still, you have survived the worst of it. I thought the child would die, I admit it, before Master Biao came."

I thought the child had died. I admit it. And me too, I thought I would die, had died, was dead already.

I wanted to die, I think. I admit that too. Not the child, though, never that.

Then . . . well. Then Master Biao came, and changed everything. Remade me, gave life back to my baby, remade the world.

WHEN MASTER Biao was absent, when he had taken the tiger-skin away, Mei Feng liked to sit out on the balcony of this new and petty palace, first build of the mighty city to come.

With all an isolated hill to build on, this had been her idea: that they should build a swift house first, compact and self-contained, alone on the slope facing south. Nothing grand, nothing that would eat time and spit out delay. A wooden house, an elaboration of their old beloved tent, sealed against weather and furnished with comfort, fit for two young people and their essential servants and no more. Business and worry could be left in Taishu-port with the generals. Closer at hand, all the noise and fuss of the workers' tents could be out of sight and out of hearing, north of the hill; all their ongoing work, building the real palace with its barracks and courts, that too, the north side of the hill.

From here she looked south to the mountains and the forest and the sky. Everything that was a trouble lay to the north, away from her: the politics of court, the dragon in the strait, Tunghai Wang and Ping Wen hopefully warring with each other on the mainland. Even Grandfather, in his anxiety and distress. North of her. Not in view.

She had never imagined sharing this little precious house with the dowager empress; but the old woman was here and the emperor was not, or not often. He came when he could and left when he must, when other men insisted or his own conscience drove him away.

She didn't argue, much or often. He was her man and father of her child, her boy-emperor and her delight, in bed and out of it, waking or sleeping, talking or laughing or silent and intent—and yet, and yet. She was almost glad to see him gone again, to feel the restful spirit of this place close again about her, almost like the embrace of the tiger-skin. Almost that close, that warm, that comforting, encouraging, uplifting.

Almost glad, bizarrely, to be left in the company of his mother.

EVEN WHEN the rain came, so long as there was no wind to hurl it in beneath the open roof, she liked to sit out here on the balcony and watch slow changes cross a world she could not reach. Inside her was what mattered, the baby that had not after all died; outside her, this house encompassed her as much as she encompassed the baby.

The old woman sat with her most days, sometimes late into the night when the hills were shadow against the vivid sky, when the moon was a lamp and the stars were silver dust flung over midnight silk. Never a comfortable companion, the empress was a comfort nevertheless, with her difficult wisdom and her trenchant grip on what mattered.

"Why do I like this so much—or no, not that, quite. Why is this all I want?"

"The tea? Because it is bitter, it speaks true to your tongue."

"Not the tea," though the empress was right about that at least. It sat in Mei Feng's mouth like a curl of steam from a hidden mountain pool, tasting of rock and depth and clarity, nothing soft or sweet. Nothing that grew. Some teas tasted of the untamed forest, or the grasslands she had never seen, or the sea-wind blowing over the paddy: greenness at their hearts. Not this. This held no light at all, no colors. It was a tea for the night, a tea for her baby in its darkness, waiting. "This," she said, with a wave of her arm across the rail of the balcony, across the dip of the valley to the rise of the hills. "All I want to do is sit here and watch the weather march across the mountains. Watch the moon come and go, watch the sun follow in its tracks," not watch any more of the world than this. Hug her arms around her swelling belly, feel the baby kick back.

Sip tea, and talk with the dowager empress; or else sip tea and sit silent with the dowager empress, when she used to eat and jabber and argue with her son.

"Ah," said the old woman, a world's worth of satisfaction in a word. "Because you have an emperor growing inside you, and this is his inheritance."

A little bewildered, Mei Feng shook her head. This was the last least shred of his inheritance, the final pendulous drop of it, the belly of Taishu hung above a desert of ocean across which not the greatest of emperors could ever reach. All the empire else lay northerly, behind them, above them, out of view. *Out of reach*, which was where she wanted it for now.

"This is the heart," the old woman insisted. "Not all the un-measured miles we have come; not even the Hidden City that we left behind, certainly not all the sordid little cities we passed through on the way. Not your grubbly Taishu-town, not even now, when the emperor must make his home there. Not all the myriad people, not all the wealth, not the armies and the power to com-mand them. This. Taishu is the Dragon's Tear, the Tear of Jade, because of this, because those mountains hold jade at their heart. All that the empire is, is jade; all that it is, is here. All that my son is, all that your baby will be. You are his eyes on his inheritance. You show him what he will be born to. Of course that seeds con-tentment in your heart. Drink your tea and go to bed, fool child. My grandson needs your sleep."

No, thought Mei Feng, *no and no and no*. The empress was wrong, more ways than she could count. She did not want to sleep, she couldn't sleep; her baby wouldn't let her. It had come so close to the other thing, to the hollow bitter empty sleep of death, she thought it clung to her awareness of the world. She didn't know if other babies slept in the womb, but this one not. If she drowsed, it would kick her awake from within. The tiger-skin could hold her under, and the emperor could do the same. Lacking either, she really only wanted to sit here and watch the night spin away under the slow rhythm of the stars.

And more than that, far more, the empress was wrong about the heart of empire. Mei Feng used to think it was the beating heart of her boy, the emperor Chien Hua, but of course that wasn't right. Now she thought it was the slow-beating heart of his mother. The dowager empress *was* the empire, she held its heart in the weak fierce clutch of her claw fingers; she was the true Hidden City, obscure and protected, unrecognized, unsought. Without her, there would be no Chien Hua, of course; every woman was empress in her own house, mother of empire. More, though: without the dowager, her husband's death would have been her son's death too, a change of dynasty, new empire built on the bones of the old. So it went, time and again—but this time it wasn't a story, this time it was Chien Hua.

Without her the emperor would never have come to Taishu, would never have been found by a certain fisher-girl, blinking in the fog.

And without her, Mei Feng thought, without her *now,* Chien Hua would hold on to what he had and let the empire slip away. He had the title and privileges of rank, which he liked; he had the jade, which he needed; he had an island for his plaything and a people to inhabit it, an army to protect it. He had his friends for company, his new palace for distraction.

He had Mei Feng, heart and body; he had their child coming.

What more could a young man want?

He would settle, she thought, without his mother. Be king of Taishu, lord of enough.

It was the dowager who clutched the idea of empire, and would not let it slip. She whose old eyes had seen the stretch of it, whose tongue spoke with the weight of it, whose pride could not conceive of yielding it. She kept it fresh in her son's mind, urgent to his generals.

Yes, there was a dragon in the strait, and a traitor in Santung— but they had means to bypass one and manipulate the other. To her the strait, even the dragon was a defense, not a barrier. Santung was held, not lost: a foothold, not a desperate vulnerable last finger's-hold. A step forward, not a falling-away.

She could be wrong and many kinds of wrong, and Mei Feng could love her for it anyway: for her stubbornness, her arrogance, her strength. For being closed off to the changing world, a high walled city, yet unbreached; and for coming down, for being reachable, for bringing her precious boy to where he might hear voices other than her own.

She was a repository for what might not yet be lost. She could be a touchstone still. She could be essential.

THE HEART of empire dozed in her chair, a small old woman too twisted by her years to be comfortable lying straight in a bed. The new fresh hopes of empire smiled drowsily, nestled in her own cushions, a small young woman too recently too sick to want her bed ever again, unless her man lay within it. Lounging like this was easier for her too, with the baby forcing all her inward organs out of shape. Fuss lingered in the lamplight beyond the balcony door; maids' hands waited to put her to bed, maids' voices to scold. This balcony was sacred space, forbidden. The old woman had taught all the household to leave them alone out here. Mei Feng would make the tea herself, to avoid intrusion; the empress would drink it for the same reason. Being entirely clear as she did so, just how great a sacrifice this was.

Mei Feng could love her for that too, for giving way on nothing, holding to her sour ungenerous temper as she did to her bitter tea, as she did to the empire.

MEI FENG could doze in the comfort of cushions and coverlets, and wake to the breeze on her face bringing news of weather and season, of forest and hills and the far sea beyond.

She could open her eyes and see first far hint of day cloud the clarity of stars. She could shift her oddly heavy, ill-balanced body and feel the baby shift itself inside her, and smile inwardly and slide a little farther down into her own warmth, and drowse again.

SHE COULD wake again and feel the shift in the wind, first breath of rain on her cheek; she could hear the silence in the house at her back and the waking hills before her, birdsong and monkey-calls and the stir of bodies through trees all melded by distance into a riverfall of noise, a susurration, almost enough to draw her down into sleep again.

SHE COULD hear a noise that was far closer and just as soft, not as alluring: the squeak of a bare sole on dew-damp lacquered wood. That must be one of the servants, risking the old woman's anger. Which might only be folly, but they had no fools in the household; which meant that it must be news. There was no reason else to be fussing out here between two sleeping mothers.

Nothing could matter that much to either one of them unless it was Chien Hua, news of the emperor himself. And no news could be good news that came light-footed on a gust of rain in the too-early morning, that had a servant standing silent over their sleep sooner than wake either one of them to break it.

Whatever it was, they should bring it to her. The old woman could have the empire; Mei Feng claimed precedence in the emperor's heart. And the right to intercept calamity before it reached his mother, that too.

There was still time. All she had to do was move: open her eyes, lift her head, slide a hand outside the covers to gesture. *Bring it here, whatever it is. Tell it to me.*

She could do that.

She could.

SHE COULD open her eyes, just that, and see—

SEE A figure bent over the empress's chair, and prop herself up on one elbow with a scowl forming.

SEE BROAD shoulders and a shaved head, dark clothes. One of the old woman's eunuchs, then, and no surprise that he went to her—

but no, that wasn't right. Even in the dim shadows under the rain-roof she could see that he wore trousers rather than the proper robe, which no eunuch ever did or would.

SEE THE old woman's feet kick suddenly beneath her coverlet, kick and kick.

SEE IT all very differently, all in a moment.

NOT A servant bringing news, no. The man was a stranger. His dark clothes said that he came skulking, that he sought to hide in shadows; his wet clothes said that he came from the rain, from the hillslope, over the balcony's edge.

His silence named him an assassin. His choice of victim—of *first* victim—named his master, perhaps. The empress had done what she could to slay Ping Wen, had failed and failed. This was surely the price of failure.

Mei Feng had done better, sending him into exile. She would be next, no question: she and her baby too, two in one, and that would be the death of empire right here, laid out in their generations in the soft fall of rain. Mother and lover and child, all together. Chien Hua could not survive this.

The old woman was kicking less strongly already. There was a cushion, Mei Feng thought, held over her head and pressed down, soft and perfumed and relentless. She hadn't even managed to free her hands. She would hate that, to go to her tomb with her nails unbloodied of her killer.

Mei Feng had nothing to throw but cushions of her own, and crying an alarm would only bring servants to the slaughter.

NEVERTHELESS.

Mei Feng screamed, and hurled cushions.

Noises in the house behind, too late, too slow, just as she was herself. The killer turned from the old woman's sprawled body, and now Mei Feng was just another victim in waiting, next in line.

He was between her and the door, and her legs were tangled in the covers and she was weak yet, not fit for vaulting balcony rails and running from assassins.

All she could do was tumble out of her long chair into the corner here, with the awkward angularity of the chair itself to shield her just a little.

She was a woman, that much he knew. Pregnant, sick, he might know those things too.

If he carried a blade, he didn't trouble to draw it. His hands were weapons enough, even in a hurry, even with footsteps pounding through the other noises of the house.

The sprawl of the chair didn't delay him long. No need to be quiet now, only quick: he kicked it aside and came at her, where she cringed back in the corner. His fingers were reaching already. One good grip of her neck, one swift snap and away. The way he had come, the way she wasn't fit to go, over the rail and drop down the hill. There were guards, of course, or there should be—but they should have met him coming up the hill.

Perhaps they did.

He might live, he might not. It didn't seem to matter to him yet, so long as she did not.

He reached down to seize her—

—JUST AS she came thrusting up, swinging her arm around from behind her back.

This was the corner where she kept the tea-things.

He couldn't see that for the spread of the light sleeping-robe she wore; he couldn't have imagined that she would find a weapon here, or be fit to use it.

He could never have anticipated the kettle.

It was a brutal heavy thing, bronze and ornate, that took a good hour over a charcoal bed to come anywhere near a boil. Mei Feng used it for the empress's sake, because the old woman treasured it enough to have brought it all the way from the Hidden City; and for her own sake, because once it was heated it would keep its water hot for hours.

Even now there was a warmth in it, after it had sat half the night half-full and disregarded while they dozed.

Mei Feng rose up swinging it like a club.

She might be pregnant, she might still be sick, she might not be fit to leap and run—but she had the strength of emperors in her bones and blood, and perhaps the lingering memory of the tiger's strength, borrowed from its skin.

And she had her baby to defend and the old woman to avenge, all her own unborrowed passion to draw on; and if she was screaming again as she surged upward, that was all for herself and her sheer fury that he would dare to do this, to bring cold death to women—and to babies, her baby!—after such a night, after such lives lived or waiting to be lived, such an empress so casually smothered.

Herself, she had a lifetime of practice, clubbing fish.

He was quick, just not as quick as she was. Strong too, he was strong; just . . . Well. Not as strong.

He flung his arm out to block hers as it swung.

She felt the impact, felt his bones shatter.

He might have screamed then, that might have been his turn to scream, but he didn't have the time.

Her arm swung on its arc, barely delayed, with the ponderous weight of the kettle in her grip.

The great thick bronze rim of it caught his skull and he fell all in a sudden, as a cliff might, undercut. And lay like a rockfall at her feet, utterly still, his crushed head blessedly lost in the shadows.

.   .   .

.

SHE HEARD the scream die out of her slowly, losing itself in a whistling kind of gasp.

SHE HEARD the kettle fall at her side, felt a splash of warmth across her feet.

VAGUELY, VAGUELY hoped that that was water.

AND THEN there were people: women and eunuchs rushing from the house, too late; soldiers from the hill, from all around the hill, too late and far too late.

THEN SHE wanted to sit down, and there was no chair.

THEN PERHAPS she broke, for a little bit.

IT WAS later, surely, some time later that she pushed her women away and made herself walk—in fresh slippers, she noticed, and this was not the robe she had been wearing, and when had she come inside the house?—back out onto the balcony, to where the empress still lay on her bed-chair, under a light coverlet.

THEY HAD taken her cushions away, except for one beneath her head.

SHE LOOKED terrible, wax-pale and cruelly gaunt and . . .

AND NOT dead.

BREATHING.

BARELY SO, a hoarse dry rattle in her throat, hardly enough to stir the coverlet across her chest, but breathing none the less.

.   .   .

MEI FENG dropped to her knees beside her, gripped the old woman's bone-cold bone-bare fingers and said, "Fetch Master Biao. With his tiger-skin. Now!"

"Lady," they said, "we have sent men already. You told us to, before."

She did? She didn't remember.

"The emperor too," she said. "Someone should go to tell the emperor . . ."

"That too, lady. You ordered it. Of course a message has gone to the emperor." Of course. Not a summons—one did not summon the Son of Heaven!—but he would come regardless. His mother, his lover, his child-to-be: he would come.

Till then . . .

"Where is the, the, the . . . ?" *The body,* but a gesture stood in for the word of it, a waft of her hand toward the wet scrubbed boards where the assassin had died. At her hand, at her feet. All over her feet.

"In the cess-pit, lady. Where you had us throw him."

She seemed to have been . . . most efficient. Ahead of herself. It was just so strange, not to remember any of it. Or to remember only those parts she didn't want to keep. The old woman's legs kicking at nothing, the assassin's face as he came for Mei Feng. The splash of warm wet across her feet.

Her hand was back at her belly where it belonged, but here was one of the women offering her a cup, a steaming cup. Some description of tea: pale gold and clear as sunlight, a scatter of dark twisted leaves settling in the bottom like a dashed character she couldn't read. She ought to learn to read. The emperor ought to teach her. Then he'd have one cause fewer to be ashamed of her, she'd have one cause fewer to be embarrassed before their child as it grew.

She reached for the tea, and hesitated just as her fingers touched the cup.

Oh.

She lifted her eyes to the woman's, wishing she had Dandan back. Dandan would have known, wouldn't need the question.

"How did you," no, try again, "where did you make this?"

"In our kitchen, lady."

Of course, in their kitchen. Not out here. Even so . . .

"What, what *with*?"

Now, at last, the woman understood. Understood and smiled. Mei Feng could hate her for that smile. Could send her back to the city, just for smiling.

"With our own kettle, lady. Not the empress's."

Of course, not the empress's, or they would still be waiting for the water to boil. Even so . . .

"Where is . . . ?" *Not here* was not enough of an answer.

"In our kitchen, lady."

Of course, in their kitchen. Not out here and not used for this, but scrubbed and standing ready, like any dutiful servant that has come a long long way with their mistress.

Mei Feng shuddered. She ought to be grateful to the thing, but, "Throw it in the pit, with . . ." *With the man it killed. The man I killed.*

"Lady, the empress . . ."

The empress loved that kettle, yes. Or valued it, or clung to it past reason for reasons that seemed good enough to her. It didn't really matter which way you said it. The kettle had its own truth, and so did the empress now when Mei Feng turned to look at her. Pointedly.

"The empress . . . will not be worrying for a while, how her tea is made." Or ever again, perhaps. Unless Master Biao came soon, unless his tiger-skin could work its miracle one more time, to fetch one more woman back from the land of ghosts.

Meantime, the empress had no voice and no will, and Mei Feng could usurp her utterly. "Throw it in the cess-pit," she said again. Otherwise it would be kept, she knew, and find its way back into use here or in the workmen's camp or somewhere. She did not want that. In her head it was crushed, broken, spilling, like a skull. She wanted it gone.

And this at least was an order she had not given already, something not dealt with yet. That was a relief. The world did move on, seemingly; she could still make it move.

"Yes, lady."

Perhaps she should watch the woman all the way, see the thing done. See the body in the pit, that too, just to know it. Not to see it everlastingly at her feet, and spilling.

Perhaps she should, but she seemed to be sitting down, on her righted chair, just here. Cup in hand, a waft of scented steam, leaves settling into new patterns, still unreadable.

Perhaps she only didn't want to leave the empress. Someone ought to sit with her, she thought. Till the emperor came.

She wished he would hurry. Master Biao too, him perhaps especially. The old woman was not too strong to fail. Mei Feng could hear her breathing, the fine thin thread of it like silk unreeling. Sometime there must come an end. Hearts beat and beat, and then they stop beating. Even infused with jade, like this water infused with tea: left to stand, it would cool, it would spill eventually or just dry up in the cup. Not even tea was eternal. Not even bitter old women.

Mei Feng sat and wished, sat and waited, sat and watched.

The balcony looked south, toward the mountains; the road from Taishu-port lay northerly, around the hill.

It was Master Biao she watched for, rather than the emperor.

THE SUN lay on the hills like a gift, like tea in a cup. The rain-shadow moved across them like a scrawl of darkness, ink from a brush, leaves in the bottom of a cup.

She saw movement, figures coming out of the trees there.

Too many of them. For a moment she was disappointed, *not Master Biao.*

She couldn't hope to see from this distance, but she looked regardless. There was a man, a tubby man with something heavy in his hands: something like the fall of forest shadow, dark and greenly. Master Biao always insisted on carrying the tiger-skin himself. It lent him strength, she thought.

Who were all these other people, then? So many of them, a parade. She was still too far away, or they were—but that tall one leading, the one that almost made her think of the emperor, that had to be Yu Shan. She was surprised that he would come, that he would leave Siew Ren even for this—

—UNTIL SHE had watched for a little while longer, and seen how the figure who walked beside him was bent and awkward, how her walk betrayed her.

That was Siew Ren herself, and walking. Not even with the skin around her shoulders. Mei Feng had not known that she could walk again. Perhaps she had not known it herself. Watching them come in file over open ground, Mei Feng saw that not only Siew Ren was hurt. Little things, really too small to be seen from here: the set of a young man's shoulders, the swing of a woman's leg. There was stiffness and the memory of pain, a lingering distrust of the physical world that was echoed all along the line.

Slowly they came, too slowly for her although they were obviously hurrying. Slowly she understood. These were Master Biao's patients, all those clansfolk he had been treating with the tiger-skin. They were the emperor's own, all volunteers, his personal bodyguard; that was how they came to be hurt. They might be following the tiger-skin, but they were coming to her. Reporting for duty. They would need her to believe that.

She watched them come and waited, then, rather than hurry down the hill to greet them. She wanted to do that and more, to urge them on faster, to appropriate Master Biao's tiger-skin and run it back up to the balcony. It was her miracle, and she was greedy for it.

But it was theirs too, held in common. They had become their own clan, these young people, bonded in blood and hurt and hardship, and they were bringing their treasure to where it was more needed now. She had to let them do that.

SAT AND waited, then, and saw them intercepted at the fence that enclosed the hill. Everyone knew Yu Shan, everyone knew Master Biao; of course they would be let through. Even so, the guards would be anxious now. Rightly anxious. When the emperor arrived, there would have to be an accounting. The men who failed him, who let an assassin by . . . Well. They should probably not expect to live. She was sorry for them, a little. Less so every time she glanced to where the old woman lay beside her, in the ragged margin of her life. It was insufferable, to see her brought so low. Those men down there had allowed it, whoever had the duty in the night.

But so had other powers allowed it, so had the world. Where was Grandfather's goddess when she was needed, or Yu Shan's tiger?

No, Mei Feng knew where the tiger was. And her cub.

Where was the dragon, then? The dragon might have intervened. People said that jade was the dragon's tears; people called this whole island the Tear of the Dragon, for its shape and its jade and perhaps for the dragon too, chained in the strait as she had been. Surely there was jade enough in the empress's blood by now, surely she had earned an intervention . . . ?

Mei Feng examined her own thoughts dispassionately, exhaustedly, and wondered if she was perhaps not entirely sane. Then her eyes flicked to the empress again, and again she was furious at all the powers of the world for letting her come so low, so late.

Well, if the dragon would not intervene, the tiger would. Even dead, it was a power in the land. The touch of its skin would draw the empress's ghost back into her body, as it had Mei Feng's own and her baby's too. It must. The old woman had not gone so far, no, not half so far; and the skin was still a potent thing, a wonder. Here came the proof of that, in single file up the hill, so many people saved from hurt or sickness, saved from death. One more would be no trouble, no . . .

THEY CAME directly to the balcony, but not to her. Mei Feng was distantly, almost amusedly aware that she was no longer anyone's first thought. She had been so for Master Biao, for everyone; now he had another patient and she was only a convalescent, pressed politely but firmly to the side of his attention. She had been Yu Shan's friend and she hoped that she still was, but his mind was all too obviously on Siew Ren: had she walked too far, should he have let her come at all? Could she manage the climb over the balcony rail . . . ?

The hillside dropped away below the house, so that the balcony jutted out a man's height above the ground. There were posts to support it, and any fit young person could swarm up without much trouble. Yu Shan leaped, seized the high rail with one hand and hung there with his feet against a post, holding the other hand down to help Siew Ren.

Perhaps she would have managed without his help. Perhaps she would have shrugged and walked around the house to the steps, to the door, and so come in as Master Biao did, with a sense of his decorum wrapped around him. Because Yu Shan was there, though—and perhaps because he had earned it, all these long days by her bed—she reached up to him with her uninjured arm, they linked wrists and he hoisted her with one easy swing, up to the rail and over.

And went on hanging there, making a fleshly ladder to help his other companions; but his eyes were all on Siew Ren through the rails, and his mind dogged along behind his eyes as young men's minds will do. Mei Feng could read him at a glance.

Siew Ren could read her too. Perhaps they all could, all these vigorous sick, but it was Siew Ren who came to her where she was still sitting in her chair, not quite knowing what to stand up for.

"Mei Feng, you look terrible." This from the girl whose voice was scratched and broken, whose face was ruthlessly twisted out of true, who carried brutal scarring like a web of white drawn over her and tugged too tight: whose life the tiger-skin had salvaged, but not her beauty. Her strength perhaps, but not as it had been. Half her body was half gone from her.

It was almost a joke, what she said. She smiled to say so, and that was worse. She wore a face now that should not try to smile.

And knew it, and shrugged, and dropped down onto her knees and took Mei Feng's two hands in her own one good one and said, "You have had a terrible night, I know it. You are not to worry anymore, you understand me? We are here now, and you are our task. The emperor wouldn't take us into war again, being as we are, being as he is, a fool," *a boy* she meant, "but even he will allow us to be useful here. He will come soon, and rant and shout and be emperor awhile, and then he will weep and whisper and be a boy awhile, and then he will go away again and we will not. And if any more assassins come, they will find us waiting long before they find their way to you. The empress will be pleased," *if she ever wakes, if she is ever to be pleased again,* with a glance aside to where Master Biao had arrived at last, where he was tucking his tiger-skin cautiously, doubtfully around the old woman in her dreadful stillness, "to find her grandchild so very well protected."

It was a long speech, for someone who had talked little for a long time. Mei Feng was grateful, and squeezed her hand. And didn't really believe that the empress would rise up to be grateful too; there was something in Master Biao's manner, even before he shook his head and muttered about time and loss and absence. Or perhaps it was in her nose, that smell of decay, familiar but stronger now, worse now.

Perhaps they were all too late, even the magic too far gone in rot. Perhaps the old woman would die after all. There were too many ways that should not have happened. If anyone in the empire should be safe, it was the dowager empress; if anyone on Taishu should be safe, it was Mei Feng and whomever she chose to spend her time with. To be wrong both ways was an affront, and not just to her. She thought the gods should be angry too, and a little ashamed.

More than a little.

Yu Shan hauled himself over the rail at last. It was still Siew Ren that he watched, but she was with Mei Feng so he came to stand beside her chair, so she could say, "Yu Shan, did you speak to the guards below, to their officer . . . ?"

He knew what she was asking. He said, "I did. The assassin killed three of them down there, without a sound from any. No one knew that he had crossed the fence."

That word might save a few lives. It might not. She couldn't tell, in the emperor's absence, what mood he would bring with him when he came. If he rode in hotly, demanding heads, she could hardly fling herself before the swinging blade.

Just now, it was as much as she could do to sit upright and nod greetings to known faces. In fact, it was apparently a little more than she could do. Someone was talking—was that Siew Ren again, or was it someone else, was it Yu Shan? and how odd, not to be able to tell the difference—but the words weren't making sense to her. Everything was heavy suddenly, her body, her eyelids. Even the babe in her belly was a weight to drag her down.

She sank back into her cushions, into a cushioning darkness. For a while she lay poised there between wake and sleep, between one world and another. Someone would rouse her, surely, when the emperor came. She only wished they could rouse his mother as easily.

Meanwhile she listened to the noises of the house, this petty palace filling up with people. Strong people, clansfolk with jade in their blood and bone; wary people, who had all been hurt before. Siew Ren was right, they couldn't have a better guard, the old woman and herself.

But these were young people too, stubborn people, her friends. Even now she could hear them arguing: how many would sleep in

which rooms and who should take the watch, how best to organize, where to watch the hillside and where to watch the road.
Where to train, where to work their damaged bodies and learn
what skills were lost to them. Who should sit with Mei Feng until
the emperor came, and afterward: how much trouble that young
man might give them, demanding a privacy they would not allow.

Like themselves, this was twisted but familiar. As best they
could, she thought, they were bringing her summer back to her,
when she had been happy living wild in a mountain valley. They
couldn't take the empress into the hills, but they could perhaps
bring the hills down here.

two

*T*unghai Wang had made his plans and laid his plans. With Ma's invaluable help—a returned Ma, a little altered perhaps by his journey north, perhaps by his best of finds there, a monksmith willing to ride back in his entourage: small and deep, the monksmith, a contrast to Ma in every way—Tunghai had gathered up and organized his forces.

None of that had been easy, and neither would the battle be to come. He must fight it without battle-lights and trumpets, at least in these early hours, when they would have helped the most. By the time his several forces came within sight and sound of each other, they would have victory in their sleeves already and not much need to talk.

His scattered generals had each their instructions. They knew what they were about, and he knew that he could trust them. So.

Even so. He would sooner and far sooner have come down upon Santung as he did before, the end of a chase, his weary exultant men surging like a river at the heels of his horse, flooding all about him as he waved them on, flooding all through the city, irresistible as water . . .

Those days were gone. Half his men were gone, dead or lost or slipped away. More than half: he had lost half in his abortive invasion, drowned or eaten by the dragon. More—not many—when the emperor struck back; more and many more in the typhoon that followed, that accursed dragon again, a weapon used against him.

Still. Ping Wen had not so many men to defend Santung, and it really could not be defended. Between them, Tunghai Wang and his generals had rallied men enough. Ma had woven them into a net all about the city: so many here and so many there, these the roads between them, these the men to run messages, here and here stabling for ponies to carry more urgent news. Ma could make a city in the desert if he chose, and feed its people too. Tunghai Wang was nothing but lucky to have Ma on his staff.

Now, though, Ma was safely in the rear somewhere with his monksmith and his boy, his other comforts. This was no night for General Ma; this was a night for soldiering.

Fire and terror are the weapons of the dark. This night they lay in Tunghai Wang's grasp, in the palm of his hand. He might lack overwhelming numbers, but he ought not to need them. A little display, death and destruction at each cardinal point of the city, east and west and north together, to say that there was no safe road away: that should be enough to bring the unreliable Ping Wen out to parley in the dawn.

No, not to parley. To submit. In support of earlier promises and plans, he would give the city and all his men—half the imperial army!—to Tunghai Wang, and in return he could keep his life, his limbs, even his position. Santung would still need a governor. Known on one side and trusted on the other, Ping Wen's could be the voice that welded two armies into one force strong enough to take Taishu as soon as the way was clear across the water.

Tunghai Wang might have written all that out and sent it into the city under a flag of truce, but he didn't want to negotiate with Ping Wen like an equal, generals who matched each other coming to an arrangement. He wanted a swift brutal victory, a surrender on the back of which he could be unusually magnanimous for the sake of all, for the future well-being of his empire.

His.

Hence this night, and the cruelties to come. Santung-city knew already how he could be cruel, but the emperor had escaped that lesson with his army largely intact. Tonight was Ping Wen's opportunity to discover just what it meant to stand in Tunghai Wang's eye, in his way, in the storm-shadow of his anger.

Tonight, fire and terror, flames and screaming and the stink of smoke. At first light Ping Wen would find himself without men at any of his careful barricades: the watch-houses burned to the ground, the walls arrayed with bodies and a double line of heads along the road to watch as he crept out in answer to the summons.

Let him make his submission with due deference, and this time the slaughter would stop there. Tunghai Wang was not wasteful, and if he were, he had Ma at his elbow to prevent it. There was a time to be savage, and then a time to be generous: both in due and proper order. Yes.

A TIME to be a soldier, that too, however high you stood. However little you were actually needed on the battlefield. Here was Tunghai Wang, then, on the westerly road, sitting high on his horse with the valley-ridge before him, the lights of the doomed watch glowing on their inadequate defenses. He wouldn't give this up. Far out of sight on the opposite side of the city, out of sight again in the river valley north, other generals would be similarly supplanting their junior officers, simply for the pleasure of remembering that they were soldiers and not bureaucrats, not officials, not Ma.

Westerly—above him and behind—the constellation called the Ghost-Dog was settling toward the horizon. Soon now, its brightest star would touch the rim of the world. That was the signal. He always liked to use signs in the heavens to direct the course of battle. Ping Wen was a dog, a cur who turned tail to betray first one side and then the other. He might think that he had risen, that he had won a high place for himself already; he might be looking higher yet; after tonight, his ambition was a ghost. Come the morning, he would find that his star had set.

Soon now. Soon.

All about him and behind, Tunghai Wang's best men packed

close. This was work they knew and could enjoy, in prospect as much as in the doing of it. A simple objective, a target they could see: *take the barricade and hold it, burn the watch-house, kill your prisoners slowly. Make a noise. Save the heads of the dead, hang the bodies by the heels.*

They were ready for this, oh yes.

Soon.

Lifting his eyes to the sky, a high moon and the broad swath of the silk-stars, the constellation called the Chariot just rising into view, Tunghai Wang saw one more light, piercingly bright and too fast for nature, too fast for anything. It climbed the dark air like a flung stone, trailing sparks; paused for a moment as if to think, as if wondering where, whether, when to fall; and vanished then, before it could decide.

Tunghai Wang wasn't sure what it meant, except no good to him. It had risen from the height of the ridge, from those surely inadequate defenses, flung surely by the hand of man, which meant the hand of Ping Wen; he thought he might have preferred to see it fall.

Then the sky erupted in a gaudy sheet of flame.

It wasn't, surely, dangerous. He fought his jittery horse to a standstill, called out to his nervous muttering men: "This is nothing, it is just fireworks," though it was burning oddly bright and oddly long for a firework. "They seek to frighten us with a display for children, that's all, flashes in the night . . ."

Then there was a drone in the air, a brief shadow occluding the stars, a shadow that moved against the wind and fell among them, physical and lethal, a thousand separate shafts.

Archers. Not an arrow touched Tunghai Wang nor yet his horse, he had always been lucky in battle, it was why so many men liked to press so close about him; but many of those men were sorry for it now. He turned his head from their screams and curses, glowered up at the ridge. *They knew we were coming . . .*

The firework might have been no more than one alert watchman catching a glint of moonlight on steel, or a boy in the paddy running scared, crying a warning below the barricade. Archers, though, a whole battery of archers, arrows nocked and ready, loosing as soon as the light betrayed their quarry—no. They knew he was coming. He had lost one man too many to Ai Guo's questioning, or else he had been more deliberately betrayed. This was almost a trap.

Over behind the city, the sky paled and flared. That would be another such firework, betraying General Chou and his force. No doubt there would be one more to the north, to meet General Ha Ten in the valley as he worked his men along the broken river road. Tunghai Wang was not going to sit here astride a fidgety horse and wait to see it. Besides, there went the stars again.

The drone of flight turned to a whistle in its fall, and then a thousand separate impacts on mud or flesh, leather or steel or stone. *Ping Wen, you may have mastered me.* Done by treachery, perhaps, or else by torture, the thing was still done well.

Nevertheless. Archers are not always swordsmen. Only let his men get in among them, and there could still be a reckoning. Ping Wen's resources were not great. This might be his only defense on this road, if he'd had to divide his forces three ways tonight. A thousand bowmen along the ridge, a firework to show them when to shoot, and hope to see the enemy run . . .

The firework had burned out at last. Darkness was some protection but not enough, in the moonlight when the archers had the range. Tunghai Wang could go forward from here, toward an enemy that waited for him, along a narrow road bordered on both sides by the soft mud and still water of the paddy where no man could run; or he could slip away into the night, humiliated in defeat. Really it was no choice at all. He called his men on in a long furious charge to the brow of the ridge.

Led them on, indeed, himself the point of the spear, dragging his army behind him as he hoped to drag his notorious luck like a net full of fish, his soldiers.

Halfway to the ridge, as the road steepened beneath his horse, as he slowed to let his men keep up, he saw another of those rising sparks, a fierce tiny light.

Expecting another flaring light to guide another volley from the archers, he urged horse and men both faster to the top.

And watched the light come tumbling toward him, there and gone and there again—and remembered his own fire-weapon from the trap he had laid along the river, and understood.

"Into the paddy!" he cried. "Quick now, quick . . . !"

Quick they might be, but of course they were too slow; they always must have been. Everything tonight was slow and late, behindhand. It was his own fault, his own lag. Ping Wen was ahead of him.

Even with his own weapons, Ping Wen had gotten ahead of him.

This wasn't, was *not* what Tunghai Wang had left behind, a potful of oil that blazed as it broke. This was worse. It exploded in the air above the heads of his men, above their chaos as they tried to scramble off the road. Immaculately vicious, it was a storm in a pot, thunder and lightning together, like a firework many times too much; and Tunghai Wang couldn't quite see how, he was too far distant and too slow tonight, too *slow*, but a number of the men fell dead and more fell screaming.

He felt like a man who had stepped heedlessly off the road and into the cloying clinging seep of the midnight paddy that would suck all strength, all movement, all heart and hope from him while his enemies ran on and on into the light. He was floundering, trying simply to keep his feet in ground that gave no purchase.

He turned to face forward again, to face the ridge, and saw twin sparks descending.

Wanted to curse, to weep, to cry vengeance on all his spies and intelligencers and the gods themselves for letting him lead his best hope into this.

Heard the double eruption at his back as those pots exploded, saw the lights of them hurl his own black shadow far ahead.

Heard the voices of his men in their hurt and terror; worse, heard the boots of his men on the road as they ran.

Away from the ridge, away from him.

It was the first time he had known himself abandoned in the field.

He turned his horse and saw them disappear, lit by the ones they left behind, those men who were burning on the road or in the paddy.

Some of them were still alive, but Tunghai Wang left them too, letting his horse pick a delicate path between the bodies and the flames, letting his luck hang like a shield at his back, letting his voice follow his deserters. Too late now, he ordered them to retreat, to pull back, to regroup out of range. If he could save their face, at least a little, he could save his own a little; he might save some remnant of his army.

He might have something to keep against another, a better day than this.

Dawn was striking in the sky at his back, and even that came too soon, before he was ready for it.

three

*Y*ou really should not be here. Really."

Really, Chung thought he might get tired of hearing that. Especially in that voice, from that man. It was becoming the chorus of his life.

Except that every time he heard it, secretly he agreed with it. Of course he shouldn't.

He was still a kitchen boy at heart, unless he was the harbor-rat he'd been before. He'd enjoyed being Mei Feng's runner, but never quite believed it. All else that he'd been, then and since, he didn't even have a name for. He could name one or two things that he wasn't, though, and *warrior* was one of those, and *companion of princes* was another.

He had been in the company of emperors, of course, one emperor at least; but that was only in Mei Feng's shadow, not by any virtue of his own. Here he couldn't even pretend that he stood in Shen's broad shadow, where almost the opposite was true.

In fact they stood side by side, but it was Chung who was invited. It was Shen who came regardless, as if by right. Also it was Shen who told Chung that he didn't belong there, in this company, in this place.

Really, he didn't need the telling.

Even so, it was quite good to be told. It helped, a little. Like standing shoulder to shoulder with Shen, enough that they were actually leaning just a little into each other, just enough to feel the pressure. That helped.

Like not looking down, not looking at what they'd really come to see. That helped too.

Just a little.

He still had to stand in the stink of it, no evading that; he still had to meet Ping Wen's gaze, which was no help at all.

Still had to meet his *smile* . . .

IT HAD been easier in the dark: working his machines, working his teams, sending his missiles as instructed. Not needing to see where they came down, or what damage they did.

Not expecting to be brought out in the broadest of daylight, to be shown.

To be praised, to be rejoiced over, *my pyromancer!*

Pyromancer. Was he?

"It, it is not my skill, my lord general," stammering because what else could you do when you really wanted to scream *no, you're wrong, it isn't me, no, no* . . . ? "It's my men who deserve your praise, their work that made this happen."

"But you brought them together, you had the ideas and gave the orders." Ping Wen was all smiles, among the bodies of his foes.

The dead were crowded around them, and if Chung couldn't blame the general he would like to blame the men who pulled the ropes, and if he couldn't do that then by all the gods who watched him he might try to blame Shen at his side, Shen the soldier, who must have infected him with slaughter-lust.

Anything, rather than look down at the corpses and think, *yes.*

Think, *yes, I did this thing, I. Me. Chung the messenger, Chung the kitchen boy, Chung the water-rat, in and out of everybody's lives. Now I am in and out of everybody's deaths, making them happen. I am a pyromancer, me.*

AFTER A long night standing to the machines, sending up a star-burst every now and then to be sure that Tunghai Wang was not sneaking back toward the barricade, he had thought it might be over: that he and Shen might seek a weary bath and a bed. They stank each of smoke and sweat and powders; careful as they were and watchful of each other, they each had burns and black oil on their hands.

Ping Wen had forestalled any thought of respite, appearing suddenly at his side: "Come, see! See what good work you wrought. It is the same north and east, but come see, this is what you did yourself . . ."

What we did ourselves, and, *at your order,* but really *I know what I did;* and of course he said nothing, none of that.

He trudged in Ping Wen's wake, and only made sure that Shen was coming too—as if that man would ever stay behind again—and dreaded everything else, every moment of this, until they were stopped in their little procession, just short of the barricade that Ping Wen had set across the road.

Stopped by two that Chung knew, the doctor-woman Tien and the fisherman Old Yen, though he hadn't seen them together before this.

It was Tien that Ping Wen stopped for, summoning her through the cordon of his guards; it was Old Yen that he listened to, at Tien's insistence, in the old man's urgency.

Chung might not have listened, perhaps—as Mei Feng's messenger he had been hours and days in the presence of great men at their counsels, and even when he was bright and alert he was seldom interested—but Shen always wanted to know everything. Shen pressed close and Chung went with him as a matter of course. It was that or fall over.

"You have a message for me, from the *dragon?*"

"Yes, my lord general—"

"—Governor—"

"—My lord governor, yes, from the dragon. She sent—"

"And she did this how?" Ping Wen asked mildly, casting his eyes about at his entourage, carefully whimsical and carefully impatient, *who let this fool near me?*

"There is a boy, who speaks her mind for her. And sometimes prevents her from attacking people. I do not understand the boy."

"Wait. He prevents her . . . ?" No whimsy now; Ping Wen was interested. "Did she allow you across the strait again?"

"Yes, excellence."

"Without one of those mute children aboard?"

"Yes, excellence."

"Hmm. I had thought, perhaps you were bringing me another of the children. That would have been a gift worth having. If you can speak to the dragon, though . . ."

"Excellence, she would want to speak to you. Directly."

"How so?"

"That is my message. She sends me to fetch you to the Forge, or if you will not come"—added quickly, in the face of his abrupt shake of the head—"then she asks that you fly a flag of her color, a banner in an open space outside the city, and she will come to you."

"She will come? And how am I to trust this accommodating dragon?"

"Excellence, she wants to parley," the old man said simply. "I have negotiated with her already, to allow the fleet at Taishu to fish with her consent. The boy said she will make the same arrangement with you."

"In exchange for what?"

"You would have to ask the dragon. All she wants from us on Taishu is that we fly her color at the mast, and not cross the strait. I do not suppose that she would want more of you."

Ping Wen grunted and stood still for a moment, gazing up at the empty sky. Then he walked again, more quiet than he had been; the fisherman and the doctor both were left behind.

It was a pity. Chung would have welcomed their company, any company: anyone else who really shouldn't be here, who really didn't want to be doing this.

Shen the soldier was looking forward to it, he thought, as much as any man might want to see the results of his handiwork. Chung the pyromancer, who might deny it as much as he liked but still knew himself to be responsible, knew that none of this would have happened without him—he didn't actually want to be anywhere near, did not want to be confronted with what he had done.

Only that he thought he ought to be, and so did Ping Wen, so here he was.

MEN CLEARED aside the barricade to give them an easy walk along the road.

There was an open stretch of ground, littered with spikes and pits and obstacles to frustrate an assault.

The assault had never reached so far. The bodies made another line of litter, farther off.

Ping Wen wanted to examine the bodies, to see the results of his new weapons in the flesh. Deep in the torn scorched flesh.

Chung didn't want to look at them.

He kept his chin up and his eyes on the horizon, except when Ping Wen spoke to him, words of considered praise like coins counted out by generous, careful fingers.

So it was that—despite the entourage, despite the guards who ought to have been watching but were all too readily distracted by the dead—Chung was first to see movement on the road westerly.

Banners and flags, designed to be seen at a distance: this wasn't another assault. A tentative party, rather, coming slowly, making themselves plain.

Chung said nothing, waited for others to notice. Hid his smile when it was Shen who saw, Shen who pointed, Shen who called an alert.

Ping Wen straightened, turned, assessed. Said no, they would not fall back behind the barricade. This was an embassage of some sort, riders flying the flag of Tunghai Wang with bannermen running before. Ping Wen would receive them on the road here, in person, right now . . .

*   *   *

IT COULDN'T have been what they were expecting. Functionaries speak to functionaries, by and large. If they had thought to be brought before Ping Wen at all, it would have been in the governor's palace, in the audience hall with perhaps a word in private after, before they were sent back to their master.

Not this, to find the man himself with such a small party, outside his defenses, surveying the night's carnage. They weren't quite ready for it, these runners and riders. Perhaps some distracted aspect of their minds was wishing they had laid a little ambush, live men among the fallen . . .

Still, they recovered. They saluted Ping Wen with respect; they conveyed the greetings of their own lord Tunghai Wang, who asked for a meeting between them, the two powers on this side of the strait.

Two equal powers was not said. Neither was anything said about victory or defeat, surrender, submission on either side. It was all most courteous and diplomatic.

Ping Wen took a little time to consider, but not too much. He stepped aside for a minute, and stood untroubled among the corpses; then he came back and said, "I will fly a banner on the ridge, north of the city. Do you tell Tunghai Wang to come to me there, and we will speak."

"When will that be, may we tell him, excellence?"

"When I fly the banner. Do you watch. A green banner; you will not miss it. It will be soon."

The green banner was the dragon's signal. Chung wondered what it was that Ping Wen might have to say to Tunghai Wang and the dragon together, or to either one of them that he might like the other to overhear.

Then Ping Wen dismissed the embassage, and watched them ride away with their bannermen running before them; and then he summoned Chung with a brisk wave of the hand, and then Chung didn't have to wonder anymore.

four

Jiao thought probably she should have gone with Ping Wen to see the bodies beyond the walls. She had seen bodies enough in her time, but these might have been interesting, handiwork of those curious boys with their curious machines. Besides, it would be good practice to establish herself at the governor's side, let her seem to be there by nature. If she really did want to act as his second voice, his shadow. It was one of her options. She was considering it.

But she would have had to take the tiger, her own second voice, her shadow. She was nothing yet without the tiger; and she thought perhaps he had seen enough of blood and death for a while. He was young yet, just a cub. She didn't want him thinking that human beings were always to be found beneath his feet. Dead by nature.

There might be no faster way to make a tiger-skin of him, and she was hoping to avoid that for as long as possible.

For now, he was worth more to her alive, and she meant to keep him that way.

For now.

BESIDES, JIAO had let that girl-doctor Tien at her with her needles, and had been feeling heavily, pleasantly sleepy ever since. And a brisk fall of rain had passed over, and now the air was heavy with that scent of hot sun on wetly green, and the breeze had picked up some of that weight and warmth as it pressed like a tender hand against her skin, and she very truly did not want to move.

· · ·

BESIDES . . .

HERE IN the governor's gardens was a pavilion that overlooked a pond. The reedy margins had been kept clear of trees, perhaps to draw ducks and herons, to let the birds and the water be seen and admired, painted perhaps, from the balcony above.

That made it a fine place also to keep watch on necessary children. Jin and her little sister lived in the pavilion, very much under the governor's eye; so did the boy Pao. They were not short of deckhands here in Santung, but he did seem to be required for the girls' ease of mind, and hence the governor's.

Sprawled in a chair on the balcony in the sun, Jiao was entirely doing her duty, watching over Ping Wen's greatest asset.

The children were playing catch beside the pond, the three of them tossing a bright feather-light ball from one to another. The little girl wasn't very good at catching; her big sister wasn't very good at paying attention. Pao had been a model of patience and encouragement.

Until the tiger came.

NOW ALL three of them were caught in a twisting wind of laughter that bent them entirely out of shape and even Jiao was grinning, struggling not to join them altogether. It had taken her till now to learn that laughing offered whole new avenues to pain.

The tiger had been lying sprawled on the balcony beside her, asleep or nearly so, his bright flank shifting sunlight as he breathed.

Perhaps the children's voices had woken him. Drowsing herself, she had been none the less aware when his head lifted to watch them at their play.

When he stirred to crouch alert on his haunches, she dropped a quieting hand on his shoulder, feeling the weight of bone there and muscles like cables beneath the dense coarse fur. She'd sensed a response to her touch, but not what she had reached for, not the discipline of submission. Before she could take a grip on his collar, he was gone: one tremendous leap took him over the balcony rail and down to the grass below, two more bounds and he was in among the children.

Jin was the unlucky one, standing with her back to the pavilion, couldn't see the tiger coming.

Which meant of course that the other two could and did, but they were as slow as Jiao. Only her mind was moving, keeping up. She saw how little Shola was wide-eyed and scared for her sister, ready to scream but she didn't have the air; she saw how Pao was just as scared but bold in the moment, ready to hurl forward between beast and girl, but he didn't have the time.

Even from the back, she saw how Jin herself was blithely ignorant, focused entirely on catching Pao's high careful lob.

Jiao saw everything, it seemed, every little detail: the ball's rise and the tiger's too, those great ground-eating bounds that sent all his lethal mass flying toward Jin's unprotected shoulders . . .

TOWARD THEM and above them, close enough to stir the girl's hair as he overleaped her; and he was turning, twisting in mid-air, stretching out one long vicious leg—

—AND BATTING at the ball as it tumbled by, like a kitten playing with a falling leaf.

SENDING IT—by chance, surely, it had to be chance—straight at Pao, who was stumbling lad-like over his own feet but still managed to hurl a hand out and catch the ball before he fell.

THEY CAME down together, boy and tiger, rolled on the grass and came up almost eye to eye. Caution or downright fear had kept the boy at a distance before this, but now he would have hot musk breath in his face, all the glitter and charm of that fierce eye in his head. Jiao knew. She was almost envious.

He stared, enraptured, and the tiger moved no more than he did.

Then, slowly—oh, so slowly!—the boy raised his arm, cocked it, flung the ball back over the tiger's head.

The tiger leaped and pivoted, couldn't quite swat it out of the air.

This time, he landed squarely on all four feet. And then just stood there, looking from girl to girl to boy to distant ball. Not a dog, quite clearly; not going to fetch the thing, no. Expecting it to be fetched.

Remarkably, it was poor hollow Jin who ran to do that. Who turned and tossed it back toward the tiger; who crouched and leaped and caught it this time on a claw, and dragged it down to earth and snuffled at it while Jin squealed and clapped her hands, while the other two stared at her, at the great cat, at her again.

No longer worried, Jiao subsided into her chair. Now she was just watching.

Pao had his courage back, but still no certainty. He glanced up at the balcony as if for consent, or else refusal. Seeing neither, he was desperately slow again but bolder than before, stepping forward, reaching down to take the ball. To take it from the tiger.

Who was growling, Jiao could hear it from here. The boy might be hoping that was just a purr made gross. It wasn't, but neither was it a dog's growl, promise of a fight. Sometimes it was an invitation. Sometimes. He growled when he ate, and she wouldn't try to take his food away from him.

The ball was only silk and feathers, and it must be torn already; Jiao saw a drift of leakage as the boy lifted it from the tiger's paw.

The tiger raised his head, and sneezed.

And crouched, his eyes intent on the ball again.

Pao tossed it from hand to hand, making the tiger's head turn and turn, back and forth. Now both the girls were giggling.

He called to Shola, to be sure the little girl was ready. When he saw her determined nod, saw her hands cup in hopes of a clean catch, he threw the ball.

High over the tiger's head, who made a wonderful unavailing effort to swat it; and turned again in mid-air to see how it fell, as neatly into the little girl's hands as if it had been drawn there on a string.

The tiger crouched again, and waited for her to throw.

She stretched her arm out and flung so hard she turned herself entirely around in a circle and so didn't see how poor the throw was, how she virtually hurled the ball straight into the turf. Instead, she recovered just in time to see the tiger pounce and tumble head-over-heels with his prey, growling mightily the while.

By the time he came to rest, he was closer to Jin. Jiao could see, she could almost measure how the boy struggled to hold himself back, not to interfere. Trust was a hard thing, and he had to trust them both.

There was no hesitation in the big girl, doing what she had seen him do. She stepped forward, bent down, took the ball away from the tiger.

Jiao wasn't sure, but she thought it was just possible that Jin had murmured a word to the tiger as she did it. Certainly Pao was staring, startled.

Then Jin flung the ball, and the tiger didn't catch it but Pao did; and then they were all three—no, all four—of them into the game, the ball flying from one child to another while the tiger spun and danced among them, taking the ball more often than any of them but always letting them have it back.

They laughed louder and louder, they hugged themselves with glee, they flung the ball more and more wildly; at last, inevitably, Jin threw it into the pond.

Inevitably, the tiger flung himself in pursuit, with a tremendous splash.

SILK AND feathers. The ball surged away on the tiger's own ripples. Before the beast could cut through them to reach the sodden mass, it had sunk and was gone.

It didn't seem to matter. A swimming cat was as much entertainment as a leaping cat, and even less expected. The children gathered at the water's margin, looking for little things to throw, in hopes that he might chase.

The tiger was perhaps enjoying himself just as much, a cool swim on a hot day. Still not a dog, he was not going to fetch twigs, but he did swim back and forth for a while before he hauled himself out, dragging a vast quantity of water with him and shaking it of course all over the shrieking children.

Then he sprawled on the grass and so did they, and it was somehow Jin's lap that acquired a heavy wet cat-head, Jin's own head that bent low above, Jin's falling hair that made a screen to deny Jiao's curious gaze, too far to tell if she were whispering.

JIAO WAS content so long as the girls were, so long as the tiger was. The boy didn't particularly concern her.

She drowsed, and kept a weather-eye open, an ear alert. In the late afternoon, the boards of the balcony creaked under a significant weight, and she spoke lightly, without looking.

"Come back to me, have you? Traitor. Don't look to me for kitten-games, you'll get none here."

The tiger didn't reply, unless his settling by her feet was a response of sorts. After a minute or two of fidget and sighs, he began to lick at still-damp fur. When he gave that over in favor of chewing and tugging at a toenail, Jiao sighed in her turn and went to fetch his chain.

five

*M*en come and take away the things you value most.

That was the lesson, the late lesson of Ma Lin's life. She used to think it was the other way around, that a man brought gifts: a home, his body, children. Company. Comfort, delight, shelter: the promises of life.

Men had taken all these things from her, one by one this year.

Her home, her security, her man: all lost, all in a day.

Her children, daughters of her flesh: they had been taken and taken, two of them ghost-first before their bodies went. One was dead now, little Meuti, and sometimes her ghost came back, *tug-tug* at Ma Lin's trousers. The other two had been taken and taken by men and men. Sometimes they were brought back, but only to be taken again.

This latest time, that might have been the last time. She had no notion of seeing them again, coming across the water in a boat. They lay in the hands of the goddess, or the goddess and the emperor together. It seemed unlikely that those two would ever agree that returning her children to her would be best for all.

She would have stayed here in this headland temple just in case. She would have waited, even if there had been nothing to do but wait.

In fact, in their absence she had found work to do. All unpracticed, she played priestess to the local people. Perhaps to the goddess too, she wasn't sure: only that she gave the people something they seemed to need, and the goddess seemed not to object.

She kept the little temple clean, she kept the weather out. She burned incense and accepted what the people brought, either for the goddess or herself. This was what mattered most, she thought: that someone should be here to take their offerings. The poor need to give. Without a priestess all these years, they hadn't been able. The goddess needed human hands to act for her, or else food rotted and the rain came in.

The goddess needed a human voice to speak through, and so Ma Lin's daughters had been taken. Priesthood was no substitute, but it was something, it was a life. A way to be, while the time passed. It mattered, to other people; she could persuade herself that that mattered to her. For now, while she waited.

She didn't try to persuade the goddess. Sometimes she would talk to one statue or another as she washed off the sticky smoky residues of lamp and censer, but only ever about her daughters, her life of long ago.

TODAY SHE had welcomed her regular women with their shy patient men, their gifts of rice and greens and gathered fruits and time. They had come and gone, as they did, as people do.

Alone again, she stood on the clifftop and watched the sky for dragon, the sea for boats or dragon, hoping not ever again to see boat and dragon come together.

After a while, she wasn't really watching anymore. There was wind and water, there was bold sun and no cloud; that seemed to be enough. Like her life now, drifting, undriven. Uninformed.

She thought perhaps the weather too was waiting, unless it was the ocean. Unless they were the same.

WHEN SHE heard men coming through the forest, she wasn't for a moment fooled by that.

This was not what she had waited for, unless it was her doom to be always waiting for disaster.

They were too many and too loud, a little lost. Not peasants, which meant they must be soldiers. For one side or the other, or perhaps the other yet: for the emperor or the governor or the rebels. She didn't really try to sort them out. She didn't care; it seemed to make no difference. Men came and took her children. For a little time they had kept them here with her, but not for long: so no, she really didn't believe these noisy men would be bringing her girls back, no. Really not.

The girls would have shown them the quicker way to come.

Besides, the girls had gone away by boat. If they came back, ever and ever, they would come that way: fetched by the goddess, returned by the old fisherman. She was sure of it.

Perhaps these men were looking for the children. If so, she had nothing to offer them, except the chance to wait. No one could cross the water, not from here. Not without her girls.

Ma Lin stood straight and waited, expecting something dreadful.

THEY CAME, shadows through the trees, men calling: this was the way, here was the headland, here the sun, the temple . . .

They came into the light in a long slow file, ones and twos to-gether. There were too many of them. Even two would have been too many for Ma Lin, even one perhaps, though she had killed one man before. This many made no sense, unless they came—unless they thought they came—to guard the children who were not here.

What use else could there be, here, for so many men?

Some carried long bamboos and coils of rope. Some carried sacks. Perhaps they were nothing to do with her at all, perhaps they meant to climb down the cliffs and harvest eggs or baby gulls, although this was not the season. Perhaps they had some other reason to go over the edge.

Perhaps they meant to work on the temple roof and thought they needed a scaffold to do it, didn't know that she had done it herself with no help but her own strong arms and legs.

Perhaps . . .

. . .

THIS WAS their captain, coming straight to her. Sending his men inside. She didn't like to see that, too many men in the house of the goddess without herself to watch.

The captain saluted her gravely, almost reverently, and she didn't like that either. If he thought her a priestess, if he offered her respect and still sent his men to do whatever their duty was, with their poles and ropes in her temple, all unsupervised . . .

She thought that was reason enough to be unhappy, even before he spoke her name.

She had not thought her name was known beyond her own people here, her little congregation, but this man knew it. He said, "You are Ma Lin, the woman of the temple?"

She nodded, warily. He had not quite said *priestess;* she was not quite prepared to believe that didn't matter. "Who are you?"

He said, "We are soldiers of the emperor, serving the governor in Santung," if those two were really the same thing anymore.

"What do you want here, what are your men at?" They were making too much noise in there, too much altogether: grunting and shouting, sounds of breaking.

"We have orders," their captain said.

And no more, but really no more was needed, because she could see what his men were at. They went in, they came out; they went in empty-handed, and came out loaded.

They carried the smaller statues ill-wrapped in sacks, slung in their arms or roped to their backs. Here came a pair of men with one too heavy to lift alone. That one hung from a bamboo on their shoulders, slung in a cradle of rope. There were men enough to carry it in shifts, and the others too, everything that could be carried.

They stripped out the temple while she watched, made an empty shell of it, left it here as hollow as Ma Lin's daughter when the goddess was not in her; and where would the goddess go now, and where Ma Lin . . . ?

six

*T*here was something about Mei Feng.

There always had been. It was more refined these days, less raw, but still powerful. Summoning, sending.

As soon as news came of what had happened to her and to the empress, of how much she needed Master Biao and his tiger-skin, of course Yu Shan had come too. What else? There was something about Mei Feng. Everybody came.

AND IT was like being back in the summer valley, standing watch and training, being together, being young and intense and impressed with themselves, comparing scars. And now here was Mei Feng sending him away in secret, in defiance—in defiance of the emperor, no less!—and here he was, going where she sent him. Because there was just something about her.

And here was Siew Ren come with him, because "Did you think you could just sneak off, and me not know about it?" and "Of course I'm coming too, you'll need me, how do you imagine you might manage by yourself?" and her tongue might be fierce in her twisted mouth and her face might glare by nature now but it was her good arm that she slipped through his, and that was enough to be going along with. More than enough, given how guilty he felt, how his life was a series of accidents but they were all bad ones and they all happened to other people, and Siew Ren most and worst of all.

He wasn't thinking about Jiao.

These days, Siew Ren made it easy not to do that, where she used to make it impossible.

It was a long walk from the palace to the city, but her legs were strong, and her stride might be stiff but it was long; and she had jade in her blood, jade at her throat, the touch-memory of a stone tiger's skin wrapped around her own. And she was Siew Ren, which meant determined. And she had Yu Shan to lean on if she needed to, and she clearly regarded that as a victory so long as she never did actually need it.

In fact they needn't have walked all or any of the way. There were always wagons clattering empty back to the city. Any one would have given them a ride. Many offered, but every time Siew Ren would pull the broad brim of her woven rain hat lower, turn her head away, refuse it with her shoulders. Every time, Yu Shan would translate that into manners, the most gracious refusal he could achieve. She had come this far, out of her hut and out of her valley, out of the hills altogether; it was enough. He was still astonished that she could face the petty palace with its strangers, guards and servants mixed among her friends and kin. She wasn't truly ready for the road, let alone the city. And was coming anyway, coming for him, unless it was for Mei Feng: and that was courage beyond reckoning. If it cost them a day's walking, it was worth the price.

If it cost her pain, she was prepared for that and so was he. Her body, her pain. So long as she never mentioned it, neither would he. His arm was there beneath her hand, and if she was leaning more weight on it by the day's end, if she was gripping it more tightly that would perhaps be his victory but it would pass quite unacknowledged.

All that long road they walked, and came to Taishu-port as the sun was setting. Siew Ren looked shocking in the low sun: her face drawn tight to the bone, all her scarring standing proud, her eyes as tense and narrow as her lips.

Yu Shan said, "You must be tired. We can sleep here," at the jademaster's palace, adopted by the emperor until his new Hidden City was completed, "and go down to the temple in the morning."

She shook her head. "I don't want . . ." Even her voice had been touched by fire. It was hoarse and scratched now, and inclined to peter out. It said enough, though: *I don't want to deal with all those people, their pity and revulsion, their superiority, their fuss.* "Can't we go to temple now?"

Let the nuns have us, she was saying. *If they keep us overnight, the morning will be easier to manage.*

Perhaps she was right. Certainly she didn't want to walk through these high and guarded gates. The temple was really not much farther, and downhill all the way. He had gawped, Yu Shan remembered, and dragged at Jiao's heels his first time here—but he was not going to think about Jiao. It was suddenly harder, in the city where all his first experience was hers, but still. Not.

There were many temples in Taishu-port: temples and temples, to offer their due to gods and gods. And goddesses. Even so—just as in the mountains there were mystical creatures that were not stone tigers, but when you spoke of a glimpse, a presence, a touch of wonder in the night, everyone knew what you meant—if you talked of temple in Taishu, there was only one temple you might mean. There was only one goddess who belonged here, who could lay claim to the island's people because hers was the strait that they depended on.

Even before she proved herself mightier than the dragon, that was true. Now it was inherent, inescapable.

No. The *last* time he was here, it was inescapable. Now, not quite so. Now the old man had done a deal with the dragon, and it was by that creature's license that they fished from here. Did that make it her strait, did that displace the goddess?

Perhaps. Yu Shan wasn't sure, and neither apparently was anybody else. The temple of the Li-goddess was thronged with people, red altar-lamps flinging shifting shadows all across the open
court and the roofed galleries that enclosed it. One voice, harsh
and female, rose above the murmur of so many, a prayer like a saw
blade biting deep, back and forth, unstoppable.

Yu Shan stood just inside the gateway and laid his arm around
Siew Ren's shoulders as he looked down into that chaotic mull,
all smoke and sound and shadow. He said, "You wait here," setting her by a pillar, something she could cling to. "I'll find the
priestess."

He couldn't see her face beneath the hat, but he could hear her
smile in the way it shaped her words. "No need," she said. "The
priestess will find us. Do you think she could miss . . . ?"

Miss you, she meant, *tall mountain boy, friend of emperors.
Jade-eater. You are famous in this town. Haven't you seen them
staring?*

Yes, of course he had, all through the streets; but all his concern
had been for her. Guilt made him over-protective. He knew it, and
could not apparently change it. Could not even apologize for it,
because she was right, of course: here came the priestess from her
prayers to greet the emperor's shadow, all unexpected in her house.

He said, "My friend and I, we need a bed tonight, and then
away early in the morning," *with our errand,* which he would not
explain until that time. "Do you have a corner where we can be
private?" meaning *do not ask Siew Ren even to take her hat off,
until we are alone.*

"Of course," said the priestess, meaning *of course not, we
are over-full already and half our people will be sleeping in the
open court,* meaning *take my cell, and I will sleep in with my
sisters.*

Ashamed, he would still use his fame or anything to buy Siew
Ren the space and shelter that she needed, to be alone with her all
night and undisturbed. Once he used to want the same thing for a

wholly different purpose—but in those days they could have it for the asking, just walk out into the forest and find a place to be. In those days, he waited for her invitation. Now he had to negotiate on her behalf. Never mind that the priestess made it easy, it was still a significant shift and he hated it.

And could see no way to help her past it, back to a place where she had the confidence to ask and the arrogance to expect. For now, he was content that she should sleep; happy that she should sleep next to him, nestling into his warmth, as though her body at least remembered.

He slept himself, a little, as much as he needed to and perhaps a little more; and woke to her wakefulness, to the bright glitter of her eye just there beside him, her body stretched against as much of his as she could reach.

She said, "You make me feel better," which made him feel as better as he could be.

He slipped one arm beneath her head, the other down to her hip, where he could hold her without hurting her. "What," he said, smiling, "like Biao's tiger-skin?"

She nodded fractionally, little more than a shift of her cheek against his shoulder; she was learning these marginal, potent gestures, when any pulling of the deep-scarred skin could suddenly hurt her extremely. "Yes," she said. "Like that, but not so . . . urgent. Like a stew that will sit all day in charcoal and cook itself slowly, slowly. The tiger-skin is a fierce flame, bamboo. Was fierce. Now I think it is burning itself out."

Like the old woman who lay beneath it, whose life was perhaps not ebbing any longer but neither was it flooding back. The skin had done what it could, they thought; it was slack water with her now, and always would be.

"Well," he said, "I can be your coals all night, every night, if it will help you heal." *Now that Jiao is gone, I can,* but he wasn't going to think about Jiao.

She smiled, that tight and savage twisting that was nothing lovely to see; it sat in her eyes and in his head like a promise received and witnessed.

THE TEMPLE woke around them, woke and rose and put itself to work.

They rose themselves, washed in cool perfumed water, dressed in borrowed robes and left the cell.

"Should we pray, do you think?" It was Siew Ren who asked, another momentary betrayal of herself, measurement of what she had lost. She used to be the one who decided, *we should pray* or *we should not*. He would have looked to her to tell him, either way.

Now she looked to him, and he didn't know. Temples and prayers were no part of their life in the mountains. The clans tended rather to respect the gods at a distance, leave them to the world beyond. Stone tigers and other creatures walked in the forests and on the slopes, the emperor himself sat at the farther end of the Jade Road, which might be any distance but it started in their hills. What need had they of other gods, or other gods of them?

He said, "We could burn joss, maybe." It would only be polite, guests in her house—but here came the priestess before they could achieve it, to sweep them up with an imperious gesture and take them to a small refectory.

"Sit, sit," the priestess said, clapping her hands for service.

"Oh, please, you've all had your breakfast; don't worry about us . . ."

"Nonsense. What, did you think we would send you out hungry? Neither the emperor nor the people nor the goddess would be pleased with us, did we so." A scurrying novice brought bowls of congee, a bowl of salted eggs, a pot of tea; the priestess smiled upon her beatifically and went on, "See, I will sit with you and drink tea, so that you need not feel awkward in our house; and when you have eaten, you will tell me why you are here and how we may serve you better than a scant meal and a cramped bed."

Yu Shan took a breath; Siew Ren dropped her face into congee-steam. He swallowed down any risk of words, picked up a horn spoon and began to eat.

WHEN HE realized that he was eating more and more slowly, when he caught himself reaching for an egg he didn't particularly want, then Yu Shan laid his spoon down, wiped his mouth, turned to the priestess and said, "Forgive me, but I must take one of your children away from you."

She understood, of course. The temple might give a home to any number of orphans; some might stay a lifetime, girls raised as nuns, gifts to the goddess; nevertheless, when Yu Shan spoke of a child, he could mean only one.

She said, "The emperor charged me to keep him safe."

"As you have." And more carefully so, since Jiao—he *didn't* want to think about Jiao!—stole the girls away in the old man's boat. "But I have come from the emperor," which was almost true, "and it is felt"—if not exactly by the emperor—"that he will be safer if we keep him farther from the sea, with those guards who protect the emperor himself and his mother," and his favorite too, whom Yu Shan was very carefully not mentioning here. She was no fool, this priestess.

"Safer, yes. Perhaps." She was thinking it through, aloud. "Safer, but less useful. Far from the sea."

Far from the goddess, she meant. From her goddess, whose interests she served, which would not always be the emperor's interests, perhaps.

At the moment, Yu Shan served Mei Feng's interests entirely, which were also perhaps not the emperor's just now.

He said, "The little boats can fish without protection, if they fly the dragon's flag," which was not perhaps a tactful thing to say in this house but true none the less, "and the emperor has no need to return to the mainland." That was pure Mei Feng and not the emperor at all; if he had said *no plans to return* it would have been a lie absolute. "Now that Tunghai Wang has the girls"—*stolen from your care* but he wasn't going to mention that, he didn't need to—"and can launch an attack of his own at any time, we want to keep the boy some way from danger."

What danger, what *other* danger, he didn't clarify: not here. He'd said enough, he thought.

Siew Ren had thought he could not do this by himself, and he had proved her wrong. Her hurts might have made the task easier, because who could distrust anyone who had given so much for the emperor? But he had saved her that, and was delighted with himself; and the priestess was nodding, saying, "Yes, of course. If it is an imperial order," and he simply stood and waited, no response necessary.

AND THEN they brought him the child, and he had not the first idea what to do with it.

HE KNEW something about boys, he had been a boy himself: but not like this, damaged and possessed, like a puppet abandoned. He hated that sense of emptiness. It was different in babies, who were waiting only to grow into themselves. This one had begun his growing, and then been emptied out; and now . . .

Well. He was something like a baby, but too big; something like a boy, but too hollow. Unpurposed. Lying slackly in the priestess's arms, then slackly in Yu Shan's. Meeting his gaze with an insensate stare, no hint of any mind behind the eyes.

Easier, somehow, to think of him as *it:* as though it were unpersoned, dead already or else not yet born. Either one, a little of both together in a living body. That might have been terrifying, if it weren't so sad.

Saddened and appalled, Yu Shan gazed down into the unresponsive face and didn't know how to move on from here. Couldn't imagine how to go from here to there, a long day's walking with an absence in his arms. He thought this child would suck his soul along the way, and still have nothing of its own. He thought it was a drain into a desert.

Siew Ren rescued him, all unexpectedly: suddenly showing something of herself again, what she had claimed to come for, *how do you imagine you might manage by yourself?*

She wore a nun's robe in somber drab, with a hood hanging down at the back. She lifted that up to mask her face, better than her rain hat ever had; and then took the child from his helpless arms.

Crooned down at it from the shadows of her hood, which made no perceptible difference to the child but he rather thought it made a difference to her. Then she lifted her head, so that he could at least see the glitter-and-twist of her eyes as she said, "Are we going, then? We have a long journey and I want him home before the day ends, there's nowhere to stop along the road."

YES, YES, they were going. They were going now. This was them, going: bidding a long farewell to the priestess, a swift one to the goddess at her altar, leaving a gift of money—the emperor's money, which he would not miss but Yu Shan felt bad about regardless—to buy clothes for the orphans, joss for those who could not afford it. It was a guilt-offering, given what they were stealing, and never mind that they had stolen the money too.

THIS WAS them on the road out of town, the Jade Road, walking; and here was an ox-cart laden with stone for the new palace, so slow that they were overtaking it when the driver called down to offer them a ride.

And, for a wonder, Siew Ren said yes; and so they sat on all that stone, as comfortable as they could be, and the laggard beasts hauled them home.

And at some point in the journey, Siew Ren dangled her jade bead on its thong and the child caught it, carried the bead to its mouth and sucked on it.

Yu Shan thought nothing of it. Only later, when they were closer to the palace, he saw her slip the bead out of the child's mouth and tuck it inside her robe again; and then, oh, then he heard the child protest.

seven

He was the one, the only one who had sailed the strait in safety without an escort-child.

He was the one who knew the goddess most intimately, more so even than her own priestesses; she was of the sea and so was he.

Also, he was the one who had negotiated with the dragon.

Of course he was a guest in Ping Wen's palace.

Guest or prisoner, and who could ever know the difference? He slept in comfort, he was brought fresh clothes every morning, there was always more food than he could eat; and he was always watched, and he could wander wherever he cared to through the palace grounds but the gates were somehow closed to him in the most polite manner imaginable.

Sometimes a captive will deliberately place himself under a stricter watch. Perhaps in protest, perhaps to punish himself for his own situation; perhaps for other reasons, darker or more hopeful, more obscure.

Once Old Yen had found the boy Pao and the children in their pavilion, of course he chose to stay with them.

That this set him too under Jiao's eye, under the tiger's—that was not quite coincidence, and not quite immaterial. Jiao had stolen his boat, his boy and the children of his goddess; she had handed them over to Ping Wen, whom both he and she knew to be a traitor; she had led him also into that dreadful confrontation on the water, himself and the goddess and the dragon.

Twice now he had betrayed the goddess. A third time would be unimaginable, which was why—one reason why—he would not be leading any men of Ping Wen's across the strait. If he had said or implied otherwise, he was lying for the sake of his head, his friends and his future. And his boat.

For all the same reasons, he would say nothing to Jiao, when all he had was accusation, truth laid bare. He'd rather talk to the tiger. That was at least an honest beast. It didn't wrap itself in a cloak of kindness, or pretend to an allegiance not its own. Jiao could only keep it by keeping it on a chain.

He had lamented, he still lamented, he was appalled by the dragon's being free of her chains. The tiger, sometimes he thought he ought to free it quietly in the night, let it run. He knew nothing of tigers, mountain creatures, forest creatures, tree and stone; still something in him thought it should be free. Even here, the wrong side of the water, far from jade.

But he was a practical man, Old Yen. He thought the tiger would rip his old frail bones apart, if he ventured to set it loose. And then he thought it would destroy the children, before it turned to Jiao and at last perhaps to its own freedom: leaping from a window, running like storm through the tame wilderness of the palace garden, taking the guarded wall at a bound and seeking the shortest road out of the city, already sniffing for mountains, for distance, for height and solitude.

Unless the call of its home would be the stronger, unless it turned to the sea and tried swimming to Taishu.

Old Yen wondered vaguely, self-mockingly, if the dragon would let the tiger by. Did power call to power, was there sympathy between one mystical creature and another?

If so, perhaps the goddess would drown the tiger, because she could not drown the dragon. Petty again, but he had seen her in his boat, he had felt her in his body, felt the weak stubborn fury of her grip.

Shrugged her off, denied her, betrayed her.

He wasn't quite sure—what weighs a lifetime of service, against a sudden betrayal?—but he thought she might be petty enough to drown him, next time he put to sea.

He thought she might try, at least.

If he took the children, would that risk their lives, or save his own? He wasn't sure, he couldn't tell. Nothing was clear anymore, in a world where his goddess was a paltry thing, a ragged twist of water on a stick, ineffectual and sour.

Not sure if he could do it, he could plan for it, at least.

He could talk to Pao while the girls were at their games, drowsy in the grass in this late-season heat:

"My boat, boy. What did you do with my boat?"

"Master, I . . . I misread the tide, and by myself I couldn't change the sails in time enough to catch her . . ."

"Yes, yes. No blame to you for that; no one can sail her single-handed. She won't yield to it, she needs a strong hand on the tiller and swift feet across the deck." Nothing about that day had been the boy's fault. He'd done well to bring the boat whole across the strait. A week ago, Old Yen would have told him to be grateful to the goddess.

Now? Well, now he was not so sure. Now he might almost tell the boy to be grateful to the boat. Stubborn determined bastard boat, beaten and broken and never sunk yet . . .

Again, "What did you do with her?"

"Beached her, master. Not," as this was confession, staring down at his big bare feet, "not by intent. The tide had us and she was too heavy for the wind, the sand was gripping almost before I had the sails set for it. We came in abeam, and . . ."

And that was the worst news so far, because she would topple for sure and might be irrecoverable without a team of men and oxen, ropes, supervision. Permission.

He said, "Just sand, though? Sand, not rocks?" only to encourage the boy; and then, "You left her there, like that?"

"She turned bow-on before we struck," good old boat, self-reliant and wise. "I think the tide would lift her. I had no choice, though, Jiao would never let me stay . . ."

"No, I am sure not. Will the boat still be there, do you know, have you heard?"

A shake of the head, a shrug; and then a lift of that head, a boy seeking comfort where he could, which was not here and not from Old Yen. Pao looked down to the pond's margin, where the girls were weaving flower-heads into chaplets of grass. The little girl was laughing, high and shrill. It was hard to tell from here, but Old Yen thought perhaps he heard a second voice, lower and more tentative, older and more damaged, coming back.

"Master, I don't know. I am not allowed to know, perhaps. I am not the one to ask. I am sorry . . ."

IT OCCURRED to Old Yen that he too might be not allowed to know, as he was so clearly not allowed to go and see for himself.

Still. He was most certainly allowed to ask, because what else was Ping Wen keeping him for, if not for his evident ability to cross the strait with or without the dragon's consent?

He asked to speak to Ping Wen.

He asked a servant, one of those attentive men who trailed him through the palace, who watched him on his walks and at his meals, who fetched him this and that and the other thing and somehow slitheringly denied him anything that might matter, those things he was too wise to ask for, his freedom or his boat.

He asked for a minute of Ping Wen's time, when the governor might be at liberty.

The servant looked first toward Jiao, who sprawled at her perennial ease barely out of earshot. She could certainly take Old Yen directly to Ping Wen if the fisherman only asked it. But if they had learned one thing in all their spying, these wary watchful men, it would surely be that Old Yen did not speak to Jiao.

The servant took his query to a sergeant. Ping Wen might pretend to a civilian rank now—with his eyes perhaps on another, a higher, the highest that could be, above all soldiers ever—but the structure of his mind, the hierarchy of his service was all military. Even inside the palace, soldiers watched the servants, soldiers made a wall between the governor and his people.

If Old Yen expected anything, it was to be interviewed through a chink of that wall by some high official allowed to pay court higher yet. More likely, he thought, it would be a brick of the wall itself, an officer of the army who fetched him a refusal.

He was astonished, then, twice astonished not to be refused and not to be summoned either: to look up an hour later and see a little procession coming to him. Soldiers and functionaries, yes, but the man himself among them, Ping Wen come at a fisherman's request.

What else should a fisherman do, then, but ask about his boat?

"My lord governor," Old Yen said after no more than a bow, just to underline that he had manners but no courtesies, that he no longer kowtowed even to the emperor, "do you have any news of my vessel?"

Ping Wen should have been furious at this interrogation, by someone so lowly. His face showed nothing, though, beyond a polite confusion. "Your . . . vessel?"

"My boat, excellence. That Jiao took to bring the children to you."

"Quite so. Your boat, yes. I regret that I do not have news of it. Perhaps I should. Every vessel in the harbor is important to me, but your own . . . Well. Let us inquire."

Inquiry involved no more than the crook of a finger, to draw one man out of his entourage.

"Master Yen's boat. What news?"

The functionary bowed—a little smugly, Old Yen thought, unless what he read as self-content was actually relief, *this I know*—

and said, "Master Yen's boat is still on the beach where it was set. It has been put to rights, and will be ready whenever you wish him to depart."

"Still on the beach? Why so," frowning, "why has it not been brought to the harbor here, to be convenient?"

"Men were sent, excellence, to do that. They were . . . they found themselves unable to bring the boat away from shore. It was felt, perhaps, that Master Yen's own hand on the tiller, his own eye on the sails, perhaps his own voice raised in prayer . . ."

Absurdly, he was proud of his boat, his bastard boat. She had brought the boy Pao in on sufferance, alive and unhurt with his companions; she would not take strangers out at all. For Old Yen, he was sure, she would lift on the tide and seize the wind and ride out where he would.

And no, next time he would not be praying. His voice would stick in his throat. If the boat did lift, if she did find the wind, she would do it by his skill and her own temper. And he would fly the green banner at his masthead, for all that he hoped to have the girls aboard. Let the goddess and the dragon fight it out between themselves, which one objected and which one let him pass.

He said only, "Thank you, excellence. When you send me, I will know where to find her."

Or anytime before then, but, "You will find her well cared for," the official said, "and well watched."

That he had been afraid of. Or anticipated, at least. Of course they would set a watch on her. There were rebels abroad, and simple runaways too, and every craft was precious.

He was himself, he thought, a runaway, though nothing simple now.

Also—apparently—he was an object of interest now. To the great, and in and of himself.

Ping Wen was not done with him. Indeed, Ping Wen seemed to have small interest in his boat, which was strange in someone who had welcomed him exactly because he could cross and cross the strait.

Ping Wen said, "Master Yen, tell me about your goddess, and her power in your waters."

It was the last thing he wanted to do, speak about the goddess who had let him down so badly, whom he had betrayed so well. Also, they were not his waters. He had spent a lifetime believing they were hers. Now, he thought not; he thought the dragon had the better claim.

He said, "I am no priest, excellence."

"Something to be grateful for. I have spoken to priests. Priestesses. They know nothing of the sea, or of the dragon."

He had not mentioned the dragon till now. Except that any mention of the goddess now was a mention of the sea, which made it a mention of the dragon too, in the way that any mention of the moon was a mention of the stars she swam among and the sun she could not outface. The one brought the other to mind as irresistibly as the tide brings in the seawrack and the ruin of men, broken wood and bodies in the weed.

Well, Old Yen knew the sea, and something of the dragon—but it was the goddess that Ping Wen asked about.

He could talk about her, of course, he had been doing it all his life. Never easily, he was not a man of words, but she had mattered intensely and he had learned to say so. And he had already betrayed the goddess to the dragon, twice. What difference could it make if he did after all betray her for a third time now? Betrayal was the spirit of the time. He stood with traitors on every hand, Jiao and Ping Wen and Tunghai Wang somewhere beyond, close by . . .

He said, "The Li-goddess can shift the sea, but only in a small way," to lift a boat across the rocks, to make a frail banner body for herself and wind it about a pole. "Nothing like the dragon's storms and tsunamis."

"And yet she could hold the dragon prisoner all that time?"

"Yes, excellence. If she has a strength, it is perhaps in holding on. The dragon was delivered by the hand of man, I think, already chained; the goddess was her jailer, not her captor. All she had to do was keep hold. It was . . . necessary, but not arduous. Native to her, I think. The sea endures, and does not let go."

"And yet she can keep the dragon from attacking ships, a whole fleet of ships, two fleets . . . ?"

Again, "Yes, excellence. If she has someone in the fleet she can possess." *Not me.* "She needs . . . solidity, I think, to turn the dragon aside. She needs to work through people. In herself she is immaterial," where the dragon was so very opposite, so very immediate, so physical.

"Well. This is interesting to me. Can you say more?"

WHEN HE had said all he could, when it was obvious to both of them that he had run high onto dry sand with the tide ebbing at his back, the governor left him. With expressions of thanks and instructions to hold himself available, as though there were anything else he might find to do instead, anywhere else he might be permitted to go.

Well, he could learn a lesson from Ping Wen. Where he could not go himself, he could draw someone to him.

HE BECKONED one of those ever-present guards. And stood his ground, waited, beckoned again.

When the man came, he said, "I need to speak to the young woman doctor, Tien. She will be somewhere in the city here. Can she be fetched?" It would be complicated, sure, a hierarchy of soldiers and officials and messengers, but he was in hopes that at the last someone would go, and the girl would come.

The guard blinked. "Tien? She is here now."

"Yes. I said so."

"No, I mean, she is *here*. In the palace."

Old Yen's turn to blink. "Why? Is someone ill?" A complex this large, almost a city in itself: at any given time, someone must be ill. But by the same token, a complex this large, it must house someone skilled in medicine. Even his village had its healer-woman. And here lived Ping Wen, the governor himself and a soldier to the bone. He was safe to keep a doctor close. His own, someone he trusted, not a new-met girl.

"Not ill, no. Broken, maybe. She keeps two old men here, fusting over scrolls older than they are. Ping Wen values them, or what they do; or she does, and he values her. I don't know. But she is here, and today she is not to be let leave. I hear she is in something of a temper about it—but she is still here."

That was curious. Old Yen could make no sense of it, except, "Don't send her to me," he said, changing his mind quite urgently. "If she is unhappy already, that would not help, I think."

The guard grunted. "I think so too, unless you are sick. She might be glad of a reason."

"Could you take me to her? I am not exactly sick, but perhaps I can give her something else to think about."

THE GUARD seemed gratified by the errand. He might perhaps be eager to see the girl raging.

He brought Old Yen to another soldier, who was transparently grateful. This man had endured the tempest; had survived it, but—he felt—barely; was glad now of any relief, any distraction for himself or his prisoner.

Tien was undoubtedly a prisoner, as much as Old Yen was, exactly as much: welcomed and watched and forbidden to leave. The only difference was that she had tried, forcibly, had insisted on her right to go.

And had been held back, forcibly; and was being held now in a closed room with a guard at the door.

Old Yen found her at the window. Might have found her out of the window and gone, he rather gathered, but that another guard stood four-square on the grass below. She had—just—too much pride to be manhandled, but oh, she was angry. She was almost spitting as she turned to face him, and only swallowed it back when she saw who he was, when she managed little by little to place and name him.

"Fisherman," she said, and, "Old Yen, isn't it? Mei Feng's grandfather? I'm sorry, I didn't . . . Why are . . . ?" And then, with a massive effort of will, setting her own mood aside as she remembered what she was, "Do you need my help?"

"I do," Old Yen said, because it was true, and because she all too clearly needed that.

"How are you unwell? I have little with me here beyond my needles," in a tube at her belt, "but—"

"But there are other doctors here who will be very well provided, and I am sure that you could raid their stores at need." He spoke that way deliberately, to make her feel piratic, vengeful, powerful. And then, to let her mull on that—Mei Feng thought he was not this subtle; but Mei Feng was his granddaughter, and knew herself adored, and thought she had manipulated him all her little life—he changed tack abruptly. "We will talk of what I need, but what of you? Why are you here?"

"I came," she said, "because I come every day to see my patients here. I am here still," through stiff lips, through a sudden wash of anger, "because I was detained by order of my lord the governor, no less. We have spoken, and even so he is keeping me here until he wants me, which will be tomorrow, and—"

"He is not sick?"

"Not he, oh no. Not anyone that I can discover."

There would be someone, Old Yen was sure, if she would only look for them less furiously; but, "What did you speak of, then, what did he want, if not your skills?"

"He wants my knowledge about the dragon," hissingly, "which he would have been welcome to at any time, if he were not keeping me from my patients. And he wants my old men too, who can make up their own minds whether to dance in his shadow up a hill, and I am not to be held hostage for their obedience," although apparently she was, "and please do not ask me why, because he would not tell me and I do not know!"

Which last was what bit deepest, apparently, what made her most angry. She was not one to forgive ignorance, even in herself.

He said, "Up a hill?"

"His excellency the governor is pleased to parade to the height of the ridge tomorrow morning, early. And he wants my two old men to drag themselves up there in his train, which is a cruelty to both of them, they are not fit for it; and that is his first excuse for wanting me, because he thinks I can help to get them there. And he is right, of course. He knows that if he takes them I will go, because I wouldn't let them face such a climb without me, even carried on other men's shoulders. And even so he locks me up like this, to be sure he has me on hand for the morning . . ."

She was working herself up into a fury again. Wise in the ways of young women, Old Yen didn't try to shush her, nor urge her to be calm. He said only, "Soldiers are not a trusting breed. They set a watch on me too, men on my boat, when I was sailing back and forth for the emperor. Before the dragon rose."

"The dragon, yes. That might be truly why he wants me, but . . ."

"I came to him from the dragon," Old Yen reminded her. "So, yes, it is no surprise if Ping Wen is interested in the dragon. He has to negotiate with her. Tomorrow, perhaps. He may be ready to fly her banner at last and draw her in. Why he wants your old men there would be another question, unless they know more than you do"—a stubborn shake of her head, that he was not too inclined to accept—"but then there is one question more, which is why he has been interrogating me about the goddess." And why he was keeping Old Yen here too, if not to sail boats for him. There was nothing more to be said about the goddess; yet the fisherman was beginning to wonder if he might not himself be rousted out of bed early, made to march up to the ridge.

Tien had nothing to offer to that question. His goddess was not hers, and, "I do not like the way she uses children."

No more did Old Yen, and he was almost prepared to say so. Better not, though, here in the heart of a palace with listening ears at door and window. Ping Wen thought him still a devotee.

Perhaps so did the goddess, despite his refusal out at sea.

Perhaps they were right.

Tien said, "How can I help you, Old Yen?"

"Not at all, I think. You have said it, you do not know the goddess, and—"

"Old Yen," quite kindly, almost laughing, temper not forgotten but set aside, "you came to me, you sought me out."

Oh. Yes. He took a breath, straightened his spine a little, wished he were at sea; what did he know of palaces, of doctors, of governors and guards?

Of lies, evasions, flight?

He said, "It is difficult to sleep here, far from my boat." *Far from my life*. It was true, this much.

She smiled at him, a little curiously. "One more night, old man. Is that so hard?"

"It may be more than one. Who knows what Ping Wen wants? Besides, he is a traitor," suddenly vehement, truth on truth, "and he worries me, what he might do next. He preys on my mind, and I cannot sleep."

Tien shrugged. "Is he a traitor? I didn't know. Perhaps he keeps good company. There are traitors all around you; half of us are traitors here, if you mean rebels against the throne. I served Tung-hai Wang before I served the emperor."

That was right, she did. He had forgotten. If she was ashamed, regretful even, she didn't show it. He said, "Well. I cannot sleep. Nor the children, whose house I have been sharing." That was better. She cared about the children.

She said, "The children don't worry about Ping Wen's treachery."

"No," not even Pao; their concerns were closer at hand. This was still, almost, true. "They are frightened of the tiger." She must at least have heard of the tiger, even if she hadn't seen it. She might have seen the bodies that it left along the shore, or the man brought in still living. Ping Wen's torturer had that man now, somewhere in this same palace, for whatever he might still be worth. Old Yen had heard the rumors, like a whisper-echo of distant screaming. Perhaps there would be an end to it now, if Ping Wen and Tunghai Wang could come to an agreement. With or without the dragon. Already they had stopped skirmishing, holding their armies strictly apart. Old Yen could feel vaguely responsible for that, when he wanted something good to hold on to.

"Well. You cannot sleep, because Ping Wen is a traitor; the children cannot sleep because of the tiger."

"Yes," he said stubbornly. "We need something to help."

"There are teas that I can mix for you . . ."

"The children will not drink a tea if it is bitter. They need something stronger, something sure. Something in quantity. Ping Wen might keep them here for weeks, months, whatever he does with us. Jin and Shola and my boy Pao. I think Pao is helping Jin, a little; I think he could help her more, but I doubt Ping Wen would allow it."

How much more should he say, how much was needful? He couldn't judge. Tien was smiling again, distantly, thoughtfully. She said, "Well. Something strong, and in quantity. Something to make them sleep . . . Come with me, Old Yen."

And she strode to the door and hammered on it, and when the guard opened she said, "Take us to the governor's own doctor, wherever he keeps his office. I need to plunder his stores."

AFTER SHE had bullied the guard and then the doctor, after Old Yen had what he had come for, heavy and sticky and warm in his sleeve like a weight of sleep compounded, she said, "Come and meet my old men. I can do them both some good anyway," patting the tube of needles at her waist, "to help set them up for tomorrow; and a new face, new conversation will be better yet. For you, too." *And we can all four of us talk about Ping Wen, and what he wants of us tomorrow:* that she didn't say in front of the guard, but Old Yen read it in her eyes.

So SHE took him to her library, a room full of books and scrolls and papers and two men. Both men moved with a pain not born of age, and one of them was introduced as Ping Wen's torturer, who had been Tunghai Wang's before; and the other was Li Ton the pirate, who had been another man altogether—another general, Old Yen remembered—in another life and was not to be trusted in either guise, was a man who stole boats and people with equal equanimity, was a traitor twice condemned, by the old emperor and the new. And by Tunghai Wang too, apparently. How these two could work together Old Yen did not, could not understand, after what one had done to the other. And yet they could, they did; and yet, he could not. He would not. It was like what the goddess had demanded of him, out on the ocean. Even at the risk of the dragon, he could not. He would not.

He made his stiff little bows, once to each of the men and more deeply, more truly to Tien; and then he left them, and took his sleevely treasure back to Pao.

And showed the boy what it was, and told him of its uses; and then said no. Said, "No, listen, you must do this yourself. I am too old for this. This is what you must do . . ."

eight

*J*iao was snoring in the back room of the pavilion.

She was quite willing to bed down alone and apart, letting her charges all sleep together in the front. Confident that they wouldn't slip away in darkness. She was the lightest of sleepers, she had told them this, alert to the slightest sound; and besides, they were not unwatched.

The tiger slept sprawled and massive along the balcony, chained to one of the doorposts. It wasn't going anywhere, and neither were they.

So Jiao thought, at least. But she was snoring, because of all the poppy in her supper; and all the rest of the poppy, the whole sticky lump of it had been rubbed into the great slab of meat that made the tiger's meal.

So. Jiao was oblivious, and the tiger—well. The tiger wasn't snoring. The tiger lay stretched across the doorway there, eyes closed. It might have been stone for real. If it was breathing at all, Pao couldn't see.

It was hard to see anything, in the dark of the pavilion. He didn't dare light a lamp. Jiao and the tiger might not be all the watch there was, and any outside guard would be curious about a light shown this late. Moon and stars beckoned, through the open door—and the tiger lay between, inert, inherent with possibility.

Oh, it was asleep. Surely it had to be asleep. So much poppy, even a magical creature with stone in its blood, even a jade tiger could not withstand so much poppy.

Could it . . . ?

In truth, Pao didn't know. Nor did the old fisherman who had given it to him.

Pao had said, "You do it, master. Please? We'll follow you . . ."

But Old Yen had said no from the start, and was immovable. "This you must do alone. I am not coming with you."

"Master, I can't . . . !"

"You must. The girls will depend on you."

"But, but, why aren't you coming? Master? If you stay—"

"If I stay, then I am not responsible and cannot be blamed. And Ping Wen would miss me before he will miss any of you. I am ordered to the ridge in the morning; I want you gone before then. With luck he will not know until after he has done whatever he means to do up on the ridge there, if the dragon allows him to do it."

"Jiao will tell him."

"Perhaps. He will be busy with the dragon, and perhaps not interested in runaway children. He may not need the children, when he is done with the dragon. Or he may not have time to spare, or men to send in chase. I don't know; but if you go—and I want you gone—tonight is the time. If I stay, perhaps pursuit will be delayed, or less whole-hearted. Besides which, I am very curious to know what business he has with the dragon, and why he wants me there, and the doctor, and her crippled men."

So too was Pao curious, but not enough to keep him here. Not if he had a chance to get the girls away.

While Old Yen talked to Jiao in the last of the sunlight, Pao had crumbled poppy into her pepper noodles. He had no idea how much was needed. "Just a little," Old Yen had said; he didn't know either, he had never done this either. Pao wanted to be generous, but there was always the fact of the tiger lurking in his mind. However much he needed to be sure Jiao was sleeping, he'd need far more to be sure of the tiger.

So: *that* much went into Jiao's supper, and then a little bit more; and all the remainder was for the tiger, rubbed into the skinned haunch of deer that he tossed out onto the balcony. The tiger had a tongue like a rasp. It lay for a while with the meat clamped beneath one tremendous paw, licking: stripping flesh away, shredding it just with that tongue, soaking in—Pao hoped—that poppy. Then it slunk off to its hidden place below the balcony, with what remained of its supper clenched in its jaws.

Pao was concerned that the drug would act too soon, that the tiger wouldn't reappear for night-duty, that Jiao would grow suspicious at its absence. Acting normally was so hard, spending time with the girls, making sure they both ate while his attention was all on that empty doorway. *Come on, drag yourself up, sleep on the boards as you always do, only deeper . . .*

And then Shola had an accident, she tipped her soup across the floor; and instead of being upset at the mess of it big Jin reached out with her chopsticks and set the spilled prawns all in line along a floorboard amid a puddle of steaming broth and said "Ducks on a lake, in mist," while Shola giggled, while Pao stared incredulous. It was so wonderful that he forgot all about the tiger until he was glancing around to find if Old Yen had heard her too, or even Jiao—and there was the great barred flank of the beast blocking the doorway as it ought to be, and the relief was almost as tremendous as the terror.

PAO WAS, entirely, terrified. They were not prisoners, any more than Ping Wen was emperor; and yet he and the children were in imperial custody here. The governor stood for someone higher, which made it something close to treason even to think about slipping away.

He wanted to be gone, though, he wanted to go home. He was afraid that Ping Wen meant to use the girls in some treacherous invasion of Taishu. With or without Tunghai Wang. Something had shifted; everyone felt it. The governor had the measure of the generalissimo, he had defended the indefensible. He would not stop there. Not here, the wrong side of the strait. He and Tunghai Wang would meet tomorrow, and what came of that meeting would bode no good for the emperor.

Pao wanted to sweep the girls up and go. Leave Ping Wen stranded without a vessel that could safely leave port, but that was a side-blow. Mostly, he wanted to see the girls safe.

It was Old Yen's plan, but Pao's to do. He had to make it happen.

Well. He had been a kitchen boy, a soldier and a deckhand, all in a year; he could be an adventurer, no doubt, a daredevil hero leading children out of danger, finding a way to take them home.

No doubt.

No doubt at all.

So, THIS.

Jiao snoring in the back room. The girls awake and dressed, a little confused, a little excited, Shola importantly explaining to Jin how very quiet they would need to be, how very brave.

The fisherman awake and watching from his corner, saying nothing, moving not at all.

The tiger . . .

Well.

The tiger was a shadow that glowed greenly dark where it lay like a wall of flesh and fur between them and freedom.

Pao had gathered up what few things he was taking against need, though he didn't really need even those. No weapons, they couldn't fight their way to safety. It was the fisherman's plan; Pao only had to trust it, and to make it happen.

Well. He could do that.

FIRST, HE had to do something more demanding.

He had to step over the tiger.

. . .

EVEN IN darkness it had weight, it had warmth. Did it move, did it breathe? Pao wasn't sure.

He stood there with the girls one on either side and waited for his courage to find him, to lift his leg and stretch it far, far over that great slump of flesh and bone and belly, the farthest step of his life.

He waited, and the courage didn't come.

Waited longer. Nothing still.

At last, it was little Shola who moved. Far too small to manage that step, too small even to leap across the tiger without touching it, she lifted up her arms imperiously, *me first.*

She gifted Pao his courage. He lifted the little girl by the wrists, swung her back and forth through the air as if they were playing monkey-in-the-tree, swung her right over the broad striped expanse of tiger and into the fall of moonlight beyond.

And had to make that step, to go with her, to give her a quiet landing on the other side.

Having once stepped, it was easy. The tiger didn't stir. Pao set Shola on her feet, steadied her, smiled at her—and stepped back again.

Took Jin's hand and swung it vigorously, much as he had swung her sister. *Once, twice, and over we go*—and they stepped in unison, long legs matching, bare feet coming lightly down together on bare boards a heel's-width from the long green fringe of the tiger's belly-fur.

No looking back now. Pao kept hold of Jin's hand, reached for Shola's, tugged his girls away—

—AND THEN looked back after all, because he felt a movement, a shift of weight and purpose at his back. Perhaps he heard the faint scrape of iron on iron, one link against another.

The tiger lifted its head, its eyes glowing jade-green at him, fierce and aware and not asleep at all.

·   ·   ·

BREATH WAS somewhere else, perhaps. Not here.

THE TIGER stared, he stared, he couldn't help it; he couldn't look away.

AFTER A long, long moment, the tiger lowered its head again. Lay watching, unengaged, much as the fisherman had. This was still Pao's, apparently, to do.

AT LAST he managed to move again, in response to two imperious tugs. Perhaps it was the girls' to do after all, perhaps they were rescuing him.

HE FELT the cold burn of the tiger's eyes, all the way down the balcony steps and along the margin of the pond. When he looked back one last time, he could still see them shine like wet stone in moonlight, two pure glints of green.

THEN HE was alone with two girls in the palace gardens, and even this seemed very big, never mind the world beyond the wall. Now it really was all his to do: no old man watching in the corner of his eye, no snoring of an enemy defeated, no vast mystical beast seeming suddenly to collude with him. Only the vast and ordinary world, full of people who would stop him if he was momentarily careless or foolish, ambitious or betrayed or just unlucky.

Best not to be any of those, then.

Here was a path that would bring them to a gate. It would be locked and guarded both; that didn't matter. He had no notion of the gate.

Here the garden was an artifice of forest, trees and rocks and hidden pools all crowded close, a wild mountain in miniature. Just before the path would have led them out of those concealing shadows, it bent around a sudden high upthrust, a pillar of rock made by man to mirror what the gods had made before him.

What man has built up, he has also climbed down again. What he can climb down, he can climb up again.

That at least was Pao's theory, and Old Yen's before him.

Where a man can climb, so can a boy. And two girls.

Shola didn't want to go first, but someone had to. The back face of the pillar was cut for climbing; still, someone had to show Jin what was possible, and it couldn't be him. He needed to stay below in case of trouble, discovery, any kind of change in the quiet of the garden.

Up the little girl went, then, climbing as though she still played monkey but peering down constantly, moonface in the moonlight, as good as a guiding lamp almost. Pao could point to her—*see what she does, see how easy?*—and urge Jin to the rock face, set her hands on the first grips and let her go. She was a natural, or else she was recovering something of the girl she used to be. Pao watched for a little and thought he could almost, almost stop worrying.

Once she was high enough that he really couldn't help her if she fell, then he started up himself.

Perhaps darkness made the climb easier. In daylight, from below, they might have been daunted. Climbing largely by touch, they found that the rock was cut almost in steps, almost perilously safe. Shola at least was not troubling much with handholds, gripping the climbing creepers more than the stone beneath; she was small enough, light enough to get away with that, but if big Jin had copied her . . .

Jin copied her little sister in many things, but not in this. She hadn't seen, or else she was too wise inside. Her body knew her own heft. Slowly and steadily she climbed, nothing at all like a monkey, rock-solid and rock-sure.

Here was the top of the pillar, and the three of them safely gathered in that narrow space. Here was a tree atop all, rooted in the rock they stood on; and Old Yen was right, the branches of the tree reached out as far as the palace wall.

The wall was a declaration, as much as a barrier: *power dwells within*. A fence, a stream, a line of trees would have served as well. A string would have been enough, if people understood it. The wall was meant to keep people out, not in. The palace was not a prison. Who would ever need to escape from the governor's own private garden?

These did, and it proved almost easy, much closer to easy than Pao had dared to hope. Shola led the way again, once he had boosted her into the tree's lower branches. She squirmed out along a stout bough, hung from her hands and dropped down astraddle the tiled ridge of the wall. Waved cheerfully at her sister, who waved back before she set herself to the same task, stretching up to grip that branch, hauling herself onto it with little help from Pao.

His heart was in his mouth as he watched her; that branch seemed not so stout beneath her weight. Indeed it was bending already, and he weighed more . . .

Still, fine branch, beloved branch, it wouldn't break, it didn't; and that bending made it simple for Jin to transfer from branch to wall. No drop at all, her legs were astride the tiles before she had to let go.

His turn: and if it had bent for Jin, it bent more for him. Bent and whipped back and bent again, up and down, springy and determined. It might almost have tossed him over the wall altogether, if he'd let go at the right time. But he held on, and clambered from branch to wall, and let it snatch itself away.

Then it was his turn to lead. He hung from his hands and slithered as far as he could down the wall, kicked a little away from it and let go.

It wasn't a long drop to ground, but the wall was built above a steep ditch. His feet hit the slope, his body toppled backward and there was nothing to do but fall and roll. At least the bottom of the ditch was dry, after days and days with no rain. Just for a moment he lay still, dizzy mind in a dizzy body; then he picked himself up

and scrambled back to the foot of the wall. Held his arms up at
full stretch, waited for Jin: who took Shola's wrists and lowered
the little girl wholesale, down securely into his grip.

Jin followed, while he was still setting Shola on her feet. Hanging as he had, she let go before he could hope to reach her. And hit
ground as he had, and tumbled as he had, and rolled down into the
ditch.

Pao held his breath, fearing shrieks of pain or shrieks of glee,
either one disaster. But Jin only lay in the bottom of the ditch,
gasping quietly. When he plunged down to her side, she lifted her
head and he saw silent laughter. She lifted one hand to her mouth
to gag herself in mum-show, to let him know she understood the
need. Then she held the hand up to him and he hauled her to her
feet and she beamed in the moonlight as though she wanted to do
it all again.

Perhaps she did. Shola too: a gesture brought her wildly running down the too-steep slope of the ditch, arms waving, on the
very edge of falling all the way, with only his body to be her brake,
to save her from calamity at the bottom.

They were enjoying themselves too much, these girls. He had to
be frightened for all three of them.

Well, he could do that. It was easy. They trusted him to see them
safe away. He had no one to trust but himself, whom he did not
trust.

With the palace behind them and no one chasing, they were just
three children abroad in the city, in the night. They might have
been anyone, going anywhere. They had good and obvious reasons to shun noise and lamplight, to sidle into alleys and avoid
company. No one who saw them would think twice, except to
wonder if they could be caught and kept, or caught and sold.

Perhaps no one saw them at all, or else no one who saw them
could be troubled to chase. They climbed the high valley side, and
here might have been harder than escaping the palace; there was

no wall but here the soldiers were watching for an enemy army, they had reasons to be alert. All their attention was bent on the horizon, though, they weren't looking for anyone slipping out of the city. Or if they were, they weren't interested in children. Perhaps they thought it made sense for children to be leaving. The edge of the city was like unhemmed silk: houses fraying into gardens, gardens into paddy. It wasn't hard to slip between one house and another, to walk the paddy paths in moonlight.

Even so it was a surprise, at least to Pao, to get away unchallenged. The girls were almost unimpressed, so much they trusted him. It seemed more than half a game to them, ducking into shadow when he waved them down, scuttling forward when he beckoned them. If terror could keep them safe, then yes, he would terrorize them if he could. Until then, he would keep his terror to himself; and them too, hug them to himself in the secrecy of his heart, his terrified heart.

AWAY FROM the city and the road, almost lost among the shifting paddy paths, he supposed that they could talk now. It was still better not, though, for fear of voices carrying over flat water.

Besides, it seemed he had nothing to say.

These paths were too narrow to go side by side and hand in hand, as perhaps they all wanted to. Also he wanted to go first, in case they ran into soldiers—the emperor's or rebels or the governor's, it made no difference now—but if he walked in front he was always looking back to check on the girls, worse than useless. So they went in order of size, and smallest first. Shola led once again with Jin's hands on her shoulders, eyes watching over her head; Pao came last, his hands on Jin's waist for her comfort, his head peering around hers.

They might have looked foolish if anyone was watching, they were certainly slow—but they couldn't go faster than Shola in any case. He could bottle up his impatience with his words, with his hope, with his fears. Step by step, bank by bank, path by muddy path they came to where they needed to be; and no one prevented them, no one threatened them, he thought it was a triumph.

He thought they had earned what they had come for.

Only now came the real adventure, now he really had to be a hero.

They wanted a boat, and there was no hope of taking one from Santung harbor, watched and guarded as it was by men and nature too, a tidal rip and a harbor bar. There were no boats elsewhere, anywhere else along the coast, except for here.

The goddess will see you safe, Old Yen had said. There was doubt in his voice, which was unexpected and not comfortable; but he said it anyway, and then he said it again. *If you have one of her children with you, she will see you safe.*

If they had a boat, perhaps. Perhaps she would. If they could get to sea.

THERE WAS the boat, Old Yen's bastard boat. Much bigger than a sampan, barely smaller than a junk: too big for one to sail alone and yet he had, young Pao, he had done that, brought her all across the strait and beached her here.

She wasn't on the beach now. He knew that. They had tried to sail her off a lee shore without Old Yen's hand on the tiller, his eye on the sails, his voice whipping orders. *Without the blessing of the goddess,* Old Yen had said, but even he didn't sound as though he meant that.

No surprise that they had failed. Ill conceived and ill made, she was a stubborn and contrary creature; she needed a stubborn and contrary master even at the best of times, in a good wind on fair water. She needed Old Yen. Pao could fake it, for a while, in the deep. Shallow seas had betrayed him; it was luck—or the goddess, perhaps her, he had best believe in her tonight—that had brought him and his boatload safe to shore.

The boat too, safe and whole. She rode at anchor, close offshore: waiting for a kinder wind, a bolder soul, fresh orders.

Not unwatched, of course. He knew that too.

Hunkered in reeds in the lee of a dune, he lay with the girls packed close on either side and peered forward.

A lamp burned on the boat herself, to show just where she swam. Closer at hand, a fire blazed on the beach. Half a dozen men squatted in its light, to show how outnumbered they were, Pao and his girls. A sampan—Old Yen's own, that normally bobbed at the boat's tail except when he had it hauled aboard—lay drawn up on the sand, close to the lapping tide and just in the flicker of the firelight.

Slowly, gently Pao pressed one girl and then the other more deeply into the shadows, *stay here. Don't move.*

He felt Shola suppress a giggle, and waited for the urgent little nod that followed, *I promise.*

Jin looked at him, all solemnity and trust—and then she nodded too, independently of her sister.

Buoyed, he wriggled back down the landward slope of the dune and then scuttled behind its shelter, parallel to the shore until he was far from the girls, surely far and far from any chance of those soldiers spotting him.

Up to the brow again, and a careful look through tussocks of sourgrass. The fire was a fierce glow that couldn't possibly find him at this distance; the boat's lamp was almost invisible, just a shifting speck above the dark mass of the sea, a star that swayed in place.

Now his nerve almost failed. He had meant to slither down to the sea's edge with all caution, and he almost couldn't move.

In the end, he could only do it at a run: his arms pushing him upright, his legs hurling him stupidly down over rocks, no chance to see where he was putting his feet, just the glimmer of moon on water to draw him forward.

He was lucky again, or else he was watched over. Once he staggered, as one leg sank knee-deep into an unexpected rock-pool;

once his foot slipped on salt-wet weed and he fell, tumbling, rolling. But he rolled on sand, and rose up unharmed, and plunged on.

At last bare feet felt the tickle-touch of water. The next step took him ankle-deep, the next up to his calf. He splashed on unheedingly, trusting that the long line of breaking surf would mask what noise he made.

A wave soaked him to the waist; the next lifted him off his feet altogether. A gasp escaped him, as much relief as anxiety. He waited for the rise of another wave, sighted the bobbing lamp of the boat and started to swim.

IT WAS a long, draining pull and he was tired already, but that was the tiredness of constant tension, trying to look every way at once, having to go slow where he most wanted to hurry. This was the weariness of honest work, and welcome.

He still couldn't forget the girls, left behind and waiting. That would be worse than this, he thought: having nothing to do but wait, obliged to trust. He would hurry now if he could, but here too he was obliged to go slow. The goddess might gift him favor, but the sea was neutral. And heavy, so heavy. He heaved armfuls of water aside, he dragged himself forward stroke by stroke, he peered ahead and thought that the boat mocked him. Holding at the very limit of its anchor-rope, maybe even dragging its anchor, drifting farther away as he struggled to draw closer . . .

Not the boat, it was the sea that mocked; and all mockery is a lie. At last the hull loomed above him, and here was the anchor-rope to hold on to, to hold and gasp and shudder in the tide's slow tug.

A wave slapped him in the face one more, one last time. Pao swallowed salt, gripped the rough sodden cable with rough sodden palms, heaved himself out of the water.

Wrapped his legs about the rope, wondered vaguely if he could be seen from shore and what the men would think, what strange

creature was pulling itself up from the sea. He wished that the
girls could see him and the men not, but that was impossible—
though the girls would be looking and the men might not . . .

HAND OVER hand he hauled himself up, feeling water run out of
his clothes, hearing the dribbles of it splash down like little be-
trayals.

No voices came at him, no cries of alarm—but one wary man
aboard would be plenty. Drawing his blade in silence, padding
barefoot across the deck, waiting for one weary boy to drag himself over the side. One swift blow, one dead boy, all hopes betrayed
and the girls abandoned to a fate worse than any he had saved
them from.

Even a skinny boy couldn't fit through the hawse-hole where
the cable ran. He had to reach up, one hand and then the other, lift
his head into view.

Bobbing up at deck-level, blinking in the sudden lamplight, appallingly visible but half blind himself, needing time to squint the
water from his eyes. He was almost waiting for the blow, or at least
the glint of light on steel as it fell, his last moment of awareness
because surely he wouldn't feel the blow itself, the split of his skull
before his ruined body fell back into the water . . .

NOTHING, AND nothing. He waited too long, not quite believing;
still nothing. No blow, no voices, nothing.

They wouldn't have left the boat abandoned. Why burn a light
on an empty boat?

Whoever was aboard must be in the cabin, unless they were
in the holds below. Pao took a breath, set his hands flat on the
deck and lifted himself over the edge in one swift thrust. Rolled
under the rail, felt the boat pitch a little beneath his weight but
surely not enough to notice, not if you were asleep in the comfort
of the cabin, he was a skinny thing and oh please let them be
asleep . . .

Squatted on the foredeck there, stupid as a moth in lamplight, listening, listening:

hearing his own heartbeat, hard and brutal in the cage of his ribs, trying to hammer its way out;

hearing the *drip-drip* of the sea still leaving his hair, dropping onto the deck, trying to hammer its way through;

hearing the wind in the rigging, the sea against the hull, both slow and soothing and long-known;

hearing another sound, regular and inappropriate, unfamiliar.

Taking a moment to understand it, and then taking a slow and tentative breath, still wary, still listening.

That was the sound of one man snoring, in the cabin there.

Only the one . . .

IF THERE were others, they were not watching the deck. He was right there in full sight and no one called out, no one came.

Even so. He did actually need to move.

Eventually, he did.

Keeping low, scuttling like a beetle, he crossed to the open cabin window and peered inside.

There was a man, yes, sprawled on the bunk. Just the one, and not likely to wake anytime soon, to judge by the dark heavy bottle that lay on its side below his hanging arm. Pao was long familiar with such bottles, and the sour oblivion they blessed their owners with.

He didn't quite believe that Old Yen's goddess could actually arrange such matters, even on the old man's boat, but still: this was perfect, ideal, and he wanted to be grateful to someone, and who else was there?

Besides, gratitude was not only owing, it might be politic. He had to go back into that puddle of light now. And take it away. Sooner or later, someone ashore was bound to notice.

Not scuttling now—pulling himself deliberately straight, indeed, walking into the light as though he was a man known to be aboard and not at all lying drunk in the cabin—Pao collected the lantern from where it hung by the steering oar at the stern.

He made his way up past the cabin, masking the light with his body as he passed the window, for fear of waking the sleeper with its dazzle. He made no effort to mask it from the shore. Let them see this; he was a dutiful man, making his round of the boat he had been set to watch. Or else he had heard something, forward: likely only a rat, but he was going to investigate anyway. The call of duty masked the call of the bottle.

Pao added a realistic sway or two as the boat rose on the swell, as she tugged a little at her anchor.

Here was the rise of the foredeck; here was the little door that gave access to the hold below. Pao lifted the latch and drew the door open softly, softly; he took a breath and ducked his head and stepped down into the dark and the dank and the ingrained smell of fish.

The lamp he carried did little to counter any of that. Its inquiring light only pointed up the depth of the shadows that closed around him; its small flame flared yellow in the salt of the air and couldn't hope to work against the damp, like the breath of sea contained; the smell of oil only floated above older, darker smells, as oil itself floats on water.

Long before Pao was pressed into his service, when he must still have been just a fisherman with never a thought of emperors or rebels or dragons freed and risen, Old Yen had filled his holds with flotsam. The boat was legendary in Taishu-port for what had come out of it this summer, what salvage and what garbage.

Even so, not everything had come out. Old Yen had not given up all his treasures. He had been compelled to make space mostly for men going back and forth, imperial soldiers rescued or raiding-parties delivered ashore; and men can duck their heads and keep low. At first glance all his holds looked empty. Until anyone looked up.

All manner of things hung overhead, in old nets stretched between hooks. There were oars and beams and ropes in plenty, everything a working boat might need for jury-rigged repairs; there were casks and sacks and baskets, because Old Yen was still a fisherman when he wasn't ferrying troops; there were lengths of ancient driftwood and other gleanings from the sea, that had no obvious use at all except in Old Yen's mysterious mind.

Setting the lamp down behind him and reaching high, Pao could just unhook one edge of the nets hung in the forehold here.

He thought he could control what came down, slide out what he wanted, piece by piece . . .

HE WAS wrong about that. It was all held more slackly than he'd thought, and the things themselves were heavier. There was a sudden cascade, and nothing he could do but shelter his head in his arms, try to shield the lantern with his body and hope, just hope that this chaos of noise didn't wake the sleeper, didn't reach the shore, *oh goddess, help me now* . . .

PERHAPS SHE did. In the silence that followed the collapse, he listened for snoring and heard nothing, heard nothing, heard—

HEARD A snort and then a snore, and then more snoring.

HE LOOKED with satisfaction now on the jumble of flotsam spilling out of the hanging nets, across the floor of the hold. So much dry wood, so much rope and woven bamboo matting, it was just what he wanted. Not quite where he wanted it, yet. He seized a bundle of worn canvas and dragged it up the steps and out into the night, letting it unroll as he went. And followed that with loose coils of fraying cable, long splintered bamboo poles, anything he could haul out swiftly.

Satisfied, he uncorked the lantern's reservoir and sloshed oil briskly over everything, wood and rope and bamboo. Pao's first lesson from Old Yen had been what a hazard fire was aboard a boat, how careful he needed to be. He was the opposite of careful now. It was just as well that the old fisherman wasn't called on to do this himself; it had been his idea, but it was Pao's to do.

Pao spread oil as far as he could over the heap while he preserved the flame in the lamp; then he swung the lamp and tossed it in among the tumble in the hold.

And watched how the flame flickered, how it reached, how it caught and spread; how it took hold in the shadows and then reached out, oily ropes like wicks drawing it into the well of the boat, bright flame leaping, high and higher . . .

WHEN HE was sure, Pao slipped over the side again, swam to the anchor-rope again. Caught hold one-handed and hung there, treading water lazily while he watched for movement on the shore.

HE COULDN'T believe how long it took them to notice that the boat was on fire. Perhaps they had more of those bottles, perhaps they'd drunk themselves too into stupefaction? If so he was wasting his time here: wasting more than time, destroying Old Yen's boat for nothing.

Cold undercurrents numbed his feet, his legs. He swayed like weed in the turning tide, and felt the water drag his dreams away. He ought to climb back aboard, quick, do what he could to control the fire before it caught hold too deeply in the timbers of the boat, before all chance was lost.

LASSITUDE HELD him, unless it was despair. He did nothing but cling on, watch and wait. Even from here, with his head barely above water, he could see the fire reflected in the dark sea's mirror, every washing wave carrying glints of it toward the shore. Oh, surely, surely one must carry far enough to notice . . . ?

AT LAST, at long last one did. There was a sudden flurry of figures, the movement he'd been watching for: a stumbling run toward the dark low profile of the sampan. It was probably funny to see, their awkward urgency, if you were closer. If you didn't care quite as much as he did, if you weren't quite so cold. *Don't laugh, girls. Keep your silence, just this little more* . . .

As THE sampan dragged itself slowly through the surf toward him, he heard voices even through the water in his ears. Panicked voices, contradictory: what was best to do, what was the only thing. How this could have happened, how that sot Sung could have let it happen, made it happen, watched it happen and done nothing, nothing . . .

THEY ROWED the sampan clumsily to the well and scrambled up, barely troubling to tie on before they were over the side. Pao counted them aboard, all six of them, all that he had counted in the firelight ashore.

Perfect again. He made his slow way down the side, listening to their confusion—Sung must have caused this, knocked something down and dropped the lamp, and where was Sung anyway? Staggered off drunk, fallen overboard, where?—while he struggled to make his own limbs work as he needed them, just this little longer.

He unhitched the sampan from the boat, gripped her stern and kicked hard to set her drifting off. No one was looking, apparently; even so, he didn't pull himself over the side until she was outside the fall of firelight. With luck they'd blame themselves, these men, and work the harder to put that fire out.

With luck, none of them would be swimmers.

WHEN HE dared, he stood up in the stern and took the oars and began to row ashore, toward that other fire.

HE CAME to land full in the light, trusting that he had counted right and there were no other watchers. He stepped onto the sand, spread his arms wide and called out.

"Shola, Jin! Quick now, come quickly . . . !"

The shouts from the burning boat had changed, he thought; no longer desperate, the men might be more angry. It might not be Sung who they were angry at.

He was still hopeful that none of them could swim.

He was just drawing breath to call again—a little anxious, a little urgent—when he saw movement beyond the flames. One figure rising, another larger at her side. Both girls, unharmed, undetained: hurrying down across the sand.

He ushered them into the sampan, saw them settled together in the bows, pushed her out into the surf again.

Scrambled aboard, seized the oars, pulled away with heavy strokes. Everything in his body was heavy now. His muscles ached and burned, he sweated and shivered at the same time and his breath was hard to catch, hard in his throat, hard to swallow down; and still he hauled, still he drove that sampan down the coast.

A mile in the dark, another mile. He counted strokes just to keep himself going, while the girls sat quiet and watched the water hiss and bubble by.

The sky was tinting pale pink and blue before he stopped, before he had to stop. He sat in the stern there and cried, almost. Sheer exhaustion inhabited his body like a dense liquid pain. The sampan bobbed in the swell; the girls didn't move, any more than he did.

The sun came up to show him the headland he was praying for, just a little farther now. Too far to row, he thought his shoulders might never pull an oar again, but there was always a paddle in the sampan. It was a different stroke, at least. He thought he might manage that little, that far.

He fished in the bilges for the paddle, found it floating; that was bad, that there was enough water down there to float it. He ought to bail, probably. But the headland was so close, and . . . Well, they wouldn't sink between here and there. Probably.

One of the girls made a noise, a soft cry of recognition; he glanced up, to see Jin pointing. Jin. How unexpected was that?

It gave him strength; he dug the paddle into the water, worked the sampan through the waves.

Into the shadow of the headland, into the creek.

Running the bows up the little beach, with a grateful last lift of a wave to carry her farther than he could have managed. Feeling her ground on sand and gravel, barely having the strength to lift the paddle inboard before he dropped it.

By the time he'd lifted his head to look for them, the girls were long gone, halfway up the cliff. Stopping there, unexpectedly; looking back, waiting for him.

Again, that gave him strength.

Over the side, one last ineffectual little drag to shift the hull a fraction higher; then he lifted out her anchor, carried it up the beach, wedged it between two rocks and left her to hope and justice.

And slowly, slowly trudged up the cliff, in pursuit of the girls; who seized his hands one each and all but dragged him to the top.

Where their mother was just coming out of the little temple there, and seemed to have fewer words even than Jin as she greeted them, if you could call it a greeting, standing there mewing helplessly while her hands made gestures not even she could comprehend.

THEY COULDN'T stay. Luck or chance or the workings of the goddess had allowed them to find Ma Lin alone; that wouldn't last. Ping Wen's men would come again, or Tunghai Wang's. There were no neutrals now. The local peasants would betray them, to one or to the other. With two armies claiming the ground and the temple empty of idols, there was no safety else.

There was no safety anywhere, this side of the water. Nor perhaps beyond it, but at least no one was fighting on Taishu.

"Will you come, mother?" It was Pao who had to ask it. Shola didn't see the need—of course she would come, it was obvious, it was essential—and Jin was rediscovering her words little by little, but not these, not yet. Not questions.

"I do not want to leave this," a look back at the temple where it sat knee-deep in a hollow, dragon-roof proud of the height. "I made a promise to the goddess."

"Mother, you gave your daughter to the goddess," though he thought perhaps that Jin was finding her own way back. "That's enough, surely. And she has temples also on Taishu."

"Not this one. There is no one else, to care for this."

"There is no one but these," her two daughters, "us," her two daughters and himself, "to care for you. You matter more than a robbed-out house. Come with us, mother."

She hesitated, but then Jin—Jin!—said, "Come," and that was it.

THAT WAS it, except he had to get them there. In the sampan, which was never meant to cross even a narrow sea; and which he could not row, not possibly, not now.

She had a mast, she had a sail. He knew how to use them.

He knew how the wind might lay her flat in its enthusiasm, might overturn her altogether if he was careless, if it was skittish, if the sea was rough.

He knew that the dragon was a jealous mistress of the strait, that she ate men when she could if they tried to cross.

He knew that the old man thought the goddess would protect her children from the wind and the sea and the dragon too.

He thought that Old Yen had been right, before this.

Before Jin started to find her own way back.

He wasn't sure at all that the goddess could still speak through her; that the dragon would avoid her; that the weather would be kind above and around and beneath her. Not anymore.

And still, he saw no choice. They could stay here and wait for soldiers, or they could chance the sea with all that she implied.

. . .

AT LAST, as they had to, they went to sea.

IN MID-STRAIT, with nothing but his own hard-acquired skill to keep them afloat and heading mostly in the right direction, they saw the dragon.

Who flew above them, over them, past them: directly on toward the mainland, from that jut of stone they called the Forge. If she looked down, if she acknowledged them, no matter. She didn't stop.

SIX

Dragonfire

one

Privately, Ma was impressed.

He couldn't actually admit to that, because Tunghai Wang was raging at his side. But this was Ma's territory, this was what he did, and he could see it being done well all around him. He knew what work must have gone into this, what thought, what planning. It was nothing easy, to make it look so easy.

He couldn't yet quite see the point of it all. Not just to enrage Tunghai Wang: that was welcome, no doubt, but incidental. Ma was sure of it. So was Tunghai Wang, which only added to his fury. Summoned here—summoned in defeat, which was a new experience, and unwelcome in itself—he had at least expected to be the point and purpose of the meeting, and was not.

Ma thought that Ping Wen had something to show them. He couldn't imagine what, except that it would be an expression of power. Ping Wen had served two emperors and betrayed one; he had committed himself to Tunghai Wang, and betrayed him too; this was a bid on his own account, but surely not for Santung. Santung was no good to anyone, a soft fruit squeezed between two fingers. Even if he had made it defensible, a soft fruit with a hard shell. For what . . . ?

THE DAY began with a banner against the sky. Long and green, twisting in the wind as the dragon did; flying above the valley-ridge, perhaps a mile north of the city.

The camp was full of the news of it, of the meaning. *Tunghai Wang, this summons you.*

Not Ma. Why would the purveyor-general go to such a meeting? He had no claim, and no reason.

And yet he came to the generalissimo at his breakfast and said, "Take me, and the monksmith too. When you go up to meet with Ping Wen."

"Why?"

Because I had a messenger in my room last night, because of course Ping Wen has spies among your army just as the emperor does, just as you have spies in Santung and on Taishu too because I set them there.

Of course he couldn't say that, it would be to say *because Ping Wen wants me there, us, the monksmith and me*, which would be to say *I am a traitor too.* He wasn't even sure that was true. His loyalty was as complex as his work, and it tended to the same thing: results. What else could matter more?

He said, "Because whatever happens today, you will call on me later to arrange matters for you, to work with Ping Wen or against him. It will be easier for me to understand the needs if I have seen, if I have heard the two of you together. If I know what he wants, and how he means to achieve it."

"I can tell you—"

"No. You don't see the same things I do. You will see his strengths, and how to break them. I will see his needs, and how to supply them."

"Or how to cut him off, if he defies me."

"That too."

It was undeniable. Whatever Ping Wen did or thought to do, he could not support Santung through a siege. Tunghai Wang would starve him out eventually; Ma might see a way to do it sooner, find something that he needed more than food.

. . .

WHEN THE generalissimo set off, then, an hour later—full of intent, but grinding his teeth none the less, knowing himself all too obviously summoned under the eyes of all his army—Ma rode with him, and the monksmith too.

The night visitor had been most particular about that. Ma understood that he himself was invited only because of whom he could bring with him.

There was some comfort in that, knowing that he was not the purpose of the intrigue. It was the same discovery that had enraged Tunghai Wang, but Ma never had been one for the front line, first into the breach. He had his courage, and it was of a different sort. Frightened for himself, he would have been no use to anyone. Secure in his unimportance, he could watch what use was made of the monksmith and add that to the account of his knowledge, use it in his turn.

Also, secure in his unimportance, he had no qualms about bringing his boy. There was comfort in that too, in the familiar figure trotting at his stirrup, holding station in the corner of his eye. If something happened—to Tunghai Wang, to the monksmith— Ma would not be alone in the aftermath. He could manage armies, solitary at his desk; he was not so good at managing himself. He would not have done so well last night when the spy came, without his boy there beside him.

With Ping Wen and Tunghai Wang squabbling like vultures over the carcass of Santung, with both of them plotting and himself only marginally privy to their plots; with the monksmith to watch, knowing that he mattered in ways that neither of them knew; with his boy to watch him, a hand when he needed help and a sharp young eye, seeing things he wouldn't think to look for—Ma might not be ready for the day, but he was as ready as he ever could be and almost eager for it.

Certainly eager to get off this accursed mule and face what must be faced on his own feet, as a man should, balanced and justified in his own eyes and in the eyes of those who loved him.

THEY SHOULD have walked in any case, he thought sourly, or else had men carry them in chairs. There were men enough, even after the generalissimo's recent catastrophe. These beasts were only for pride, the arrival of a soldier and not a surrendered man; and the generalissimo's pride would not let him ride the road where he personally had met his catastrophe, all too recently. Black scars on the road, ash in the air—no, he could not ride through that.

So he turned aside too soon, to follow wayward paths through wood and scrub where the beasts were confused and unwilling, untrusting. Ma at least had his boy to take the mule's head and lead it forward through mud and shadow and bamboo. Trained to the open battlefield, horses of a more delicate temper twitched and shied as this unfamiliar world closed around them. Even where it opened into paddy they were uncertain of their footing, on narrow mud paths between stretches of still reflective water. Their nervousness delayed the whole procession, fed Tunghai Wang's temper, fed it more when at last he surrendered his pride and summoned bannermen to the horses' heads.

The paddy was empty, where the season's second crop of rice should have been ripe and ready for harvest. Only these lowest stretches still held water. No one farmed on land where soldiers lurked; and as the men climbed the ridge, they found walls down and ditches blocked, whole terraces crumbling. That was the bitter residue of the dragon's typhoon that had brought ruin to the generalissimo's plans before, calling an end to a battle half-fought when he was poised to win it.

The higher, the drier. It hadn't rained for days, for weeks; springs and streams still fed the lower paddy, but not the height of the ridge. The path there was easier for the horses, all dried mud. Tunghai Wang dismissed his bannermen to the fore again, but Ma kept his boy at the mule's head. If he needn't watch how he rode, he could ride with his eyes ahead, high ahead, on that flirting banner and the curious structure rising beside it.

The banner spoke of a northerly wind, blowing steadily offshore: fine wind for an invasion they could not mount, either of them, Ping Wen nor Tunghai Wang. The generalissimo had no means to cross the strait. The governor might have both boats and safe passage—Ma's spies spoke of a child blessed by a goddess, able to repel the dragon, fetched unexpectedly from Taishu—but he dared not deplete his forces in Santung for any adventure against the emperor. If his attention slackened, if he let himself be distracted, the generalissimo would find a way in behind his guard.

So: two men caught in a sullen squabble, neither of whom could reach for what he wanted more. Ma was intrigued to learn how this tale would turn next—and what that was, that angular construction close by the banner there.

Before they reached it, he had recognized its bones. Had he not seen to the erection of such machines himself, and the feeding also: numbers of earthenware pots, quantities of oil, of black powder, flowers of sulfur, more?

He knew by length and weight and substance just how those machines were put together and how used, how many men they took. This was similar, and yet not the same. Its arm was longer, and there were too many ropes; it had a net sling rather than a solid cup to hold and hurl its projectiles. It had two young men climbing all across its gaunt height and arguing tightly, while its team squatted in the poor shadow of the rocky ridge.

More to the point, Ma couldn't see the point of it. There were its missiles, familiar pots and curious woven baskets that wouldn't hold the liquid fire he knew. He remembered sheets of flame in the sky, fireworks as weapons—but at whom would Ping Wen hurl them, up here? Not at the generalissimo, surely. That man had learned their lesson already, which was why he came when summoned. Giving him—and, more to the point, giving Ma—close sight of these new machines would not be useful to Ping Wen, whatever he had in mind.

His boy clicked the mule to a halt and Ma slid off, awkward and ungainly as ever. He was sorry to let Yueh see him this way in this company, but what could he do? A man was what he was, whatever circles he moved in, however high he rose.

This had been the topmost terrace of the paddy. Now, in the wake of the dragon's ruinous storm, it was a field of bare flat mud: dry mud, his boots found on landing, sun-baked to a desert dryness. He still didn't understand why they were here, why Ping Wen would have chosen such a site for such a meeting.

Or why the war-machine, or why that other structure men were working at, a rough forge built from stones out of the broken wall. Smoke wrapped itself around them; the air shimmered and rang with hammer blows, iron on iron on stone.

Ma found the monksmith at his side, alert and interested. "They are making chains."

"Are they?" Ma couldn't see so much.

"Of course. Excuse me . . ."

And he was gone, to join the smiths around their furnace. Ma felt more confused than ever, looking around. Beyond the forge was a little group alone, two men sitting on the broken wall with attendants. One at least seemed to be a cripple. Squinnying across the distance, Ma thought that was Ai Guo the torturer. Tunghai Wang had left him behind in the city, intending to reclaim him later. Well, he was in another's hands now; that was the price of confidence. The other man might be General Chu Lin, who had turned pirate and then traitor. Why he would still be with Ai Guo, why either of them would be here—these were questions wanting an answer Ma did not have.

Beyond them was an older man even more alone, standing where he had presumably been set, among a group of temple figures. More were set at intervals all around, like fence posts, like a ring of torches in the night.

Beyond him again, Ping Wen with an entourage. Among his followers was a woman with . . .

A woman with a tiger. On a chain.

A jade tiger. Ma had never seen one living, though he'd owned a skin once, a gift of the old emperor, long lost and left behind.

This was madness, and yet not. There was purpose here, grim purpose, and nothing to do with Tunghai Wang. Who knew it, perhaps. And was walking across the baked ground to join Ping Wen, to discuss it, perhaps. Ma should be with him, but he preferred to stay here, to hold himself apart, to watch this all work out. He had played his part already, bringing the monksmith here.

Also, he distrusted everything suddenly, including the assumed truce that had brought them here. There was violence everywhere, in that machine and all these machinations, in chains and hammer blows and heat, in the tiger and its woman and every man here: violence contained, potent, ready. Even the temple idols were a trap.

Ma had his courage, and he would keep it here, beside his boy.

THE TWO great men, governor and generalissimo, met on open ground and bowed respectfully to each other, just as much as they each thought protocol demanded. Ping Wen had served Tunghai Wang before this, both openly under the late emperor and covertly under the new; he stood now as imperial governor, and might reasonably claim an equality he had lacked before. One outside the city and one inside, both held absolute dominion.

If Tunghai Wang still thought they were here to discuss the city, dominion, he was swiftly disabused. Ping Wen ushered him to the side, to the rocky shadow of the ridge—and left him there. Went back to his entourage, to his woman with the tiger, seemingly just to wait.

To wait and watch the sky.

The banner turned and twisted in the wind. It was a summons, meant to do more than fetch the generalissimo. Now it was to fetch the dragon.

Ma understood that, just a little too late to pretend that he was ready when she came.

HE COULDN'T understand why she would come, but that was only one of the many things he did not understand today. It was easier than many to dismiss. Why should he ever pretend to understand the dragon?

She came. He knew it when the men were suddenly pointing, as suddenly snatching back their arms, not to draw attention to themselves. Her attention. She might not like to be pointed at.

SHE CAME, and blocked out the sun. Deliberately, Ma was sure.

She hung in the air and peered down at them. Staring back, Ma saw an excrescence on her neck, a shadow that moved: the boy that was said to ride her. He had assumed that to be a myth, compounded of fear and mystery together. He was perhaps a little more afraid, finding it true. An immortal creature is one thing; an immortal mediated by a human, something else entirely. A tiger on a chain.

The impression of control was too easy to misread or overvalue. The woman held the chain; she didn't hold the tiger. The dragon might bear the boy, but not the way Ma's appalling mule had borne him here.

He stepped up to the beast's head, only to be closer to his own boy. Let people read that as they would. No one was looking anyway. Not with a dragon in the sky.

It was Ma's business to watch not the battle, but the men who served it. The habit of long practice brought his eyes down from the dragon.

He might have been the only one—apart surely from the dragon, and perhaps her boy—who saw the team working on the warmachine, dragging down the arm and setting a missile carefully, carefully into its net. One man running to the forge, running back with smoke swirling from the cup of his fingers.

Those two young men whose charge it seemed to be, shifting the aim of it with poles and spikes. Carefully, carefully.

Everyone around them, their whole team worked blindly, heads tipped back to stare—but they were well drilled and their duties were mechanical, they seemed almost part of the machine themselves as they heaved and hauled, as the world seemed to pause on its moment.

Even Ping Wen wasn't watching the men, or the machine. He must presumably have given the order for it, which left him free now to follow his soul's desire, do as every man else did, watch the dragon.

Ma's own soul was torn. The intense draw of the dragon—almost a passion, almost a craving, he was fascinated by the sense of his own self reacting—balanced, cruelly teasing, against the fascination of watching all these others react.

One last glance around the margins of the bare open field, and he saw the woman too with her head cocked, looking upward into that vast shadow. The tiger's eyes gleamed through the gloom of it. Ma thought they gleamed at him: as though he held some interest in himself, as though simple dragons could be discounted.

Ma would have discounted that, only that it was hurled suddenly and entirely out of his head as one of the young men called an order, men heaved, the war-machine creaked and an object rose startlingly, almost vertically into the sky.

It was a missile-pot, trailing smoke. It climbed a little higher than the hovering dragon, and seemed to pause a moment before it began to fall, directly toward her.

She appeared to be watching it with as much interest as anyone.

Then it exploded.

MA HAD seen fireworks all his life. Just a couple of nights since, he had seen fireworks made into weapons, or at least instruments of terror.

He had never seen this, never imagined how a missile might

erupt into a sheet of viscous flame, which might fall like a curtain over the hindquarters of an immortal.

Who might lift her head and scream, a dreadful sound that could shatter rocks and hearts together.

Who might twist and tumble out of the sky all unexpectedly, coming down in a broken spiral to land in the dry paddy there, too close, too desperately close and writhing, hissing, all pain and all fury all at once.

She needed the sea, Ma knew, and could not reach it. Fire clung to her tail, though she slammed it and slammed it into the dead dry earth, raising nothing but dust, no quenching mud, no relief.

The boy slid from her neck and ran helplessly to and fro, away from her and back again, crying out almost in the voice of her own pain, until men seized him and dragged him to the forge.

two

Old Yen knew.

He knew when he saw the monk in his robes join the smiths at the forge; when he saw the doctor-woman with her dreadful companions, with all their acquired dragonlore; when he saw the boy Han on the dragon's neck, innocent and ignorant and doomed.

He even knew what he was here for himself, that too. When he saw that ring of idols, set like guards all around the plateau and clustered like a troop of soldiers—or else like a templeful of worshippers, that too—just here where he was told to stand himself, then he knew. Really, it wasn't even hard.

PING WEN meant to chain the dragon.

As AN expression of power, it would be immense. Under the eyes of his significant rival, it would be majestic; how could Tunghai Wang surpass this? He would lose his prestige, his authority, his army. All in a moment.

The emperor had lost already, so unimportant he had not even been fetched. When the thing was done, Ping Wen would lead a flotilla across the strait—but it would be in celebration, not an invasion force. He wouldn't need a single soldier. If the Son of Heaven had any sense, he would himself usher Ping Wen to the throne. If not, his own people would hurl him down in contempt, in casual dismissal.

. . .

EVEN JIAO and the tiger, even they were here for a purpose, to show how mortal can chain mystery: to teach the people that it could be done, to ready them for it before showing them the thing itself. And then, of course, to look small and insignificant afterward. *A tiger? What means, what matters a tiger? He chained a dragon, he!*

Their day, Old Yen's and Jiao's had begun in silence, in conspiracy. Dragging herself out of bed in the dark of the morning, she had seen the children's absence, of course, first thing. And had understood it, perhaps, despite her thick head; had understood her thick head, perhaps, that too.

And laid no blame for it, apparently. Called no guards, set no hounds to the chase, said nothing at all. Ping Wen would learn it, no doubt, sometime today. The servants fetching food to the pavilion were safe to report the children missing; that news would climb to him even in his triumph.

He would be furious, Old Yen thought, even if he was triumphant. Doubly furious with Jiao, who had failed her watch and then not confessed it.

Even so. She said nothing, showed no interest. Rose and washed and took the tiger on its chain, set off to climb to the valley-ridge where Ping Wen had gone already.

Old Yen had followed, had caught up even despite her longer legs; the tiger was a dawdler, it seemed. So they walked together, climbed together, spoke not at all.

HERE ON the ridge, they had separated. She stood with Ping Wen, his object lesson, clear to be seen. Old Yen found himself alone among his host of idols, too many for one temple to supply.

He watched Tien and her companions when his gaze was forced from the dragon, from her repulsive pain; saw how they moved toward the forge, where the boy Han was being chained again. Tien was urged forward between the two men, pale, reluctant, determined. Old Yen knew her kind. She would do what she thought was her duty, at whatever cost to the boy or to herself.

And then, oh, then . . .

IT HAPPENED, as it had to happen. The boy struggled and lashed out, cried the dragon's pain and his own distress, and was chained regardless.

Even that first step served to still the dragon, at least a little. She made one frantic attempt to be airborne, to climb away from this, but the war-machine hurled something high and the sky above her blazed with fire and she fell back again; and then the boy's chains seemed to cramp her, even before Tien and the old men went to work.

Old Yen couldn't see what they did, and he couldn't have read it anyway, but he knew. They were cutting spell-words into the chains, to draw the dragon ever deeper into their captivity: to chain her terrible mind along with her monstrous body, stillness and silence and sleep.

It ought to be a good thing, it had to be a good thing. It was what he had wanted most, all summer long. Her freedom was what he had dreaded most, all a long life long.

And for all their chains and spells and dreadful fire, they couldn't do it alone. He knew.

HE FELT the goddess in his gut like a sour rising, fetid and insidious.

He felt her steal into his mind. She was a long way from the sea, but he had salt in his bones, and all these idols drew her.

He had refused her before, but this was different. This was a thing he wanted to see happen, a thing his people needed, freedom on the water and no terror in the sky.

She could take the dragon back into the deep and keep her

there, once men had chained the creature—but she needed a man
to work through, a man of the sea, one of her own.

She needed Old Yen: his body, his voice.

HE REFUSED her again.

three

Standing close by Ping Wen, Jiao could feel his confidence, his incipient triumph.

She could see his future, the swift parade to the ultimate height, the Jade Throne itself and the empire reunited under his rule.

She could see the slow return to the Hidden City, in glory all the way: trumpets and banners and cheering crowds, every city's gates flung wide in welcome. She could see herself right there, marching beside the new emperor's carriage, paced by the tiger: part bodyguard, part mascot, the very symbol of Ping Wen's success.

For a bandit, that was quite a climb. She might—

SHE COULD see, the moment that the old man refused his part.

She didn't know what it was, but something shifted in his face, in his body, enough to catch her eye and her attention.

The tiger growled. The dragon turned her head.

That seemed to be as much as the dragon could do, against all the magic they were working on the boy in his chains that chained her too. Her last freedom, and even that was limited; it was the boy she looked to, not the old man. She had nowhere else to look.

Understanding it afterward, working it out slowly moment by moment, Jiao got this far: that it was Han's choice, and not the dragon's. She had no choices left. He sat the throne in her head, he wore the chains that bound her; any decisive move had to come from him.

Whether it was consent or commandment, her idea or his, Jiao couldn't say and didn't want to guess.

However it worked between them, this was how it worked in the world: that the dragon looked to the boy, and all the monksmith's chains and all the doctor's spell-words were no use when he enabled her.

She moved with his authority. She stretched her head out on that impeccable neck, further and far further than seemed possible; she showed her dire gape to everyone who stood around, gaping at her—

AND THEN she swallowed Ping Wen.

JUST THAT, swift and neat and immaculate. Her head came thrusting down—so close, Jiao could smell the rank salt reek of her, could feel the wind of her strike—and her mouth engulfed the man, gave him no time to cry out. She lifted him in those terrible teeth, tossed her head back, swallowed him like a bird that takes a fish whole and flapping.

Jiao saw his legs still kicking as he went down.

THEN THERE was mayhem. Panic. If she was free to eat one, she was free to eat them all.

SO HALF his entourage believed, at least. They fled, and others followed: scrambling along the ridge or tumbling down the broken slope from terrace to drained dry terrace, soldiers and officials, smiths and servants.

Not Jiao, and not of course the tiger. They stood and watched it happen all around them, one at least with a bitter twist to her smile. She never could work out how the tiger felt about anything, its chain included. It was a traitor to her, it had let the children by in the night and done nothing—but she hadn't much cared even this morning, when Ping Wen might have proved angry. Now . . .

Well. Now they stood and watched the people run, and counted the few who remained, and weren't surprised to see the old fisherman still there—his fault this was, she thought, as much as Han's, though she wasn't clear how—and the doctor with her two slow men and their servants. And the monksmith, and over yonder the general who had brought him, with his sweet pretty boy and Tunghai Wang who would not flee, of course, not him.

The dragon seemed not to rate him as important enough to swallow. That would be a blow, another blow to his much-bruised pride. No matter.

What mattered to the dragon more, she flailed her smoldering tail into the war-machine and smashed it, broke it piece from piece, broke some of the men who still dared to attend it.

At the same time her head thrust toward the forge, toward the chained boy and the monksmith. Who stood alone to face her, and oddly she didn't eat him; only nudged him aside, almost gently, if such an atrocious creature could be gentle. Jiao didn't understand that at all.

The chained boy she seized in those terrible teeth, but didn't swallow him either. Only lifted him and then herself painfully into the wind, and flew away with no one to gainsay her.

JIAO WATCHED till she was out of sight, then looked around again.

There was Tunghai Wang, already reckoning how he could rank this among his achievements, how he could reclaim Santung and be the generalissimo and not lose face. *I faced down the dragon, and she quit me*—he would claim that, no doubt, and who would gainsay him?

The runaways would never have the nerve. Of those who had stayed, none of them would have the interest. Tunghai Wang could do as he liked, she thought, and it would never matter.

She could attach herself and the tiger to his side, and rise with him as she might have risen with Ping Wen.

. . .

Or—

Well. There was the monksmith, gazing after the dragon. She was interested in the monksmith, and especially now. She thought the dragon and the smith between them knew something that she didn't, held something that she couldn't see, some secret. There could be something to be learned from the monksmith, and she had missed learning new things since she left Taishu.

Or—

There was the ruin of the war-machine, and they could all be grateful that ruin had not encompassed fire and explosions, but still: there were broken people among the broken pieces, and she knew a way to help mend broken people, better than the doctor could even once she stopped staring after the dragon.

Jiao looked down at the tiger, and it looked back.

She fingered her tao and said, "One stroke to take your head off, traitor, and a quick skinning after. I could save lives."

It wrinkled its lip, showed her its teeth like a challenge.

She laughed harshly and turned away, tugged the chain to bring it after. "Come on, then. There's nothing here I want."

She had a blade at one hip, a tiger at the other. She had a secret little stash of stolen jade, always on her person now, since she no longer spent time with people who would know. The tiger knew, of course, but that was a different matter.

There was a path along the ridge, running north: away from Santung, away from the sea and any distant thoughts of Taishu. She might have forgotten it for a while, but she was still a pirate at heart. A pirate with a twisted shoulder, but still. A land-pirate with a tiger. She should stick to what she knew; and the land lay this way, more land than even she could walk, even in a long, long lifetime.

four

They went up, they came down.

Uphill is the harder work, or ought to be: but going up, Dandan had a ream of men to help her. She sat Li Ton in a chair and had him carried on poles, shoulder-high. What he consented to, Ai Guo could scarcely refuse.

Up they went, then, stately in their dignity, like people of importance. Dandan and the boy Gieh followed in their dust.

THEN THERE was the matter of the dragon. Other things happened, perhaps, but it was the dragon that mattered. She came, she burned, she raged, she went away.

Ping Wen in her belly, her own boy in her jaws.

BY THEN almost everyone had run off, everyone who could. Some were too proud, or too busy, or too broken.

Dandan thought she herself was perhaps too slow, no more than that. By the time she thought, *I could run, I suppose,* it was already too late. She had looked for her old men and seen them stranded, abandoned, helpless in the dragon's glare.

Of course she hadn't run, then.

The only surprise was that the boy Gieh stayed with her.

THE DRAGON might have eaten more, she might have eaten them all, but she took her boy between her teeth and left the rest to one another. *Perhaps she thinks we will eat one another,* and perhaps they would. There was a masterless city down below, and at least one man up here who had wanted long to master it, and others who had spent blood already to prevent him.

After the dragon, though—after the dragon, all the mortal world seemed drab and short of meaning. War not worth the effort, a sword too dull to draw. Tunghai Wang might not even claim Santung now if he felt at all the same way she did—emptied-out, adrift, like a bubble in the eddy of a stream—but Dandan thought it would fall to him regardless. She thought he would walk down and find it in his hand: not won and not gifted him, not surrendered, only heedless.

He would have to walk, because all his horses had run away and all his bannermen after them. He might have armies at his beck and call, but not just now.

Just now he was walking less far, perhaps with greater purpose: from there to here, picking his way around the vast rubble crater this paddy had become in its ruin. *Dragon Hollow* they would call it, she thought, and never dare grow rice in it again.

Were they the ones to decide this new dispensation, then, the men still standing here: Tunghai Wang, the monksmith, the pirate and the torturer? Power resides, she supposed, where people leave it. Ping Wen had left much unspoken-for. She wanted to press her two old men back from it, spirit them away. But all their bearers had run, and she was slow in any case, slow again. What should she do, hurl herself between them and whatever Tunghai Wang meant to offer, whatever he meant to demand? She was too small to matter, a sparrow to mob a hawk.

He stopped to speak to the monksmith. Behind him, here came his general: *too fat to run,* she thought, watching how he leaned on the shoulder of his boy.

Dandan didn't want to watch, didn't want to overhear.

Tien the same, she thought. At least, Tien was moving toward the smoking chaos of the shattered war-machine, not lingering to listen in. There were men hurt over there; they mattered more.

Dandan had been playing nurse awhile now to Tien's doctor, to men in pain. It was something to do.

She seized Gieh by the shirt and tugged him after.

BROKEN TIMBERS, splintered bamboo spars, torn bindings. A serpent's nest of ropes all tangled. In among that ruin, bodies too: broken, splintered, torn and tangled.

Fire too, fire everywhere. They were lucky, she supposed—if anyone remotely wanted to call this luck—not to have seen the whole paddy engulfed in that same fury that had brought the dragon down. Or else the dragon had been careful even in her agony, not to risk still more harm to herself.

Her flailing tail had crushed and scattered, even as it spread fire through so much that was flammable or explosive. Looking around—because fear was only common sense, it was the stitching that held her together when she was being brave—Dandan couldn't see a single projectile left whole and deadly. Powders and oils mingled and burned in streaks and puddles, wood cracked and snapped in heat, smoke wreathed the scene and made her cough but nothing erupted or threatened to erupt.

She didn't feel safe, no, the opposite of that. Still, she went with Tien into the smoke, among the flames.

Among the bodies.

SOME OF them were at least moving, dragging themselves toward some dream of safety. Some were barely hurt, except perhaps in their heads. More than one was wandering numbly through the devastation, stumble-footed and directionless.

Tien was the doctor. Dandan herself could be most help to those who didn't quite need doctoring, only someone to guide them in the smoke.

If an inner voice suggested that she was performing the same service for herself, it was very deep down, a moment of recognition rather than thought: *here I am, being me again. Doing what I do.*

It was a comfort, or it would be, later. Set it aside.

HERE WAS someone who needed other comfort: a young man not noticeably hurt, not moving either. Squatting dangerously close to a pool of flame, not even shifting the tatters of his ripped and blackened clothing from its licking edge.

She said, "Come. Come with me, let me—"

Then the smoke shifted on a breath of air and she could see past him, just that little way she needed: just far enough to show her why he wouldn't move, why her voice would never draw him, why encroaching fire couldn't drive him off.

Another man, just as young: lying sprawled on the ground there but not dead, nothing like dead. Hurt, to be sure; and awake, alert, feeling the pain of it. That was a good sign, by all that Dandan knew.

What was not good—not good at all—was the litter of timbers that lay haphazardly across the lower half of his body, thick heavy beams that made a better job than the smoke of hiding whatever damage had been done him.

More than one of those beams was smoking, and there was live fire somewhere underneath.

His friend should have been frantic, should have been heaving at the timber with his bare hands for want of any better tool. And was not, was just crouched there unmoving by the young man's head. Holding one hand, she saw, in both of his.

That said plenty, more than was needed. Even so, she said, "Gieh—!"

The squatting one shook his head. "Don't bother. I know how much these beams weigh. And everyone's run away, who was fit to help."

"Even so." This time she said it aloud. "We can at least try. You'll have to get out of the way."

And still he didn't move. "I have tried. It's hopeless. All you can do is make things worse for him." By stirring hope in the trapped man's heart, he meant, perhaps; or else that any effort to shift the beams only helped them settle, to hurt him all the more.

Well. He would hurt more soon enough, when that fire caught better hold around him. She understood his friend's despair, and wouldn't buy into it: not yet, not ever. She could be furious with him, but there wasn't time. Not yet . . .

At least she could stop him burning up with his friend. Whether he wanted that or not.

She bundled up the hem of her own skirt, and went to beat at the flames that licked toward him—and did at last, at least startle a movement out of him, a sudden hand that snared her wrist like a cuff of iron. This close, seeing through the filth, she realized that she knew him: Mei Feng's runner, he had been, in and out of the palace all summer long.

"Not," he said, "unless you want to burn too. I *made* that," a jerk of his head toward the flickering oily pool, "I know how it works. Your skirt will be a wick to it, no more."

"Then if you *made* it," she hissed, edging away, "you will know how to *kill* it, will you not . . . ?"

A shake of his head: he didn't know, or it wasn't possible. Or he didn't care, or he couldn't think. Any of those.

Unexpectedly, it was Gieh who spoke, behind her: "The dragon knew," he said.

And then he loomed up beside her, with something in his hand—a long pole with a spike at the end, that might have been a weapon or a tool, she couldn't tell.

She hitched herself urgently out of the way as he drove the beak of it into the soil, that narrow margin between the young man and the fire. An hour ago this ground had been baked brick-hard; she didn't think mere iron would have dented it. That was before the dragon crashed to earth. Her simple weight had cracked it and cracked it, the whole terrace, from the natural rock to the retaining wall; her brutal writhing had ground much of it to dust beneath her belly.

Gieh had seemingly no weight at all, all bone and leather, but his wiry strength was inexhaustible. He broke through the soil's crust and built a hasty rampart to hold the fire back. Then, when Dandan thought he'd dig more clods and scatter them to soak up the oil and smother the flame entirely, he said instead, "Move, both of you. I can't help unless you move."

"You can't—" the young man began, hopeless as before. Gieh ignored him, driving his spike hard into the ground between him and his trapped friend.

And leaned on it, rocked it back and forth, split the crust again; said it again, said, *"Move!"*—and now at last Dandan at least understood.

And took action on her own account, two hands under the squatting man's shoulders and dragging him away by main determination.

"It's no use, it's no *use* . . . ! He can't shift those timbers, not even with a lever, he'll just—"

"No, he won't. He's not trying to shift the timbers. Look."

The young man dashed tears and smoke out of his eyes, shook the dread out of his head, and looked.

Gieh was digging away instead beneath the trapped man's body: breaking the earth with relentless effort, the long handle of his pole rising and falling, rising and falling . . .

"Oh." For one precious, terrible moment the young man was still in Dandan's grip; then he had wrenched himself free and run to seize a tool of his own, an iron bar. On his knees beside Gieh— and now suddenly careful of the fire behind its dike—he seized his share of the work, slamming iron into earth, wrenching out clods in a storm of dust.

. . . .

BETWEEN THEM, they hollowed out the ground beneath the trapped man and so tugged him free, out from under the grip of what they couldn't shift. Dandan saw how his jaw clenched as they dragged his legs across the rubble, how he bit down on the scream he would not utter.

Unexpectedly merciful, she stopped them before they had hauled him all the way to the paddy wall. "That's far enough for now. Gieh, you did really well. Now do better, go and fetch Ai Guo."

"Ai *Guo*?"

"Yes. Hurry."

Meantime the injured man's friend looked worse than he did, pale and shaking and needing this respite. Needing to kneel, apparently, with his friend's head in his lap, needing to see nothing else for a while; needing to murmur, "Oh, why is it always you?" which made small sense in a field of catastrophe and drew an answer so private it had to be expressed without words.

Dandan peeled back ruined clothes while they were distracting each other. She looked, she touched, wiped blood aside and decided not to press more deeply, not to test what moved and what would not.

Instead she lifted her head, spoke to the other one, said, "What's your name? I don't remember."

He just looked at her.

She sighed. "All right, then. What's *his* name?"

"Shen. He's called Shen . . ."

"Shen, can you hear me?"

His eyes glittered in the drifts of smoke, his head nodded fractionally on his friend's lap. Pain had pushed him away, but not entirely; he was finding his way back. Hand in hand with hope, perhaps, if he would dare it.

"What's your friend's name?"

The ghost of a smile. "Chung. He's called Chung."

Chung, yes. That was it. "Good, then. My name is Dandan. I

am no doctor, but here," looming in the smoke, shuffling forward between crutch and boy, "here is Ai Guo, who—"

"Who is no doctor either," the old man said above her, patiently bewildered. "What game is this?"

"No game. Here," she said, meaning *here where I need you,* "you are doctor enough. You know exactly what harm a body has taken, who better?"

He grunted, in acceptance of a self-evident truth. Seemed not displeased, but still said, "Where is Tien?"

"Being a doctor, in ways that you cannot. You can at least tell me whether this one needs her wisdom," which almost certainly meant *whether this one is dying,* which she thought he probably understood.

All he said was, "You will need to lift him up." He might have made it a point of pride, *I am not accustomed to stoop to my work*—but that would only have seemed to be cover for the truth, *I am no longer able to stoop to my work,* and he was too proud to allow that.

Gieh was willing, Chung could be bullied; between them, they built a hasty scaffold of wood and stone, and hoisted Shen onto it with what care they could achieve. Which was more than they had shown in pulling him free, but not enough, not now that urgency was gone. He hissed, and turned his face away.

Ai Guo took his time, his professional time overlooking the body before him, assessing its hurts. Touching, twisting in ways that she had balked at, bringing degrees of knowledge to the task that she couldn't approach. Never shy of making Shen flinch or hiss again or cry out loud: satisfied, seemingly, when he did, because that was information.

At last he stepped back and said, "There is nothing here to concern me."

Chung had been silent so long, he was suddenly boiling, boiling over: "*Nothing?* What kind of doctor are you? He's in so much pain . . ."

"Pain, yes. I am . . . the kind of doctor who seeks truth in pain," without so much as a glance down or a gesture to draw attention to his own visible damage or the constant pain he lived with. "Burns hurt, and so do broken bones. Shen has both. But these are simple burns, and simple breaks. I have looked for deeper harm, crushed organs or interior bleeding. I cannot find either. I may be wrong," though he clearly didn't think so, he presumably rarely was, "but I believe your friend will mend entirely, with time and care."

"Meantime," Dandan said swiftly, for fear that might prove altogether too much for Chung, "pain can be managed. Here," she still had a lump of poppy in her sleeve, fetched up against her old men's needs. They might need it yet; they would have to share. She broke a little off and gave it to Chung. "Feed him this."

"So little?"

"Yes, and less than that. Less at a time. Rub it on your thumb, and let him suck it." They'd both enjoy that, she guessed, once they had started feeling easy in this new dispensation. Easier. "Give him more and he'll sleep," which would be no bad thing but Chung would worry. "Make him comfortable, and yourself too. Ai Guo will help."

The old man blinked. "I will?"

"Of course. This is your special study. What else would you do here?"

His hand gestured tightly toward the group gathered around Tunghai Wang: where the world presumably was being meted out, where he might have seized his portion, if he could have held it.

He had perhaps not anticipated Dandan. He was in part her portion, and she was not prepared to let him go.

She wouldn't willingly let anything go, and she was hoping to use all this smoke and fuss to gather around her what was hers, and what ought to be. She thought all those important people would go soon, walk back down to the city, leave everyone else here doing what they could amid the wreckage. It would fall to her anyway, no question, to bring her old men down at a pace that they could manage; she wanted to let everyone else get far ahead, just keep her own people close. There would be turmoil, she thought. It would be important first to keep out of trouble, and then to rebuild amid the chaos: to emerge stronger, better placed, more secure.

She'd forgotten, though, her own people were not hers alone. Or at least, no one else recognized her claim. The old men, the boy Gieh, any of them would have squabbled with it; and then there was Tien.

The whole of Santung would squabble with her over Tien. Here came Li Ton into the smoke now, stiff and stately, looking for the doctor.

"Oh, are you hurting too?" Of course he was hurting, he always hurt. Like Ai Guo, though, he rarely asked for help.

"Not for me. For Tunghai Wang, he wants her."

"And what, he sent you to fetch her? You who can barely walk?" Disappointment made her snappish. She'd hoped power would just walk away and leave them here, leave them all to her.

"Why not?" the pirate said equably. "This at least I can manage. I can play messenger, so long as there is no hurry. And Ai Guo is over here already, and you had taken our boy too. There was no one left but me."

That was clearly not true, Tunghai Wang still had an entourage of sorts; or there was the monksmith, or the fisherman, or . . .

Still. Li Ton it was that came, one of her own; and he came to take it all away from her.

"Gieh," he said, "now that I've found you, run and fetch the doctor."

"She's busy," Dandan asserted, last desperate defense, "she's being a *doctor* . . ."

She was; but Gieh went anyway into the thick of the smoke, and he came back coughing with Tien in tow.

She said, "There are people hurt here, badly hurt . . ."

"Ping Wen's men," Li Ton said, with a shrug. "Eventually, Tunghai Wang will remember that they are his men now—but not yet. Just now, all he remembers or understands is that you and I and Ai Guo know more about the dragon than anyone else in Santung—I have been at pains to impress that upon him, in case his spies had missed it—and that he needs dragonlore more than he needs anything else in Santung. She has made a dragon-shaped hole in his head, and he wants us to fill it for him."

"I'm a *doctor*," Tien said—but even she sounded unconvinced, and she couldn't keep her eyes from the southerly horizon, where the dragon had gone.

"Then you shouldn't have made yourself an expert in something he values more. The generalissimo has been a soldier all his life, there are few things he values more than a good campaign doctor; and yet here you are, and he will take you away from all your doctoring. Come."

"No, wait, I can't"—and yet she was, already moving unhappily in his wake, looking back only to say, "Dandan, you'll have to look after them up here, until I can arrange—"

Dandan surprised herself perhaps as much as anyone else there, perhaps more. She said, "No. If Tunghai Wang wants Li Ton too, he will need me to come too. If he wants Ai Guo too, he will have to wait; I can't manage more than one of them at a time down that hill."

"There's always Gieh."

That was Li Ton, and Dandan laughed at him. "Would you trust your pain to that boy? Or Ai Guo's? Besides, in Tien's absence, Ai Guo knows more about bodies than anyone else. No," she said, astonishing everyone, taking charge entirely, "we will leave Ai Guo up here for now. With Chung's help, he will organize a hospital for you, Tien. Chung, there are all these others you can use," the walking wounded and the merely shocked, those she had guided herself out of the smoke, who were still milling around or else just sitting and nursing their memories and griefs. "Round

them up and make them busy. See the injured as comfortable as
they can be, with whatever you can gather," coats and flags abandoned by the fled. On beds of earth at first, but at least the dragon
had broken it up for them. "I will give you the rest of this poppy,
here, and you are not to give it all to Shen," which—said aloud—
meant that Shen would refuse even what little Chung might offer
him, and so save more for others who might be in greater need. Or
not, but the two young men would feel better for it. Ai Guo should
probably take some too, and would not. "Tien may have more that
she can leave with you," if she hadn't used it all already, knowing
that Dandan had some to spare. "Ai Guo will use his own knowledge, to help you make them easy. I will go down with Li Ton, and
come back with more help. With Mu Gao and a squad of men."
Dandan was forming another plan as she spoke, as all these more
important people unaccountably stood and listened and allowed
her to do it. It was necessary to be changeable, in these changeable
days. "Be as useful as you can, Chung, and as patient as you must.
It will take me half the day, but I will be back; and we will make a
camp of tents for everyone who can't be moved, and live up here
until they're better. And you can make fireworks while you wait for
Shen to mend, and we will let them off in triumph when he does."
And then—well, by then she would count these young men among
her people, these and perhaps more, because that was what she
did, she cared for those who needed it and so made them her own.
Her outraged heart took seize.

Took seize, and let not go. She had seen Jiao watch everything,
and quietly walk away; she thought perhaps that she would do the
same, in time. With her people around her, a family, a tribe. They
would all be better away from this. Ai Guo away from his torture-
chambers and his generals who abandoned him and used him and
abandoned him again; Li Ton away from the sea and his lost
Shalla, his pirate life; all of them away from war and soldiery and
death. There must be country somewhere inland where they could
settle, build a home and a new life. Gieh was a peasant and so was

she at heart, they knew how to farm, they could teach these rough bewildered men . . .

SHE'D MEANT Gieh to stand as crutch to Li Ton's slowness on the path down to the city: to pace the old man on his other side, lend a youthful arm at need and on instruction. Apparently he was too distracted to be dutiful, his head full of dragon and smoke, his legs full of bounce. He had slithered ahead and involved himself with faster walkers, more important men, the generalissimo and his party.

Or not quite that, in the event. It was the monksmith that he skipped beside, at the tail of the generalissimo's party; the monksmith that he listened to along the way, insofar as he was listening at all.

For some obscure reason—or under some obscure instruction— he had rescued the dragon's green banner from the ruin of the paddy and was flying it aloft like a kite, like the boy he was.

No matter. Dandan could manage Li Ton by herself, so long as they didn't try to keep up; and she thought she could likely reel Gieh in again once they reached the city, once he remembered who he was and what he did when he wasn't playing among the great. If she were wrong, if the monksmith decided to keep him—well. Boys were cheap, and plentiful.

There was another one ahead and below her on the path, giving an arm to his master the fat general. Not abandoning his duty, though he was constantly looking back over his shoulder, all too clearly itching to fly kites alongside Gieh.

It was turning into quite a parade ahead, as stray runaways came awkwardly back to their commanders. Shuffling along behind, Dandan had a view all the way to the city's edge. That was more than a guard detail waiting there in greeting. News must have run all through the city like a breaking wave, far ahead of any running soldiers. Everyone could have seen the dragon and the fires that brought her down. By now, that growing throng should know not to expect Ping Wen among this returning troop. Tunghai Wang was back instead, their master by default, and—

AND THEY were looking, the whole city was looking to the north, to the valley road, to see him come.

No one was looking up or back, into the southern sky.

Perhaps Dandan was the first to see her, when the dragon came as well.

They all knew soon enough: when men pointed and cried out, when Gieh let his kite-banner fail on the wind and fall down, when her shadow overswept the crowd packed close at the city's edge, waiting for Tunghai Wang.

When her bulk came down, right there, at the city's edge. Blocking the road, breaking the road and the buildings to either side, crushing anyone too slow or too stupefied to run.

Dandan wondered if she'd come back to eat Tunghai Wang after all. Or to eat them all.

But she seemed content just to squat there, magnificently in the way. She hadn't eaten her boy either; he slid down off her neck and stood beside her, one arm against her claw. Leaning against her strength, it seemed to Dandan, his new chains dark and heavy under the weight of sun.

After a long time, after a *long* time, two men walked out of the generalissimo's party where it had tangled itself together into a knot of reluctance, and went slowly forward to speak with her.

One of them was Li Ton, and the other was the fisherman, Old Yen.

It was as well to be changeable, these changeable days. Dandan thought she might need a new plan.

five

*H*ere on her balcony, looking out over the forest and the rising peaks, Mei Feng was farther from the sea than she had ever been.

It didn't seem to matter. These days, she thought she carried a sea inside her. Within her swelling belly, her little spawn-of-emperor swam in tidal salt. That was enough, apparently. She hadn't thought she could be happy away from the coast and boats, storm and surf and far horizons, but she was happy here.

Happy with herself among others, with her subterfuges and her plots. Little things that made life better for someone, and then for someone else. She could save the empire, she thought, if she could only do it one person at a time.

If the emperor would only stop arguing with her.

She was happy with him too, with her man. Even when he was angry. He was still magnificent about it, and still prepared to listen. Eventually, she thought, she could bring him to see that she was right. Until then—well, she supposed that they would argue. And she would get her own way, because she plotted and subterfuged, because she was sneaky where he was plain and forthright and didn't quite understand that being emperor wasn't quite enough.

She looked down the length of the balcony, to where Yu Shan and Siew Ren and the boy were playing a game with little round beads of jade. Rules didn't seem to matter much, and every now and then the child would pick up a bead and suck it instead of rolling it. He had decided, apparently, that jade was meant for his mouth.

It made him laugh, which made Siew Ren smile; that was good enough.

He spoke sometimes too, a word or two. Her name, or Yu Shan's. Not his own, not yet; but they called him Yaya, and he lifted his head when he heard it and came if it was called, if he was interested, if there was food.

The emperor was troubled by the changes in the child. It was what they argued about most often.

"Mei Feng, you should have left him at the temple. He'll forget the goddess if we keep him here, she'll lose her grip on him."

Yes. Exactly. "He's good for Siew Ren," she said, "and she's good for him." Someone, and someone else. All the empire, one person at a time.

That was only today that she had said it, though not for the first time; and she had gone on, "Bring Pao back with you, and the girls."

"Mei *Feng*!" He had been on the point of mounting a horse, to ride to the city; a runner had come with news, a little boat sailing in from the mainland all unexpectedly, with an unexpected crew of mostly children.

"And their mother too, of course, bring her. She's a priestess, all but. She'll make sure they don't forget the goddess." Even so Mei Feng thought, she hoped, the goddess might lose her grip on Jin too. This far from the sea, this far from her influence. If the girl could be induced to talk again, if she could learn another kind of life . . . "They'll like it here, I think, this little house," this far from the sea. Four more people, they had room for another four. One at a time, she would find a way to settle them.

"Do you *want* us to be stranded here, with no means to cross the strait?" The question was serious, and so was he. But he slipped his arms around her waist as he asked it, because he needed to be touching her—or touching them, perhaps, her and their baby, two in one—whenever she was close enough, whenever he could. Whenever she allowed it. Even when they were arguing.

Yes. Yes, I do. No more adventuring in pursuit of a lost empire. She wanted to keep him close, in protection of a child who had been nearly lost and an island the same, a life that she would cling to as much as could be saved. She couldn't quite say that, not yet, that was too big an argument. She said, "Send Grandfather back to the dragon, he can negotiate." For a boat, perhaps, a truce-boat that might even be true. Not for an army. Not again. Secretly, she rejoiced at that. She could almost bless the dragon.

"Your grandfather is on the other side of the water, as far as we know. And he doesn't have either of the children anymore, to help him cross back."

"The dragon will let him by," she said. That had to be true; she insisted on it. "But you," with her hands clenched in the silk of his robe, little fists of determination, "you bring the children here to me. Tomorrow. Promise me."

"Or?"

He knew there had to be a threat to follow. It made her smile, even as she growled it: "Or I will come and fetch them, all that way and back again. In that nasty jolty carriage I will come, with all the upset and the danger and . . ."

"Little liar. You like it here, and you hate going to the city, and you would never do anything to upset our baby." Laughing, he bent to kiss her, while his hands stroked the bowl of her belly. "Perhaps," he said. "Perhaps I will bring them back. For a while, for a little. If I don't, you will only send someone to steal them again."

She nodded, firmly. That was true. It was her best weapon, so long as he believed it. Plots and subterfuges, one laid within another. He would bring the children here, and she would do what she could to draw Jin back from the goddess, and if that made her a traitor so be it; it was only the empire that she betrayed. Never her man.

She thought the empire was the old woman in the silent room

behind her, under a skin that did her no good now. There was someone who could not be drawn back, from wherever it was that she had gone. Mei Feng sat with her an hour dutifully every day, listened to the slow rasp of her breath and saw no reason why she should ever leave this state, caught half and half between life and death, favoring neither one above the other.

Should Mei Feng pity her? She wasn't sure. On the whole, she tried not.

THE SKY darkened. Siew Ren fetched lamps, and then led Yaya and Yu Shan off to bed. People had learned not to try to chivvy Mei Feng. It was harder than ever to lie comfortably in bed, unless she had her man there to nestle into. If she was alone, she'd often drowse the night in her chair here, as she used to with the empress. She liked waking to the sounds of wind and distant trees and night-creatures, waking and waking. She liked moonlight on her face, the bright strewn ribbon of the silk-stars overhead. Not so much the occasional night-creature on her skin, a curious moth or a spider dropped from the roof above, but those were as likely indoors as out, and they did no harm. Nothing seemed to bite her anymore, or if they did bite she didn't feel it and her skin didn't swell or bruise.

Perhaps there were mosquitoes out there now with stolen jade in their bellies, in their blood, that had trespassed and departed all unseen. *Go well, little thieves*—she could be placid even about mosquitoes now, apparently.

Perhaps there were mosquitoes out there somewhere that had tried to bite the emperor. Mosquitoes with sore bent noses.

She giggled on a breath, and missed her man, and hoped to remember to tell him that.

And looked up, and saw something occlude the stars.

Something big, too big. Monstrous big.

Dragon-big.

She watched it come, thinking that surely her heart should be in her mouth, she should be running, screaming for help, alerting the guards.

But the guards would know soon enough if the dragon came to ground, and what could they do? What help should she scream for, where should she run?

She sat where she was, and watched. Waited.

She was unreasonably sure that it would come to her.

IT SWOOPED low over this petty palace, and settled on the hill above.

Now Mei Feng didn't need to run or scream or alert anyone. They knew. Everyone was running and screaming on their own behalfs, alerting themselves and one another.

She sat in her chair and waited.

Yu Shan came out from the house still lacing his trousers, barechested. He told her to stay, as if she were a puppy uncertainly trained; then he vaulted the balcony railing and was gone.

A little later, a boy hauled himself up over the railing, much less gracefully.

A boy with broken chains hanging from his neck and wrists, trying—with small success—not to let them make a noise as he came.

Having come, he seemed to have nothing to say to her, but only crouched warily in the shadows.

She said, "How did you ever get past Yu Shan, jingling the way you do?"

He said, "I held still under a bush and let him go by me. He went up to the dragon."

Of course he did. Everyone would have done that, except those who were running away. One stray boy, slipping from the dragon's side, clinging to the shadows—he would go as disregarded as a moth tonight. He could depend on that.

She said, "So can you really have the dragon take you wherever you want, whenever you want to go?"

He snorted laughter through his nose, which she took to mean *no*. "Sometimes," he said, "I can persuade her that it's in her best interests if we go somewhere together. Though she never quite believes me. Which is wise of her, because it's never quite true. Like tonight," with a jerk of his head toward the fallen silence that must exactly describe the location of the dragon, the awe that Mei Feng could almost feel even through the width and height of the house, the weight she was sure she could feel, that the hill itself seemed to complain about. "I had an excuse, but really I wanted to see you."

Why me, what can I do for you?—but what she actually asked was, "What's your excuse?"

For answer, he shook his chains at her. "I need these cut away. I told her we'd both be easier, with them gone. She bit through the links, but she couldn't get her teeth under the collar and cuffs," great bands of iron hammered around his flesh, "without biting off bits of me." Important bits, she gathered: his head, his hands. There was a livid gash on his neck where she must have tried, tried and failed while he kept very still or screamed and thumped puny fists against her snout or . . .

She couldn't really imagine their life together, how they did ever deal with each other. It was just too extraordinary, beyond the reach of her mind, she who had gone from fishing boat to emperor in one night and onward after. She said, "Well, I can have men from the site remove those for you."

"Tell them to be careful," he said, very earnestly. "She will be watching. She doesn't quite trust me, and she won't trust anyone else. At all."

"I will do that," solemnly agreeing, as though any man would need to be told, with the dragon's great head thrust at him and her eyes aglow. "Will it make much difference to you and her, when the chains are gone?"

"Not really. I still have all the old words written on my skin," shifting his shoulders gently. She might offer him a shirt before he left. One of the emperor's, perhaps; this boy would be lost in it. "But these are stronger, some of them. That monksmith . . ."

"The monksmith?" she said sharply. "The monksmith's dead."

"Well." He didn't sound convinced, though the way she'd heard it, he had himself seen the old man die. Long ago, that seemed now. Back at the start of everything. Lost in the fog. "If so, they found another. Who looks, well. Like the monksmith."

"Perhaps all monks look alike," at least to a boy in confusion.

"Perhaps. Anyway. I'd like to be rid of these. And so would she. Nothing I can do about the words on my skin, but it's better if they don't jangle in her face."

"I'm sure. So," coming to the point at last, "why did you want to see me, actually?"

"I thought you ought to know what's been happening," though his eyes glinted as they shifted in the lamplight and the shadows, and this wasn't the truth either, though still not a lie. "Your grandfather wanted to tell you, but he's waiting for Li Ton to find his crew, what he can of it, and . . ."

"Wait." Her grandfather, and Li Ton? The fisherman and the pirate, the loyal peasant and the traitor general? "What do those two have to say to each other?"

"Quite a lot, actually," and the boy Han was grinning in the darkness. Nice to know that he could still do that. "Li Ton chained me and your grandfather freed me, more or less, but since then they've been talking about boats. They'll be coming across in Old Yen's soon enough, and then Li Ton wants to find the *Shalla* and crew her again, reclaim her. He thinks she gives him a better claim on me," and his fingers strayed to his ear, a sliver of metal, a piercing ring that he might have plucked out at any time but oddly hadn't.

"Is he right?"

"Mmm? Oh. No. But you may be seeing more of him, in these waters. I think the dragon wants to keep him, to be her voice to the people."

"Li Ton? I thought you . . . ?"

"Oh, me too. She just doesn't like to let me out of her sight. I'll be her voice to Li Ton, I think, and then he'll sail up and down the strait and talk to people. Talk to you, on her behalf."

"Han." Mei Feng's mind was failing, a little, at the thought of the pirate as ambassador. For the dragon. "What's *happened,* that she should want him to speak for her?" Or to make him agree—but one question at a time.

"Oh—yes. That's what I came to tell you. She ate Ping Wen."

"She did *what*?"

"Ate him. He tried to chain her again, but your grandfather wouldn't let the goddess take her back to the strait; and they were trying to control her through me," with barely a shudder at the memory of it, whatever they had done to him, these fresh chains and more, "and I . . . Well. I let her eat him."

Mei Feng heard more than that, *I told her to eat him* or *I saw the chance* or something on that order, his decision almost, his incitement, something. His the guilt, at least, except that he didn't feel guilty.

Nor would Mei Feng, on his behalf or her own. Ping Wen had been a traitor, and undoubtedly deserved a slow death in a dragon's belly. She hoped it had been slow. She cradled her own belly and said, "Well, then. Who rules in Santung now?"

Expecting the obvious answer, *Tunghai Wang* and themselves no better off, she was startled when he said, "She does, the dragon does, if anyone."

"How . . . ?"

"She was angry, after Ping Wen tried to chain her. After he did chain me. She took me away, to the Forge. She liked the Forge, we both did; I thought that was the home she wanted. I do still think it was. Only, she was angry, and she doesn't trust people. You, Taishu, she trusted you, your grandfather made a pact with her; she thought she could do the same the other side, and they betrayed her. So now she won't let anyone have Santung, she wants it for herself. It's going to be . . . complicated. The Forge was *easy*," a sudden protest, all boy, "but that's not good enough anymore. The palace in Santung is hers now, that's where you should come if you want to speak to her. I think she'll let people cross the strait, some people. Your grandfather, Li Ton. The emperor, perhaps, if he wanted to come. You, but I don't suppose . . ."

He blushed, unexpectedly. All boy again, all human. She was delighted to see that.

"No," she said, "I don't suppose either." She didn't know what to suppose, this was all too much, too sudden, too new; but she didn't think anyone would let her cross the strait to visit a dragon, either pregnant or with a babe in arms. "What about your friend, the doctor, Tien? I liked her, and she helped me. I wanted to bring her back here, but she wouldn't come."

"No," he agreed. "She wouldn't do that. She . . . does what she thinks is right. She tried to help Ping Wen, she chained me again, tried to chain the dragon."

"Oh. Han, I'm sorry, but I'm sure . . ."

She wasn't sure what she might be sure of, when it came to putting words together.

He was more sure, apparently; he was smiling, somewhat, as he said, "It's all right. I know why she did it. And she knows more about the dragon than anybody. She stays with us. We belong, she and I."

Which wasn't quite *we belong together,* but it was perhaps the next best thing. Even if it meant *we belong to the dragon,* for now.

Mei Feng shook her head; their story wasn't important, except to them. She gazed out at the night, felt the weight of the dragon at her back, thought she ought to be sending for men with chisels and hammers, against the beast's impatience; realized she still didn't understand.

Said, "Han. What does she want," *she* the dragon, to be understood, "with ambassadors, with a voice? With a city? Why deal with us at all? She doesn't need to."

"Oh," he said, "yes. I think she does. I think she's like you," and he was blushing again, staring at her belly and twisting his head suddenly away, "I think she's nesting."

six

Voiceless, senseless, the old woman drowses, lost in her lost body, adrift on tides of salt, slow salt.

VOICELESS, PATIENT, the goddess waits.

SOMEONE WILL come, again. Someone always comes.

about the author

DANIEL FOX is a British writer who first went to Taiwan at the millennium and became obsessed, to the point of learning Mandarin and writing about the country in three different genres. Before this he had published a couple of dozen books and many hundreds of short stories, under a clutch of other names. He has also written poetry and plays. Some of this work has won awards.